Ella Cerulean

BOOK 1 OF
THE CONNECTIVE

BY
TRIMID DEW LANNS

Ella Cerulean: Book 1 of The Connective
© 2014 by Trimid Dew Lanns

Printed in the United States of America

First Printing, 2014

ISBN: 978-0-9905458-1-1

Published by Stoicheion Limited
www.stoicheion.com

For Matthew, who lets me be myself, no questions asked.

For J, who really liked that I am weird.

For Sara, who got me through my mom's passing when I barely knew her.

For my mom, who gave me the best advice ever, despite her disaster of a life.

For Emily, who loves me without bounds and makes sure I get comics.

For Dan, who feeds me, and when I forget, reminds me to be better than I am.

For Bahb, whose insanity matches my own, and who stays up all night talking to me when I need it.

For Lindsey, who says nice things to me even when I don't deserve them and has let me talk her into many projects.

For Kyle, who reminded me who I was when I got lost.

For Miranda, who once saw that I won a short story contest and told me she was proud of me.

For Katie, because she encourages me to do EVERYTHING.

For Tom, who challenged me on why I read young adult books, making me realize their importance.

For Jon, who kept asking me what I was waiting for.

For Erika, who became my friend at the worst time of my life.

For Skaht, who was the first person to let me run wild with my party ideas.

For Nicole, for her unwavering support and generosity.

For Drew, who randomly sends me nice messages.

For Sam, who keeps offering to bring me things.

For Bob, who taught me about peep jousting.

For Jeff, who, no matter how much I just yelled at him or how awful I look, will tell me I am beautiful.

For Alexis, who always thought it was cool that I was different.

For each and every one of you who has danced with me, come to events I was co-hosting, listened to me rant, and just been my friend.

And the last, but really the most important, thank you: For Christina, because without her I wouldn't be here at all.

"As language is in the alphabet, so is entire nature, the play of all its laws, in one atom."

Emerson

Prologue

The tribe's leader came running. They had come back from the mines with his son. They came to him in urgency and told him his son had fallen ill from angering the spirits. The leader knew it would happen. He had begged his son to stay away from the mines. The son insisted he was stronger than all the others who had fallen ill. He was the leader's first born, after all. Spirits dare not make him ill. In addition, his son proclaimed the greatest entitlement to the wealth that was to be found in the deal with the stranger.

"But, my son, we are very wealthy. We have food, a home, family. There is much comfort here. A great and wise simplicity."

"Father, we could have vehicles and many foreign goods. Comfort beyond our wildest dreams."

"What do we need with that?" the leader replied. "These are material things that complicate the soul further, my son. It has come to me in my dreams. The stranger uses the spirits for great evil. Your soul should not carry this burden."

The leader's words were lost on his headstrong son. The son saw trips to foreign lands, and living what he thought was high above everyone else. He wanted such things. He had been touched by the stranger's greed. The promise of a "better" life was what the gold-ringed man used to lure the people with a simpler way of life to their death. The leader, in his frustration, had forbidden his son from going to the mines. His son left the next day to lead more and more people into them to search for their better lives. This was six full moons ago.

As the leader entered the shelter, the medicine man and the caretakers stepped aside. He knelt next to his son.

"Father," he reached his hand out, struggling to lift it even the slightest bit, "you were right. The spirits will destroy us all." His breathing was labored, and he was shaking with a heavy sweat all over his body.

"Shh, my son, carry not these burdens now. It was a mistake to be learned about and left in the past." He turned and caught the worried eye of the medicine man.

"What is it?" The leader snapped at the medicine man.

"I'm sorry, Overseer, I just thought you should know, your son has been muttering of the other caverns. I fear he may have done something regrettable." He looked away quickly.

The father looked down at his son and feared the answer to the next question. He knew he had to ask and find out if his son had told the gold-ringed man of the cavern.

With a breath that he thought might burst his chest, he leaned close to his son. The smell of the sweat and the poison that was eating his son alive filled his nostrils.

"My son, ease your burden as you pass from this life to the next. You must tell me if you told the stranger of the cavern of power." The leader leaned closer.

His son opened his eyes with a great shame in them. "He promised to give you real power, Father. In the world of the wealthy and white." His eyes closed and he began to choke.

"My son, please... Did you tell him of the cavern of power? Let me take this pain from you! I must know, my son. It is our duty to care and protect this secret and our people!" His voice was nearing hysterical. The medicine man put a hand on his shoulder, but the leader pushed him away. Reaching over, he pulled his son up and lifted his head to him.

"Please, I beg you that you free yourself. Let us still bound to this plane, to the responsibility, take it so you may be judged mercifully. Did you tell the stranger of the cavern of power?"

His son struggled to open his eyes. "Please, forgive me, forgive me, he knows of the cavern of power." He choked again and then lay still.

The leader held him silently and then gently laid him down. Closing his son's eyes, he turned to the caretakers. "Prepare him for the next journey."

The leader turned to the medicine man. "I have to go into the city. I will ask you to oversee for the village while I am gone."

"How long do you believe to be gone?"

"I have to find the gold-ringed man. He has knowledge no one was to possess but the elders of this tribe. I believe him to be searching for the cavern of power for his own personal means. To what end, I do not know. But he must not find it."

"How long do you believe this to take?"

The leader looked him straight in the eye, "I don't know that I'll ever return."

The leader walked from the shelter into the village. He felt his eyes burn from the smell of the spirits. He saw the children playing in the glowing mud and fishermen pulling dead fish from the river. The baskets of mud on top of scantily clad teenagers had great weight to them and some spilled the glowing mud onto their faces and into their eyes.

The evil was spreading quickly now that it was in the water. The leader came to the frightening realization that he may be too late to save anyone.

Chapter 1

The pain spread through her shoulder as she hit the marble, missing the cover left on the floor meant to soften any falls. *So much for that,* she thought irately. It wasn't the pain she minded, it was losing the advantage. Looking up at the hand her instructor held out, she considered yanking him down and over her head into the hard wooden walls behind them. A snicker nearly escaped her mouth, and she was glad he couldn't see her face behind the mask.

"You really need to pay better attention," he said as he helped her up. "I'm supposed to be teaching you fencing, not hand-to-hand combat. Your father would be very unhappy."

"My father is always unhappy with everything that I do," she replied. "Besides, you are teaching me fencing. You're also just teaching me something interesting." She bent over and picked up the forgotten weapon. Fencing was boring to her. She much preferred the intimacy of a fight, face to face. Almost always able to anticipate what her opponent was going to do when coming in contact with them, she was pretty sure the fencing mask had hindered her ability to focus on the instructor. Though it seemed likely she could anticipate him because he was the only opponent she ever had, since they had to keep their extra sessions a secret from her father. During each of their day-long fencing lessons, they spent an hour on the forbidden work. Thus far, no one had said anything about the black and blue streaks and spots she seemed unable to avoid. Of course, it helped that most of the time she was covered in head-to-toe clothing, and none of her caretakers dared speak ill about her to her father. *He is as kind to them as he is to me,* she thought bitterly.

Frowning, she stepped forward and thrust out her arm. "Shall we?"

He came at her and they sparred for several more hours. She was a good fencer, not great, simply because she did not care to be. Her thoughts continuously wandered as they parried and thrust, parried and thrust.

They finished the day-long lesson with a final session of Tai Chi. A sacred exercise in meditation that she had pleaded with him to teach her after she had come early to a lesson one day and had seen him moving elegantly and calmly through motions that appeared to flow with an unseen force.

The quiet emptiness that filled her mind as she moved with him blocked all the unpleasantness of the pain in her body, which had grown more and more persistent as the day went on.

As they stood in silent contemplation, the door to the room burst open, ripping her out of meditation. Jolted to attention, she and her instructor turned to see her caretaker running in. Fluster and fear colored her face.

"Bleu!" The term of endearment her caretaker used for her. "Bleu, your father is home and he is not himself. He seems to be very unsettled and angry. He is demanding to see you immediately."

This news shook her. "He's home? He's not due back for at least another month?" *This is very bad,* she realized. *Something terrible must have happened.*

"I know, love. But he is here and he wants to see you. You better go to him." Holding a hand out, the hurried woman took the weapon from her.

"I'll go get changed and meet him at dinner," she started to turn back to her instructor.

"No!" her caretaker nearly shouted. "I'm sorry, darling. No, I think you should go to him as you are."

This did not amuse Bleu. Her father always demanded she be fully and formally dressed when she went to see him. Her caretaker was right, this was not good. She turned to the instructor, who had been standing silently at her side, calm as always. "I'm sorry that I have to cut our time together short today. At the end of the week, then?"

He nodded and turned to leave. Before he reached the door, he looked back and said, "I'm here if you need me."

She found herself surprised by these words and the seriousness with which they were said. But she nodded curtly. "Thank you for your support, as always, my friend."

He nodded back and left the room.

Ella Cerulean

Sighing, she removed her gloves and started towards her father's office. All the while, her caretaker struggled to keep up next to her and fussed with her hair.

She smiled at the woman, "I'm assuming my father knows I was in my lesson."

The woman nodded her head.

"Then I am going to guess, since he demanded to see me now, that my hair style is the least of his concerns." She had to smile and leaned over and kissed the woman, her truest friend, and confidant, in the world.

The caretaker dropped her hands to her side, then hugged the girl back swiftly and tightly. "Whatever is going on, I am here for you as well."

With that, Bleu opened the door to her father's overbearingly opulent and intimidatingly grand office, created to impose an air of importance upon whoever entered it. She tried not to come in here as much as possible. It was filled with heads, and statues of animals, and places both killed and conquered. These trophies were supposed to be a badge of honor, but to her they were violent and disturbing.

Her father sat behind his desk, shuffling impatiently through stacks of papers and signing with a large pen with such ferocity it seemed as if he was at war with the words. He was still wearing his traveling clothing.

He did not look up as she crossed the floor and stood in front of his desk.

"I told her to hurry and get you. Does anyone obey me the way they are supposed to?" He spoke with an even tone despite the way he was handling the papers. It frightened her.

"No doubt you have noticed that I have returned from travels sooner than expected." He continued to write. "My plans have been interrupted with an incident. I am unclear of the details, but I do know some of my men have been killed." She drew in her breath sharply. Her father was many things, but careless was not one of them. He took great pains to see to it that everyone under his direction was suitably compensated and protected in their positions. Especially those abroad. Which could only mean that something had happened somewhere far away. What this had to do with her, she did not know.

"It has been suggested to me that there is a possibility you could be of some assistance in this matter."

"What? How could I possibly..."

He cut her off, "I am, Daughter, as surprised by this as you are."

In spite of herself, those words stung.

"You are to pack and get ready to leave with me immediately." He said it as if the matter were closed.

"What? Wait, what about my studies? The horses? Fencing? We are due to have guests in a week." She sought desperately for any reason to stay. She did not want to leave. Some of those guests were very important to her.

"You are not to decide what guests we will have nor will you tell me of your studies. I've seen you fence, Daughter. You are, at best, adequate. Your tutor will travel with us and you will continue uninterrupted. The house is tended to as always, and, I dare say, will survive without you here to ride the horses. Now you are to be ready to go by the end of the day tomorrow. Upon inspection of our arrangements we leave no later than two days from now. This matter cannot wait." He didn't look up as he pointed her to the door.

She stood, unmoving, waiting. She felt defiant. An indulgence she rarely thought to entertain. But she was so angry.

The silence in the room grew until her father finally deemed to look up at her.

"Why are you still here? I gave you an order."

"I am not one of your men that you can tell what to do." Her heartbeat thundered in her ears. She could feel her face flush with resentment.

"I am WELL aware, Daughter," he said the word daughter as if it burned his tongue, "that you are not a man. A fact, I am generally kind enough not to point out, that you would be much better suited to my life if you were. Your inadequacies as a female are a struggle with which I continuously contend, and do so admirably."

"I am realizing," he continued, with a measured malevolence, "that taking you with me is a more than righteous choice, as it is obvious by the way you think that you are allowed to speak to me that I have indulged you long enough. Since I have given into your every whim, you will get ready to leave with me and you will come. Do as you are told, or things such as fencing lessons and horses will no longer continue to be a consideration in my planning for your education, no matter how well-rounded I've been told it needs to be."

She shifted uncomfortably and the rage coursed through her. She never asked for anything. She was always told what to do. Her whims? She barely knew the meaning of the word. Her life was a rigorously scheduled program of whatever her father's advisors said she should be doing to attract a husband of prestige and money. The thought of a husband turned her stomach, someone being chosen for her. That's what she had to look forward to. But she didn't have a choice and she knew any more petulant behavior could cost the members of the household their jobs. Her father had done away with people he had decided were a bad influence on her before, and she knew he'd do it again.

All the while speaking, he had not looked up in her direction once. Then he did, and she wished he had not.

"Why are you still standing there?" he asked her. "You know, you're tall enough that in your fencing attire you almost look like a man. Now get to your room and get ready to leave. Furthermore, I expect to see you properly dressed for dinner. We have important company this evening. I will not repeat myself. Go."

She wanted to scream at him. She wanted to smash the trophies in his horrible office. She wanted to run from this oppressive place that had never felt like a home. Nothing she did was ever good enough. She wasn't the right sex, she wasn't smart enough, she wasn't strong enough, she had never lived up to whatever standards he created. She didn't even know what he wanted, and that angered her most of all. How could he fault her for something she didn't know existed? But, as always, she turned with her legs barely staying beneath her to walk, and left to do what he wanted. She didn't have a choice. There were people here who depended on her good behavior to keep their jobs. Once they were let go from her father's employ, he made sure they couldn't ever work anywhere else in the city. His reach was far and cruel. No one knew this better than her.

She walked silently through the ornate, unfriendly halls to her room. The place was so beautiful and so devastating. Stopping only briefly to stare out a window, she saw that a gloom had settled over the city. One that matched her mood perfectly. Her mind wandered to what lay beyond the borders, as she had never been farther than the countryside. And even then it had been in company limited to only those approved by her father. Men mostly, many of whom were quite possibly the most uninteresting creatures to ever curse this planet. That thought actually made her smile a tiny bit. Being bored out of her mind, at least one of them had taken pity on her and taught her to ride a horse like a man and how to wield a real sword. Not like the weapons in fencing. The sword was ghastly heavy and at first made every bit of her hurt when she tried to hold it longer than a minute.

As she continued back to her room, her father's workers hurried by her, clearly preparing for the arriving guests this evening and for the journey they were to take. It occurred to her that in her anger she hadn't bothered to ask where they were going, nor had he deemed to tell her.

The door to her room was open, and her caretaker was already packing her things for the trip.

"Bleu, I'm sorry we have to go," she said, as tears leapt to her eyes which made both of them embrace and share a moment of sadness together. There was a lot more to be sad about than either of them wanted to admit.

"I hate him," she whispered into the woman's soft hair, which smelled of oranges and wood smoke from the fires in the kitchen.

"No you don't, Bleu. He is your father and he does care for you in a way we do not understand." She let go of her and continued to pack.

"He doesn't care for me," she said stubbornly, hating herself for sounding like a child. Still, she knew the woman was wrong. Her father didn't care about anyone except himself.

"Wait," she said to Cathryn, whom she trusted more than anyone to love her despite her mood swings. "Who is coming to dinner?"

"I do not know, but it's best we get ready for it. Whoever it is, your father has spared no expense preparing for dinner or for the trip."

"Do you know where we are going?" She started to gather her books. None of them were getting left behind.

"I am not entirely sure, but whatever happened, I am most sure it was in Africa."

"Africa?" Startled by this statement, she dropped the books and turned to look at her friend. "What is going on in Africa? I didn't even know my father had ever been to Africa."

At this question, the older woman looked nervous and worried.

"Why do you have that look on your face? What has my father been doing in Africa?"

"Bleu, darling, I do not know for sure. I only hear rumors when the men return from traveling. And even then, you can never be sure what is true because it's always talk when they are drinking. You know your father spies on the spies and makes sure to keep the gossip out of this house." She hurriedly shoved clothes into a trunk and went into the next room.

That was true. Her father did not like gossip or rumors, and he had lectured her about it on many occasions when she was younger. When he bothered to take any time to acknowledge her in the first place. Once, after too many glasses of wine, a rare truth slipped out of his mouth when he said, "Rumors destroyed your mother." It was the only moment she ever knew that he was honest. And it had taken several bottles of wine at a wedding they were attending in the city for that small bit of truth to appear. It had not since, and she had no idea what it meant. When she tried to ask him about it later, he punished her for imagining nonsense by forcing her to sit in on relentless hours of tedious government meetings. People came and went with complaints, many without evidence, and her father decided who was guilty or not based on whatever rumors they presented to him. Or so he said during those meetings. People were mercilessly punished if they had no evidence of the grievance they proclaimed had victimized them. A lesson of great importance, he had repeated to her over and over. At some point during the proceedings, however, she started to notice that several men who worked for her father seemed to take a special interest in certain complaints. She was nearly positive that these men were intimidating many of the people coming before them and destroying whatever evidence they may have had to prove their innocence. Of course she had no way to prove this, only observation and feeling, and she was pretty clear on what reaction that would get. Wandering around her room mindlessly touching things, she felt sure some part of this puzzle was missing. The idea that somehow she could be useful to her father in Africa was confusing, and for the life of her she had no idea what that meant. *What could I possibly do?*

Her caretaker came back into the bedroom, and Bleu turned to face her. "You need to tell me what you've heard. How can you think it's better for me not to know? Keeping me in the dark is what he does, not you." Her voice cracked a little at the end and she hadn't intended to cry, but she was overwhelmed by all these thoughts and questions.

It did, however, make her caretaker soften her nervous look. She hugged her tightly and whispered in her ear, "All I know is that there is a business in Africa that no one is meant to know about. I have no idea what it is nor who works at it nor what its purpose is. I was told at one point your father was advised not to explore the region. He had the man removed from his position and found someone willing to do what he wanted. As we know, your father is not one to have his decisions questioned. I also do not understand what purpose taking you there would serve. But what choice do we have?" She said the last part quietly.

"I am going to go with you and make sure you can study and do whatever I can to keep you safe. If men have really died there, I truly do not know why your father thinks taking you there is a good idea in any way except to perhaps right some wrong we are yet to see."

"Right a wrong? What could I possibly do?" This idea confused her completely.

"Darling, we have a lot to do, and I imagine on our long journey we will have time to talk more. Let's pack and get you ready for dinner."

"I won't get to see him." Bleu said it so softly she wasn't sure she said it aloud.

"I know you won't, and I'm truly sorry. But your friendship won't go away, my love. He will still be here when you get back."

"Whenever that is," she replied, not in anger but in defeat. There was no way for her to win this. She had to go. Turning around and unlacing her boots, her eye caught a glint on the table. She pulled off her cumbersome fencing boots and picked up the charm. Hung from a soft black cord was a stone so blue it seemed to glow from within, shimmering with a silver moon sheen. You could only see it when it caught the light a certain way.

"Get out of that awful uniform and into the bath," said the woman, sounding as close to a mother as she was ever going to get. "We can tie that under your dress and no one will know it's there but us. We ladies, after all, have to have some secrets."

This got a smile out of her as she continued to undo the fencing uniform. It felt good to get the heavy material off her skin and get into the warm water of the bathtub. And really, she did have some pretty dresses to wear to these wretched formal dinners.

Later that evening, as she was dressed and ready for dinner, her stone tied safely out of sight, she took a moment to pull out a map she had and looked at Africa. It seemed so close to them, yet she knew it was very far away. The world spread out before her on the table, she realized that she did want to go on this trip for no other reason than to see what the world outside this city might be. Whatever purpose the trip, whatever reason her father had for bringing her, she was about to do something she had always longed in her heart to do: Explore. And, short of running away, this may be the only chance she'd get.

As she walked down to the formal dining room, her skirt swishing about her and heels clicking the floors, the halls seemed strangely quiet, considering the great bustle only several hours earlier. She passed by huge displays of flowers and large, lit candles. Carpets normally reserved for only the most prestigious of guests had been laid out in the rooms she passed. The rooms were exceptionally clean and presented, which was saying something, as the whole place was normally as immaculate and imposing as it could get. As she walked, distant sounds of piano music started wafting toward her. This really took her by surprise. Bleu enjoyed music and so did the staff, but they were very careful not to disturb her father with it. He allowed her to learn the piano, but he did not want to hear it. One of the cooks had once said her mother played the piano so beautifully it would break your heart, and Bleu had often wondered if that is why he loathed the sound of it so much. Because it made him think of her. The woman who shadowed this place and her father, but of whom she knew so very little.

She reached the dining room before anyone else had arrived. The table was set with the most luxurious and ornate linens, crystals, and silver you could find in the world. The room was aglow, with soft light glinting off all the highly polished pieces. The household staff came in and out, wordlessly setting dishes on the buffet and onto the table. Each and every one of them dressed as formally as Bleu was garbed.

Who in the world is here for dinner, she wondered for about the millionth time. In spite of the curiosity, her stomach grumbled. It had been a while since she had eaten. She looked at the food on the table and picked out in her mind what she would eat. As always, carefully avoiding the things that had made her sick in the past. A secret she worked hard to keep. She stood, waiting for her father to arrive. It was taking much longer than she had anticipated. It wasn't like him to dither. The household kept a rigid schedule when he was here and sometimes even when he wasn't. Bleu made it clear when she was in charge no one should worry too much over dusting the ugly family paintings a hundred times a week. But some of them ignored her, treating her with disregard, and continued to work as though a military general was constantly sitting on their shoulder. The men, of course, most loyal to her father. They treated Bleu as if she was a silly little girl, if they troubled themselves with her presence at all.

When the door finally opened, it wasn't her father at all. It was Cathryn, her face an impenetrable mask of calm. She began to say something to the woman, but Cathryn raised her hand and came to stand next to Bleu.

"I don't understand..." she started to say to her friend, as the doors to the dining room opened. In walked her father in full formal dinner dress, as the servants came in and lined up, one by one, on the far side of the room. Several people followed, carrying glasses of wine and engaged in conversation. Her father seemed to well be ignoring them and stepped to the side of the large, ornate wooden doors to let everyone pass by him. Slowly and elegantly, a tall, stunning woman with white blonde hair and a shimmering silver velvet dress walked through the door. She was wearing white gloves that seem to sparkle with light as she held her hand out to Bleu's father and smiled charmingly at him.

"Your home is beyond lovely, Leopold." She spoke with an accent Bleu didn't recognize.

"It is made ever more lovely by your presence, Fraulein."

The woman strode so confidently around the room she seemed to glide across the floor. Everyone stood by their seats and waited while she stopped to admire each and every painting. A scent of lavender seemed to be following her through the room. Bleu had to resist the urge to sneeze.

Nobody spoke as the fraulein moved to her seat. She stood at one end of the table next to where her father would sit. No one dared sit there without his invitation. It was a seat reserved only for those who interested her father, usually for business or political reasons. Bleu had never been asked to sit there. He kept a minimum of three to four people between them at dinner. She was not expected to talk to him at all. Only to listen if he chose to address her. The woman's presumption she would be welcome to sit there angered Bleu, and she waited for her father to correct the woman in front of everyone.

Instead, she smiled across the room at him and said, "I absolutely cannot wait to eat. I am famished." One of the servants moved to pull a chair out for her as her father strode across the room to the head of the table.

He smiled broadly at the woman and turned to the table. "Please, everyone be seated and enjoy your dinner."

All the guests sat down in their seats as they were pulled out by the servants. Each of them was then given a napkin in their lap. Nearly everyone who worked in the estate seemed to be on duty for the dinner. *Yet another surprise for the evening. Who were these people? Who was that woman?*

As the food was being served, she appreciated greatly that her caretaker tailored a dinner for her to eat, knowing what would make her ill and what would not. No one ever noticed that she did it, and Bleu was always grateful. The one time someone had noticed, her father gave her a lecture on being thankful that she could eat so well when so many could not. That she was served the finest of everything and to reject it was self-centered and unappreciative. What he didn't realize was that she was grateful to eat well, she just had to eat carefully. Something about much of what she was supposed to be grateful for made her ill. But to argue was only to invite more criticism, so that night she ate everything set before her, and for the next two days was as sick as she had ever been before in her life. Her father had left for business and had not been around to hear of this happening. Which was for the best, as he didn't really believe you should take days to be ill. He found it weak and of poor character. He never seemed to get sick or injured.

One of the many intimidating and unusual things about him, she thought as she carefully looked around the table at each guest that evening. She only recognized one face, an ambassador who dealt with many of the relationships that needed to be formed with other countries. That was the extent she knew of his job. Though she had inquired further, she was given abstract answers about his position. He sat to right of her father. It was always his seat. No one else was ever permitted to sit there.

Each one of them was dressed and behaved in a manner which indicated to her that they belonged to wealthy families, whoever they were. The women were bejeweled from head to toe and each smelled of a different flower. None of them, she thought, were as dazzling or as regal as the woman who sat next to her father. The men, like her father, were dressed in formal regalia. One of them seemed to be a military man of sorts but not of an insignia she recognized.

Not a one of them was paying attention to Bleu. She carefully watched them until her glance reached the head of the table where her father sat. He currently was engaged in a conversation with his ambassador, and that was when she realized the blonde woman was watching her and smiling a wide, frozen smile at her that did not seem to reach her eyes. The woman held her gaze for only a moment before holding her crystal wine glass up to servant and waiting for it to be filled. The ambassador turned to the fraulein and said something Bleu could not hear. The woman's laughter rose above the din and caught the attention of several of the other men at the table, including her father. He leaned into her and said something only she could hear and that seemed to widen her smile. Her father smiled, clearly pleased with himself.

Bleu absolutely could not believe this sight. She turned to Cathryn, only noticing then how lovely the woman looked. The red dress she had chosen to wear was more formal than anything she'd ever seen her caretaker in, and it stood out against her skin in a way that lit up her eyes. She had been so distracted by the arrival of these people and the proceedings she had not thought to compliment her. She felt a bit ashamed for being so absorbed in something that probably did not matter at all.

"Cat," she said, "you look really beautiful."

The woman smiled. "Be careful not to call me Cat in front of your father. You know how much he dislikes our nicknames for each other. How is your food? Mine is wonderful, I have to say," her voice dropped to a whisper, "much more than normal, isn't it? Who are all these people?"

"You don't know?" Bleu thought Cathryn would know, and the fact that she didn't drew her attention back to the party in progress.

"I know the ambassador, of course, but I have only guesses as to who the rest of them are, like that woman. She is ravishing, I must say, but when I asked about who she was or where she was from or even why she was here, no one seemed to know. Except the ambassador, and he seemed uninterested in telling me what was going on. I was pretty unhappy with him."

Bleu heard the note of hurt in her voice. The ambassador had been her friend for most of her life, though their positions kept them from each other's social circles most of the time. Bleu had often wondered if there was something more than that between them, but when she had asked, her caretaker had changed the subject and told her not to worry about silly things. Though Bleu didn't find it silly. She would never admit it, but she found it somewhat romantic.

Dinner lasted several hours, most of which Bleu spent talking about her studies with Cathryn. No one seemed interested at all that they were there. Which was fine by both of them. By the time dessert was being served, both of the women had figured out exactly what they needed to bring on their mystery journey.

Dessert was an unbelievable concoction made with flavors she couldn't identify. The light in the room had dimmed as the candles had melted further down. It seemed several of the conversations had stopped while some had turned either intensely heated or completely flirtatious.

Cat leaned over to her and whispered, "Everyone seems to have had their fill of wine. Including your father."

She had barely bothered to pay attention to her father as her studies were the most important thing to her. Glancing over, she saw her father's cheeks were quite red. He and the ambassador were gushing over the fraulein who had a brilliantly coy smile on her face.

Her father said loudly, "You must stay here until we leave. We have accommodations that I am sure will meet your approval and needs."

"Really, Leopold, it's not necessary. We are settled into a hotel further into the city. It is quite lovely," the fraulein said demurely. Bleu didn't know why but she felt like it was a pretty false statement.

"Hotels are for commoners," the ambassador declared. "You are most certainly not common. We will have all your things and your staff brought to the estate." As he said it, Bleu's father nodded to the head of the household who quickly left the room.

"Well," Cat whispered, "I do not know if your father has ever invited a woman to stay here. I have to say, I'm pretty astounded to hear this." Bleu didn't know what to say. She had never known her father to show interest in any woman unless he needed something from her or her husband, and even then it was never flirtatious in nature. He stuck with figuring out what charitable cause they seemed to support or political issue that was of importance to them and used that as a way to garner their attention. She was going to find out who this woman was before they left.

As everyone at the table was finishing dessert and started to rise, it seemed an after-party of sorts had been planned in the formal living room. And it was made clear to both Cathryn and Bleu that they were not required to stay, "though they could if they wished." Her father said it in a way that indicated he did not really care what they chose to do.

"I want to try to find out who that woman is, Cat," Bleu said in a lowered, hurried voice. She was nervous as to what her caretaker's reaction would be to that statement, since she was always telling Bleu not to concern herself with her father's affairs nor with who the people were coming in and out the house. She always told Bleu to focus on her studies, on fencing and riding. Cathryn seemed pretty determined that she not be troubled by adulthood for as long as possible. A sentiment Bleu was starting to feel she was truly outgrowing.

The older woman smiled at her and said, "Don't we all?" This made her laugh. Definitely not the reaction she was expecting but glad for it nonetheless.

They moved into the formal living area that was filled with the unfamiliar sight of fresh flowers. Candles twinkled against the many gilded frames, vases, and polished-to-a-shine furniture. It was the first time in a long time that Bleu thought the room looked appealing. It seemed to have a little bit of life in it for once. Something a lot of the house seemed to be missing most of the time. Having generally avoided the larger formal rooms, she realized how uncomfortable she usually felt in her own home.

Her father sat down in a large, kingly wooden chair, and the fraulein was never far from his ear. She was surrounded by the guests nearly all evening, making it impossible for Bleu or Cat to get in to talk to her. Her father's personal assistant came into the room and whispered something to him. Her father, by that point, was drunk. He, in turn, loudly announced that all of their rooms were ready and their things had arrived, so they should feel free to make their way to them whenever they would like.

As the hours went by, Bleu was starting to feel tired and Cat noticed, though neither of them made a move to leave. Bleu knew how stubborn her caretaker could be, and it occurred to her that she may very well have picked up that trait. The guests started to drift out one by one, the women fading and no doubt wanting to remove their pounds and pounds of jewelry, she thought. The men were drunk and loud, though not her father's ambassador, she noted. He seemed to have grown more quiet through the evening. The fraulein was still in top form. She always had a glass within reach, but Bleu was pretty sure she wasn't drinking much from it. The conversation between her father and the woman seemed to have grown more private. The ambassador was the only other one of them that seemed as involved as they. He stopped continuously to write notes in a tiny book he carried in his vest pocket.

Cat leaned over to Bleu. "We don't seem to be getting anywhere, and what I wouldn't do to look in that notebook." She set her glass down on the table with a clink.

Bleu looked at her and realized that she seemed more than a little displeased. She put her hand on Cat's arm. "Maybe we should just go to bed for now. We can always try again tomorrow."

Cat seemed about to reply when the fraulein got up and strode directly over to them. She stood above them, making Bleu feel as though she were about a foot tall. She and Cat stood, and the woman smiled her brilliant white smile.

"I am terribly exhausted," she said in a voice that sounded anything but. "I do hope you ladies have been enjoying your evening as much as I have." She looked over her shoulder and raised her glass gracefully to Bleu's father. He returned the gesture and went back to talking to the ambassador but never took his eyes off the fraulein.

"I would very much like to get to know both of you," she continued. "Women must always stick together so we shall not be outdone by the men." Something in her tone struck Bleu, and she was pretty sure this woman had never been outdone by any man.

"I don't think you have to worry about us. This one," Cat gestured to Bleu, "is as smart, clever, and resourceful as any man I've ever met." The note of pride in her voice was unmistakable. Bleu felt a little silly at the sudden burst of praise but also happy to hear she felt that way.

"No doubt," said the Fraulein, though her voice sounded as if she had her doubts. "Your father is a charming man. He doesn't speak much of home. Only business matters, affairs of state, things of those nature." Bleu felt her stomach turn. It didn't surprise her that her father didn't talk about her, but she didn't need to have it pointed out to her by a stranger.

"He is a busy man." Cat definitely sounded annoyed now. "Let's go upstairs. No doubt the fraulein has many important things to discuss with your father." She took Bleu by the elbow and led her from the room. Bleu felt the words ringing in her ears, and, even though she didn't want them to, they hurt.

"She's right," her voice flat and hard. "He doesn't talk about me because he doesn't think I'm worth talking about." They were walking down the hall, and Cat stepped in front of Bleu, putting her hands on Bleu's shoulders.

"Look at me," she said. "Your father is an important and powerful man. He is a good leader and generous. But he is not perfect, and one of the ways he is not perfect is that he takes for granted having you for a daughter. That is not your fault. He cannot handle you because you remind him of a loss. A loss he could not prevent. And that is something he has not been able to get over."

"I don't care," she replied defiantly, knowing it wasn't true at all. "I'm used to him not caring about me, I'm used to knowing I embarrass him."

"You are not an embarrassment. I do not know who that woman is, but she does not know anything about you. She knows nothing about who you are, the person you're becoming. Her words do not matter." Cathryn wrapped her arms around Bleu protectively and held her as the tears she resented having washed down her face. "Your father does not know you either, and that is going to be a great sadness to him soon. I am sorry that I cannot fix his behavior, but I will tell you every day that it is not your fault, if I have to."

This slowed the tears a bit and got a small smile out of her. Cat would tell her that every day, she was certain.

"You don't have to tell me every day, and really most of the time I don't care anymore because what choice do I have. But sometimes I wish..." she got a little choked up again but swallowed hard. She hated tears. She hugged Cathryn back and then started back to her room. She did not want to be out here if anyone else left the party. Namely that woman or her father. She heard the door to the formal room open and turned to see Cathryn with her arms crossed waiting for the ambassador, who was making his way to the front door.

Cathryn stood right in his path, and Bleu went around the corner in the hall and held back to peek at them. She couldn't hear what they were saying, but

Cathryn was clearly giving the ambassador a piece of her mind. He had always seemed to Bleu to be a nervous man, and he was clearly more agitated than normal as Cathryn continued to talk. It went on for about ten minutes before she finally stepped aside so he could leave. He did not move right away, only looked at her with hurt and confusion on his face. Which is exactly how Cathryn was feeling. She was sure of it.

With a dramatic swish, Cathryn turned on her heel and left the ambassador standing in her wake. He seemed more than a little shaken by whatever it was she said to him. Bleu leaned back out of sight but not soon enough for Cat not to see her.

The woman turned the corner, took Bleu by her elbow again, and guided her firmly to the bedroom.

"I wasn't eavesdropping ..." she said. Cathryn didn't look at her but the corner of her mouth twitched a little.

"If, Dearest, I thought you could hear me from that far away, I'd have you spying on more important matters than my annoyances," she said sarcastically but not without humor.

She let go of her arm and laughed a little. "We still have a lot to do. We should probably go pack as many things that make us happy to take with us as we can, if we have to be stuck on this arduous journey with all these insufferable people." Bleu snorted at this statement. Cat had a hard time keeping how she really felt to herself. A trait, she suspected, her father both liked and loathed in her caretaker. She was the closest thing Bleu had to a real parent, and a rush of emotion came over her so she threw her arms around the woman. Cat hugged Bleu tightly but briefly and opened the door to her room.

"Now go to your room, Bleu. I will be there in the morning to help you finish gathering things. Then we'll sneak to the kitchen and make sure all the teas we like best get packed, as well as the simpler foods for travel." Bleu nodded her head and continued down the massive hall as Cat shut her bedroom door.

Bleu decided she wasn't quite as tired as she thought just a bit ago. Instead of heading right to her room, she decided to go to the library. She went down the steps and noticed how quiet the halls seemed to be now, after all the music and chatting at the dinner party. Not even one of the servants was around. She wondered how late it actually was and glanced around as she stepped off the staircase. Many of the lights had been put out in the house, and it was mostly dark, except for bright moonlight leaking through the grand windows. Clouds moved across the sky, shadowing what bit of light there was as Bleu realized someone was coming out her father's office. For the second time that evening she moved out of sight to see what was happening.

The woman moved as soundlessly as a ghost when she shut the door to her father's office. It was so carefully done, Bleu was sure her father was not in the office. The woman had something in her hand. She wasn't sure what it was as the complete darkness came and went. It seemed as though it might be a rolled up piece of paper. The fraulein's voluminous dress made the only noise in the dark as she came down the hall towards where Bleu hid.

Bleu moved further into the shadows, holding her breath as the woman grew closer. The fraulein seemed to stop moving for a moment, as Bleu could no longer hear the swish of the dress material. For what seemed many minutes, there was no movement. Bleu dared not even breathe. She didn't know why but she was pretty sure she should not let the fraulein know she had seen her come out of the office. Just as suddenly as it stopped, the sound of the woman's dress moving away from Bleu started again. She waited another long moment and glanced around the corner just in time to see a sliver of the glimmer of the dress move up the back stairs toward the guest rooms.

She finally exhaled. The woman had turned away at the last minute. *Did she think I was down here?* It appeared as if the fraulein was coming this way to go up the stairs but then changed her mind. *Should I tell my father what I saw? What would I say? Maybe he knew she was in his office? They did seem to be working on plans together. Was it possible he had given this mysterious woman access to the one room that was off-limits to everyone else without his presence? That was very unlikely.* As far as she knew, her father ran the world from that room. At least the world they lived in. *If there wasn't anything strange about the woman being in the room, why was she in there in the darkness and silence of the middle of the night? No, something is definitely off.* Bleu had no idea what or why. Her mind was running away with a million possibilities. Now she was never going to get to sleep.

It had grown cold in the hall, so the warm familiar library was even more inviting than normal. She closed the door as silently as she could behind her and moved to the desk in the dark. Of all the rooms in the house, she knew this one best. Besides her own room, this was her favorite place in the house. She ran her hands across the desk until she felt the box of matches she had left there. She opened one and struck a stick. It flared to life and she lit several candles on the desk. As always, everything was as she left it. No one ever came in here. All the books that interested her father were in his large, dark library in his office. This had been her mother's room, and as far as she knew it was left exactly as it was before she died. She picked up one of the volumes left open on the desk and touched the tiny, perfect handwriting in the margins. She wasn't completely sure, but she believed this was her mother's handwriting. Most of the books Bleu had ever picked up were filled with delicate notes her mother had written in them. All carefully kept in the margins, never marring the printed words themselves. Most of the notes were easy to understand, thoughts and feelings about certain stories or philosophies. But sometimes the notes made no sense that was discernible. Even after reading an entire book, sometimes multiple times, the notes were confusing.

Some of the notes in science books could perhaps be theories or questions simply constructed out of experiments, but the real mystery was: When was her mother experimenting with anything scientific? Not knowing enough about the family's past led her to draw a lot of conclusions that had no basis. It left her to wonder endlessly about them. As she had gone through the books for many years, it had started to seem as though her mother had been looking for an answer to something. What that could be, she really had no idea. She had wondered before if it was an answer to some of her father's businesses. It seemed at times that not many people knew what exactly he did outside the country. When she had asked what his dealings were she had been shrugged off like a child. Even Cat seemed to either be in the dark about them or was unwilling to share what knowledge she had. And sometimes Bleu was left to wonder what secrets Cat kept from her. She didn't think they were kept with the intention to hurt her. Knowing Cat, it was exactly the opposite. There were, however, books with notes written in them that Bleu could not even begin to imagine had anything to do with whatever the business outside the country might be. Books about the heavens and night sky. Books about myths that her mother seem to take very seriously. Odd notes in art books with pictures of dark, fantastical paintings and sculptures with names written under them with question marks. Names she did not recognize as being any people her father knew now. *Maybe friends from the past?* The other part that raised questions for her was that they were in fact not all in places that her father was known or had ever had business, so far as she could guess. She had thought that perhaps these were the artists or their muses, but further research on her part had yielded no evidence of that being the case. She had read and reread everything in this room multiple times and kept notebooks of her mother's notes to reference when she tried to guess or cross-check things she thought might match. None of it helped. In fact, it usually just caused more questions to come out of what possible answers she might have had.

Her restlessness caused her to pick up the books that were laid on the desk over and over and flip through them, unsatisfied with the idea of rereading them. It's not that she wanted anything new. She always had new books being brought to her, thanks to Cat and her fencing teacher. Even books she had surmised her father wouldn't want her reading. But Cat didn't worry too much about telling him what they were doing most of the time. She was also very good at making sure that the servants more loyal to him than to them saw and heard only what they needed to see and hear. Cat was extremely good at managing the information about Bleu's life when he cared to show interest in it. Which made his sudden command that she come to Africa all the more unusual. *Never mind his astonishing behavior with the fraulein.* Thinking of that woman irritated her, and she set down a book so carelessly it knocked over an ink well.

"Dammit," she muttered under her breath. She reached for sheets of old blank paper to catch the ink before it touched the antiquarian wooden desk. As the indigo ink ran in little rivers with candlelight glinting on it, she realized the paper wasn't blank at all. The ink that soaked into the sheets filled indentations on the paper that appeared to have once been written there but had faded long ago. She picked up a sheet and moved it around slowly to spread the ink. More and more words started to appear between the blotches. She set it down gently, opened a drawer to pull out a soft cloth meant for caring for the delicate covers of the old books, and blotted the ink away carefully, not wanting to smear too much and make them unreadable. She moved delicately over the sheet, trying to move the ink in the dim light to make out what it might say. As more and more of it became clear, it seemed some of the notes were familiar to her. Many of the names she had puzzled over under artistic masterpieces were written in the same handwriting as in the books, but they seemed to be in a list. With what looked like hieroglyphs next to them. Although there was something about them that implied to her that they weren't Egyptian. Though vaguely familiar symbols, they didn't match in her mind anything she had read or learned in her Egyptology studies. Knowing she certainly didn't have all the knowledge of Ancient Egypt that she'd like to, she did have a lot. Much of her youth had been spent poring over books filled with the magical history and language of the great kings and queens of the fascinating world away. As she was looking as closely as possible, another indentation caught her notice. Her name was written next to one of the drawings, and it was written in different handwriting.

That could only mean that someone else had written this list with her mother, and it was not her father, as the markings were not in his hand. Nor were they in Cat's or anyone else's that she knew now. And furthermore, HER name was on this list. *What in the world was this list?*

She couldn't believe after all this time she had never looked at this paper closely. It was always stacked here. On the rare occasions someone came to clean the library besides her, it was moved but always replaced as it was when they began to clean. Bleu always brought her own notebooks with her to the library to write and make notes. It had never occurred to her to use anything in here that wasn't easily returned, and thus the stack of paper had sat there for years. She stared and stared at the sheet. She rifled through the other sheets, wondering if she should try to see if there was more written on them. Lifting the ink well so the flame of the candle shone through the glass, she could see there wasn't much left in the bottle. *I can do part of another sheet and come back with more ink tomorrow.* She closed her eyes for a moment and thought about all she had to do. The opportunity for time alone in here tomorrow was unlikely to present itself. Packing and readying for that blasted journey had to be done, and with that thought, the melancholy of leaving behind her home and the few friends she had washed over her again, as did a feeling of overwhelming exhaustion. She held the sheet and sat down in the big, soft, velvet chair behind the desk. It was a chair so big she could sit with her legs tucked under her. Made slightly more difficult by her formal dinner dress, she adjusted the skirt beneath her knees and feet. Pulling a throw that was one of the few things she had ever brought to leave in the room down over her, she settled in and studied the sheet more closely. It was getting into the late hours of the night, and she could hear the clock ticking out in the great hall entrance. A sound that with all the people in the house you would normally barely notice. Her mind wandered as the list slipped from her hand to her lap. The cold, beautiful woman passed through her thoughts, and one more time the question of who this person was sat at the end of consciousness. Drifting between awake and asleep, the image in the mysterious handwriting danced in the unnatural colors produced with the twinkling glow.

Her eyes started to feel heavy with sleep, and as they began to close, the vague impression that someone came in the room made her sit up quickly and look around. Thunderous, her heartbeat sounded in the hushed, book-filled room. The door was closed and latched as it had been left upon her entry.

"Hello?" Her voice falling off into the dark empty corners of the library. It was a relatively large room with plenty of secluded spaces. But sleep-clouded eyes made out no one in the shadows, and it was still as the night before dawn. Leaning back into the chair, clutching the sheet of paper tightly in her hand, an uncomfortable sleep washed over her. Images of someone going through the desk and shuffling through the books, as she sat in the chair only partially awake and unable to move with the bone-weary tiredness that comes with emotional strain, kept her from fully resting. As did the continued worry about what the day of preparing would bring. And ultimately, leaving for Africa. She awoke several more times, once with tears on her face she knew were because she would miss her friend's visit, she had longed to see him so much. It had been two years since she last saw him and he'd been sent off to school by his father. Her own father made it well known that he didn't want them to be in acquaintance. She didn't know why and when she asked Cat about her father's harsh words about their friendship, Cat didn't have much of an answer beyond that Bleu's father didn't think his young daughter should be entangled with any male companions at this point. This made Bleu indignant to say the least.

"We are not entangled," Bleu told her irritably.

Cat had smiled at her and replied with, "Of course not, love, your father just thinks all your focus should be on your studies, and so do I."

Despite that statement, a few chance encounters with her friend when she and Cat had ventured off the grounds of the house had made her wonder if Cat really felt that Bleu was "entangled." *We are just friends,* she thought ever more irrationally as she tried to get comfortable in the chair, not really knowing why she didn't want to go sleep in her room. Knowing only that she would miss this sanctuary of peace when they left, something about leaving the room would make it real again. Whatever reason she had to go with these people on this trip, Bleu had a growing suspicion that it wasn't a good one. Trying to put it out of mind at least for now, she closed her eyes to sleep.

There was sunlight streaming through the window, catching the dust particles, and making them glint in the bright spots in the library. Taking a minute to focus, Bleu realized someone was over by one of the bookshelves picking up volumes, flipping through them carelessly, and putting them back.

"What are you doing?" Bleu demanded of the fraulein. The woman was fully dressed for a day in the city, with her hair pinned back tight and boots polished to a shine peeking out of her long, full skirt.

"Be careful with those books, they belonged to my mother," Bleu stood up and straightened her gown. She frowned and realized she looked very disheveled in front of her father's guest and no doubt would hear a lecture from Cat about it.

The woman continued to ignore her and wandered around a minute more before she turned to acknowledge Bleu.

"Your father invited me to visit anywhere in the house," she said with an emphasis on the word 'anywhere' which made Bleu wonder again if the woman knew she had seen her coming out of the office. How she had seen Bleu, she could not figure out, but something made her feel the slightest bit nervous about the woman's tone. *Of course,* Bleu thought grumpily, *SHE is the one sneaking around MY house, not the other way around.*

"Well, that's nice that my father invited you to visit the house," she replied in a tone so sweet that she almost laughed. "But those books still belonged to my mother and they are old, fragile, and valuable. So I'd thank you, Fraulein, to be careful with them."

For some reason, this made the fraulein smile. "Your appearance notwithstanding at the moment, which is a mess, I would very much like to be friends."

That caught her by surprise. She hadn't expect the fraulein to say that, though something about it didn't sound genuine, Bleu decided. She was pretty sure this woman could not be trusted. *Who sneaks around someone's house at night and goes into rooms that I am positive my father locks every evening?* She did not trust her nor did she want to be her friend, whatever that meant to this woman. *However, maybe the best way to figure out what she is really doing here and why my father seems to care so much is to accept this offer of friendship.*

"I would very much like that as well," she replied. "I should probably go change my clothes before my father sees me," Bleu said it in a light tone. "He'll get cross with me if he realizes I slept in here."

"I shall not tell him. We women must stick together," she said as she reached a hand out and brushed a piece of hair off of Bleu's face.

She had to force herself not to pull away from the woman's ice-cold hands.

"Thank you," Bleu smiled at the woman. "I'd appreciate that. I should probably get going. I have a lot to do today and you look like you're on your way somewhere." As she said that, the door to the library opened and Cat stepped inside.

"Is everything alright in here?" she asked in a cautious tone.

"Everything is great," Bleu said to Cat in an overly cheerful tone. She bowed her head to the fraulein and held her arm as a gesture for the woman to leave. Cat stepped aside and held the door as the woman turned and walked down the hall out of sight without another word.

Cat arched an eyebrow at Bleu. "What was she doing in here?"

"She said Father told her to visit anywhere in the house." Bleu set about picking up books and replacing bookmarks. "I don't know that I've ever known him to invite anyone to look anywhere they wanted. Do you think he also meant his office?"

"I think you know he didn't mean his office, Bleu. Why would you ask that?" Cat started collecting books and waiting for nods of yes or no as to which ones she should bring to pack. Bleu hurried over to the library door and closed it. She glanced around quickly, as if expecting someone to jump out of the corners.

"Because when I came down here last night I saw the fraulein coming out of the office and Father was not with her. In fact, no one was around and she seemed to be overly cautious with any noise she was making and was taking her time to see if anyone had noticed her."

"Well that is very interesting indeed. Did she see you?"

"I don't think so. As soon as I saw her I hid out of sight. I don't really know why. All I can say is that I just had a strange feeling about it." Bleu was standing and saying the words quickly, her heart racing. She was sure that whatever was going on was very big. Though she had absolutely no reason to think this other than a feeling.

"Your face is flushed," Cat said. "Do you feel okay?" She put her hand on Bleu's forehead.

"I'm just tired. I didn't sleep well. I don't want to leave on this trip. I have a dreadful feeling about it and I want to see Dorran but obviously I can't." She felt the tears welling up again and hated it. She felt like a child whenever she was going to cry, and she didn't want to be treated like a child anymore.

Cat sighed. "I know you want to see Dorran. I want you to see him too."

"What? I thought you agreed with my father that I shouldn't be distracted from my studies." She said it bitterly even though she didn't want to. She couldn't help it. A big part of her was getting really tired of being told what to do.

"Bleu, I want you to be happy, and he is your friend. Despite what you think sometimes, I do have your best interests at heart. He is a nice boy and someday he will be a nice man, and that is better than what you can say about a lot of people."

"I don't guess there's any possible way to get out of this trip?"

"I doubt it, sweetie." Cat continued to sort books and started to shuffle through the papers on the desk.

"Oh, the papers... I almost forgot," Bleu walked over to the chair where she had fallen asleep and bent to pick up the books and papers that had fallen to the floor. "I found these sheets. They have invisible symbols on them, or I mean, I guess invisible notes. I don't know, it's strange. I was wondering if maybe they made sense to you." She continued to dig through the pile and flip through the papers over and over. "I don't understand where they are, though. I had them last night when I fell asleep, although..." Bleu's voice trailed off and Cat stopped to look at her.

"Although what?" She walked over to where Bleu was pulling the cushions off the chair and tossing the pillows onto the floor. "What are you looking for?" Cat bent over to pick things up off the floor.

Bleu was on her hands and knees now, looking under the desk, chair, and shelves.

"I'm looking for these sheets I found last night. I swear... I swear they had invisible notes written on them. I know that sounds really crazy. But they were here and I don't understand where they went, unless..." she paused and looked at Cat, who stopped and stacked a bunch of papers onto the desk. "Unless someone took them." She looked directly at the door.

"You certainly had an eventful evening after I left you to go to bed." Cat went back to picking things up.

"You don't sound like you believe me." Bleu stood up and dusted off her gown, which was absolutely a mess now. She had to get back to her room before her father saw her or she would be lectured for eternity.

"No, it's not that I don't believe you. But I do think that you're under a lot of emotional stress right now and may be looking into things more than you should."

"I'm not looking into anything," Bleu snapped. "That woman was coming out of Father's office and she was acting strangely. It wasn't my imagination." She sounded defensive. She didn't want to sound defensive. She was still tired.

"I didn't imagine the symbols. I spilled ink on the desk, and when it spread onto the sheet these words and symbols started to appear. I'll show you the cloth I used to clean up the desk." She stalked over to the table where she left the rag and it was not there either.

"What the hell?" Staring at the stacks, she had to resist the urge to throw them off the table.

"Stress or no stress, do not use that language," Cat came around and put her arm around Bleu.

"I'm not being crazy," she insisted.

"Okay, then where is the rag? Where is the paper?" She squeezed her a little tighter. "Maybe you're not making it up, but you do sometimes remember things wrong." She finished the sentence gently.

Bleu couldn't argue with that. She did sometimes remember things wrong and she could never explain why that happened.

"I know I do, but I thought someone was in here last night."

"Why did you think that? Did you see someone or hear someone?"

"Well, no. I just thought... It just felt like someone was in here." She looked down at her hands. *No way that didn't sound crazy.*

"I see." Cat stepped away from her and turned her to face her, eye to eye. "Is it possible that maybe after seeing the fraulein you just might've been feeling a little paranoid? That would be understandable."

"So you do believe that I saw her down here?" Bleu looked at her caretaker. If Cat didn't believe her, she would have to wonder if she was going crazy. She wasn't remembering it wrong. Not this time.

"I do believe you and do think there is something very off about that woman. Not to mention that I have the oddest feeling that I know her."

"You think you know her? Why didn't you tell me that?" Bleu demanded.

"Because I couldn't put my finger on it last night and you were already so upset. I also don't know why I think I've met her before. It's sitting off at the end of my mind, just out my reach, love."

"She was coming out of father's office and she was in here this morning. She must've taken the sheets," Bleu said stubbornly.

"What would she want with those?"

"Why else would she be in here? Why was she in father's office? Who is she? We don't know her at all. We've never heard her name. No one said anything about her. Father had the house decorated and prepared for her arrival. When does he act like that? For anyone? He'll have the house cleaned regularly and even extra for the politicians and when he needs money for the country or a business venture. But for a person? And the flowers and the music and the wine and the party. I mean, who is SHE?" Bleu's voice raised, and as it did, Cat put a hand on her shoulder to calm her down. She shrugged it off.

"You need to listen to me, Cat. Something is going ON!" Her head ached, she pressed a palm into her temple.

"Bleu, what's wrong? Your face is getting pale. Are you okay?" She put her hands on Bleu's face.

"I don't feel very good. My head is starting to hurt." She almost fell onto the chair. As Bleu sat she heard the sound of paper crunching but she was starting to have a hard time seeing and breathing. Cat was saying something but she couldn't understand her. Cat was so far away and Bleu didn't understand why she had gone so far away.

That seemed wrong. Bleu shook her head hard, and as clearly as the pain came, it was gone. Her eyes focused and Cat's worried face was right in front of her. Cat's eyes filled with a familiar concern. Bleu smiled and massaged her forehead as Cat walked to the desk, picked up a pitcher filled with water, and poured a glass. Bleu took the glass from her and drank it slowly as little bursts of color popped up in her eyes every time she blinked.

"Do you feel better?" Cat asked as she smoothed Bleu's hair down. Bleu nodded her head yes as she drank water and heard the paper-crunching sound again. She handed the glass back to Cat, stood up, and felt a bit dizzy. Bleu pulled the pillows and cushions off the chair.

"What are you doing, sweetie?" Cat sounded worried again. "You're being a little odd this morning and it's starting to really concern me. We have a lot to do today, plus there's an errand I need to do in town and I thought you might want to come with me." Her tone of voice gave Bleu a moment of pause, and she turned to look at the older woman.

"What errand do you have to do?" She momentarily forgot what she was doing and went over to the woman.

Cat smiled slyly.

"Well," she started organizing the desk and not looking at Bleu, "I need to pick up some gifts. Your father asked me to have some things at the ready to bestow upon leaders where we are going." She kept cleaning without stopping. "Conveniently, there's a certain jewelry artisan who happened to arrive in town earlier than he originally planned, and I made arrangements by courier for us to go meet with the artisan's assistant." She stopped and smiled at Bleu. "I figured you might want to join me. But I will tell you that we don't have a lot of time, and, bothersome enough, your father also wants me to pick up a gift for you-know-who." Cat frowned, "I didn't want to keep that from you since he'll probably give it to her in front of everyone at tonight's going away gathering."

"Wait, going away gathering?"

"Yes, Bleu, your father is having a banquet this evening with a dance. The house is utter madness right now with the preparations. Never mind all the workers who ran into the city at dawn to invite everyone your father expects here tonight. But no doubt it'll get done. Because, well, that's how it goes here."

"I cannot believe we are having another social."

"Last night was just a dinner, darling. Most officials have them frequently and keep their homes filled with guests, wine, and flowers. As we all know, the head of this household tends to find these things a waste of time and money. Not that he has always," she added at the end. "Tonight will be different, and you will wear a ball gown and be as gorgeous as ever."

"I don't have a ball gown." She was so confused. *Why is my father acting like this?*

"You do have ball gowns. Many of them, in fact. They were made for you over the years by friends of your mother's. She was a great patron of all arts, as you know. I've had the gowns stored for a long time, and I am having one brought up as we speak and tailored for you to wear this evening. We will also be bringing some of them on this journey. I was told there would be ample opportunities to wear them." Cat sounded pleased by this possibility, and Bleu had no idea what to think. Except that she wanted to know more about her mother.

"My mother decorated this house, right?" She had to be careful about how she asked her questions, otherwise Cat wouldn't give her any more answers.

"She did, love. But your father had a lot of the art taken down and stored when she... when she left us." Cat sounded a little choked up, but she had her back to Bleu, who couldn't see her face.

"But a lot the stuff that's still up? She picked that out?"

"She did. And the furniture, piano, silver, these books," she gestured around the room.

"The house was magnificent, and I am sorry you cannot remember it. You were so young when she left us." Cat stood still and stared out a window as the sky was lighting up with the morning. "Your mother felt fortunate to have access to so much wealth. And as such, she used it to make other peoples lives more comfortable by commissioning them to create, most often, the greatest works of their lives. And it wasn't limited to art. She took care of farmers, florists, musicians, wine makers... Everyone, really. And because of her kind generosity and support, everyone adored her."

"Where is all the art now? Was some of the stuff we used last night things she had made?" Bleu's words rushed out. She had so many questions and wanted to know every little detail. But she knew at any moment her caretaker would stop answering them.

"I told you, love, they are stored. They are in the farther parts of the house, and we never go over there. Your father has not exactly forbidden it, but he has made it quite clear that the staff is not allowed into that wing of the estate. NOW! Enough questions. I really do want you to come with me on this errand, so are you sure you're feeling well?" She fussed about more as Bleu chewed on her lip.

"Will you answer one more question?"

Cat looked at Bleu with sad eyes and nodded. "I will. But then you have to promise me that you will get upstairs and get ready for the day. Everyone is dashing about to prepare for the gala, and us for the journey. We must do our part."

"Okay, I promise." A million questions raced through her mind and she knew Cat wouldn't answer most of them. But she had always wondered something. "Was my mother an artist? Did she paint? I once thought I overheard Father say that she used to paint."

"Wow, Bleu, you have quite successfully been a spy all these years, haven't you?" She laughed a little. "Yes, your mother was an artist. A very talented one. And you should know her art was the first to be taken down and moved from this part of the house."

Bleu took this in and wanted more than anything to see what her mother had painted.

"What did she paint?"

"Nope, no more questions. You promised. And have you already forgotten we have an appointment?"

"Right," Bleu said impatiently, "with the jeweler."

"Yes, but a jeweler who has an assistant of whom you happen to be very fond..." her voice trailed off and even sounded the tiniest bit smug.

"Wait, what? You did say... oh my... they made it into town early? That's what you meant."

"Yes, silly, that is what I meant. Now pick up those cushions off the floor that you threw there for whatever reason, and go get ready."

"The cushions..." she looked at the floor. "Oh right, yes, I know why I did that."

Cat laughed. "You're really not making any sense."

"NO, I found these papers last night, and I think when I fell asleep I must've forced them between the cushions." She pulled the last big one off the chair, but only a torn fragment of paper was there.

"What? Where are they? I know they were here." She dug through the pillows and shook the blanket that was on the floor. "Did you take anything off here, Cat? Did you put those papers on the desk?" A frantic feeling was rising in her. She didn't know why, but she wanted those papers.

"Bleu, I did not take any papers. Are you talking about those papers with the symbols? What is that piece on the chair?"

Bleu picked it up and looked closely at it. It was torn and it looked as if nothing was written on it.

"This must be one of them," she muttered to herself. She brushed past Cat and put the piece of paper down on the table, smoothing it out as she reached for the bottle of ink.

"Are you really going to dump that on there?" Cat asked and shook her head. "Well, fine. Let's see. What are these symbols?" Bleu ignored her and carefully let ink drop from the bottle to the piece of paper, trying to not flood it with too much liquid. Nothing happened as she stared at the paper. They waited as a minute ticked by and no symbols appeared.

"I don't understand. I thought there was something on them."

"You are so overwhelmed right now, and you were so tired maybe you imagined it. Our minds deceive us sometimes when we are not expecting it."

"I didn't imagine it." Bleu snatched the paper up and put it over the candle light that had burned low to the holder through the night.

"You really were lucky that candle did not catch anything on fire. You must be more careful," Cat lectured.

Bleu was about to respond when the ink started to take shape.

"Look, here. See what I mean? This is so strange. The ink, it's like it's reacting to the light or something."

Bleu was so intent on watching the symbols appear she didn't realize that Cat had fallen completely silent.

She looked up at her. Cat's face looked stressed.

"What's the matter?" she asked. "Have you seen these symbols before? You look like you've seen a ghost. Or, you know, a creepy woman coming out of a dark office." The joke fell flat in the room as Cat took the paper from her hands.

"Hellllooooo?" She waved her hand between Cat's face and the torn sheet. Cat kept staring at the sheet until Bleu tried to pull it from her hands. That seemed to snap her out of it, but she held tight to the paper. Bleu let go as Cat smiled and handed it to her.

"Sorry, love. They are just doodles. They are nothing important. I just hadn't seen your mother's handwriting in a long time," she finished sadly and started picking up all the pillows and cushions on the floor. "You need to hurry if we are going to make it to our appointment on time. We shouldn't waste a minute. I'd like to see them too."

Bleu watched as Cat went around the room cleaning and picking up things to be packed. Bleu was positive she wasn't telling her the truth. Or at least not all of it. *All of the adults in my life are going insane.* Clearly Cat was not going to tell her anything else, and she really did want to see their friends. She grabbed a stack of books and blank sheets off the desk.

"Take the back stairs," Cat called to her before she walked out the door. "Most everyone is busy but your father's ambassador is twittering about like a dolt, and we don't need him telling your father how disheveled you are this morning. Now, hurry. The girls laid out your clothes on the bed. Wash up and I'll meet you out front."

"Okay, Cat." Bleu stopped. "Thanks for answering some of my questions about my mother. I know you could get into trouble with my father for it."

"You're welcome, and don't worry about him. I'll see you shortly." Cat shooed her out the door. Bleu dashed off down the hall to the stairs, being careful to be quiet and avoid any of the houseworkers.

When Bleu made it back downstairs thirty minutes later, Cat was speaking to the ambassador. She did not look happy.

When he saw Bleu making her way over, he nodded to her and walked away.

"What's the matter?" Bleu adjusted the strap on her bag.

"Nothing is the matter. Are you ready to go?"

"Yes, I'm ready. Are you sure you want it to be just us by ourselves?" Bleu asked. "I mean if we are carrying gold jewelry we should be careful right?"

"We'll be fine. Let's go."

They started on a walk into town. It wasn't a long walk, but her father probably wouldn't be happy if he found out that they went alone. Though they did when he was out of town. No one dared report on Cat to her father. A lot of people in the area of the city knew who they were, since her father ran the country. *It is somewhat awful.* She wished more often than not that no one knew who she was or who her father was. Most people didn't dare say anything negative to her, but on the occasions that it had happened it had been pretty terrible. She felt for the people. So many of them had known her father when her mother was still alive, and one thing Bleu knew for sure was that his compassion had all but disappeared when she had died.

"Cat?"

"Yes, love?"

"Sometimes I hate going into town."

"I do too. But why do you hate it specifically?"

"Because it can be awful to see how some people are forced to live. I don't understand why my father doesn't help them."

"He believes we all have to help ourselves."

"That's not right, though. Life is not always fair to everyone, and people don't get choices in a lot of the things that happen to them."

"That's true. So what do you think we should do about it? What do you think you should do about it?"

"I don't know, I guess. I've never really thought about it before."

"Well, love, why don't you think about it. And maybe whatever you think you should do, I can also do it when we come back from Africa."

"Do you think people need help there too?"

"I think, and forgive me for saying this, love, that if your father and his men have been there, it is likely at least some of them need help just like people here."

"If I had thought about this more, Cat, I would probably think that too."

They walked the rest of the way to the town in silence, with the exception of nodding hellos to the people who passed them on the path, or to turn down offers of carriage rides from passing friendly families.

Right before they went through the main gate to the shops, Cat stopped and looked at Bleu.

"What?"

"I just wanted to see how you looked."

"Uh... why?" Bleu felt fidgety already and this was not helping

"You're just so grown up. It is a wonderful thing, and terrible feeling that you're no longer a child for me to protect and spoil." Cat seemed a little teary again and Bleu was starting to think she was not the only one who might be about to crack up.

"I'm not completely grown up," Bleu said, taking Cat's arm in her own. She was glad to hear the woman acknowledge for once that she wasn't a child, but she knew there were plenty of things that she would never be able to figure out on her own. Like what was going on with her father, or why no one talked about her mother. *Maybe just life in general,* she thought grimly. Then she laughed.

"What's so funny?"

"I'm just so... dramatic in my head," Bleu kept giggling. "It's always the end of the world in there."

"You're not just dramatic in your head, dearest." Cat continued walking and started to giggle as well. Bleu swatted her on the arm and linked elbows with her as they finished the trip to town.

As they arrived at the main street of businesses, it seemed to Bleu that it was strangely quiet.

"Cat, does it seem...?" Her voice trailed off as she looked around at so many of the buildings that appeared lifeless and empty.

"A bit empty for a workday? Yes, it does seem as such." Cat wandered over to a shuttered flower shop and tried to look into the window. "I can't really see. The curtains are drawn. I don't think I've ever known this place to be closed during the week. Let's walk to the grocer and see what is going on. The grocer is never closed."

As they made their way further into the streets, not a single soul appeared. There was little noise and even the animals that usually wandered the neighborhood had disappeared. Bleu started to feel uneasy as they rounded the corner to the grocer. The door was open, which gave her some relief. Cat walked ahead of her and into the building. Bleu glanced around her and thought she saw the drapes on the tea room window flutter. As she stopped and watched for a minute to see if anything would move again, Cat came back to the entryway. "It's open and the shelves are stocked but there is no one here. This is very very unsettling."

"I thought I just saw the drapes move in the tea room." Bleu started over to the small, quaint space and rapped on the window. There was not a single sound. "I know I saw them move." She turned to look at Cat, and as she did there was noise at the window.

She and Cat moved closer and saw there was a young child staring back at them.

"Hello, dear," Cat said, her voice sounding unreasonably loud in the silence. "Are you okay? Do you know where everyone has gone?" The child shook her head no.

"Will you open the door?" Bleu gestured and smiled, not wanting to frighten the little one. The child stood there for a moment. "I'm not supposed to open the door for strangers but I think I know who you are." She pointed at Bleu. "You live in the castle."

Bleu shifted a bit uncomfortably. She really did not like that the girl called it a castle.

Cat touched Bleu's hand. "We both live in the house on the hill, yes. Have you been there?"

"Only to the grounds for a walk. My parents said we're not welcome in there."

"Do you mind opening the door so we can come into the tea room and maybe have a cup?"

"My mom isn't here," she stood still, unsure what to do next.

Bleu bent over so she was level with the girl in the window. "I want you to know that you are welcome to the castle. Always. You just ask for me. My name is Bleu."

The girl's eyes grew wide.

"We are going to go, now, and see if we can find anyone else. Thank you for talking to us." Bleu stood up and took Cat's hand for them to go. They started back to the road.

"Wait!" They heard a ruckus of feet running and the click of the door being unlocked. The girl was dressed in a simple green dress and pinafore. "I hope I don't get into trouble, but you can come in." She ran back into the little cafe as Bleu and Cat made their way up the ramp to the door.

Cat looked around the lovely space as the girl was behind a counter gathering teacups.

"How old are you?" Bleu asked and began to remove her gloves.

"I'm 8 and I've been helping serve the ladies in the tea room all year. I'm very good at it," she said proudly as she carefully dropped sugar cubes onto a delicate plate.

"I have no doubt," Cat said as she sat at a table.

"Can I help you?" Bleu moved to take the tray, but the girl shook her head.

"You go sit and I will bring the service to you." She hurried to the back where the stove was lit and water was being warmed.

"I do not know what to think. I hope she can give us a clue as to where everyone went."

"Is that what people really think about us, Cat? That we don't welcome them? This town and country help pay for the managing of the estate. They should be allowed to visit it."

"I knew that statement bothered you. We can talk about it more later, but we need to pick up a great many things today. The citizens seeming to have disappeared is not going to help us accomplish that."

"The tea is ready to be served," a loud voice announced. In spite of herself, Bleu smiled at the high pitched, serious formality.

"What is your name, dear?" Cat spread a napkin in her lap as the child began to lay out the service from the cart she had rolled to their table.

"Emily," she said, as she carefully set a cup and saucer in front of Bleu.

"That is a pretty name," Bleu told her. "I have always liked that name."

"Thank you ma'am."

"Emily, do you know where everyone is today? Why are you left on your own?" Cat asked, as she sipped the tea. "The tea is perfect. You have mastered the service wonderfully." Emily curtsied to her and looked at Bleu and Cat sincerely.

"Well, ma'am, this morning a man wearing full uniform with quite a lot of medals on it came into town and announced that the country was in need of men for a trip to the Dark Continent. He said that it would be a once-in-a-lifetime opportunity, and no one should miss the chance to be hired. I heard my father say it paid well enough to pay off all our debts and buy the tea room outright. My mother was not happy about him going to the application place. My father will be gone a long time if he gets chosen to go. I am left here as my mother did not think it was a good place for a lady to go, and I am a lady."

"Why would would the trip need more men? My father had sent quite a lot of people on the expedition that left?" Bleu looked at Cat. "Do you know anything about this? Why are they looking to empty the town of its people?" Bleu was getting anxious. *Why are there always so many damn questions?*

"This is the first I know of it. We should go."

"Emily, do you know where everyone went for the application?" Bleu pulled money from her bag and set it on the table.

"I heard my mother say that they were going to the harbor this morning."

"You are quite handy with your hearing skills. Thank you very much for your excellent service and hospitality. Please keep the extra for yourself for a new ribbon." Cat walked to the door and motioned for Bleu to come.

"Make sure you remember what I told you. You can visit the castle anytime. I'll make sure of it." Bleu hugged the little girl and hurried to the door.

Cat walked determinedly down the street in the direction of the harbor.

"CAT! Wait!" Bleu ran to catch up to her. "Cat, what is the matter? I know we need to get down there, but what good is it going to do? Can we do anything about it? What would we do? I mean these people want to work and should get a chance to see the world, I guess." Even as she said it, Bleu didn't believe her own words. She knew something wasn't right about this expedition.

"My darling, I am tired of not knowing what is going on. I am the female head of household and you are my charge. The entire estate is responsible for the well-being of the town and country. I am going to find out what is going on and exactly what you are getting dragged into. Your safety is at risk as it is when we travel. My instinct is telling me this is even more dangerous than we've been led to believe. I am not your actual mother, Bleu, but I may as well be." She continued her brisk pace as Bleu struggled to keep up with her.

"And anyway, I would guess that our jewelers are also down on the docks witnessing what I can only imagine is quite the spectacle."

"Actually," said a deep baritone voice coming closer behind them, "I am not, and have managed to avoid the mess so far. But I'm not sure for how much longer since my father went down there this morning to our ship and has not returned yet."

Bleu spun around and threw her arms around a surprised young man.

"You're here!"

"I am here," he laughed. "Did you think I would not come to see you?"

"No. I mean, I guess, I don't know. I have to leave in the morning." Her words tumbled out her mouth, as she stepped back from her friend and straightened her dress.

"Yes, I heard that you may have to leave and that means we have few precious hours together, so let's get on with the day."

"I have so much to do today," Bleu said. "I don't have time to just visit, irritatingly enough."

He grinned at this, "I will do them with you, all these things. I'm somewhat useful, occasionally."

Cat smiled at both of them. "I'm glad we ran into you, Dorran. Maybe you can share information about what is happening? Do you know why they are taking more people from town?"

"I know that they've gone to many towns across the country and recruited men. I've seen them out more than once, these soldiers of fortune. They proclaim service to the royal family and to the creation of a new world with a new race of people."

"I see." Cat circled around to look at him. "Now tell me the rumors. As we know, there is more truth in the whispers."

The look on his face darkened. "The rumors are not those fit for decent people."

"I think you underestimate how courageous Bleu and I tend to be, young man."

"I have no doubt of your courage, ma'am. I doubt the integrity of both rumors and these expeditions into a land of mystery. Cowardice and fear make men behave in horrifying ways, and I suspect that might be part of what is happening."

"What ways? Do you mean the men who work for my father?" Bleu looked at Dorran and Cat, who seemed to share some sort of secret. It made her mad.

"Look, can't one of you for once give me a straight answer? I am not a child and I am not oblivious to things that are happening around us. I am really sick of all these half answers I get. Do you think not telling me things keeps me from thinking about them? Do you think I am that empty headed or self absorbed? I might be in charge of these people someday. At least maybe somewhat. Don't I deserve to know what is happening with them, or to them?"

They both stood silently for a moment and looked at Bleu. Her frustration melted a little, seeing both battling with wanting to protect her. She knew in her heart, even though it was so very infuriating sometimes, that they cared about her. But still, she wanted to know. It was her choice.

"Yes. You are right. Dorran, tell her. Tell us what you have heard, so we can possibly make sense of all this confusion and understand what we are being forced into."

He didn't speak. Bleu stood right in front of him and looked into his deep brown eyes. She had never before noticed they were flecked with amber. Putting that out of her mind, she took his hand in hers and said, "Please. I know you only don't want to tell me because you care about me, but it's time I start to hear the truth."

"I do care about you," he said rather quietly and covered her hand with his. "Alright, I will tell you. Both of you. Let us move out of the way so no one can overhear us. Then we will make our way to the harbor to see what we can see." He took Bleu's hand in his arm and led her and Cat to an abandoned bench.

"What I have heard is troubling. The rumors surrounding the expeditions into Africa are numerous. Despite having the public face of being charitable missions of mercy and help, there are rumors of murder, corruption, and enslavement. Talk of people being hunted for sport."

"What? That cannot be. That is the most ridiculous thing I've ever heard." Bleu refused to consider it. "I see now why you don't put much weight in rumor."

"I warned you, Bleu. But yes, much of this is obviously embellished falsehoods. We all know how people behave and hear what they want. Gossip is a pastime in the towns and homes of many people," Dorran said.

"Except," said Cat, "we do know people have died. We do not know how or why, but we know that much."

"Yes," he said, "but there are a few of us who believe it's more people than we are being told, and we do not know why families would not receive answers as to where their loved ones have gone. Many of them are told that they are not reachable because they are so far into the interior of the continent. Whereas I am sure this is partially true, many of those men have been gone much longer than they were supposed to be, and it is making some of the wives suspicious. They are no longer buying into the public face of the trips."

"This is... I don't even know what to say." Anger burned in Bleu's mind. "My father is a lot of things, but I never thought he was a murderer."

"The reality of being a leader and many of your men being so far from you is that you cannot always control what they do." Dorran looked away from her.

Cat moved to embrace Bleu.

"Please don't, Cat. I know I said I wanted to know, but it's a lot to process. I guess I didn't know what was going to come of asking. I mean, I'm not stupid. I didn't think you were going to say good things. But slavery? Murder? People hunted for sport? What does that even mean? I cannot begin to fathom." Bleu stood and began pacing back and forth in the street.

"This is odd, I agree, Bleu," Cat said it in an even tone. "But please remember not all rumors are true and not all whispers are lies. Somewhere in there is the truth, and what we seek at the moment is reassurance in taking more precautions. Which I feel we just received. Your safety, darling, is my number one priority."

"I know it is and I appreciate it. But that doesn't mean we shouldn't find out the truth. Our lives are no more important than anyone else's. If people are being hurt that are supposed to be under our family's protection, we need to help them."

"One step at a time. Let's go down to the harbor to see if we can find out anything else." Cat stood and turned to Dorran. "Will you join us?"

"Of course. Like I said, I need to go find my father anyway."

"Why is he down at the harbor? He's not thinking of going to Africa is he? I thought your business was doing so well here," Bleu did not want to hear that her dear friend's father was thinking of leaving him behind.

"Not at all. Do not worry, Bleu. He just went to pick up pieces we are delivering to clients today."

"Oh good. I'm so glad. Did you have a lot to deliver today?"

"Yes, we did. More than ever before. Europe prospers a great deal these days."

"I guess." Bleu started to walk down the street and then she remembered something.

"What does that woman have to do with any of this? She is going with us isn't she? Why would she be doing that?"

"What woman?" Dorran asked.

"I don't know who she is, Dorran. She showed up here a day ago, and my father is a completely different person around her. We had a formal dinner last night, and the house was full of people, music, wine, flowers. He seems determined to impress her. But I don't trust her. Plus..."

"Plus what?" Dorran looked at Cat and at Bleu, and Cat nodded her head.

"I'm pretty sure she went into my father's office without his permission." Bleu didn't mention the symbols on the paper since Cat didn't seem to think they mattered. *She is wrong. I am positive they mean something.*

"Without permission? What do you mean?"

"It was late, after dinner. I was going to the library and I saw her sneaking around in the dark. I got such a strange feeling about it that I hid out of sight."

Dorran smiled at her. "You hid out of sight? Like a thief in the night?"

"Do not make fun of me. This is not a joke."

"Indeed it is not." The teasing tone in his voice annoyed her.

"Look, are we going to stand here or are we going to go and find out what is going on? I'm pretty tired of all this already, and apparently I have to go to Africa tomorrow."

Cat turned her face, but not before Bleu caught a smile on it.

"Great. You think it's funny too." Bleu got up and walked off in a huff.

Dorran and Cat, of course, followed her, but she could hear Dorran stifling a laugh. *God, he irritates me sometimes. Forever. Since we were little kids.*

They both caught up to her, and the three of them made their way to the harbor. As they drew closer, it grew louder and louder with talking and yelling. Someone was trying to holler directions over all the noises, telling prospective hires where to go for exams and questions. It was one thing to walk through town and hear that nearly everyone was in one place. It was entirely another thing to see it.

It was more hustle and bustle than Bleu had ever seen. She recognized the grocer, the tea shop owner, the florist, and many other people whom she had encountered over the years in town. But there were also a lot of unfamiliar faces. Men in uniforms she had never seen. Many of them had guns and swords attached to their sides, and their faces bore hard looks and scars.

"Who are those men in the uniforms?" Bleu asked Dorran, trying to be heard over the noise but also trying not to draw too much attention to them.

"They are men who have returned from Africa. Many of them are not from this part of the world."

"They look so angry," she said.

They walked in silence, taking in the activity around them, as Dorran led them as carefully as he could through the crowd and down to his family's ship.

Just before they reached the landing where Dorran's family ship was docked, a woman stepped in front of Bleu with tears streaming down her face.

"YOUR FATHER IS A MONSTER," she screamed at her. "MY HUSBAND WOULD NOT HAVE TO GO IF YOUR FATHER WOULD TAKE CARE OF THIS COUNTRY LIKE HE IS SUPPOSED TO!"

Just as she was about to say more, a man ran to her side. "I'm so sorry, miss. She's upset that I'll be gone so long, but it'll be good for our family. Your father is offering us a once-in-a-lifetime opportunity."

"HE IS NOT! HE IS A LIAR!" The woman was inconsolable, crying as her husband tried to pull her away.

Bleu reached out a hand to the woman. "I'm sorry you're so upset, I didn't know this was happening."

The woman jerked away from her and spat on the ground in front of her.

"You are a spoiled brat and your whole family is cursed. You ruin our lives and take our livelihood, but you will pay. You'll all pay for this!" Her husband pulled her away, muttering more apologies to them as Bleu looked at Dorran, not knowing what to say or feel. He took her hand and they continued to the ship.

"It's not your fault," Cat said to her when they reached the dock. "People worry for their loved ones."

Bleu didn't say anything. Lost in her own thoughts, she pulled away from Dorran, walked to the end of the dock, and stared out across the water. Taking a few deep breaths before turning around, she made up her mind that she was going to try to figure out what to do to make this whole mess better. As soon as she learned the truth, she would figure out how to fix it. Whatever that meant.

As she turned back around, the Amadello family ship caught her attention. She hadn't seen it in a long time.

"Dorran! I forgot how beautiful the ship is, I have not seen it in so long." It was truly breathtaking, glittering in the sun. Unlike most of the ships docked at the harbor, the wood was carved and polished to a shine. It was decorated with carvings from historical battles, each one detailed with what Bleu suspected was real gold and real jewels. She had always wondered how it was no one stole such treasure. Cat had once told her that Dorran's family had a reputation of fearsome qualities but also of generosity. If someone was caught stealing, she had told her, if they could prove they truly needed the gold or gems for a good reason, the Amadello family would gift them whatever it was they needed. If you were just a thief seeking fortune without working, well, Cat had said, there was a punishment to suit the crime. Bleu had tried to get Cat to tell her what that meant, but if Bleu thought they told her nothing now, Cat really told her nothing when she was younger.

There were many people who worked for Dorran's family, and more than a few of them were rushing about on the ship as well as polishing the sides, and obviously working very hard to keep it in top shape. It was a famous ship, Bleu recalled, none other like it in the world. She stood, admiring it, when someone called her name from up above.

"Bleu! Beautiful girl get up here and give me a hug!" Dorran's father walked to the top of the ramp and held his arms open to her. She couldn't help but smile, he always made her feel so welcome. She went up the ramp, picking up her skirt until she almost ran. He caught her in a huge, warm embrace, smelling of clover, tobacco, and the sea.

"My goodness, you are so tall," he bellowed loudly, letting her go and motioning for her to step onto the ship. "AND YOU! CAT! Have you always been such a goddess?"

Cat shook her head. "You always seem to remember each time we see one another." Her sarcasm made them both laugh as they embraced. Dorran came up the ramp behind them.

"Son! What is the madness down below? I came to pick up the most precious of our deliveries and have been stalled time and time again as I wanted to leave. The patrols say that it is not safe for me to move through the town. Which is just preposterous! They clearly have no idea to whom they are talking. Let's have lunch and then we should go as we please. Do you ladies have time to join us?"

"If it can be brief. As you know we were coming to pick up gifts from you as well."

"How about, my dear Cat, we have lunch, and then we shall take you into town and back to the estate ourselves? I have a delivery for the man himself." He guffawed as he said this, and Bleu was happy to see that he still was not intimidated by her father as so many men seemed to be.

"That should be fine. We do have to eat, after all, and we certainly will not get a chance for a while to lunch with you."

"Excellent! He turned and rang a large bell that seemed to set in motion an unseeable flurry of activity. Wonderful food smells started to waft through the air as Mr. Amadello showed them around the newest additions to the ship.

"We will be at the gala this evening," Dorran whispered to Bleu. She pulled herself away from all the marvels around her to focus on her friend. She was so lost in thought she had not paid much attention to him, even though she had wanted to see him so much.

She smiled. "It will be wonderful to have a friend there."

"Yes, a friend," he muttered and abruptly walked away.

"Okay, that was weird. Just like the rest of this day," she said aloud to no one in particular.

"Dorran, like so many his age, cannot actually say what he means," Cat said near her ear and started to laugh. "He will not be the first of them to annoy you and confuse you."

Mr. Amadello heard that statement and laughed heartily. This reassured Bleu that all adults were insane, as she had previously theorized.

They didn't see Dorran again until lunch was served, and he did his best to not directly speak to Bleu. She decided to not care. If he could not tell her what his problem was, amidst of all the other things happening today she was not going to worry about it.

As they finished all the amazing food, much of which Bleu had never eaten before, their host ordered all the boxes they needed to be packed and readied to be taken to the estate. Bleu gathered her things and thanked her host over and over for the wonderful meal.

"I know leaving this place is a big, scary imposition to your life Bleu," he said to her, "but your natural curiosity and sense of wonder will be glad that you do. I believe it is good for young people to travel as much as possible." He looked right at Dorran. "It makes them understand that there are other problems out there that are much bigger than theirs."

Dorran frowned and tilted his head at Bleu. "Shall we go?"

"I suppose," realizing that she did not want to go, but instead to stay on this marvelous ship with this loving man. That seemed so much a better idea.

They went off the ship and onto the road where there sat an old-fashioned, gilt-decorated carriage, complete with a family crest, flags, and horses. Men attended to them, as women who bore the Amadello family crest passed out bread and sweets to the children.

"Your father certainly knows how to make friends," Cat remarked to Dorran, who said nothing in return. He held the door open for them to get into the carriage and climbed upon a horse to ride back to their home.

"Good grief, what is his problem?" Bleu asked Cat. "Actually, I decided I do not care so I still do not care."

"Sure, not caring seems to be good cho..."

"I mean, seriously? What is his problem?" Bleu interrupted her caretaker, not seeming to notice.

Cat did not say anything.

"Don't you have something cryptic and annoying to say?"

"Bleu, darling, you are doing just fine all on your own." Cat folded her hands and looked pointedly out the window.

The rest of the trip back to the house passed without any further incident, much to Bleu's relief. She did not even realize how tense she felt, waiting to hear or see something else horrible, until they passed through the gates of the estate.

They got out of the carriage as Dorran and his father disappeared into the house. Cat gave out instructions to all the workers and sent Bleu up to her room.

There were more people and activity in the house than Bleu could ever remember. Piles of flowers and food being brought in, animals being groomed and adorned, chandeliers being cleaned, rugs being batted. Everything that was already polished last night was getting even more polished. It was all she could do not to be under foot. It was a bit suffocating, and she was glad to get behind the closed doors of her bedroom.

"My room..." Bleu's shock and sadness was matched only by her anger at seeing the fraulein in her room.

"Hello, darling," she said, ignoring Bleu as if she was just someone who wandered into the wrong place. "I thought to be helpful and had all your things packed for the trip and everything carefully stored."

"Who do you think you are?" Bleu snapped and walked over to the woman to snatch a satchel she used for carrying books from the woman's perfectly manicured hands.

"I am just helping. Traveling for a woman can be vexing, and you were in town a long while, which I am sure was exhausting for you." The fraulein said it to her as if she was a helpless child.

"Yeah, great, you're a treasure." Bleu put the satchel on her bed, crossed her arms, and faced the fraulein. "You can go now."

"You should not be so rude to your guests." Her voice was icy cold as she drew nearer Bleu. "You would not want to offend the wrong people."

"I think I'll survive hurting someone's feelings."

"Do not be so sure." The woman's gaze was hard and steady. Her eyes were a frigid blue and seemed so flat yet filled with something sinister.

"Did you just threaten me? I am not afraid of you," Bleu retorted. *Though honestly, I am a little.* "I do not care who you are to my father, you are not my guardian and you have no control over me. I do not know who you think you are coming into my life and packing up all my things like they belong to you, but you can leave now." She didn't flinch as the fraulein did not blink. The woman held as still as a statue. *She does not even seem real.*

As though nothing had just passed between them, the fraulein smiled brightly. "Your gown, darling, is just amazingly gorgeous and is hung in your dressing area. I took the liberty of having matching flowers sent up for your hair as well as having shoes found for you. They are divine. We shall have a grand time tonight." She reached out and patted Bleu on the shoulder, then turned dramatically and left.

Bleu sat on her bed, more than a little stunned. The day had been filled with the strangest, most shocking, craziest sights and behaviors she had ever dealt with, and the day was not over yet.

Cat came in and looked around the room.

"Why did you have all your things stored? Besides your bed, obviously. You did not have to do that, though I am glad you got them to pack your room up for you. I am a little surprised you let anyone pack up your books and notebooks."

"I did not ask anyone do to this, Cat. I was planning on dealing with it all myself this afternoon. When I came in, the fraulein was here and she had everything packed and stored."

"What? That is infuriating, isn't it? Who does she think she is?" Cat raged and stormed around the room.

"Obviously she thinks she is someone very important," Bleu responded absently. Seeing everything packed or gone from her room made her feel that this was really happening. She was leaving her life here behind to go who knows where, to do who knows what. She wished she had Mr. Amadello's optimism.

"I am going to go have words with her. You rest a bit and then you should start to get ready for the evening. Make sure all your small, personal things you want to bring are nearby and packed where you can find them." Cat left Bleu alone again as she gazed off into the empty room.

She was overwhelmed, bewildered, and livid, but she was certainly not tired. Knowing it would be a long night, she did what Cat suggested and looked through all her smaller bags, making sure they were organized in the way she wanted and filled with what she meant to bring. Much to her surprise, the attention to detail was meticulous, and she found everything she had wanted to bring along.

After a couple of hours, Cat came back with a light dinner for them to eat and chattered away about not being able to find the fraulein.

"It's going to be a long trip indeed if that woman is with us the whole time. Bleu, you've barely touched your food."

"I'm not hungry. I ate a lot at lunch. The food was wonderful and not like anything we eat here."

"It was wonderful. The Amadello family certainly knows how to entertain."

"What is the matter with Dorran? Should I worry about it? I don't want to leave with things bad between us."

"Things are not bad between you. I promise, you'll see. Let's get ready for the gala. One of the girls should be bringing my dress here. We can get dressed and go down together. I had all my things packed and stored as well, so we'll both be ready for a fresh start when we come back."

Something about Cat saying that made her feel immensely better.

"Thank you, Cat. That sounds wonderful."

"We may not be able to count on anyone else, but we can count on each other, can't we? Now finish up and get washed. You certainly do not want to smell funny, though it would probably keep some of the more boring guests away from you tonight. On second thought, let's neither of us bathe." Bleu started laughing and so did Cat as they started to prepare for the evening.

It took some doing to get ready for the dance. There were a lot of pieces to being dressed so fancy, and Bleu was trying not to lose patience because the gown she was wearing truly was a work of art. She just wished wearing art wasn't so cumbersome, and yanked at her petticoat for the millionth time as Cat laced up the back of the bodice.

"Do I have to wear the flowers she left for me? I really do not want to give her the satisfaction." Bleu glared at the dark red roses as if they were poisonous.

"Well, they do look nice with the gown. Let's put them in your hair. I know you don't want to do it, but you know the saying, 'You catch more flies with honey than with vinegar?' Let's consider this some honey." She adjusted the roses with pins in Bleu's long dark hair.

"Are you saying you think I should be nice to her?"

"I am saying that perhaps we should be nice in order to seek what we want. That certainly seems to be her plan, at least on the surface."

"Fine. I will wear the flowers but I will not wear the shoes. I want to wear the shoes my mother had made to go with this gown."

"I would not expect anything less." Cat handed her the silver lace brocade boots with delicate stitching all up and down the side. The stitching was a pattern of flowering vines with carefully created dark blue roses hidden in the design. Bleu laced the boots and stepped back.

"How do I look? Completely silly, no doubt."

Cat smiled and pulled her to the full length mirror left on the wall in the dressing area.

"Tell me, do you think you look silly?"

Bleu could not believe that was herself in the mirror. She always had nice clothing and was always pressed, clean, and well presented, but this was something else entirely.

"I think I look like someone else."

"You are not someone else. It is you that looks back at you. Your gown is exquisite and has been fitted to you perfectly. Your mother always had an eye for color and talented people."

"Yes." Bleu was studying the black-blue gown in the reflection. The material shimmered subtly and was carefully tailored into a bodice on top that was laced in the back with silver ribbon. The front was embroidered with a silver forest that carefully wove around her waist. There was a tiny doe outlined in the trees. The sleeves were made to run over her shoulders in a delicate metallic lace that belled out slightly at the wrist. Cat was right, the dark red roses contrasted well with the blue and her hair.

"It's like something from a fairy tale." She ran her hand over the bodice, imagining the person her mother had make the gown. It was wondrous.

"Indeed it is, and we even have our own witch." That made both of them laugh very hard.

"We have to stop laughing. You'll be red when we get downstairs." Her caretaker fussed with her hair a little more and blotted her face with a handkerchief.

"Now, we know that you are, in fact, the fairy queen of the known heavens. How does your old nanny look?"

Cat's gown was also dark blue but it was made with a velvet that was soft to the touch. It fell in waves around her waist to the floor, and it showed off the blue in her eyes which was not always noticeable. The top was decorated with a simple line of silver stars at the neck.

"You look like a queen." Bleu ran her hands down the velvet sleeve of Cat's dress. The statement got a laugh out of Cat.

"So both of these gowns are blue and silver, a lot of the colors in the house are blue and silver, and I don't know why I've never really noticed it before. Is there a reason for that?"

"Yes, the reason is simple. They were your mother's favorite colors, and they used to be even more prevalent than they are now. Well, you know the other part of that story. But we've had enough sad things for one day. Let's go see if we can manage some fun on our last night, for who knows how long, in this old house." Bleu laughed as Cat bowed melodramatically and opened the door with a flourish. They stepped out in the hall and almost ran right into Dorran.

Bleu's breath caught when she looked at him. Not that she wanted to think this. *He does look very... very... very... well... something. Nice. Yes, nice.*

"Good evening, ladies. My father has ordered me to escort you both to the ballroom." He turned to Cat and handed her a box. "He asked if you would do him the kindness of accepting this small token of appreciation befitting a goddess." He said it so seriously that Bleu giggled until Dorran raised his eyebrow at her. Cat opened the box and gasped.

"It may be small but it is quite perfect. It's quite the skill to always know the exact gift to give. Bleu, help me put it on." She pulled the necklace out and handed the box to Dorran. The necklace was a crescent moon pendant that hung just above the stars on her neckline. *It really is perfect*, Bleu thought as she carefully hooked the chain.

"What is the material?" Cat admired it in a mirror that hung in the hall.

"We do not have the name of it yet. It is rare and quite malleable to make such creations." The metal had a highly polished, silver look to it. The moon was set with tiny midnight-colored stones.

"And you, madam," Dorran continued very formally. "Your father asked that I give you this." The box was larger than Cat's by quite a lot. Bleu took the box and opened it carefully. Inside sat an impressive tiara made with the same metal and blue stones as Cat's moon. It was made to look as vines and the stones as tiny blue roses.

"It is for you to wear around your head," Dorran said, as he pulled it out of the box and demonstrated how it was to be worn.

"My father had you make this for me?" Her father always had things for her and never said no to anything Cat asked for her, but this was different.

"He did," Dorran said, and handed the circlet to Cat, who began arranging it around Bleu's hair. It was so light she could barely feel it.

"It is an important day, after all, Bleu." Dorran produced another box, smaller this time, and handed it to her. "Happy Birthday, Bleu."

"My birthday? I completely forgot." She opened the box. Inside was a necklace with a locket fashioned as a silver book engraved with a rose. It was the single most lovely thing anyone had ever given her.

"Look on the back," he said quietly.

Bleu turned the locket over. On it was a her name and a symbol she had never seen before.

"What is this symbol?" She ran her finger over it as Cat finished fixing her hair. Cat stepped back to give them a moment.

"Quite simply, it is a symbol of knowledge. Anytime I see it, I think of you. May I?" He took the necklace and stepped behind her to fasten the chain. She held very still.

It was over so fast it seemed like it never happened, but she was sure he brushed her neck with his finger. *He is so odd.*

Cat came over and looked at the locket. "Did you really think we would forget your birthday? One does not turn 16 every day. Doesn't she look beautiful, Dorran?"

"Yes. Of course," the awkward stiffness from the afternoon returned. Cat looked at him, shook her head, and began to lead them down the hall.

The house was filled with people. It was loud and shimmery and fragrant. Cat and Dorran were quickly swept off, leaving Bleu to wander through rooms she had been in her whole life but barely recognized tonight. When she rounded the corner to the ballroom, which as far as she knew had never been used, the sight of it amazed her. Everything had been cleaned, restored, and decorated, seemingly overnight. There were musicians set up to perform and women in gowns of every color in the rainbow ready to dance.

"Do you like your gift, Daughter?" Her father came up beside her.

"Yes, Father, it is very beautiful," she replied as she turned to face him.

"The fraulein thought you might. She has a wonderful eye." He said it in a way she had never heard him speak, and she did not really like it.

"Your gown is quite a piece of work." He looked it up and down and noticed the locket about her neck. "Where did that come from?"

"It was a gift from Dorran for my birthday. Isn't it lovely? And yes the gown is unlike anything I have ever seen. Cat said Mother had it made a long time ago." She was feeling emboldened for some reason. She never mentioned her mother to her father.

If only for a moment, his gaze seemed to soften.

"Your mother always felt the need to buy things we did not need." His words were meant to sting and they did. "I do not want you to spend too much time with that boy. His family is surrounded in rumor, and he is not good enough for your company." He left just as suddenly as he appeared.

Bleu felt as if she had been kicked.

Cat came up to her with a glass of champagne, on the arm of Dorran's father who handed Bleu a silver rose.

"Bleu, what's wrong?" Cat handed her glass to Mr. Amadello and smoothed Bleu's hair.

"My father, he's just so..."

"Now stop right there, young lady. It is your birthday," Mr. Amadello set down the glass, took both her hands, and pulled her to the dance floor as the music began. "Your father is a right old bastard, but he was not always this way, and he is not your problem to worry about tonight. Let's dance, darling, before you are swept away by every young man in the room." Bleu unknowingly made a face that made him laugh. "Yes, I agree. 'All those young men' is a terrible thought." Despite herself, she joined in laughing.

By the time they were done dancing, Cat had wandered off. Bleu wove her way around the room, saying hello to everyone, and trying very hard to examine all the newly uncovered art in the room. She had no idea there was so much in here. The room was glorious, covered from floor to ceiling in murals and paintings of everything she could imagine.

"Bleu, would you like to dance?" Dorran's familiar voice startled her and she smacked her elbow on a nearby pedestal.

"Ow! I don't know. Are you going to keep being so weird?" *That really hurt,* she thought, and rubbed her elbow vigorously.

"I do not know that a leopard can change its spots." Bleu burst out laughing at how serious he said it, as he reached over and massaged the last of the pain out of her arm. It made her feel a little shy.

"Fine, let's go dance." She took the hand he held out to her and followed him onto the dance floor.

The first dance kept them apart and moving as did the second, but as the music slowed he moved closer to her, put his hand lightly on the small of her back, and began to lead.

"Did you look in the locket I gave you?"

"No, not yet. Should I?"

"Do not look at it until you need to."

"What does that mean? I swear I would die of shock if anyone ever gave me a clear answer."

"Well we wouldn't want that, would we." He didn't say anything for the rest of that dance. Then the music picked up the pace again, and they were separated once more. They danced until Bleu could not dance anymore, and the crowd in the ballroom had thinned a bit. She gestured to Dorran that she wanted to take a break. He went over to the refreshment table and brought her a glass of punch.

"I'm too warm and would really like some fresh air. Would you join me?" Bleu said nervously. His behavior had made her feel unsure.

"Of course." He led the way to the back veranda. It was a mild night. Spring was alive and colorful, especially as it neared summer. Bleu wondered about the weather where they were going.

"Dorran, do you know anything about Africa?" He was looking out over the grounds, all of which were perfectly kept. The outside of the house was always beyond presentable to the world. Flowers seemed to glow in the moonlight.

"Yes, I have been to a small part of it."

"I didn't know!" Bleu was surprised to hear this, though she did know that he and his father worked all over the world. "What's it like there?"

"Mysterious and beautiful. I think, Bleu, you will like it a great deal." She stood next to him and put her hand on his arm.

"I am glad I got to see you before I left, Dorran."

"I am glad as well, Bleu."

They turned and faced each other. Bleu dared not move. She didn't want this moment to end. She was happy that he seemed to be relaxed a little.

"I love my gift, Dorran. The tiara is lovely, as well, even though my father said it was ordered by the fraulein," she said sourly.

"She ordered it, yes, but she did not design it or make it," he said. "I did both the tiara and the locket, and you should take both of them with you."

"I was going to take them, though I fear losing them." Her hand went to the locket and she felt the engraving.

"When you need them you can use them."

"Will you please explain what that means?"

"I just did, Bleu. Trust me, you will know when you need them." He leaned a little closer to her, and just as she leaned in to him the door opened and the fraulein came onto the veranda with her father.

"Move away from my daughter, young man." Her father's words came out slurred. He'd clearly been in the wine again.

Dorran stepped away from Bleu.

"I'm sorry, sir. I meant nothing by it."

"Yes, that's exactly the problem isn't it. You and your father have no idea what anything means." He struggled to stand and the fraulein held tight to his arm.

"FATHER! Do not talk to him that way. They are our friends." Bleu was embarrassed and she glanced at Dorran, who shook his head at her quickly. Bleu blinked. *He doesn't want me to say anything back?? My father or not, he is being so horrible.*

"Now, now, Leopold, they are young, silly children," the fraulein said in about as phony a sweet voice as any human could manage. "Leave them be."

At that point Cat came out to the veranda, took one look at Bleu's father, and led both Bleu and Dorran back into the ballroom.

"Let's not end the night on a bad note since we do not know when we will see each other again. It is the early hours of the morning, though, and we do still have many things to do before we leave, so you should say your good-byes and good-nights soon," Cat said to them both, and then went back to Dorran's father, who was clearly expressing his displeasure at ending the night.

"I guess I have to go," Bleu said. "I never did tell you that you look very handsome tonight."

"You look very beautiful, Bleu. The most beautiful I have ever seen anyone look." He stared directly into her eyes as he said it.

"Thank you, Dorran, and thank you for my gift. I wish I didn't have to go." She said it quickly and truthfully. She wanted to stay here so much. "I don't know when I'm going to see you again."

Dorran bent and kissed her hand.

"It will be sooner than you think," he said confidently.

Chapter 2

Ella put down her paintbrush and looked at the clock. 5:00 p.m. She had only a couple hours left until she had to go to work. Painting today had been for almost 13 hours straight. Waking up in the early hours of the morning and unable to go back to sleep, it made the most sense to get up and start working on the project.

Having spent the majority of the last few days in bed and not feeling well had kept her from working on painting, and she felt behind. Which was nuts. Because she was the only one who even knew about it. It wasn't due anywhere. Ella just always felt that if she did not keep some sort of schedule she'd never get anything done. A lesson she learned the hard way when in school. She began cleaning up her supplies, putting away paints, and washing brushes. Taking great pains to care for each individual piece since she had to be careful with her money, as always. If she could avoid wasting anything she always did. She didn't want to have to work more than she needed most of the time. She'd rather be spending her time painting. After everything was washed, folded, and carefully organized into containers, Ella sat down on her big, velvet couch and stretched out. Feeling stiff, sore, and tired, as well as the disjointed feeling from reality that was all too common in her life, Ella leaned her head back onto the arm of the couch. Staring at the ceiling and thinking about her struggle with the ever-elusive rest, she wondered once again what it was that kept waking her every night. Pain, dreams, and constant inner battle.

The dreams had started when she was kid. Sometimes when she was younger they scared her. Ella would wake up terrified and covered in sweat. Feeling the heat of the fire from them, she would panic and scream. The teacher who watched over the younger children would come running to her in the middle of the night and try to calm her down. Often the teacher had to stay with Ella until she fell back asleep.

What about the dreams that scared her so much carried over into her teenage years? Ella would spend weeks, sometimes even months, not sleeping. It made life difficult.

Sleeping in classes and making lots of mistakes while doing chores led the teachers to seek outside help with her. They thought she was a troubled youth who was deliberately trying to avoid her responsibilities. After all, they had dealt with many teenagers in the past, and that's what they all did.

Ella was put into therapy. Endless hours of tests and questions kept Ella away from her peers for the majority of her teenage years. Over time she began to figure out all the things the doctors and teachers wanted to hear from her. She doubled her efforts in studying and spent countless hours doing chores slowly and carefully. All in hopes of keeping them at bay so she could be left alone. At night, she would take the sleeping pills they gave. The pills' effects were supposed to last through eight hours. The best nights, Ella got four hours of sleep.

The dreams would burst through the drug-induced barrier and force her awake at the darkest hours of the night. Having learned to be careful not to arouse attention, she would lay quietly in bed, writing poetry and drawing with paper and pens she'd hide between the mattress and box spring.

As she grew older and continued dutifully to go through therapy, they began to leave her alone more and more and deal with real troubled teenagers. In this school, there seemed to be a lot of them.

She tried each night to remember what she had dreamt. To make sense of the terror and chaos that poured through her every night. What was she so afraid of? The question plagued Ella constantly. Not knowing why she believed this, Ella knew her dreams were trying to tell her something. But the harder she tried to hold on to the memory of them the more elusive they seemed to become.

"Ella, would you come to my office?" asked a female voice in almost-too-perfect English.

"Yes, ma'am." Ella stood up from the floor and brushed off her apron. She ran her hands down the front of her skirt to smooth it out. She had been washing the floors and the rubber cleaning gloves over her black uniform gloves were making her hands sweat uncomfortably. Grateful for the chance to remove the rubber gloves, she pulled them off and put them in the pocket of the apron.

"Take a moment to collect yourself. One must always look a lady," the headmistress said.

Ella nodded and reached behind her back to untie the apron. Everyone knew to always look the best they could in front of the headmistress. Appearances were very important to her. She carefully folded the apron and put it on the cleaning cart.

"I'll just step into the ladies room, ma'am, and freshen up quickly." Ella turned, walked a few feet down the hall, and let herself into the restroom. She was nervous. She looked at her reflection in the mirror. Her cheeks were flushed and hair a bit mussed, so she checked to make sure no one else was in the room and then pulled off the uniform gloves.

Turning on the faucet, she wet her hands and shook them out so there was almost no water on them, then smoothed down her hair. Ella turned to get a paper towel to dab her face and then another that she used to carefully dry the sink. She couldn't leave it wet after she'd been there.

When she felt a little more together but still terribly nervous, she put the gloves back on and took a deep breath. She pulled open the door, and the headmistress was just outside waiting for her.

The headmistress gave Ella a queer, almost unnoticeable, look. She turned gracefully and began to walk toward the office. Ella followed closely behind. The woman had perfect posture and her hair was tied in a bun. Not a single strand was out of place.

She walked around to the chair behind her immense desk. Everything was in perfect order.

"Have a seat, Ella."

Ella sat down, crossed her legs, and put her hands in her lap. She looked around the austere, stern-looking room. A room of which she was, admittedly, a little afraid. All the students dreaded getting called in here. The headmistress was not known for kindness.

There were always rumors flying around the students. Even Ella knew some of them, despite distancing herself from everyone as much as possible. The most disturbing thing about some of the whisperings was that they looked to be true.

There were basically two schools on this large, private piece of land where Ella had grown up. Most of the children in these schools belonged to wealthy and powerful families. Some of them spent their entire childhood and adolescence here and away from their families. Many of them did not appreciate this.

Despite being given any material thing a young person could hope for, most of the students here were bitter and resentful people. They often acted out, hence the need for a stern headmistress, one would suppose. But there seem to be more to it than that.

When Ella was first moved into the house for high school age children, she briefly attempted to open up to another girl she met soon after the change. Ella had been lonely for so long she consciously made the choice to try and share with someone. To find out what it might be like to care about someone. She was curious, she told herself. It was an intellectual project. After all, she didn't really "need" someone. Perhaps what they thought of her might teach her something. She may even share her secrets and see what this person might think of those. Especially the one.

Timid and more miserable than she cared to admit to herself, Ella involuntarily found herself drawn to a girl with the lightest blonde hair she had ever seen. It was so blonde it looked nearly white. Her name was Alexandra Francis. Alexandra had been through both schools and was near graduation. She was nearly two years ahead of Ella in education, though Ella sometimes felt many years ahead of her.

Alexandra was a very animated girl. Telling vivid tales of love and betrayal between many of the students and many famous people from around the world. More often than not, she was the heroine in some way or another.

. Ella suspected that many of her stories were not necessarily true. Nonetheless there was something charming about Alexandra, and despite her obvious embellishments, Ella was drawn to the older girl. She was so different from the other girls in the school. She told her stories with unbridled enthusiasm and didn't seem to care in the slightest what the other students thought. Not too many of them seemed to actually believe anything Alexandra said.

Something else about Alexandra was her confidence in her beauty. Ella was fascinated by this, not caring much for the reflection she faced each day. Alexandra's white-blonde hair and gold-flecked, dark brown eyes made her lovely to look at. She stood about 5'-2" high, and Ella, at 5'-10", seemed to tower over her. Alexandra described herself as an artistic muse, explaining to Ella that women were meant to show off what the universe gave them. With that as a mantra, Alexandra was constantly in trouble for making her uniforms "inappropriate". Ella never bothered with her clothes. She always wore what she was supposed to. She had enough attention from the powers that be at the school.

She did think Alexandra's brazen defiance was amusing. There was no love lost between Alexandra and the headmistress.

"There isn't much the headmistress could really do," Alexandra often told Ella.

"My father has paid for half this school," she would remind the woman.

Often the headmistress, who never lost her cool, seemed a bit on the edge when Alexandra had pulled yet another stunt of some sort. Nothing seemed to get Alexandra expelled. Not smoking, cutting class, getting caught with boys. Even once with a teacher. Nothing. Ella knew that plenty of other students had been expelled over the years. Some with parents as wealthy and powerful as Alexandra's father. Maybe some even more so. But the headmistress just bit her tongue and sent Alexandra to detention over and over again. It was strange to Ella. It seemed as though the woman was waiting for something. Biding her time until she could do something to Alexandra. But Ella just brushed off that feeling as paranoia based on her experiences with anyone in authority. *What could she possibly do?*

Alexandra would be graduating in about two months and she could barely contain herself. She'd be inheriting her trust when she graduated. As it came closer and closer, Alexandra became even more excitable than usual.

"Ella! I am gonna leave this wretched place and leave that witch in the dust. I'm gonna travel 'til you graduate, find the best place in the world, and then I'm gonna come back–and let me tell you, I wouldn't come back for just anyone–and we're gonna go live in paradise on my miserable father's money. You can be an artist and I'll find us boys... Who knows? Maybe even men. And think of ways to embarrass my family." And on and on she went.

Most of the other seniors were just as ready to go as Alexandra but not quite as vocal about it. Everyone who would listen heard how "the witch" was getting left in the dust and not one more penny from Alexandra's family.

It all made Ella laugh. Secretly, she did in her heart believe that this was to be Alexandra's and her life together. Ella found herself getting caught up in the fantasy. She would daydream about beaches and mountains with villas and picture Alexandra laying on the beach surrounded by handsome men telling them silly stories. All of them laughing and dutifully telling her how perfect and beautiful she was as Ella would be more serious. Always drawing, writing and finding a way to contribute to the world. Perhaps she may even meet someone. Someone who was smart, strong, and handsome. Who knew? These were all the wonderful hopes for the future that Ella held close to her heart. She would record them in journals that she kept hidden from everyone, even Alexandra.

The graduating classes at the school had always been a subdued bunch. Probably out of the fear put into them by the teachers. The fear of bad references and résumés. How could they get into an Ivy league school if they didn't get stellar recommendations from the headmistress? No university meant no future which meant they would bring shame onto their families. The school had a lot of power over them. But not Alexandra. She didn't care about that stuff, and her father didn't have the time to pay attention to her or anything she did. She was free to do what she pleased, and what she pleased was for everyone to remember that she had been through the school. That she alone the headmistress never challenged, and she was going to pull one last stunt to prove the woman had no power over her.

At first Ella thought it was only a joke. Surely Alexandra wouldn't want to push it at this point. It always felt to Ella that the other shoe was going to drop when they were least expecting it. Obviously, Alexandra even knew not to push it too much more. Not when she was so close to being free.

This was in fact, not the case. Alexandra was planning something grand and humiliating. She was being extremely secretive about it, not telling Ella anything that was happening. Ella continuously asked what was going on, but Alexandra would just smile and tell her not to worry. But she did worry. Endlessly. The headmistress was getting haughtier and haughtier as graduation drew nearer and nearer. There were to be some very important people at this year's event. The entire school was being cleaned and trimmed. Even all the students were expected to participate in the preparation. Rooms were to be scoured clean top to bottom, all uniforms mended and pressed. The meals as of late were the best they'd ever been. Even all the students notebooks were being inspected for doodling, and anyone with any bad grades was being kept for tutoring and being required to retake or redo any and all work below an "A". Ella started to suspect, as she was working on scrubbing the floors in her room, that this graduation might have guests attending that had many a deep pocket and would present many a chance for the headmistress to raise her social standing in this world of money and power. That would certainly be a perfect chance in Alexandra's mind to get the headmistress "back" for all the misery she had pushed onto her.

"Ella, I am concerned," the headmistress began in a voice that sounded not concerned at all. "I fear there might be some students that do not understand the importance of the coming graduation events. Important to the school and each and every student's future."

"I'm sorry ma'am, I don't understand what you mean?"

The headmistress smiled patiently as if talking to a young child and not to a girl who was nearing seventeen. "No, of course you don't, Ella. I know that you are a good student, trustworthy, and that you represent what is great about this school. That is why I'm coming to you with this." She paused and stared at Ella expectantly.

The room was painfully quiet. Ella could hear her heart pounding in her ears. *Does the headmistress really think I would betray my friend?* She never would, no matter what the price. Alexandra meant more to her than anything else in this world. Even her future. She couldn't afford an expensive university anyway. She hadn't applied to any and with her condition still being the "second" most controlling thing in her life, she didn't think too much beyond just getting out of here undiscovered and getting on with life.

My life, she thought happily. *Not much longer.* Although, the headmistress' face made it clear that it was about to get a whole lot longer. Well, she didn't know anything. None of the plans had been shared with her no matter how many times she'd asked. All she knew was that Alexandra was up to something. *But that's like having no information at all,* Ella decided. Alexandra was always up to something.

"I really don't understand what you're trying to get at?"

"Ella, let me make myself as clear as the air you breathe. All your bad dreams, strange little quirks, and inept social behaviors are already going to keep you from ever making anything worthwhile of yourself. The only hope you have is that you do get good grades and that I will allow this school and its teachers to give you good recommendations so you can get into some sort of respectable university. But only if you give me what I need will I then give you what you need."

Ella was fuming inside. *Inept social behaviors? Like any of the spoiled, idiotic kids in this school are worth talking to anyway.*

"Headmistress, I really don't understand what you're talking about. I mean, is this about all the guests that are coming? Are you worried something's going to happen? What exactly do you think is going to happen? Because maybe you should warn the students? Is it a threat to our safety? I'm sure all the parents would want to know if their children were in danger or something. They count on you to take care of them and some of those people are very important, aren't they?" Ella couldn't believe she'd just said that, and so smugly too. The head-mistress didn't respond for what felt like an eternity. Ella could hear a clock ticking and her breathing felt labored. *It's all in your head.*

The steely, straight-backed headmistress didn't even blink, as far as Ella could tell.

"Very well, Ella. You don't want to cooperate. That is your decision. I am left with no other choice. Since you do not care about this school's future, the school does not care about your future. When such time arrives for you to apply to university and you need a recommendation, you will not get one. I hope you understand how this is going to damage your future. If you decide to cooperate before the ceremonies, all will be well."

Yeah, for you. There was no way Ella was going to snitch on Alexis even if she did find out what was going on.

"May I be excused?" She shifted uncomfortably in the hard chair.

"Yes, Miss Cerulean, you may be excused. But don't forget... I'll be watching you. I will find out what is going on, and the perpetrators will be punished. Best take care you're not one of them. Your record will really not withstand much more on it."

Ella blinked at that last part. *Not much more on my record? What's that sup-posed to mean,* she wondered as she left the office as fast as she could without seeming too eager to get away. She walked down the hall quickly and turned a corner. Stopping to lean on the wall to catch her breath, she closed her eyes for a minute.

"The old cow is already threatening you," said a familiar voice.

"I'm not afraid of her," Ella said without opening her eyes. Her friend tugged her gloved hand.

"Come on," said Alexandra. "Let's go get something to eat." She turned, pulling Ella off the wall, and began to head to the courtyard of the school. They wandered over to a grassy area under some trees. Some students were mulling around here and there, but they were too engrossed in their own worlds to pay much attention to them.

"I'll go get us food," Alexandra said. She walked off toward a door that led to the dining hall in the main part of the building. Sitting in the grass, Ella kept her eyes on her friend as she walked away. *Why was the headmistress so much more concerned with what was happening this time?* It's not like stunts hadn't been pulled in front of visitors before. The platinum-haired Alexandra wasn't the first or only person to despise being at this school with that woman. She sat thinking for what seemed like a long time.

She looked up at the sky. There seemed to be a large black mass moving quickly towards the school.

"What in the world...?" she said aloud. The students were gone. Trees began to whip violently. Dirt, rocks, and leaves blew all around, obstructing her vision.

Suddenly the sky grew forbidding and ominous. She looked up and there seemed to be a thick cloud of gray dust starting to spread above her. Standing up and trying to take steps towards the main building where Alexandra had gone, the space between Ella and the building seemed to grow with each movement. Her friend had come to the doorway. She was saying something, but Ella couldn't hear her. The wind was getting louder and louder all around her. The school began to melt away, then the trees, then everything disappeared. The confusion was setting in and it was getting harder and harder to breathe. She was having a difficult time keeping her feet on the ground. There was a sharp pain in her chest, and she heard someone scream. Alexandra screamed, and then... thousands of screams.

Ella sat up straight, panting and sweating. Trying to calm herself down, she looked at the clock. Its glowing face said it was now 7:15. She had to get up and get ready for work or she was going to be late. Again. Throwing back the covers, she painfully moved her legs over the side of the bed. As much as she didn't like to do it, she was going to have to take painkillers tonight. Work was a must. All the money she had saved up was gone and she had to pay rent shortly.

The living room was getting dimmer as the hour got later. Her eyes were still adjusting a bit from having fallen asleep. She put a hand to her chest. It still hurt as if she had been suffocating. *What a strange dream.* Not the part about Alexandra, but the rest of it. She had dreamt of Alexis before, but not with the intense ending. The ending had nothing to do with the school. In fact, she had no idea what that was. *Dreams can be very random,* she supposed. It was just so disorienting when they included a real memory.

"I really miss her," Ella said aloud to the empty room. She had to be honest with herself. She was a pretty lonely girl these days.

"There's no point in feeling sorry for yourself." She slowly started to stand up and had to grip the table from the sudden rush of blood to her head. Steadying herself, she reached for the bedside lamp and flicked it on. She looked down at her chest and saw that her shirt was stuck to her with sweat. Glancing at the table and spotting the painkillers, she popped off the lid. Really hating the need, she dropped one in her hand and walked slowly to the kitchen. Each step was stiff and painful. The kitchen wasn't far off, but it took a few minutes to reach. She picked up the blue glass she'd left on the counter earlier and filled it with water. Swallowing the pill and drinking most of the water in one long drink, Ella, without thinking, reached her hand into the sink and poured the rest of the water over her hand and down the drain. Smiling to herself, she still loved not wiping the sink out. It was nice to be a grown up.

Feeling a bit better after drinking the water, she wandered to the living room and began to stretch. She had discovered that a little yoga before work could help loosen up her almost constantly stiff joints. It was the only natural thing besides painting that helped. Not having a lot of time, after just a few repetitions Ella went back to the bedroom and into the bathroom. Turning on the light, she blinked and peered at her reflection. Her dark blue eyes were a little bloodshot, no doubt from the restless sleep.

"Hmmm, maybe I should try to get a haircut sometime soon..." she ran her fingers down her long, dark hair, stopping momentarily to touch some of the silvery strands that ran randomly through it. When she was younger she had really disliked the silver hair. Kids had tormented her endlessly about being a witch, but now Ella decided she liked the silvery-blue hair. It was something that set her apart, but not in an overly noticeable way. *Alexandra pointed that out.* With that thought, Ella felt the sadness set in on her again.

"Just stop," she said to her reflection. "That was a long time ago. Deal with now or you're gonna be homeless."

Leaning over and turning on the shower, she promised herself she wouldn't think about her old friend again. *Think about something pleasant, like painting.* Waiting for the water to get lukewarm, she stepped in the stream after undressing and let her mind stray over some of her new ideas for a painting. She was leaning toward some sort of prehistoric creature. She had seen a magazine a few weeks ago that had some digital renderings of dinosaurs. Particularly water creatures, the grand majestic beasts that once ruled the oceans. She was drawn to them and she felt like the renderings didn't do them justice. The ones in her dreams were so vivid and lifelike. She was fascinated by the theories and the pictures of what the past had to offer. The idea of everything being connected and evolving really appealed to her.

The strangest thing about her interest in the ocean was that she had only been to it once when she was young and could hardly remember it. But part of her felt like she knew it very well. *Of course. It's because you're a big freak.*

The warm water felt good on her aching body, and she lingered for longer than she had time. After one final rinse, she turned around and reached to turn off the water. In the process of doing so, she banged her hand on the faucet. It sent a shooting pain up her arm and she slipped against the wall. Ella sighed. *It's not going to be an easy night.* She stepped out of the shower and wrapped a towel around herself to dry off.

Stiff as ever, it seemed to be worse than usual. A long-standing prescription for the pain meds with the pharmacy near her apartment kept up the supply. The workers were always odd to her when she went to pick them up. Not too many young girls had standing prescriptions for strong narcotics. As much as she didn't like them, she knew they had gotten her through more than a few tough nights. Though they still didn't help with sleep much. But nothing helped her sleep.

Wandering into the bedroom and sitting down on the bed to breathe deeply for a minute helped the tense shoulders relax a moment. Getting up to get dressed, Ella donned the usual self-imposed uniform of black tights, black skirt, and long-sleeved black top. Opening another drawer, she took out a pair of black gloves and set them on the dresser top. She reached for a brush and pulled her hair back into a pony tail. There was nothing she could do about her eyes being so red. All that could really fix them was sleep. That didn't appear to be in the immediate future.

Hurrying to put on the gloves, she glanced at the clock, grabbed her bag, and ran out the door. Walking away, she almost forgot to lock the apartment. Sighing with relief, she ran back, locked it, and ran out of the building.

The night was relatively clear. The sky was a deep purple with sprinkles of stars here and there. It was a warm spring night, and the city was happy for it. The walk to Alchemy, the club where she worked, was a short one, and this one in particular was shaping up to be pleasant. There were a lot of people around. Teenagers sitting on the porch of a coffee shop. Couples holding hands and smiling hopefully at each other. There was a light breeze coming off the lake. The smell of fresh water in the air made her smile. It was a beautiful night. Staring up at the stars and not paying attention to where she was walking, Ella turned to avoid a light post and smacked right into someone.

"Oh, I'm so sorry," Ella started. She stopped to look at him and let out a gasp that she quickly tried to cover up. His eyes looked like they were made of liquid gold. It had to be the light from the street lamp above playing tricks on her. Her eyes were so tired from lack of sleep she knew she probably shouldn't trust anything she thought she saw.

"No, I'm terribly sorry. But I need to add that getting to look at those stunning eyes, I don't regret the happy accident," the man said smoothly.

Feeling the heat spread from her neck to her face, "Well, excuse me," Ella stammered and turned to get away from the embarrassment.

"Wait!" he called. "Why are you in such a hurry?"

"I'm late for work! Sorry again!" Rushing down the street and paying extra attention to where she was going this time, she made it to the club in record time. She ran to the back room and threw her bag in a locker. Putting on an apron and stopping in front of a mirror to put on lipstick, she got out to the counter just as the music started and the doors opened. The manager looked at her disapprovingly but didn't say anything.

"Hey, sweetheart, can we get a little service over here?"

Ella grimaced. She hated being called "sweetheart". She wondered for about the millionth time if she would get fired if she hit someone with a bottle.

"Sure, pal, what'll it be?" Standing in front of the patron and two of his friends, she picked up a couple of glasses and set them on the bar. People were slowly trickling in as the bouncers checked IDs and decided who could come in.

The patron smirked. "What's your specialty?" he drizzled out as he leered at a couple of blonde women who walked by him.

Ella controlled the urge to roll her eyes and said, "Whatever you want."

He turned to her, his eyes flicked up and down, and she felt her gag reflex kick in.

"That's what I like to hear. Give us," gesturing to the guys behind him, "some top shelf whiskey."

As she reached behind her to grab the bottle, a hand moved across the bar to grab her. She stepped back just in time for it to miss. The patron had an annoyed look on his face that Ella pretended not to notice. Pouring the whiskey into the glasses she pushed them across the bar to the guy who, in turn, handed her a fifty dollar bill. She reached to take it from him, but he didn't let go of it, forcing her to lean a little closer.

"Keep the change, sweetheart, and be good. There's plenty more where that came from."

Forcing a smile and replying with a cheery, "Thanks," she moved down the bar to the next group of people.

"How is everyone tonight? Can I get anyone anything?" Out of the corner of her eye, Ella saw a guy standing under one of the lights on the dance floor. It looked like he was wearing all white. With all the lights going in the club she wasn't sure. That was unusual in this scene.

"Can I get a gin and tonic?" a pretty blonde asked. Ella noticed her looking at the guy in white on the dance floor. He was very tall. As he turned his head in their direction, the blonde stood up straighter and brushed her hair away from her face in time to give him a radiant smile. He nodded at her with a slight smile on his face and turned away.

"Well, it's shaping up to be an interesting night," she said to Ella. "Am I gonna get my drink or do I have to make it myself?"

"I was just waiting to ask you what kind of gin you wanted. I didn't want to interrupt."

The blonde glared at Ella. "Whatever. The best you've got of course."

"Of course," Ella muttered under her breath. When she looked up again the blonde was still glaring at her.

"What's your problem? Is it my fault you're dressed like Wednesday Addams?"

What Ella really wanted to say was it was better than being dressed like a... a... well, she didn't know what and didn't care. Instead, she smiled and handed the drink to the blonde.

"It's on the house, sorry if I took too long."

The girl tossed her hair, took the drink, and turned toward the guy in the white clothes.

Ella sighed as she looked down the bar and saw that the man from earlier who had called her "sweetheart" was beckoning for her to come down to him.

"Three for three," she muttered as it occurred to her that perhaps she would like to find another job. If only her options weren't so limited. Taking a deep breath, counting to ten, picturing water, and thinking about all the other things that supposedly help you keep your patience. *Yep. They probably aren't going to help tonight.*

"What can I get for you, sir?" Annoying Customer was his name, she decided. "Another round of whiskey?"

Annoying Customer winked at her. "You know what I like, don't you, sweet-heart?" He snorted at his joke. She just stared at him for a moment and realized he was not only obnoxious but, wow, did he really look the part as well.

He was wearing a shiny black button-down top, except most of the front wasn't buttoned. Around his neck he had a long gold dollar sign on a thick chain dangling in between the open shirt, and his dark hair was slicked back. Annoying Customer had a rather large nose and squinty black eyes. He was chewing on a cigar and had crusty white bits at the corners of his mouth. There was a musty smell coming off him, Ella realized. She had originally thought it was just coming from some stale sewer water.

He winked at her again. "Like whats you see, babe? You can see as much as you like."

She blinked and laughed. *Does he really think I was admiring him?* He seemed to take her laugh as encouragement. He leaned further over the the bar and reached out to run his finger down her arm. It miffed Ella and she stepped back to move out of his reach. Annoying Customer did not like this reaction. He forced himself further over and grabbed her arm tightly, forcing her forward.

"Hey, let go of me!" she looked quickly around. No one else who worked at the club was paying attention to them. They were all busy with other people. Pulling as hard as she could from him, she couldn't get out of his hand. She felt herself start to get angry as the man sneered at her. She pulled again. His grip was iron.

"Don't worry, sweets, I gots nothing you don't want."

Ella pulled away from him as far as she could and started to feel around the bar for something to hit him with. She didn't want to start a fight but she wasn't about to let this creep harass her either.

"Let her go." The voice was low but loud enough to hear over the music.

The shock distracted her for a minute and then Annoying Customer squeezed her arm tighter.

"Ow! Listen you cretin, let go of my arm!" Pulling harder and getting really mad, she was feeling a little warm. *Ugh, I can't get away from him.* To make matters worse, she was starting to sweat.

"Mind your business, pal," growled the cretin. He didn't turn around to acknowledge the stranger.

"I will if you will." His voice was solid and distinctly clear despite the loud music.

Out of the corner of her eye Ella saw the stranger step forward. Annoying Customer must have noticed as well because he gave her arm one last hard pull and then pushed her back into the shelves of glasses and bottles. Glass shattered all around her and more than one of the bottles hit Ella's head and shoulders. The manager came running to the bar with two security guards in tow.

"Knock it off!" The manager stepped between the two of them. Ella's shoulder was starting to throb. Feeling slightly dazed she rubbed her shoulder and realized it was warm and wet.

"Crap," she muttered.

The security guards were pulling Annoying Customer out of the club and he was shouting the whole way. He pushed the security guards off and glared at the manager.

"I'm going to go get my company and then I'll be off. No hard feelings, pals." All the while he said this, his eyes were focused on the stranger in white.

Flustered, and possibly starting to let loose a stream of veritable bad words, Ella turned and ran to the bathroom, the manager calling after her.

Her shoulder was throbbing where the bottle hit it. Rushing to the bathroom through the throngs of people, she pushed open the door so hard it slammed against the wall behind it. A couple of girls in the bathroom looked at her warily.

"Um, uh, yeah, everyone needs to leave, uh, someone said the toilet is about to overflow," she stammered, clutching her shoulder. She noticed gratefully that the only lights on in the bathroom were the dim ones over the mirrors and stalls.

A girl with streaked blonde hair and a loud, low-cut top squealed and ran out of the room. Several more flicked their lipsticks closed and lazily sauntered out.

Thinking that was everyone, Ella locked the door.

Pulling paper towels out quickly from the dispenser she wet them and started to dab her forehead. Leaning close to the mirror she noticed streaks down her cheeks. Wiping furiously, she didn't notice the girl with glazed eyes come out of a stall until she was standing right next to her.

The girl stared at Ella and slurred, "Where'd myfriendsgo?"

Irritated with herself for not checking the stalls, Ella looked away from her scrubbing. "Uh, they left because the bathroom is closed."

"That's weird," the girl replied, swaying forward a bit as she spoke. "You have hair dye on your shoulder."

Ella blinked. "What?" A finger poked a spot of her shoulder a little too hard. "See, hair dye," she repeated.

The wetness suddenly disappeared off the girl's finger as if into her skin.

"What the..." she leaned what she thought was closer to her finger but instead slipped and fell onto Ella, who in turn pushed her up. The sweat was on her and Ella hurried to wipe it off before the girl recovered completely.

"What's going on?" she demanded in a rather three-year-old sounding voice.

"You've just had too much to drink." Ella finished steadying her and directed her towards the door. Unlocking it she said, "Go on back out there and tell the manager at the bar that we owe you one for kicking you out of the bathroom. He'll take it off your tab. And have some water please."

The girl perked up at that, straightened her skirt, and moved out the door. "Cool hair color anyway," she said before ambling off.

Re-locking the door, Ella pulled out her ponytail. She was going to have to wear her hair down for the rest of the night. That would make it harder to work, but she had to be careful.

"Oh, well," she said to the somewhat ghostly girl in the mirror looking back at her.

Wiping out the sink, the counter, and even the mirror to be safe, she finally unlocked the door and went back out to the bar.

All the bottles were picked back up and the cretin was gone. She thought she saw the guy in white but there were so many people around now she couldn't tell for sure. All the black hid any white. The manager was tending bar and saw her come back out.

"You okay, Cerulean?"

"Yeah."

"Want to take over, then?"

"Yep! I have rent to pay." She turned and smiled at the nearest available goth boy.

Chapter 3

The rest of the night passed without incident. In fact, it was so busy any thoughts of the evening's events were pushed to the back of Ella's mind. Her shoulder was still dully aching as she counted out tips from the shift. She was pleased to find she'd made almost half the rent money already.

It was still a beautiful night at 2 a.m. when Ella left the club. There were a few grey clouds in the sky and it smelled slightly like rain. Since it was late, Ella decided to take the shorter route home.

When she walked to Alchemy she went down the main street around the block from her apartment. Now she was cutting across a normally full, but empty at this hour, parking lot. It made the walk a lot shorter and there was just enough light for it not to be creepy.

When she reached the lot, there were a few more cars than normal but still not many. There was one beat-up, dark-colored four-door that was there late nearly every time she passed through the lot.

"Must be security guards," she mused aloud.

Glancing around, she saw a black car on the street slow down a little too far from the red light. That made her heart speed up ever so slightly. Assuming it was her overly active imagination, she decided to ignore it and picked up the pace of the walk home. To her relief, the car turned when the light changed, and she let out a long breath she didn't even realize she was holding. Not slowing the pace, Ella crossed the parking lot quickly and reached her block in record time.

When she spied her building she let out a laugh. "Wow, I'm so jumpy." The incident had bothered her more than she had originally thought.

Rounding the last corner to her place, she saw a somewhat familiar figure with their back to her. It was a bit darker in front of the building than under the streetlights on the block. The figure stepped directly under the light above the door of her building. Ella's eyes widened. It was the guy in white from the club. The outfit he was wearing was amazing. Even without much light, it was luminescent.

Why is he in front of my building? How does he know where I live? A hundred questions raced through her mind.

She stepped on a stick, giving away her presence. The guy in white whirled around. The look on his face was unreadable except for a the smallest bit of surprise that flitted quickly across his features.

"Hello," he said softly.

"Hi," Ella stopped.

"I'm Ry..." he was cut off by the door to the building opening. The pretty blonde from the club stepped out. She smiled broadly at the guy in white and didn't notice Ella at all.

"My roommate is nowhere to be found, Ryan," she reached out her hand to him. "So, if you want to come up..." she moved suggestively toward him.

Ryan peered at her and then turned to Ella. "Well, good night," he said as he pulled the door open far enough for her. The blonde finally noticed Ella standing there.

"Oh, the nun from the bar lives in my building. Must be time to move," she said snidely to Ryan.

He seemed to barely glance at the girl. He was staring at Ella so intently she felt a bit undone.

"Nun? Really? How clever. The 1950's called. They want their insult back," Ella was tired and pretty well sick of everyone at this point. This girl was officially on the list. *Whatever that means. But yeah, the list.*

There was no way to walk past without brushing against him. Which she did as quickly as possible and was so self conscious she thought her bright red face must be very evident, even in the dim light. She felt more than a tad grouchy as she moved past him.

Walking quickly up the first flight of stairs, Ella dared a look down at Ryan. He was still looking at her even as the blonde girl draped herself on him.

Ella took the rest of the stairs to the third floor two at a time and briskly walked to her door.

Her hand was shaking as she dug out the keys and fumbled with the lock. Once inside she locked the door behind her and leaned against it, closing her eyes. That was the strangest reaction she'd ever had to anyone. Boys did *not* embarrass her. There was no room in her life for them. Generally, they had no interest in her anyway, as far as she could tell. *What is wrong with me?*

The encounters from the evening had left a wound-up feeling, so she decided to be productive. Looking at a blank white canvas that she'd prepared the night before, she began to imagine a dinosaur. Letting her mind wander, she absently plopped down on the floor, dropping her keys, which made a loud noise in the dark, quiet room. Ryan's face came to her mind's eye.

"Oh, Ryan." She knew his name and didn't even realize it until now. Feeling herself frown, she unlaced her boots and set them aside. Leaning against the wall with closed eyes, she tried to picture the dinosaur again. Instead, his face floated into her head. Her eyes flew open and a groan escaped her lips.

"This is stupid," she said aloud to the room. "Okay, okay, focus. He's cute. So what? He's with that dumb girl so obviously his taste is terrible. Probably a jerk. Likely a jerk."

He wouldn't leave her mind. Sighing loudly and deciding this was not a good time to paint, she got up. There was no way she was going to be able to sleep yet. She was wide awake from work and not in pain. The pills had a while before they would wear off. Deciding to do some cleaning to work off the nervous energy, her mind wandered to the evening's events. The creepy cretin was not really anything new, although he was far more aggressive than anyone had ever been toward her. Ryan's behavior was a tad surprising. Any guy who had "defended" her before had always stuck around, trying to keep Ella's attention on him. He didn't bother her at all after everything was taken care of, and he wasn't asked to leave. Thinking back to the bathroom, one thing she'd almost forgotten was the wetness from her shoulder on the other girl's finger, and how it seemed to disappear or dissolve into her skin. *Well, that was crazy. It was pretty dimly lit in that bathroom. It probably just dropped on the floor and I didn't notice.* The girl was tipsy, and Ella was trying to get her out of the bathroom and take care of the throbbing shoulder. She stopped wiping the counter and touched her shoulder. It was tender and definitely going to have a bruise.

Picking up the cloth again, she looked around the room. Truth be told, it didn't need to be cleaned. It was always clean. Ella sometimes wondered if she had some sort of disorder. It was really important to her that the apartment stayed clean, she would rationalize. She could not work in a mess. Painting in a chaotic, messy room was uninspiring. *Who are you kidding? The headmistress totally made you crazy about cleaning.* Ella was not happy. This was the second time tonight that woman had popped in her head. This did not amuse her in the least. The headmistress was someone she really wouldn't mind forgetting about, even if she had to get hit in the head with a bottle at work to do it. *That woman may have made me a clean freak but not an austere, boring minimalist,* she thought, grinning to herself and looking around. Everything had its place, but there was a lot of everything.

Straightening and dusting, she started to hum to herself. After about an hour she was feeling hungry, so she put away the trusty cleaning cloth and went to the fridge. It was a little bare. There was a twenty-four hour grocery nearby. *I'll stop there on my way home tomorrow night. But for now some strawberries and an apple will suffice.*

Somewhere in the quiet building, Ella heard a door close. It was muted, not slammed, but in the stillness of 4 a.m. it was distinct. Footsteps followed. They grew louder and louder. Since her apartment faced the front entrance, she could almost always hear everyone coming and going. *Maybe it's Ryan,* the random thought popped into her head, unwelcome.

A little peek isn't going to hurt anyone. She walked to the windows that faced the street. The glass was covered with heavy, blackout curtains to keep out all the light. Carefully moving them aside, she glanced down just as Ryan stepped to the sidewalk. He stopped to put on the jacket that he was now carrying, a thought that bugged Ella. He looked up in her direction.

"Damn," she stepped back, and the curtains fell into place. *Did he see me? I should've shut off the light.*

"Great! Now he thinks I'm weird." Hazarding a second glance, this time she turned off the light. "Couldn't do it the first time?" She really annoyed herself sometimes.

He wasn't there. The curtain fell back into place. "What are you so worried about? You'll probably never see him again, and if you do see him at the club, he'll be with that girl."

Going back to eating the fruit, she decided to go to bed and put an end to this stupid night. She lay in bed for over an hour before she finally drifted off.

Pleasantly surprised upon waking up, she found she'd slept for six hours peacefully. Even more surprising, the spot where the bottle hit her last night wasn't sore at all, and neither were her joints. Getting out of bed was much easier than the night before. Making the bed and tidying the bedroom before start-ing yoga stretching, Ella really couldn't believe how much better she felt.

When she was done stretching, she went over to the mirror and pulled down her sleeve. The top of her shoulder only had the slightest hint of discoloration. However unusual her good health was today, it put Ella in a great mood. It was 3:00 and she still had six hours until work. Mentally making a list of things she could do before and after work, she ambled over to the computer to read the news. Since being unable to do much but lie in bed and eat, she was feeling pretty out of the loop from the world. Moving her favorite chair in front of the desk, she noticed a pen in the crevice between the cushion and the frame. She pulled it out. She thought the name on it was not one she recognized. It was the name of an art gallery. Not remembering if she pocketed the pen accidentally at work, she thought to look up the name of the gallery online. She wandered over to the window with the pen in hand and pulled open the curtains.

It was a gloomy day. Just the opposite of yesterday, it would seem. Mildly concerned about rain, she momentarily forgot about the pen and thought about the forecast for the evening. Setting the pen aside and sitting down at the desk, she pulled up a page with the local radar and weather. It appeared it would be gray all day and evening with mild drizzle throughout the night. Ella loved the rain despite the trouble it caused her. The extra preparation for work was a trial even after all these years. It did, however, make her even more curious as to why she was feeling so much better than she normally would be on a day like this. The pressure changes and humidity were murder on her joints and most of the time would send her to bed for days unless she took many painkillers.

Suddenly she remembered the name on the pen. Clicking back to the search, she typed in "Soap Factory". Several possible pages popped up. To her surprise, it was a local art gallery she'd not been to, which was something she made a point to do. It literally was an old soap factory that was currently seek-ing to display unknown local painters. The request was for thematic, color-driv-en collections. That got her attention. Never having had the nerve to put any of her work in public was a battle, truth be told. Knowing logically she had to be careful with everything that she did, but at the same time she longed desper-ately to be a part of the artist community. It wasn't a possibility. Staring off into space, her mind wandered to Alexandra. She was constantly telling Ella not to be afraid and to put herself out for the world to see and admire.

"You're unique without trying," she would say. "Look around at all these spoiled brats spending tons and tons of money trying to set themselves apart from each other, and they're all the same. You're special and lucky to be so." Alexandra certainly didn't try to hide.

Ella realized with sadness how much she missed her friend, and how much she seemed to be thinking about the past lately, something she really tried to avoid doing. Looking back at the web page, she noted the contact info for the man in charge of the exhibit. It also mentioned exhibitors that were accepted would be a given a portion of the admission fees that were collected as well as an opening evening and a chance to sell their pieces. It was so tempting. She could take extra time to get ready and be careful. She could play the overly eccentric artist, demanding low lighting other than that on the paintings. Assuming her collection was even accepted. She smiled to herself. Trying to imagine demanding anything from anyone made her feel silly. *Can I really live the rest of my life hiding from the world? What is the worst that could happen? People thinking I'm a freak? That already happens.*

Standing up, she looked around the living room. It was full of paintings. On the walls, on the ceilings, lined up and stacked on each other. She hadn't realized until that moment there were quite a lot of them. *What will happen to my art? Am I going to continue to make it and share it with no one? Continue sharing nothing with no one?* She reached for the phone.

"Hi, uh... My name is Ella, um... Ella Cerulean. And I was calling about an advertisement on your website about looking for collections for an upcoming exhibition... Right... Oh, okay... Yes, please. I'll wait." Her hand was sweaty as she listened to the phone ring on the other end of the line.

"Evan speaking."

"Hi, Evan, um... wow. So, look, I was calling about the ad on the website about the um..."

"Yeah, well," he cut her off, "I need to see a portfolio and some of your pieces. We are looking for something very specific." His completely no-nonsense attitude made her even more nervous.

"Oh, right. Okay well, I have some pieces but not really a portfolio."

"Not really? Do you have one or not, and should I waste my time looking at it?"

Ella swallowed nervously. "Yes, I have a portfolio. No you would not be wasting your time looking at it."

"Fine, be here tomorrow, 4 o' clock."

"Right, yes, I will be." He had already hung up. She hung up the phone. *What in the world was I thinking? I don't have a portfolio at all!*

"No time like the present."

Forgetting all previous plans for the afternoon and evening, she started to dig through the closet and look for a camera. *There is so much stuff in here.* Pulling out folders and boxes, pushing things aside, she came across a folder she hadn't laid eyes on in a long time. It was full with all the drawings of dreams and nightmares from when she was a kid. Having pushed them out of her mind so long ago, seeing them now was numbing. Thumbing through them, she stopped on one that had not slipped from memory. In it there was a girl standing under a tree. All around her, wind was filled with pieces of trees and books and pieces of a building, all the way to the edge of the page where it looked as everything was melted together and blurred. The only thing completely clear in the picture was the girl, who had a look of fear and confusion on her face. As she picked it up, it was a vivid reminder of the recurring dream Ella had been having for most of her life. Including two nights ago. *All my work to forget,* she admitted, *was rather pointless.* Once again she thought of Alexandra.

Groaning, she shoved the drawing back into the folder. Her need to be melancholy the last few days was not going to help her present her work. Finally finding the camera in a container on the bottom shelf, she pulled it out and found it had no battery. No battery wasn't helpful. She was going to have to go and buy one. Going outside during the day was not her favorite thing to do. It made her apprehensive, but she had to do it or no portfolio. It was necessary.

Ella decided she would drive her car somewhere a bit farther away in order to avoid anyone she might know from work. She knew a lot of them lived near here. Looking around her apartment to figure out if she needed to buy anything else on this daytime adventure, it occurred to her she was going to have to stop working on the portfolio to go to her job. She couldn't get out of it because rent was due in a few days. All the time she felt she had today was suddenly gone. As she grabbed the Soap Factory pen and a piece of a paper to make a shopping list, a sudden pain flashed behind her eyes. It was sharp but brief and included a random yellow light spot and an image of an unfamiliar man's face. As quickly as it was there, it was gone, and she rubbed her eyes. She decided that if she could remember what he looked like she would draw him later. Maybe he could be used in a painting.

She finished writing the list, and quickly got dressed. Packing a bag with a towel, a water bottle, a few pills, an umbrella, an extra pair of sunglasses, a hat, a jacket, a couple pairs of gloves, a scarf, Band-Aids, some snacks, and water. Ella was ready to go. Grabbing her car keys and purse, she went down the stairs to the front door where the blonde girl from last night was checking her mail and talking on a cell phone.

Noticing Ella, an evil looked crossed her face and she loudly said, "You wouldn't believe how amazing he was and his body…" Ella pushed past her and slammed the door before she could hear the end of the sentence.

Feeling a little annoyed with her reaction to that girl, *because seriously, who cares*, she went over to where her car was parked on the street. Balancing a bag and purse to unlock the door made her drop the keys. Bending over to pick them up, out of the corner of her eye she spotted what she thought was the car she had noticed slowing down the night before. She stood back up, but it drove around the corner before she could get a good look at it. Not sure, and wondering what it mattered anyway, she got in the car and turned it on.

She pulled away from the curb and slowly drove down to the corner. There was a lot of traffic because the university was in session today. As she waited for a few minutes, Ella thought she saw the car merging into the lanes of slow-moving vehicles. *They probably just live around here.* Although she had never noticed the car before. She was abruptly pushed out of her reverie when the car behind her honked loudly to let her know there was an opening. Thoughts were lost as she moved into the traffic and started on her way out to the edge of the city.

Wondering when the rain was going to come, Ella turned on the radio and flipped through channels. The trouble with her joints hadn't started despite the obvious humidity, although she was repeatedly checking her appearance in the mirror. Head-to-toe black clothing was a savior, but she usually couldn't do much about her face unless it was cold enough to cover it with a scarf.

On what seemed like her hundredth nervous face check, the car from earlier made a brief appearance in the mirror. Turning off the main street to take a less used way to the suburbs she saw the car turn behind her. It definitely seemed like this car was following her, and she still couldn't shake the feeling it was the car from last night. Turning again, it again followed. She sped up and decided to stick to the main streets. *Why in the world would anyone be following me?* The destination was near so she put it out of her mind and concentrated on getting to the store.

Five minutes passed and she reached her destination. She didn't see the car pull into the lot behind her. Only now did she notice she'd been gripping the steering wheel tightly. Promising herself she'd get a handle on her imagination, she parked the car and climbed out. She grabbed her bag, then threw it back in, sighed and grabbed it again. Sometimes she really hated carrying around all this stuff. *Better safe than sorry.* Locking the car and involuntarily glancing around the parking lot, she walked into the store.

She took off her sunglasses, and the lights hurt her eyes for a second. It had been a while since she went shopping other than for groceries. It wasn't often she needed even art supplies. Not really liking stores because there were so many people, Ella would buy off the Internet and at various garage sales. The bright lights of stores caused a problem for her not just by hurting her eyes, but also by illuminating some things she tried to keep people from noticing, like her hair.

Kind of short on time and looking quickly at a store map, she dug the list out of her bag and, of course, dropped a bunch of things on the floor. She picked them up as quickly as possible while the other shoppers stepped over her. A shiny black shoe stepped exceptionally close to Ella's hand.

Fumbling around, she mumbled, "Excuse me," stood up, and narrowly missed colliding heads with a man in sunglasses as he was bending down to help her. He dropped his bag on her foot and she felt it knick her toe. She let out a sharp breath of pain.

"I'm really sorry I dropped my bag on you. Are you okay? I'm guessing by that gasp you may have been poked by my wife's craft items. I brought them with to find matching ones for her. Are you okay?" He took off his sunglasses and looked at her with concerned eyes.

"It's fine, I'm okay. Thanks for trying to help me, but I'm a klutz." She smiled brightly as the man put his glasses back on, smiled in return, and walked away.

Ella gathered her stuff together and picked up a shopping basket. The light was awful, her eyes stung. *All the more reason to get this done quickly and get back home.* Glancing at the signs, she headed toward the art department. Looking down the aisles as she breezed by them, she saw the man who walked into her in the front of the store. He was wearing those dark glasses, which almost made her laugh. She wanted to put hers back on. He turned to look at her staring at him. She felt stupid and walked away.

Continuing on, she stopped and bent over to look at painting cases. The store suddenly seemed oddly quiet. As she examined one of the cases, the sound of stiff shoes clacked on the tile floors. The sound was unnerving. Listening for a minute and then shaking her head, she zipped open the case. It expanded fully open, and then more, and then a little more. The lights were getting dimmer in the store. *Why is this case so, so very big? Why is it so dark?* The aisle narrowed and she couldn't keep her balance. The man in the glasses reached a long hand out to grab her as she slipped to the floor that was falling out beneath her.

The tree was on fire. It had a secret beneath it, someone told her. But she couldn't remember who. It crumbled to dust before she could get to it. She was in a desert. Though it hadn't always been a desert. It was so windy that dust clouded most of the air. She couldn't see well nor breathe. The dust burned her lungs. All the wind produced no sound, and it was eerily silent. Turning her head, she saw that some of the dust was whirling around to form an oval that was clear. In the oval was an explosion that made no sound but looked to be devastating. The image faded away and was replaced with a view of a building unlike anything Ella had ever seen before. It was triangular and seem to rise up into space. Though one couldn't tell because it was hovering above a mountain range. The mountains themselves were spectacular. Dark red and burgundy caps blending into deep purple bases. They were reflected in the building's shimmery, silver, glass-like surface. A heavy gust of wind hit Ella in the chest but she didn't move from the spot where she was standing. It was as if she was stuck in quicksand, just not sinking. The top of the striking building started to break apart and large chunks of it tumbled into the tops of the mountains, causing some of the caps to fall with the pieces to the ground. Every bit of the building collapsed and landed in a crash. Once it stopped, several strange, large, gray animals that looked a bit like lions wandered up to some of the debris. One lowered its head as if to investigate, suddenly jerked back in surprise, and raised its head as if to cry out in pain. The other creatures followed suit, though no sound actually escaped from their mouths. The oval burst apart and Ella shielded her eyes. Blinking furiously she looked up and saw a torrent of water rushing toward her. It didn't seem to be just an image. It made no sound but was moving at an unbelievable speed, and it was growing quickly in size. She pulled at her legs as hard as she could, but they didn't budge in the slightest. The water was closing in quickly. Panic started to rise. She was going to drown. Feeling the drops hitting her face, she closed her eyes. She could feel the pressure starting to build around her. The water knocked into her but still didn't move her from the spot. The pressure was now building on her chest. What felt like a hand wrapped around her arm and pulled her with more strength than she could ever imagine existed. It wasn't until she nearly was unconscious that she realized she was breathing underwater.

She jumped when the horn honked. The car was running, and her bags blocked the mirror so she couldn't see behind her. The horn blared again.

"Gah! Okay, okay. I'm moving, geez." She pulled the car out of the way so the person could pass. The driver turned her way. She caught a quick glance while trying to figure out why she'd spaced out so much. It wasn't unlike her to get lost in thought. But Ella didn't remember shopping. Only a vague recollection, really. *That was stupid, of course I shopped.* The car was full of bags. She looked at the clock. She had done it in record time, too. Only twenty minutes. Plenty of time to get home and get work done on her portfolio.

As she drove home, she didn't once spot the car that she thought had been following her.

Which, she reminded herself, *is obvious. Because it hadn't been.*

"Wow, Cerulean you really need to get a hold of yourself." She turned on the radio so she didn't have to listen to her thoughts, and a song she loved came on. Singing along as she drove home, a troubling feeling came over her as she tried to recall shopping. The painting case had fallen out of her hand. It made a loud, disconcerting noise. Not exactly sure she had bent over to pick it up, she pictured herself picking it up. It was a fuzzy image. She turned the radio up louder.

Walking through the store, she had picked up things on her list, though she didn't look at the list at all while there. *Waited in line, checked out, went to car, loaded car and started to drive home. Everything is there. I just lost track of time.* Pulling onto her block, she parked at the nearest available spot. Getting out and opening the door to the back seat, she started pulling out the bags. Slowly her head started to have a dull pounding. As she closed the door, the pounding grew a bit worse. Gripping the bags and hurrying to unlock the building door, she got in and quickly walked upstairs. When she turned the key in the apartment door and threw the bags inside, the pounding stopped.

Ella stared at the bags. She had fleeting pain, yes. But sometimes she knew. Knew something wasn't right. Reaching a hand out to the bag that fell nearest, she gripped the handle and light flashed behind her eyes. She turned the bag over quickly and dumped it on the floor. There was nothing in the bag that wasn't on the shopping list. She grabbed the second bag and dumped it on the floor. Nothing unusual. One more shopping bag and her tote. Looking around, she didn't see the tote.

Thinking it was still in the car, Ella opened the door and ran downstairs to the front door. Just as she was going to go outside, the car from earlier caught her eye. It was parked more than a few cars down, but she was positive it was the same one. Not knowing what to do and staring at the car for a few minutes, thoughts raced in her mind. The man behind the wheel was the same one who nearly collided with her at the store. The sound of his shoes clicking loudly on the floor echoed in her head.

Moving away from the door, she had to decide what to do. *Go out to the car or back to the apartment? If I go outside what if something happens? What if he is going to attack me? Or worse?* Of course, that seemed illogical because it was bright daylight outside. Somehow, though, she had a nagging feeling that wouldn't matter. Not having a way to defend herself if he did decide to attack her, *because he is a psycho or something*, Ella turned and walked back up the stairs. She decided she would wait to go to the car. There was no one she could call for help if she needed to, and she definitely didn't want to scream and draw attention to herself. Besides, she had to get the portfolio together and there was still the chance she was imagining things. A voice in her head told her she knew better, but she was not going to listen to it. She couldn't waste any more time on this possibly paranoid fantasy. It was going to have to wait. And anyway, her head wasn't hurting anymore so she could think straight.

Walking through the door, she saw the supplies scattered all over the floor. Scooping up as many as possible and depositing them on the dining room table, Ella began arranging them in a meticulous fashion. She lined paints up in groups with the coordinating brushes. She sifted through piles of paintings and sketches and put them in protective coverings. Looking at the plain cover of the case, Ella decided to paint it. Picking up a pencil she started to sketch on the material. Starting with mountains and oddly shaped clouds, she formed them into a pattern she made up.

The shapes seemed slightly familiar. Putting down the case, she rifled through some drawings and picked up one she was sure was from when she was about ten years old. The note she wrote to herself on the back said, "Dreamt this again, I don't know what they mean, but they mean something important." Smiling to herself at how dramatic the note was, Ella put aside the drawing and continued to work.

Daylight began to fade, and after what seemed to be no time at all, Ella looked at the clock to see that she had to get ready for work. The portfolio was nowhere near where she wanted it to be, so as soon as she got off she would be rushing home to work on it.

She didn't want to be late again like last night so she set aside the work and started to get ready, running out the door with time to spare for once. Hoping it would be a profitable tip night, she had made the attempt to dress up a little and decided to work on being in a good mood during her walk. She glanced around nervously now and again, but the car from earlier was nowhere in sight. Ella went over to her car and noticed the missing tote from earlier was sitting on the driver's seat. She did not remember putting it there, but she also did not care. She was glad it was not lost.

Feeling relieved that she was just paranoid, she made it to work before the club was even open. Something she almost never did.

Her boss was in the back room going through paperwork and looked up when she came in.

"How are you doing tonight, Ella?" He looked concerned. "I was worried that imbecile from last night had shaken you up a bit."

"Oh, it was not great," she laughed warily. "But what can you do? Sometimes there's going to be a jerk."

"I was glad no one bothered you after work," he said casually.

Ella looked at him blankly. "No one did bother me. But how would you know that?"

Looking a bit red in the face, he mumbled something about just keeping an eye out while she walked home last night.

Ella had to giggle and resisted rolling her eyes. She knew he had daughters of his own. He was always telling the staff about them and the "miserable sacks" they brought around as boyfriends. Most of the boyfriends didn't seem to last too long with the papa looking over their shoulders every second. He made no secret that he didn't think any men were good enough for his "girls." And he made it clear that "girls" included Ella. She knew he meant well, but truth be told she found him somewhat narrow-minded and outdated in his way of thinking. She tried to carefully say this to him, but he wouldn't hear it. His daughters were his daughters.

"Pretty girls have to be careful is all. You know I'll be perfectly happy when you meet someone worth your time, but I can't say I've seen anyone at this point," his slight southern drawl came out in his words. It wasn't always there, Ella noticed, but when he got sappy it would make a minor appearance.

"My girls neither. They just bring home the idiots. I don't put up with it though. You know I don't. They need to finish school. Then maybe they can get serious with someone. But until then…"

"You're a good dad," Ella cut him off. If she didn't he would go on for a while and she wanted to get set up at the bar. It was often not cleaned or arranged the way that worked best for her. "I'm going to go get up and running for business, Jack. Thanks for looking out for me."

She headed out to the front end where the lights were still on and the blinds over the windows were yet to be drawn. Glancing out the window, she saw the boy in white from the night before. Only this time he was wearing what appeared to be silver. He saw her and held her gaze for a moment before turning and walking away. *What is he doing here again?*

Wiping down the bar quickly and lining up glasses, she slipped away to the bathroom. Ella peered in the mirror at herself. Dark hair pulled into a bun, silver streaks very apparent. Tight black top, long black gloves, the norm. At least her eyes weren't bloodshot from painting all day. Pulling a red lipstick from her pocket, she paused a moment before putting it on. She grimaced at herself for being in denial about wanting the guy in silver's attention. "Ryan," she reminded herself. She slammed the door when leaving the bathroom.

"You ready, Cerulean?" the bouncer shouted from the door.

"Yeah!" She walked behind the bar as the lights went down, and she tried not to think about Ryan.

The night started as normal, girls in long flowing velvets and rich asian fabrics like perfect artistic dolls. The guys dressed in boots both of gothic romance and of futuristic warrior looks. Some people mingled and others danced while some skulked around the outlying goings-on to avoid talking to anyone.

Ella stayed busy most of the first part of the evening pouring dark red wines and making purple martini drinks, not having any time to really notice if anyone she sort of knew was there. There were a few people Ella had a casual rapport with. When she finally had a down moment near midnight, she glanced around the club. It was busy and darker than usual. The lights had been covered in mercurial purple gels, giving every corner of the club an eerily surreal look. Her eyes were searching for a familiar face when she heard her name.

"Ella, right?" a male voice said some what softly to the side of her. She almost didn't hear it. Turning around she saw Ryan and her heart skipped a beat.

"Yes, and you're Ryan. I never really said thanks for the help 'defending my honor.'" She air quoted with her fingers and smiled awkwardly. Ella wasn't sure but she thought she saw him blush a bit. *It's probably the weird light.*

"It was nothing. I didn't want to seem like I thought you couldn't take care of yourself. I just, he just..." he stumbled over his words. "That guy overstepped his bounds," he finished quickly.

Ella felt herself smile and reached out to shake his hand. "Well, it is nice to meet you for real this time."

Ryan shook her hand firmly and held it a minute longer than he should, staring at her glove. "Those are pretty," he said.

She reluctantly pulled away. "Yeah, thanks, I guess they're my thing." At that moment she heard someone shout for the bartender and she turned around. "I'll be back in a minute. Well," she stopped. "If you want."

"Of course," he finally smiled. Unfortunately she didn't get back in a minute as more and more people lined up to order drinks. After about ten minutes of mixing and collecting money she glanced over to the spot where she'd left Ryan. He wasn't there.

She didn't see him for the rest of her shift. Working later than normal cleaning up and counting out, she didn't leave the club until after 3 a.m. She admitted she was disappointed that Ryan had decided to leave. Though she wasn't surprised. The blonde from the other night had shown up, and Ella had a feeling he was a bit preoccupied once she found him.

Distractedly walking home, she thought about how much she would really have liked to talk to him more. Cutting across the school parking lot, she noticed that some of the lights normally on at night were dark. She could barely make out the dark-colored car that was always parked in the distance. Walking a little more leisurely than normal, mostly because she was lost in thought, she heard a loud slam and someone cry out. It startled her beyond belief. As she turned around in the darkness, it momentarily crossed her mind to run home.

"Coward," she chided herself.

"Hello? Are you okay?" She started moving further into the parking lot. *The darkness is so weird.*

"I'm, well, ugh," a man with a strained accent groaned.

"I'm sorry, Sir, it's really dark and I'm having a hard time seeing. Oh, I think I see you." Ella jogged towards the dark-colored car she had seen so often. Tossing her bag on the ground, she knelt beside him.

"Are you okay?"

Moving to gather up the papers that had scattered from his fall, the man groaned again. "Oh, thank you, miss, for coming over to assist me." He struggled to straighten up. "I seem to be having some complications."

"I sort of see that." She finished gathering the papers and stuffed them in a folder that was lying upside down on the ground. A street lamp flickered on in the darkness above them.

"Well, that's a spot of good luck," the man said. Ella could better see his face now. It was not too clear but he looked a bit sallow and tired. He was older, maybe in his forties. She was never any good at guessing ages. In the distance thunder clapped loudly. *I need to get home soon.* She helped the man struggle to his feet. He smiled gratefully and adjusted his glasses.

"Thank you so much, miss. I couldn't have ever imagined that someone would be out at this late hour who would help an old man to his feet. Especially not a nice young lady."

"Oh it's no big deal. I was on my way home from work. Incidentally, I need to be going. If you're okay?" Lightning streaked across the sky. She really didn't want to get wet.

"I hate to bother you more, miss, but to be honest I do think I may need a bit more help. See, my arm has gone limp. It's a side effect of some of the drugs I'm taking, and I need to get all this into my office before it rains. If you could possibly carry some of it to just under the awning, there, I would owe you tremendously."

Ella couldn't leave him without helping. And besides, it was mostly dark, even if it did start raining.

"Sure, no problem. Do you work here at the school?" She asked in a cheerful voice. She bent over and picked up his bag, some folders, and a box.

"Ah, yes, I teach chemistry." He was fumbling around to find keys in his pocket.

"Chemistry? That's great. I wasn't very good at it. I tried, but I often couldn't understand my teachers so I spent a lot of extra time getting tutoring." Ella was rambling. Lightning streaked across the sky again. Thunder jarred the glass on the car. Her worrying was making her ramble. A gust of wind blew some of the folders off the pile.

"Crap!" She dropped the boxes and went chasing after the folders. She grabbed most of them, but one seemed to keep moving just slightly out of her grasp. She chased it and stomped a foot down on it before it could blow away again. It started to rain and the wind began to pick up.

Bending over and stuffing the sheet of paper under her jacket, she started to run back over to the door. The rain started coming down hard. It was causing Ella's hair to fall out of the bun and into her face. She could barely see where she had dropped the stuff she had been carrying. The man she had stopped to help was nowhere to be found. The chaos from the storm was picking up as Ella started toward the door. Someone yanked her from behind and caused her to fall to the ground hard. She hit her tailbone on the concrete, and the pain shot through her back, forcing her to drop what she was holding. Struggling to see who had come up from behind, she tried to get up on her knees only to be shoved to the ground again. Swearing as rocks ground into her palm, she swung out an arm, trying to hit whoever might be near her. Not making contact with anyone, she pulled herself up. Lightning cracked the sky in a jagged line, and Ella caught a glimpse of the creepy man from the bar the night before bending over to pick up the papers that had flown from the box.

"What the...?" *Is he following me? IS EVERYONE FOLLOWING ME?? GAH!* Now she was mad.

"Hey!" She yelled but knew that there was no way he could hear in the storm. She ran over to where he was and threw herself against him as hard as she could. He was a brick wall. He turned and tried to push her again, but she dodged out his way. Grabbing at the papers, she yanked as hard she could to pull them out of his hand.

"Dammit, those are not yours." She pulled as hard as possible, trying to kick him in the shin at the same time, and the papers tore. This seemed to make him angry and he looked like he was reaching for something in his pocket. It was hard to tell in the wet wind. Grabbing everything she could as quickly as possible, she took off running toward the door, not stopping to check behind her. It was propped open, so she pulled it the rest of the way with her foot and dropped everything on the floor. Jerking the door closed and listening to a lock click into place, she wiped the hair out of her face and watched out the window to see if the man had come after her.

As quiet as it was in the building, the storm raging outside was matched only by the noise in Ella's ears as her heart raced. Lightning lit up the sky one more time, and she looked intently but couldn't see anyone. She waited another moment, expecting at any second that the man would appear in the dim lights that shadowed the building. For what she was positive was an eternity, breathless and anxious, the sounds of the rain continued pounding on the roof and windows, echoing loudly through the halls of the building.

She couldn't stand here forever, and she was fairly certain the man had gone. Despite her fear, she was more angry than anything. She could not deal with people encroaching into her space. It freaked her out too much. Getting a grip on herself, she hoped, shaking water off her clothes, and smoothing her hair down, she pulled a tissue out of her bag and wiped her face off as best she could. Her black clothes were wet but wouldn't betray anything. Looking down the hall, she saw there was only one room that had a light shining out of it, so she picked up everything and walked down the hall. All the while her shoes were making squishing wet sounds on the tile. Feeling a bit absurd, she started to laugh.

There was only a small light on in the classroom. The man was standing over the desk, closing the lid on a bottle of pills. He had an intense look of pain on a face marred with concern. "Are you alright? You look upset. I am very sorry you are so wet."

"No, no," Ella said as she tried to get her mind around what had just happened. That man attacked her to get this box, and she could not even begin to guess why. "Some man just grabbed your papers. They are ripped in half. I tried to get them all back but I couldn't." The words came out fast and she hoped they made sense.

"What? A man grabbed my papers? From you? Are you okay?" He moved toward her, and she stepped back into the hall.

"I'm sorry." He stopped moving toward her. "I didn't mean for this to happen. I have no idea why someone would want all these old files. I would not think they mattered to anyone but me." Unsure what to do, they both stood there with only the sounds from outside the room paired with the ticking of an old-fashioned alarm clock on the desk.

"Thank you for getting those. I've been terrible trouble to you this evening. I really can't thank you enough for helping me. Let's get you inside my office. You're a little wet. I don't have a towel but I do have an umbrella you can take with you." The professor gingerly reached out to take the box and bags. She didn't let go of everything right away as she was sort of staring off into space. Ella really wanted to get home. *Like now.*

"Oh that's okay. If I run now I should be fine." Ella shoved the pile at him and took off running before he could say another word.

"No problem. Thank you, miss! Perhaps I'll see you again!" he yelled, but she was already down the hall, and with the thunder he doubted she heard him.

"What a strange young woman." He mumbled to himself and dragged what he could of the boxes and folders into the building. He decided to leave most of it by the door. At this late hour no one would be here except Security, and they were used to his late nights.

Carrying what the girl had shoved into his still-usable hand, he shuffled to the office in the back of the classroom. The numbness in his arm was starting to diminish, and he shifted more of his weight to the pained side.

He struggled to unlock the door to the office, though less than when he was outside, and used the folder in his hand to flick on the light. As he lifted it up he noticed a smudge on the white, type-filled sheet. Looking at it more closely, he flicked on another set of lights in the office. It looked like a smudgy fingerprint. Holding it up to the light, he saw that the marks were on the back of the paper as well. They had to be the girl's fingerprints. He had just read this paper an hour or so ago and there was nothing on it. Not normally something that would be interesting, really. People have dirty hands all the time and leave oil marks on glass, desktops, you name it. No, what was interesting about this was first, the color, and second, he was almost positive she had been wearing dark gloves. So how would her actual fingerprints have smeared onto the paper?

Chapter 4

The doctor examined the fingerprints closely in the light. He could make out some faint lines in the prints. Maybe the prints were just dye from the gloves. Nothing else made sense. Odd as it was, he had other work to do, so he put aside the paper and walked back down the hall to get the rest of his boxes. Saying hello to the night security guard, he was feeling a little better except for a sharp pain running occasionally through his arm.

As he was picking up all the papers that had drifted to the floor, one of the lighted signs caught a shimmer of a drop of water just outside the door. Stepping closer, the doctor didn't notice anything about the water that would make it shimmer. As he turned back to the papers, the shimmer caught his eye again. Thinking that maybe he had a drop of water on his glasses, he took them off and rubbed them dry on his shirt. He put them back on and winced in pain from lifting his arm too quickly. The water shimmered again. Stepping back to the door, he bent over and peered through the glass. This time he could see there was something swirling around in the water. He pushed on the door. A gust of wind blew it open, and it clanged loudly against the wall.

"Doc, are you okay down there?" the guard shouted to him.

"I'm fine. Just getting the rest of my things in," he hollered back and watched as many of his papers blew down the hall. The wind had kicked up considerably since the rain first started. He didn't remember anything about a storm in the forecast. Leaning as far over as he could in the bursts of wind and squinting his eyes, he could see colors swirling around in the water. It was probably just oil, but it seemed to be such a bizarre color in this light. Pulling a tissue out of his pocket, he dipped it into the puddle.

The tissue absorbed the water quickly and he stood back up. The wind kicked up even harder, causing the door to swing and hit him squarely in the back. There was a sickening crack and he fell on the ground, crying out in pain. The door swung open and hit the building again, shattering the glass. In the chaos he felt the tissue fall from his grasp. His head was spinning and he was seeing white spots in front of his eyes. The last thing he saw was a man in a black suit standing over him. The man in the suit raised his left hand, the wind stopped, and all that was left was a gentle rain. He bent over, picked the tissue up from the ground, and disappeared into the night.

Ella hadn't run this quickly in a while. Gasping for breath, she slammed her door shut and started to shed damp clothes, all the while dripping water on the floor. She had to dry off, change quickly, and go make sure she hadn't left any wetness throughout the building. Luckily the stairs and halls of the building were covered in dark carpet and dimly lit, so if anything dripped on them no one would be able to tell.

Throwing her clothes in a pile and pulling on others after drying off, she grabbed some black towels and ran down the hall, trying to be as quiet as possible. When she had run in, she had tried to touch as little as possible, but now she noticed smudges on the bannister and door handles. Wiping them off quickly, she went down to the bottom floor and opened the front door with the towel covering her hand. She propped the door open against her foot and leaned out. There was a smudge on the door where she had stuck the key in the lock. She dried it off and was about to go back inside when she thought she heard footsteps.

"Hi again," a male voice said. "I'm sorry," he said. "I didn't mean to startle you." It was Ryan.

"Oh, it's okay. I'm just usually the only one up this late at night." She was having a hard time looking at him. His shirt was made of reflective material with an ultramodern look to it.

"I'm guessing you want to come in and see your friend." Ella put a sarcastic emphasis on the word friend.

This time he smiled.

"Well, this is going to seem even stranger than our meetings thus far." He reached into a pocket on his silvery pants. "But I was actually bringing you back your glove. I don't even think you realize this, but you left one of them at the club last night. I happened to notice it on my way out when you were helping another customer."

"You did leave somewhat suddenly." Her voice sounded slightly hurt. She made a mental note to adjust it.

"I didn't want to tie you up all night. I know you have to work." He sounded so sincere, Ella felt like a jerk. He was just trying to be nice.

She reached out a hand and took it from him. She thought she felt something in it but didn't reach inside. Ella wanted to talk to him.

"I'd like to talk to you sometime, but I have to go right now." He paused. "And not to see my 'friend.'" The last word came out almost as a laugh. Ella felt her face getting hot, and with a little wave, he left.

Taking her glove and her embarrassment back inside, Ella walked down the hall to her door and squeezed the glove. It made a noise like there was a piece of paper inside. Puzzled as to what it could be, she went back in the apartment, locked the door behind her, and looked inside. There was a crumpled piece of paper in it.

His name was on it as well as a phone number and a note that read, "Are you a painter? You should show me."

As far as hit-on tactics it is an unusual one. She was pleased, though. He wanted her to call him. Doubting very much that she would, she realized that she had to wash the glove and all the other clothes from the night. She really didn't remember leaving the glove at the bar, but last night had been odd. *In fact, this is turning into a bizarre week completely.* Including that he asked if she was painter. *How in the world would he know that?*

Running a hand through her hair nervously, she reflected on the chaotic week she was having. Really not used to so much personal interaction with people in her private life, she wasn't sure what to make of all of it. She threw the glove across the room and folded Ryan's note into a neat square. And then she unfolded and folded it again.

"UGH! I am not as good at anything as I am about being indecisive!"

She took the note and stuck it into a wooden box sitting on her desk. She needed to work on her paintings. There was no way she was getting much sleep tonight.

Pulling out the case that she had begun working on, she set to painting the drawings on it, carefully selecting brushes and mixing paints. It was therapeutic to push out all the strange events of the last few days and carefully fill in the lines. Giving life to her pictures was the thing Ella loved most in the world. In fact, it was her world she created every time she painted. Having the picture in her mind form on the medium in front of her helped her think more clearly. It helped separate the dreams from the reality, especially when the painkillers made things so hazy sometimes.

The dead of the night was filled with the steady patter of rain on the windows and roof.

Ella worked through it, taking only one break to stretch and eat. She wandered around to the kitchen and was taking some food out of the fridge when she heard a car pulling into the lot behind the building. For no reason other than to stretch her legs a bit, she wandered over to the window and pulled back the curtain. There was a dark-colored car sitting in the lot. It looked an awful lot like the car in the school parking lot. The one belonging to the professor. It was pretty dark, but Ella thought she could see someone sitting in the front seat. She looked down for a moment more before dropping the curtain. All these car sightings she was having were starting to make her batty. She decided that it couldn't be the professor's car and started back to work. After about an hour, Ella heard the sound of an engine starting and a car pulling away. She made up her mind not to cut across the parking lot any more. In fact, from now on she would take an entirely different way home from the club.

She started to slide drawings and smaller paintings into protective covers and place them into the lovingly painted case. She was pretty happy with the way it had turned out. Holding it up and admiring it, she was reminded once again of the days back in school.

Ella had been a very good student. She graduated at the top of her class. But more than that, she was an artist and a writer. She kept most of the writing to herself, although every now and then she would incorporate some of it into a painting she was doing, sometimes writing short stories or poems for pictures or for series of pictures. Her art teachers throughout the years would encourage her to submit her work to competitions in the school and through other organizations. Every time she did, Ella won an award. In fact, every year she won "Best in Show" at her school's art fair. Most of the other students would joke about not even bothering to enter anymore, but it was often required that they produce.

As Ella grew older, the art teacher she had throughout her high school years encouraged her to use art to get a scholarship or fellowship at an art university. An accomplished artist herself, she was convinced that Ella could get into any school she wanted. The teacher wrote her a glowing recommendation letter and collected others from teachers at the school. But Ella never applied, much to her teacher's disappointment. She assumed she wouldn't be able to pay for the schooling, even with a scholarship, and she also knew that the headmistress would do what it took to humiliate her in front of any admissions board. Ella's art teacher was not afraid of the headmistress. She was the granddaughter of one of the school's founders and the woman couldn't touch her. She, like Alexandra, would remind the headmistress of her place. She would also often step in when Ella found herself at the headmistress' mercy.

Ella was never quite sure why she had earned the art teacher's affection, but she really cared for the older woman and respected her. Her classes were not only educational but completely enjoyable. The teacher helped her explore so many different genres of art, and Ella would be lost without them. She couldn't have made it through school without Miss Magritte.

All these thoughts about her old life were puzzling Ella a bit. It had been some time since she had felt nostalgic for her school life. Not that she missed it, but she did miss a couple of people.

On the opposite side of Miss Magritte was the headmistress. The intolerant, controlling woman always seemed to be hovering over Ella's shoulder. That woman's beautiful, cold, hard face never had a smile on it unless she was wooing some well-to-do businessman. Then she could sparkle and charm like no other.

The rain softly splashed against the window's glass through the night. Ella touched up old works and carefully considered each one. She took photo after photo with both a film camera and a digital camera. She loaded them onto the computer and watched the images flicker before her. There were many paintings of imaginary places and of the ocean. A dragon, a rose, a tree sitting on a cloud in a midnight-colored sky.

She really wanted to start a prehistoric painting but she didn't have time. She worked until it grew impossibly dark around the apartment. That was when she knew how close to dawn it was. She decided to stop for a bit and lie down. She could get by just fine with only a few hours of sleep.

Padding into the bedroom, she stripped off her clothes and hopped into bed. She laid back on the pillow, feeling good about all that she accomplished tonight. She hadn't worked to put together an actual project since before high school graduation. She rolled over to set an alarm for about four hours from now, and her eyes closed immediately.

She was standing behind a thick glass window. There was a terrible dust storm. The golden sand blew in terrifying, blinding swirls around the stumbling animals outside. Animals... they weren't just animals, they were dinosaurs. Even from this viewpoint, partially underground, Ella could see the immense size of them. There were hundreds, maybe even thousands, trying to make their way through the storm. The sun was covered by thick gray clouds. But they weren't ordinary clouds. They seemed to begin from the ground and reach like a choking hand up into the sky. Only every few minutes would the strength of the wind clear them away, and then Ella could make out the animals once again.

Looking away for a moment, Ella noticed she was wearing a suit of thick, dark material. It was a full body suit with small glowing boxes on either of the shoulders and on the top of her legs. There appeared to be some sort of silvery substance in them. She reached down to tap on one and it made a clicking sound like plastic. The material also brightened at her touch. She looked at it closely and curiously, but her attention was drawn away by a loud noise that was not recognizable to her ears.

Looking back up to the window, she saw some of the dinosaurs move closer to it. None of them seem to notice that she was there. Ella stepped forward, closer to the glass, and looked down to see that she was standing in some sort of wet, greenish substance. She lifted her foot out of it and it dripped back down with a sizzling sound. There was steam rising from it, and that's when Ella noticed a buzz.

It was constant, steady, and not very audible, but something about it made Ella feel she needed to find its source. It was stiflingly hot in the place where she was, and as she had that thought the suit loosened slightly. She was pretty sure it just got cooler.

She put a hand against the window so she could lean closer to look at the substance on her feet, and then something collided heavily with the structure she was standing in, knocking her into the goo. The noise was deafening and the buzz grew louder. She thought she heard her name.

She reached over and turned off the alarm. Only four hours but she felt great and excited again. She didn't have to work at the club today, just get to the appointment at the gallery. And she really needed to start that dinosaur painting tonight. She had them on the brain.

The first thing she needed to do was get her film developed. There was a one-hour photo place not more than a few blocks from her, which would do since she was crunched for time.

Sitting down at the computer again, she sorted through the images that had downloaded from the camera last night and picked ten of them to print. She threw on some clothes to walk and drop off the film. She was being careless, she knew, going out with few precautions, but she didn't care today. Grabbing her purse and running out the door, she hurried from the building and down the street.

Rounding the corner, she saw that the streets were full of people. It was a pleasant day despite being so gray. She quickly reached the photo shop and checked in the film. Deciding to get something to eat while she waited for it to be done, she went to a café not far away.

It was crowded inside. There were a lot of students weighed down with bags full of papers and books. Ella got in line behind a few of them.

"Yeah. I heard he was going to be fired," one of them said.

"No way. You can't just fire professors, they often have tenure," said another.

"I don't know. They say he stole all this money from some company," the first one said.

"I doubt it, and if it's some pharmaceutical company who cares anyway," the second one replied.

"I, for one, would hate to see him get fired, I really like Dr. Reynolds," the first student said.

"Yeah, me too," agreed the other one.

They stepped up to the counter and ordered their food, and as they were done, they looked over Ella's shoulder and in unison said, "Hi Dr. Reynolds." There was a look of embarrassment on both their faces. Ella, feeling uncomfortable, didn't turn around but stepped up to order food when she heard a mildly accented voice say, "You ran off so fast last night I never had a chance to thank you for helping me."

Ella didn't realize at first that the comment was directed at her. Then she turned around.

It was the teacher from the parking lot. She smiled. "It's not a big deal."

"It is a big deal. Not many people help strangers these days and never mind in dimly lit parking lots."

"Uh, seriously, no big deal." And she turned back around to pay for her lunch as the man reached over her shoulder and handed the attendant some money.

"My treat," he smiled kindly at Ella.

"You really don't have to do that," she stammered.

"My treat to say thank you," he insisted. He was being so friendly Ella couldn't help but smile back.

"Well, thank you," she replied and began to look around for a table.

The man ordered his food and also looked around for a table. There was only one empty.

"I'd be happy to share the table with you, miss." The professor smiled again.

Ella wasn't sure what to do. Her amazing lack of social skills bugged her. She had to keep her guard up, but for some reason she heard herself say, "Sure."

They went to the table and sat down. There was a minute or two of awkward silence with Ella looking around nervously, brushing hair out of her face over and over again.

"So," said the doctor, "do you attend the university?" He could see she was nervous, but he really didn't understand why. She was quite fidgety.

"Uh... no, I don't." She tugged at the fingertips of one of her gloves.

"I just realized I don't know your name," he chuckled. She seemed to grow more uncomfortable when he pointed that out. "My name is James Reynolds. Dr. Reynolds, if you like." He said it hoping to make her relax a bit. She was a curious girl.

"Um... my name is Ella," just as a server brought their food to the table and set things down in from of them. Ella immediately began fussing with the food and arranging things on the plate.

"Ella, I am pleased to meet you." He held his hand out across the table. She slowly lifted one gloved hand and shook it.

"Gloves? Neat. Very old-fashioned. My mum used to wear gloves all the time," he held her hand a minute and examined it closely. Ella tugged her hand away.

"Oh, I am sorry. I didn't mean to seem kooky. I was just wondering, when you helped me the other night, were those the gloves you were wearing?"

Ella looked at him warily. "I guess. I don't know. I always wear gloves."

"Oh, yes. Are you a painter?" He looked at her through his glasses, waiting for an answer.

Great. Why does everyone suddenly want to know? I am being too careless lately.

"Yeah, you could say that. Look, Dr. Reynolds, I appreciate the food and conversation, but you know, I have to go. My film is probably done and I have a deadline." She grabbed her purse and started to get up.

"Oh, well, maybe I'll see you some time, Ella." He stood up but she left without saying goodbye. What a strange girl, he thought. Though not as strange as the fingerprints. They were not just smudged. He could make out the patterns on the tips clearly in the light. He sat back down and began to wonder how he could find her again. Someone had told him to check that apartment building, but it felt so presumptuous just to show up where someone lived without having been invited. Old men stalking young girls was generally frowned upon.

Ella hurried back to the photo place. When she arrived, the clerk said she hadn't been gone long enough. Waiting and twisting her fingers over and over, she didn't know why she was still going to take the portfolio to the studio. There were going to be more people asking more questions. *How am I going to handle it?*

Waiting the final ten minutes for the film was agonizing and served as a good reminder as to why everyone used digital. She talked herself in and out of going to the gallery a hundred times by the time it was done.

Throwing her gloves across the living room in frustration, she strongly considered not leaving home ever again.

"I am going to do this," she said aloud to the room and set back to work.

A couple hours before she was due to meet the gallery owner, she made final decisions about what to take and put everything by the front door.

She got ready to go slowly, and periodically stopped to breathe in deeply to calm her jangled nerves. When everything was ready and she was dressed, she gathered up all her things and made a vow not to look for any cars. Not to be a paranoid weirdo. *Well not to be paranoid anyway.* She got in the car and went to the gallery without a second thought about all the possibly creepy things that had been happening. The music was up very loud just in case.

The gallery owner smiled when she walked in. She had decided to wear a shorter black dress with fluttery sleeves, silver tights, and knee-high black boots. The tights were risky if she started to sweat, but she figured since it was so temperate out she'd probably be okay.

Feeling beyond nervous, she kept fiddling with her hair. *I really need to break this habit.*

"Ella! It's nice to meet you. I see you brought a lot of your work. You know, just in case, for future reference I can come to your studio." He was well-dressed and self-assured. It intimidated Ella but she drew in a deep breath and resolved not to show it. Yep, he is cute. That thought did not help. She wanted to sigh dramatically and leave herself at home. *Why am I so boy crazy lately?*

"Hi, Evan, it's nice to meet you," holding out her hand, which he shook. "I am happy to bring my work here. I thought I could meet with you, and depending on how it goes between us I was going to look around the studio for placement ideas."

Evan took the portfolio from her outstretched hand. He brushed her arm slightly with his finger.

"Well, Ella," he was flipping through the pages, "I have to admit I am impressed with your work, I am going to be honest here when I say I see a lot of 'interesting' art. I can't help but admire your sheer amount of work and the cohesive theme of color usage." He put the portfolio down on the desk and ran his fingers over the symbols she had painted on the cover.

"Do these stand for something?" he asked her.

"I guess. I don't know yet. There are a few on there that I used to draw as a kid, and I know I've seen them somewhere before," she finished vaguely. She knew exactly where she had seen one, but he didn't need to know that.

"They are cool," Evan said and looked up with a flirtatious smile.

Crap. If there was one thing she was absolutely, positively terrible at it was flirting. With all the years working in the club one might think she would be very good at it. Really she mostly awkwardly drove people away. Pretending not to notice he was being flirty, she kept on talking.

"I brought some of my actual paintings. They are in my car if you'd like to see them."

"Sure," he said and got up as if to come help her.

"No, that's okay, Evan, yeah, Evan, um, I can get them," she fumbled around with the keys and went back outside.

She went and unlocked the car, somehow managing to not roll her eyes at herself, and pulled each painting out one by one, carefully leaning them against the car.

When she finished taking them out, she locked her car and saw the dark-colored car. This time she was sure it was the same one. The man who had walked into her at the store was sitting in the front seat. *No, not now. Paranoia is going to wait until later.*

She picked up the paintings as fast as she could and went back into The Soap Factory. She leaned them against the wall in the office while she waited for Evan to finish a phone call.

"Nope, it's going well. Yes, the show should go as planned. Yes, right. I'll let you know. I have to go. I have 'someone' in my office." He flashed his perfect smile at Ella again. He got out of his chair and came over to her. She tried picking one up to give it to him and it slipped out of her hand. They both bent over at the same time to pick it up and nearly hit heads.

"Oh, I am so sorry," she started apologetically.

Evan laughed. "It's okay. Relax, Ella." They both stood upright and he handed the painting to Ella. "I'm not opposed to chick-flick moments. We can pretend sexy soccer mom music is playing in the background." In spite of herself, Ella laughed at his joke, then thought better of it and stopped.

He put a hand on her shoulder. "I like them."

He sounded sincere, not flirtatious. Ella stood stiffly still, hyper-aware of his hand on her shoulder. She was not sure that she cared for it. It seemed sort of arrogant.

"Relax," he said again. "I'm giving you a show." Dropping his hand, Evan went to sit at the desk.

"You're giving me a show?" Her voice stammered a bit.

"Yes. Your paintings are complex and unusual. Which is what I meant when I said interesting. I actually meant they were interesting. A lot of stuff is not interesting, believe me when I tell you. But you know, I run a gallery. I have to be open to exhibits, even if they abuse the definition of art." He smiled that perfect smile again, like a Cheshire cat. "I am sure you will draw a lot of people. So the next step is picking a date and planning an opening party."

"Party?" Ella hadn't thought of that.

"Of course," he said. "Getting attention is how you and I will make money. Sadly that is the reality of being an artist, and it's something I'd say we need to do."

This time Ella laughed. "Yes, I need to make money. It just never really occurred to me it could be from art."

"That is a cute thing to say. If only all painters were as adorable as you. Now, Ella, do you have any special requests for the party?"

"Special requests?" She didn't know what he meant. "I'm not sure I understand?"

"For the party," he said. "Details. Haven't you ever had a party before?"

"No, actually, I haven't," she said quietly. For some reason it made her feel kind of bad.

"Oh, sure, don't worry about it," though his tone suggested she should worry about it. "This is gonna be great! No worries, Ella. I can take care of all of the details. I'll tell you what, why don't we make a plan for me to come over sometime this week and look at more of your work? We can pick out pieces for the show."

Ella wasn't sure what to say next. She didn't want him coming over. She knew that much.

"There are pictures of a significant amount of my work in my portfolio," Ella said carefully.

"Sure, and that's great, but I need to plan for sizes, placement, labels. Don't worry, it's painless," he joked.

"Oh, no. I know. I just have to work a lot. I don't have much free time," Ella rambled on.

"Ella, it's cool. You're protective of your creative space. No big deal." He put a comforting hand on her arm and she couldn't help but look into his eyes. He was really good-looking and he *seemed* like he was being nice. She just did not *feel* like he was being nice. She maneuvered herself away from his reach.

"Cool gloves, by the way, and I like your boots."

"Thanks," she said, trying to match his nonchalant tone.

"Why don't you just bring me a bunch of stuff tomorrow and I'll go through it."

She let out a sigh of relief, which made Evan snicker.

"No worries, doll. This is the start of a beautiful friendship."

He was pushing her to the door.

"Should I take my portfolio and paintings?"

Evan quickly glanced over his shoulder at his desk.

"Actually," he said in a tone Ella could not discern, "let me hold on to them and use them to get some ideas. Then the paintings can go right into the show. You should decide what is just for showing, and what is for sale and for how much."

Ella stopped, forcing Evan to bump into her. She turned and they were only inches apart.

"Evan, thank you so much. I really can't begin to tell you what this means to me."

In her excitement she hugged him awkwardly. When she tried to pull away, he held on to her for a moment.

"Oh. I'm so excited!" She smiled brightly at him.

"Good. Great!" For the first time since she got there he seemed a little unsure of himself. He ran a hand through his dark, wavy hair.

"This is so great! Bye!" She hugged him again and left the gallery.

He stood in the office looking at his hand. Where he had briefly returned Ella's excited hug, a warm substance had come off her dress. Must be paint or hair dye, he thought.

As he turned to walk into the bathroom to wash his hands he felt a slight tingling sensation. He looked at his hand again just in time to see the last of the substance absorb into his skin. "Weird."

Crossing back to the desk, he picked up the phone and dialed a number.

"Yes, she came in. She is, well... pretty great. A real talent. She is beautiful, if a little twitchy." For a moment he said nothing, just listened.

"Yes, Sir, unusual? No. Not really. She's never had a party," he laughed sarcastically. "Okay, Sir. Yes, we are setting up a show for two weeks from now. Sooner? Um, yeah. I'll try." Silence again.

"No, she wouldn't invite me over."

"Yes, Sir. It'll be done," Evan hung up the phone, picked up Ella's portfolio, and left.

Ella was on cloud nine, or ten for that matter, when she left the gallery. It really wasn't so bad. She thought she'd have to spend more time trying to sell her work to him. But now she had a show and a party!

The idea of a party made her anxious. An art opening meant lots of strangers and questions about herself.

Well it is done now, she thought. She wasn't going back out. She never backed out of anything no matter how scared she was.

Geez, lighten up! This is a good thing.

In her excitement over the day she forgot completely about the man in the car.

Chapter 5

Ella practically skipped home. *I have a show! A real art show! He thought my paintings were great.* She ran up the steps to the apartment and flung open the door. Looking around, she tried to see her art from a new perspective. *What did he see when he looked at it?* Ella saw places from dreams, unfulfilled wishes, worlds that didn't exist and generally just things she loved. She was feeling brave.

She went over to the desk, took out the note she had stuffed in a box, and spread it on the surface.

The numbers looked at her. She ran a finger over them and they told her to call. Staring at them for a minute longer while trying to decide what to do, her mind wandered to the party. *Who would be invited?* She didn't have anyone to invite. She ran her finger over his number again. Walking over to the phone, she picked it up and dialed.

It rang only once before he picked it up. "Hello," came the sleepy voice.

Ella swallowed. "Hi, um... Ryan, this is Ella."

"Ella! I am so happy you called," his voice perked up. "I wasn't sure you would, since all of our encounters have been rather odd."

"Yes, well my life lately has been kind of odd," she giggled. *No. No giggling.* "I have to say I am not entirely sure this is a good idea, but I was feeling brave today."

"I am so glad. Hey, listen. How brave are you feeling? I'd love to meet you for a coffee or something?"

She hadn't considered that he might want to see her, and she didn't respond for a long time.

"Hey, it's okay if it's too weird," Ryan said congenially. "If I were a girl, I'd be weirded out by me, too." He chuckled. "I can come down to the club again. We can talk a little more, and then you can decide if you want to be seen in public with the likes of me."

That made Ella laugh and put her at ease. "No, coffee sounds great," she bit her bottom lip. "Um, maybe sometime in the early evening tonight. I do have some things to do today."

"That sounds great." He sounded genuinely pleased. "There's this great place near where you are. We could meet there." They agreed on a time, and Ella hung up the phone.

Oh, wow! I just made a date. Now she had to decide what to wear. She looked down and decided everything she had on was wrong.

She spent the next hour tearing through the closet. She was freaking out and it was starting to show. She was sweating intensely. Taking a moment to sit down and try to put some of that yoga "training" to work, she closed her eyes and took a deep breath.

In her head she could hear footsteps. Heavy, clacking footsteps. They were precise, determined, searching. They fell on the carpet in the hallway, as if supporting the immensity of something. The weight of it leaned on Ella's mind. She opened her eyes, her pulse racing. Maybe she should call Ryan back and not go out with him. She felt completely off her rocker.

That's when she remembered the man in the car. *Had he been outside the gallery?* In the excitement of the day she had forgotten about him. *Had he followed me home? There are too many coincidences. He is following me. But why? Why would anyone be following me?*

Ryan, the teacher, this man. She had to be careful. Something strange seemed to be happening. *The man must be from the incident at the club the other night. He is angry about getting thrown out and now he is trying to scare me!*

That has to be it. You're just used to your boring old life where nothing ever really happens.

Looking at the mess she had made in the room, she started to pick it up slowly, contemplating each piece as she folded or hung it back up.

Boys had asked Ella for her number before. They had asked if they could see her after she got off. She always said no. She wasn't exactly sure why this was different to her. There was something about Ryan she couldn't put a finger on. Since it was to be the week of new things and weird things, why not a date too?

After she put the clothes away and finally decided on an outfit–dark purple tights, black skirt with silver ribbons running through it, black mock turtle neck, knee-high boots, and a strand of sparkly antique beads–she began to pace the length of the living room. She picked up paint brushes, pillows, books, and vases and rearranged them, all the while wiping dust carefully from them and gently placing them where they would sit. She adjusted lamps, straightened pictures, wiped down mirrors, arranged the flowers she had picked some nights ago in a vase, put away dishes she had washed. She cleaned the apartment carefully, deliberately, and tried to ignore the fact that she was going on the first date of her life.

She went in the bathroom, applied a careful bit of glitter to her eyelids, and brushed out her hair. She smoothed out the skirt and folded the towels carefully on the hanging bar.

Then it was time to go.

Ella looked at her outfit in the mirror one more time and sighed. She wished she would consider that this might be fun. Pulling on a pair of long black gloves made of satin, she left to meet Ryan.

She made it to the coffee shop before he did. It was a cool place. Built into an old victorian house with thick green rugs thrown over hardwood floors. There were lots of nooks and alcoves you could sit in to avoid being bothered. The lights were dimmed and there were candles everywhere.

Deciding to order before he arrived, she went up to the counter where a girl of about eighteen was waiting behind the large etched-glass counter. There was an antique espresso machine behind her.

"Hi. Can I help you?" The girl stopped folding napkins and set them aside.

"Yes, thanks, um... I'd like a medium soy mocha," Ella replied.

"Sure. For here or to go?" The girl moved to the register and punched in a few numbers.

"For here. I'm meeting someone." Ella reached over the counter and handed the girl some money. She had a nose ring and a tattoo of a rose across her chest. It made Ella think of the mark on her own chest. She unconsciously reached a hand up and touched it to the spot where the mark was.

"Okay." The girl moved to the espresso machine and put the coffee shot glasses underneath the spouts after filling them with the grounds.

"I wasn't sure you'd actually come," said a male voice jokingly behind Ella.

She turned around slowly and couldn't keep from smiling at his comment.

"I'm not going to lie. I did consider not coming on the off chance you might be, oh, I don't know... a serial killer?" she joked back.

"It's a good thing I suggested a public place," he smirked. "Witnesses and all for you."

Ella laughed as the rose tattoo girl handed her the coffee.

"Could I get a green tea please?" Ryan reached in a pocket and pulled out money that he set on the counter. His skin was very fair, Ella noticed. He was wearing an unreal outfit. It was stylish. Sleek black pants that had a silver sheen to them and dark blue, long sleeve fitted top with some sort of design on it that she didn't recognize.

"What is the design on your shirt?" she asked him sipping the coffee. She wasn't nervous anymore.

"It's a fractal," he told her. "I bought it in an awesome artist's space in the Camden Lock. The guy was really talented."

"The Camden Lock? That's in England?" Ella had always wanted to go there.

"Yes, it's in England. It's a really cool place. I hope I get to go back." His voice suddenly sounded a bit melancholy.

"I've never been." She tried to keep her voice cheerful. "I'd love to go, though. I have not done enough traveling in my life, for sure."

"Yes, traveling is great," he said as he reached for the tea. He smiled brightly at her. "Who knows, Ella? Maybe we'll travel together."

When he saw the surprised look on her face he said, "I'm an optimist." He laughed and she couldn't help but join him.

"Shall we sit?"

He led the way to one of the further corners of the coffee house. Large velvet pillows sat on the wooden benches. Each table had several candles on it and a vase with a single flower.

They settled on opposite sides, and for a moment they were quiet. Ryan stirred the tea slowly and stared at Ella. He seemed very interested in her. She wasn't sure if she had anything interesting to say.

She flipped a hand over her hair. *I am so fidgety. Again.* She sighed and sipped her coffee.

Ryan looked at her, puzzled.

"I am sorry these last two days have been rather odd and I've been doing things I wouldn't normally do," she said.

"Please explain." He lifted the large white tea cup to his lips and took a sip.

"Hmm... Well I guess first could be calling you and being here right now," she laughed. "But so far, so good." She felt great, relaxed, maybe even a smidgen confident. Although she also felt slightly dizzy.

Ryan seemed completely relaxed. He was watching her intently, waiting for her to keep talking. *Like he actually cares what I have to say. Why?* She couldn't help but wonder. The thought made her falter for a minute. *I need to work on my crap attitude.*

"Is there anything else?" He looked puzzled. "Because calling me can't be all that exciting," he smiled with a perfect smile. "I can't imagine that, as pretty as you are, you don't go out on a lot of dates." He calmly took another sip of tea. He said it just like that. Matter-of-fact.

She decided to pretend he didn't say that. Instead she concentrated on taking a sip of coffee and looking around the room.

"Well," she continued, without looking at him yet, "I took some of my artwork to a gallery called The Soap Factory to try and get a show." She placed the cup carefully back on the table and looked at him. "It went really well. The owner was very... helpful, and gave me an offer for a show. So I'm excited about that, if a little perplexed, since I've never done one before."

"That is very cool! So you *are* a painter. I thought that you might be because of the paint on your glove." *He is too nice,* she decided. Ryan actually seemed interested to hear she was an artist.

Her head hurt a bit. *Maybe I am drinking too much caffeine?* She decided to stop and get some water.

"Yes. So I got a show at the gallery. The gallery owner seemed to really like my work, which was a great feeling. I haven't shown anyone my work for a long time." *Why am I giving out so much personal information?* She never talked to people, never mind telling them so much about herself. *Today is a day of many firsts.* Ella smiled broadly.

"Yes, so I got a show. And I get to have an opening party and I am pretty thrilled about it." She finished in a rush. "I am going to go get some water. I'll be right back."

"Okay, Ella. I'll be here, waiting with bated breath to hear about your show." He said it dramatically and made her giggle. That made her feel silly, but she decided not to care.

She got up and walked back to the counter. It was a busy place filled with couples and friends. The soft lighting of the evening in combination with the candles really did make it a rather romantic place to be. Ella poured a glass of water from the pitcher sitting on the counter and turned to walk back the table. The man in the suit from the car was walking in the front door. She turned around quickly and went back to the counter, putting her back to him. *There is no way I'm imagining that he is following me.* People were shuffling around her, and she was trying to watch him without giving herself away. The man walked toward the other end of the back room opposite where she was standing. She wanted to get back to the table as quickly as possible. *This is so insane. What could he possibly want from me?*

She made it back to the table swiftly, only to find Ryan not sitting at it anymore. *Maybe he went to the bathroom.* She didn't know where it was, so trying to spot the man in the suit and find the bathroom at the same time, Ella tripped on the corner of a carpet. She stumbled, but as luck would have it, somehow managed to catch herself on a table. Ryan came out of a door and saw her leaning on the table. He strode over to her and put his hand on her back. It was hot. She felt very warm. Ella felt her knees lock and everything lightened around her.

The buzzing in her ears was almost unbearable. *What was the sound?* The heat continued to rise as Ella walked further into the cave. She couldn't tell what it was. There were high, heavy, metal pieces standing out and boring into the ground. There seemed to be broken glass, yet it was hard to tell where it had fallen because of all the green liquid flowing through the floor. Some of it was seeping into the walls.

"Ella?" a voice sounded from faraway. *Where am I?*

"Ella? Are you okay?" Ella blinked her eyes and saw Ryan above her, as well as many other curious faces. He seemed to be lit up. She blinked again. It was the light behind his head. Rubbing her eyes, she realized she was lying on the floor. She moved to sit up quickly and became woozy, which caused her to slip back into Ryan's arms.

"Wow, be careful, Ella," he said, concern marring his voice. He looked up. "Could everyone back up a little so she can sit up, and could someone grab a glass of water?"

"I'm so warm," Ella said and sat back up slowly. "Don't you do trust exercises on all your first dates?" she joked in a dry, cracked voice. It felt like she had swallowed broken glass.

People started to wander away, and someone handed Ella a cold glass of water that she sipped slowly. It felt good in her hands. She looked around at the faces and people meandering about to see if she could spot the man in the suit, but she didn't see him anywhere.

"Do you think you can get up?" He put his hand out to her. She nodded and he pulled her up slowly.

"Wow, I'm really sorry to be so much trouble." Her face was blisteringly warm, and she held the glass up to her cheeks.

"You're no trouble at all," he said sweetly. "I'm just worried that you're okay."

"I've just had a lot of excitement today. Much, much more than normal." She tried to laugh but ended up coughing. *Great. I'm a helpless basket case, first impressions are awesome.* She tried not to choke on the water.

"Maybe we could go for a walk," she continued. "Fresh air could do me some good. Unless you've had enough excitement for the evening." *Maybe he didn't want to be around some lame girl who fainted and had hairy-chested men give her a hard time.*

"Of course! I wanted to hear more about your art." He let her hand down gently and smiled at her. "Are you sure *you're* up for walking around?"

"Oh, I'm fine," replied Ella. "I just got too warm, and you know I actually just tripped on the carpet so I'm not so much unhealthy, just kind of clumsy." She tried to sound cool and sarcastic. The words did actually come a bit better this time. Not so much a cough but almost a snort. *Fabulous, this is going wonderfully.* But a voice in her head said, *he still wants to spend time with you so all's not lost just yet.* She'd have to make up for this disastrous start to her first date with some dazzling conversation. She almost snickered aloud at the thought but was afraid this time she would actually snort. She bit her lip and set down the glass.

"Let's go have a walk, then." She looked around one last time for the man in the suit, but there was still no sign of him. *Is there any chance I was just imagining him?* she wondered for the hundredth time.

Ryan held the heavy, leaded-glass door of the coffee shop open for Ella as she stepped through.

The sky had grown cloudy. *Definitely a cause for concern.* Ella had not read anywhere that it was going to rain. *Perhaps it isn't and it is just cloudy.* She really didn't want anything else strange happening tonight.

They walked along in silence for a few minutes. Ella was unsure how to restart the conversation. She didn't want to monopolize the whole evening, and everything had very much been all about her at this point.

"So, Ryan, where do you live?"

"Not too far from you, actually," he said. "I have a loft."

"Oh, cool. Where do you work?" She fiddled with the tip of a glove for a moment, then forced herself to drop her hands to her sides.

"I actually don't have a job right now. I am spending time working on personal projects." He was looking off into the distance. "What else would you like to know?" he asked with a teasing tone and a bit of an edge she couldn't help but catch.

"Oh, I'm sorry. I just... I've just been talking about myself this whole time, and I thought it'd be nice for me to get to know you a little bit." Ella thought she could faintly smell rain. There was light breeze kicking up around them. It was subtle but it felt like another storm was coming.

"No, it's fine. Of course I want you to get to know me, if you'd like to." He smiled brilliantly. Very brilliantly, even. "That is kind of the point of dates, isn't it?"

"Dates? Yep, dates." She was back to being slightly embarrassed. *It's truly impossible for me not to be an idiot.*

"Though this isn't a great date," he kept going, not noticing her embarrassment. "I really didn't think this out very well. I guess I didn't want to intimidate you. All of this already got off to a freaky start. And really, I didn't think you'd call me. I figured you'd just think I was a creep from the bar." That statement made her feel, well, somewhat defensive, and she wasn't sure how to respond. Though she did want to respond sarcastically.

He stopped walking and turned to face her.

"We should try again," he said emphatically.

"Try again?" Ella stopped walking and looked at him. *Okay, maybe hold it on the sarcasm.* The night was enveloping more of the remaining daylight, and he seemed to stand out brilliantly against the dark. His blonde, golden hair gleamed.

"Let's walk you back to your place and start over. We'll go to dinner and then we'll take a walk. What do you say? Oh, but first I have to go do something. It's not weird. I promise."

"I don't know. You really don't have to do this, plus if you have things to do..."

"You know, Ella, I really like the silver in your hair."

"Fine. You don't have to overdo it." She grinned. "I'll go back to my place and you can come and meet me there. And also you can explain to me how you knew where I lived in the first place."

"I got lucky," he said. "That girl–that really annoying drunk friend of my cousin–asked me to walk her home. She told me which apartment was yours."

"Friend of your cousin?"

"Yes," he looked at her suspiciously. "Did you think I actually was out with her?"

"It might've occurred to me."

"I have better taste than that... obviously." He held out his hand out to her.

"Obviously." This time she did roll her eyes but took his hand, and they walked back to her apartment so they could start their date again.

Overhead, thunder clapped loudly and lightning blazed across the sky.

Ryan left Ella at her apartment. She wasn't sure what to think at this point, but she went inside as he reassured her he would be back in no time.

Yet another unexpected storm that seemed to be moving in worried her. She wasn't sure now what the plans were going to be, and considering the dismaying aspects of the evening she thought that maybe she should tell him to forget it. Despite it growing darker, if she were caught in the rain many more things than she currently cared to share could be revealed. She just didn't want to risk it yet.

But really, she didn't want to think about it either. She couldn't help but like Ryan. He had been kind and patient. He also hadn't been freaked by the odd things that had happened so far this evening.

Unless, she thought begrudgingly, *he dropped me off here to ditch out on me.* Suppressing that thought as fast as she could, Ella began to pace the apartment.

Why was that man following me? It was racing in a circle in her head over and over again. *Who was he? What did he want? This was just too many times for it to be a coincidence.*

She thought back to her shopping that day. It still seemed so hazy. But she was certain it was the same man. The pain meds messing with her head were making it hard to remember. Even with yoga and meditation the pain could occasionally become unbearable, and the cost of relief was high.

The mixed-up memories aside, she had to decide what she wanted to do with Ryan. He wanted her to pick somewhere to go have dinner. She didn't go out to eat often, so she didn't know many of the places that were around.

Lightning struck outside, and thunder rolled loudly over the city. Ella sighed. *This night is getting worrisome. Are dates always so complicated?*

She pulled off her gloves and went into the bathroom. *Do I look silly with glitter? Is the outfit wrong? The gloves strange?* Looking at them as skeptically as possible, she decided they were not weird. The world was full of green hair, facial piercing, and tattoos covering chests. Gloves were not strange. Nothing was weird anymore, and, well... that pleased her. *At least nothing on the outside.*

Walking out of the bathroom, she heard the buzzer go off. Heart quickening, she hurried to the front door, forgetting to put the gloves back on. She had to go get them and make him wait. Almost running back to the bathroom, she grabbed them off the sink and was trying to pull them on as she opened the front door and stepped out. Ryan was there as she was pulling them on.

"Oh," Ella said, surprised. "You got in."

"Yes." Ryan smiled as he handed her a bouquet of flowers, unusual purple-colored roses. "One of your neighbors was outside and he let me in. I hope that's okay?"

"Of course, um, these are so beautiful. Thank you. No one has ever given me flowers before." She inhaled their scent deeply.

"I find it hard to believe no one has ever given you flowers before, and really, I should have just brought them in the first place." He bowed low in front of her. "Please forgive me, My Lady. It was a mistake on my part. A proper date requires proper behavior."

Ella giggled. He stood back up and winked at her.

"I can wait while you put them in water," Ryan said.

"What?" Ella looked at him questioningly.

"The flowers," he pointed at them. "Water?"

"Right! Um... duh..." She didn't know what to do. *Do I have to invite him in?* She wasn't ready for that. *What are the socially acceptable answers in this situation?*

"Yea, I'll uh... be right back. You don't mind waiting a minute, do you?" she fumbled for the doorknob.

"Of course not," Ryan smiled slyly. "It's only the start of the date. Maybe you'll want to invite me in later."

Ella arched an eyebrow at him. She was quickly starting to remember why she didn't date.

Backing up against the doorknob and not taking her eyes off Ryan, who gave her a questioning look, she turned the handle and went in slowly. She opened it a tiny little bit so she could barely fit in. Once she clumsily got through the crack, she managed to trip on the small black rug in front of the door and nearly fell. Some of the petals of the roses drifted to the floor. Her foot landed with a heavy thud, and Ryan knocked on the door. Groaning internally at her continued self-sabotage, she checked the flowers to see if she'd broken any of the stems.

"Ella, are you okay?" he called through the door, his hand turning the door-knob. She grabbed it and leaned on the door heavily, not letting him open it more than an inch. Her eyes met his through the crack.

"I'm fine, just my usual gracefulness. Let me get these in water and then we can go." As she finished, there was a loud thunder roll that seemed to shake the building, and the lightning streaked across the sky, illuminating the room. The storm was starting to move closer.

"When you're ready, we might want to hurry. The rain is coming fast. My car isn't too close to here, unfortunately." He moved away from the door and Ella shut it.

She couldn't go out in the rain, and the storm was imminent. A decision had to be made.

Then a clap of thunder struck again and the decision was made for her. She looked around to sum it all up. The apartment was spotless, there was a movie to watch that had come in the mail, and she did actually have some food, or they could order a pizza. *I think normal people still do that.*

Now to just get up the nerve to invite him in. The lightning became more insistent and was now lasting longer than just a few seconds. The thunder that followed grew louder and louder. The rain struck the window with large drops that rattled the glass.

Besides herself, no one had been in this apartment in a very long time. She took her boots off, placed the roses on the table, and for the third time that day decided to do something she had never done before.

The rain was steady and it sounded as though it was windy outside now.

Ella slowly opened the door and Ryan smiled.

"The rain has gotten the better of us," he said and noticed her boots were off. "Um, I think you might be missing something," and pointed to her feet.

"I was thinking," she started cautiously, "the weather is really terrible and it's starting to get past decent dinnertime. This might seem not as exciting as it could be, but do you want to hang out here? I mean I am guessing you're not a serial killer so... I have a movie, some food, or we can play a game, get a pizza?" *The last part sounded dumb.*

"Are you sure? Because you seemed a little nervous about me coming? Which is not a big deal. I understand, you're kind of shy. I can go get an umbrella?"

He is so nice. She really wanted to spend time with him, but she couldn't risk the rain.

"Yes, I am sure. As long as you don't mind wasting the evening." Waiting for his answer she played with her hair. Then forced herself to stop. *Bad habit, bad habit, so knock it off.*

"This evening is not a waste, and this is a great way to be able to talk. So let's hang out here."

Ella stood, staring at him for moment. He waited without saying anything and looked directly at her. She opened the door all the way, and Ryan stepped inside.

"This is your place?" his voice sounding amazed. "It is absolutely stunning." He didn't move from in front of the door. Taking it all in, he stood there carefully looking around the room. Ella walked around the living area and turned on the carefully placed lamps. She didn't say anything to him. She was very interested in watching his reaction.

She quietly walked over to him and moved to take his jacket. He took it off wordlessly and then, tearing his eyes away from the room, bent over to unlace his boots. When he pulled them off, Ella noticed he had unusual socks on but didn't say anything about them.

"I have never seen anything like this before," he walked into the room across from where Ella was hanging his coat. "You are full of surprises, aren't you?"

The living room was large. There was one full wall with no windows. That is where the biggest mural was painted. It was an ocean. It was the entire length and height of the wall. The background was a lighter blue with waves at the surface crested with silvery coloring. The sky above the ocean was gray-blue and filled with clouds, like a storm was rolling in over the water. There was a silvery ship on the horizon, carefully detailed with a mermaid on the front bow, and with seagulls flocking around the sails. The focal point of the mural was a large humpback whale. The whale was surrounded by fish and plants. Each individual creature was intricately lifelike and yet had a surreal feeling of the fantastic.

The tail of the whale was full and majestic. The look of its solemn head gave an impression of wisdom and history. Two glistening, blue dolphins swam at its side. Their expressions gave the idea of a younger playfulness. There was plant life covering the entire bottom of the wall. Long, sinuous leaves that gave the appearance of swaying slightly in a current. Hundreds of different kinds of fish swam around in every open spot.

The occasional lightning streaks lit up the room and gave an unusual look to the wall every few minutes. Ryan studied it with attention and was lost in thought for some time. Ella didn't bother him. She watched him out of the corner of her eye as she attended to the roses, carefully cutting them, matching heights, and putting them in a vase with water.

Ryan finished looking at the ocean and turned to the other main wall. It had two large windows that were covered with dark purple curtains. Between them Ella had painted a field of surrealistic flowers. While he studied the flowers, Ella took things out of the fridge and and set a table with various fruits, bread, and cheeses. The lights flickered in the storm, which hadn't lost any of its intensity. Ella took tall crystal glasses out of the cabinet and filled them with a sparkling raspberry juice. After folding midnight-blue napkins carefully on the table and arranging silverware, she ran out of things to do.

"What do you think?" No longer able to contain the question, it slipped out. Her voice sounded shrill and cracked. She felt stupid for asking. Maybe he thought she was crazy. *Well, you are.*

"What do I think?" Ryan stood upright and lightning lit up his face.

He always seems to be brighter than the room he is in. The lights flickered in the apartment a second time as Ella waited for his answer.

"How could I think anything but that this is amazing? You are so talented. Your place is so beautiful, just like you. Is the whole apartment painted? Not that I expect you to show me." As he said the words, he stepped further into the dining area where Ella stood, and noticed that those walls were also painted. Ella, not able to bear watching, went to a drawer and pulled out matches to light candles, hoping the supposedly calming aromatherapy would actually help. She inhaled deeply and nearly singed her hair. *So much for that.*

Ryan continued to wander the dining room and examine the paintings closely. He walked back to the living room and looked again at the whale, wandering around the room as if in a trance.

There was a strike of thunder that shook Ella a bit.

"That was a little unnerving," she said and picked up a glass.

"What?" Ryan didn't look up from the tail of the dragon that circled the dining room wall.

Ella laughed, "The thunder startled me." It struck again. The storm seemed to be here for the length of the evening.

He turned to look at her. "I didn't even notice." He looked down at the table. "Or that you set such a lovely table."

"I thought since we weren't going to dinner that maybe you would be hungry and want something to eat." She set the glass down and picked up the second to offer him.

Accepting it, he pulled a chair out for her.

"You are very chivalrous," she joked. "I noticed when I was lying on the floor."

"I feel as though your unique talent and unusual taste, even sophistication," he pointed to the crystal glass on the table, "requires it."

"Don't be too impressed. I bought those at a garage sale." Ella reached for a plate as Ryan walked to the other side of the table to sit down.

"Recycling is sexy." He laughed as a particularly harsh torrent of rain hit the windows.

"Wow, the storm is really something." Ryan picked up a plate. "I wonder if the power will go out." As he said it the lights flickered again.

"No worries," Ella said as she filled a plate with strawberries and cheese. "I have lots of candles. I love them, in fact. I frequently paint by candlelight. I like the way it makes shadows on the canvas. Sometimes I can see pictures I hadn't thought of," she paused. "I guess I sound kind of nuts." She stopped and put the plate in front of her. Ryan was looking at her with that intense interest again. She shifted in her seat, wondering if there was any graceful way to eat with your hands. She'd only set out finger foods. *Because I eat like a kid.*

"No, you don't sound crazy at all. Well, not crazy in a bad way," he took a sip from his glass. He held it up to the candlelight and stared into the liquid for a moment. "I love bubbles," he finished. Ella looked at him questioningly.

"Sorry. Random thought." With that, the lights went dark and the fridge stuttered to a stop. The power going out didn't make too much difference in the room since the candles were lit, but the only sound now was the ticking of an antique clock on the bookshelf and the storm that was getting overwhelmingly windy.

"The storm is unexpected. I haven't really heard about any serious weather moving in," Ella chewed a strawberry thoughtfully.

"Who knows? Weather is very unpredictable these days," Ryan said. "Especially with global warming taking its toll."

"Yeah, I try to only use my car when I absolutely have to," said Ella.

"Cool, yeah, I bought a hybrid. It's great but not a complete solution." Ryan took some more cheese. "These cheeses are great. What are they? I think this is gouda. My mom loved gouda." His voice sounded sad again. Ella wanted to ask him why but decided it was to soon.

"Yeah it is, um... organic and all that," Ella ate a piece. More thunder rattled the windows. Even harder this time. She stopped eating and stood up. Ella walked over to a window and pulled back the curtain. It was a mess outside. It was almost impossible to see out of the glass, with the constant stream of large water drops hitting it. She could make out branches on the ground and leaves covering cars. The sky lit up momentarily, and that's when she thought she saw the man in the suit. *How can that be?* She leaned her forehead as close to the glass as possible. It was cool on her skin. *Is he out there?* She couldn't see anything.

"What are you trying to see?" Ryan came up behind. He was very, very close. Her body grew very warm. She stepped carefully to the side and turned to face him.

"I know we don't know each other very well, but I have something somewhat strange to tell you." She crossed her arms and walked across the living room.

"I'm open-minded," he joked. "What is it? You're an alien? I could've guessed from your unusual personality and great taste. Most girls your age are definitely not like you. I knew you weren't human."

"Most girls my age? What?" She frowned. "Never mind. Look, this is very weird, but I think someone is following me. I know it sounds really paranoid and strange, believe me. And I have no idea why they would be following me. I paint, I bartend at Alchemy, I read, I am not a terribly exciting person." She looked at her gloved hands. *Okay. There may be one reason someone would follow me, but why? And how would anyone know?*

"Someone following you?" His reaction was not what Ella expected. Rather than tell her she was certainly a nut and laugh it off, he walked over to the window and looked outside.

"Yes, well maybe it's just some bizarre coincidence but I have seen this man in a dark suit several times. It's just really odd." Walking back to the window and standing next to him, she looked out the window again. *Where is he?* She knew he was out there. *Why would someone be out in this horrible weather? To follow her?*

"What did he look like?" Ryan asked her, still searching outside.

"He seems very tall. I haven't gotten the best look at him. Something strange always seems to be happening. Why don't you think this is weird?" Ryan didn't answer her but continued to look out the window.

"What do you mean by something strange seems to be happening?"

"Ryan, could you please look at me? I don't know. Fainting, things I can't remember well. It's just my overactive imagination." A huge chunk of something slammed into the window.

"What the hel..." Ella walked back to the window. There were large bits of hail starting to fall and hit the windows.

"Ella, we should probably get away from the glass." It was too late. A giant piece of ice hit the glass and it shattered, sending water, leaves and glass flying into the perfectly immaculate room. Shielding her eyes, she didn't realize what happened at first and was stumbling around trying to grab hold of the curtains that were flying around. Her hair was blowing wildly in her face. Ryan's strong grasp pulled her away from the window and out of the wind for the moment.

He ran down the hall looking for a towel for her.

"In the bathroom," she shouted. He grabbed it and hurried back to her. She took it and dried her face, blinking at the mess.

"This has got to be the most crappy date ever," she said ruefully to him. In spite of herself she laughed and so did he.

"Ella, where's your caretaker? I'm going to see if he has a piece of wood to cover the window until we can get it fixed. Are you okay? Did you get cut anywhere?" He reached his hand out to touch her arm, but she yanked it away. More abruptly than she meant, but there it was.

"I'm fine," she said curtly. "The caretaker is one floor below me. Across the hall."

"Um, okay. But, are you sure you're okay?" Ryan was looking at her with a concerned and curious look on his face.

"I said I was fine. Why are you looking at me like that?"

"It's hard to see in here but there seems to be a dark-colored smeared something all over your face." His finger touched her cheek. "Was there something on your towel?" he examined the tip of his finger.

"Mm... Maybe," Ella didn't know what to say. "Maybe paint or... or... hair dye. Sometimes I get a little sloppy and forget to wash the towels."

Ryan looked at her curiously. "Somehow I doubt that, but I am going to go get some wood before this mess gets any worse."

"I am going to try to clean this up." She tried to smile like it was no big deal that her window blew out in a freak storm after she told a strange boy she was being stalked. *No big deal.*

Ryan walked out of the apartment without another word. He wasn't gone long and came back with a board, a hammer, and nails.

"Your caretaker said he can fix this tomorrow when you're out or at work. Just leave him a message." He set to work and had the board up quickly. The hail had stopped almost immediately after the window had broken. They didn't talk for the next twenty minutes. They just cleaned up the mess together, and when they were done, with the exception of the board on the window, no one would be able to tell anything had happened.

The room smelled richly of rain and the scented candles. The rain had finally calmed to a steady stream of water on the windows, but the power was still out.

"I think maybe we should eat." Ryan smiled but there was a struggle in it. He looked as though he had a lot of things he wanted to say, but for some reason he was holding back.

"Yes, that is a good idea, but you shouldn't feel like you have to stay. I can't imagine this is your dream date." She brushed a hand across her hair which was soaked, she also felt a cut. "I really appreciate all your help, and the least I could do is feed you. But I think maybe I should clean up first."

"I don't want to leave. We were just starting and it's not very late, assuming it's okay for you to be up." He sat down back at the table and waited for her answer.

"Nope, I doubt I'm going to get much sleep. This has been an exciting, adventure-filled day for me. So just give me a minute to change and wash my face."

"Of course." He set about filling his plate. Ella could make out the troubled look on his face in the candlelight.

Going down the hall to the bedroom, she closed the door behind her and went into the bathroom.

She was a mess. Not realizing her tights were wet, she slipped and hit her head on the sink. She cried out in pain.

"Ella," Ryan called out. "Are you alright?" His footsteps hurried down to the room and he wiggled the door handle. Coming into the room with a candle, he found Ella holding her head in her hands.

"I'm fine, no worries," tears stinging her eyes. She moved and sat against the wall by the tub.

Kneeling down in front of her, he gently pulled her hands away from her face.

"You're not alright. It looks like you cut your forehead." He held the candle up closer to her face. "Oh my god! What is on your face? Something is wrong!" He grabbed another towel and held it against the cut.

"Ella, I think you're bleeding!" His voice sounded strained.

She sighed loudly. "I think maybe you should probably leave."

Ryan moved the towel from her face, and Ella looked him straight in the eye.

"I can. I mean I will if you want me to. I just wanted to make sure you were okay." He sounded rejected, a little hurt.

"I can't imagine this is how you want to spend the evening, and I for one have had enough excitement for one night." She could feel something wet on her forehead and once again thanked her lucky stars that it was dark. *Wait, I don't have any lucky stars, tonight proved that.*

"I am fine. Just annoyed and frustrated by the way this evening is going." She took the towel out of Ryan's hand and held it against her forehead.

"I am sorry you're frustrated. I know the evening has been a bit discouraging, and now you're hurt. But I got to see your place and it's incredible. I, for one, would like to keep talking if you're feeling up to it."

There was silence between them while Ella tried to decide what to do. Her head hurt a little, and she was a bit shaken with the broken window. Seeing the man in the suit outside her window hadn't helped. *I just know that I did! Maybe it would be better if I am not completely alone all night.*

"You're right," she said, trying not to sound hesitant. "I have all that food still sitting on the table, and you've certainly earned it." She laughed, and after a moment so did he.

"Let me just try and clean myself up. Do you mind leaving me the candle?" She started to stand up. As she did, he leaned in to hand over the candle. Their heads collided. As Ella slid back down to the floor there was no sound except her clothes rustling.

"Ella, are you okay?" Ryan reached his hand out in the shadowy light. He felt a shoulder and it was shaking. Ella was laughing uncontrollably with her hand over her mouth. When Ryan realized this he started to laugh as well. For a few minutes, other than the noise of the storm, the room was filled with the sound of nonstop hilarity.

"You're really the most accident prone person I've ever met," Ryan said while gasping for breath.

"I think you're a jinx on me," she jabbed back. Her laughter subsided and she pointed to the door. "Just give me a minute and I'll be out."

Ryan finally stopped laughing and caught his breath. "Yep, just don't fall in the toilet or anything."

"Ha, ha," said Ella as she stood up and closed the door behind him. Moving the candle as close to the mirror as she could, she saw that a fair amount of blood had trailed down her face.

She turned on the faucet to let the water warm up for a moment. She reached for a clean washcloth, wet it, and started to wipe her face. She brushed her hair after she thought that maybe she had cleaned all the blood off her face. Trying to wipe out the sink in the candlelight was more difficult. She couldn't tell if there was blood on the sink or if it was shadows from the candlelight.

The rain had slowed to a drizzle. The wind seemed to have subsided completely. Picking up the candle after she thought she was cleaned up well enough, she opened the bathroom door and went back into the dining room.

Ryan was waiting for her and he smiled, well, vibrantly at her in the dark room.

"My turn," was all he said as he gently took the candle out of her hand, his fingers grazing her softly. She felt herself warm to his touch. She turned in a circle, her socks sliding on the wood floor, as he walked away from her and shut the bathroom door.

The candles on the table had burned down quite a bit since the evening had begun, and the juice had warmed. Ella went to the fridge, opened it quickly, and took out more to refresh the glasses.

With that, all of Ella's beautiful lamps flickered to life.

"Ryan," she called. When he didn't answer she made her way back to the bathroom. Just as she rounded the corner, something blue on his finger absorbed into his skin.

He turned and stared at her. "What is all over your bathroom?"

Chapter 6

The lights seemed excessively harsh to Ella at that moment. She could feel her body start to overheat. *The lights picked a great time to come back on.*

Ryan looked at her and laughed. "Are you okay? What did you spill in here? I'll help you clean it up."

Her head was spinning. Ella thought with horror that she was going to faint again.

He turned to pull a towel off the rack behind him, and Ella tried to say, "Don't worry about it. I'll take care of it later," but the words were being highly uncooperative. Reaching a hand out to touch the back of his arm, she felt herself starting to slip. One of her knees locked and she tried to bend it. Grasping the door frame, she slid her hand down the jamb and leaned carefully against it. Then her door buzzed. Ryan looked up from wiping up the mess all over the sink, and Ella jerked her head around, surprised to hear anyone ringing the buzzer. The startled feeling from the sudden noise pulled her out of the sinking heat.

"Where you expecting someone?" Ryan asked in a friendly, casual tone.

"No, not at all." Ella pushed herself off the door frame and shook her head to clear it.

"I'll finish wiping this up and be ready to eat in just a minute." He started to hum to himself.

Ella walked to the front door. *Who could possibly be here?* She pushed the button on the intercom phone. "Hello?"

"Ella?" the slightly accented voice was recognizable to Ella in a second. The professor.

How did he find out where I live? Did he follow me? She sighed. *This whole night is just plain stupid.*

"Yes, Hi, um... I am not sure how you figured out where I live, but this is not a good time," she said as politely as possible.

"I am sorry to bother you," hurried the professor. "I just wanted to ask you a few questions."

Sighing loudly, she thought for a second. "Fine. Ask away, if you promise you'll go away." She hadn't meant to be so rude, but she was getting crabby.

"Actually, Ella, I think maybe these are questions best asked in private. If you could just let me up for a moment, I'll be very quick about it."

"That is out of the question," she responded. "I don't know you. It's weird and more than a little creepy that I seem to keep coming across you. I mean, seriously, you're at my apartment. I didn't tell you where I live. Did I even tell you my last name? I don't even remember, but boy, am I learning to keep my personal info to myself."

"I am sorry Ella. This is an awkward way to have a conversation. Why don't you just come downstairs for a minute and we can talk. I understand the strangeness of this situation, but I promise I mean no trouble. I found some interesting material in a puddle of rainwater that I wanted to ask you about."

With that, she nearly slammed the phone into the wall. Instead she kicked the wall childishly and looked around the room to the broken window. She heard Ryan humming in the bathroom, rain trickling behind the buzz of the intercom, and of course, the mess in the bathroom.

"I'll be down in a minute." She hung up the phone without waiting for an answer.

"Ryan?" She could still hear him in the back. "I have to run downstairs for a minute I'll be right back." She slammed the door before he could respond.

Crossing her arms and staring at the floor as she trudged her way down to the front door, her nerves felt on edge. She inhaled deeply and opened the front door. The professor stood in the rain under an umbrella, wearing a long trench coat. His glasses had splatters of raindrops on the lenses. He tried to smile at her. Ella felt her annoyance showing.

"Again, Ella, I am really sorry to bother you, but I really just wanted to ask you a couple of questions."

"So ask." Ella's tone was uninviting and she could feel more of the stiffness in her joints returning. A shiver ran across her body. *Ryan should leave soon.* She was tired, irritated, and pretty sure he thought she was crazy. *Oh, and possibly cursed.*

The rain was starting to pick up again, and the umbrella the professor was carrying made conversation difficult since it didn't exactly fit all the way against the door. He had to stand more than a few feet back from Ella. She thought that was fine until it occurred to her that someone might hear them talking. She moved back, and the professor smiled gratefully, turned away from her to close his umbrella, and then stepped inside. He was leaning slightly out the door and trying to shake off some of the rainwater when there was a sound of footsteps.

"Hey, Ella, I heard you say something, and the door closed. But I didn't hear what it was that you said." Ryan was still humming as he came down the stairs. He was smiling when he looked at Ella, until he noticed the professor in the doorway.

"Are you okay?" Ryan asked. Ella thought there was a sharpness to the question.

"I'm fine," Ella furrowed her brow. "Do you know the professor?" That was when the professor seemed to notice Ryan standing there. He shook the umbrella involuntarily. The look on his face was unreadable. *Strangely unreadable.*

She looked between the two men, neither one of them moving nor willing to engage in the first word.

"Uh, this is, uh... Dr. James Reynolds, and this is Ryan," she said, gesturing to each one in turn. The professor opened his mouth as if to say something, then shut it and instead stuck out his hand. "Pleasure to meet you, Ryan."

Ryan didn't step forward to take the offered hand. He simply inclined his head and then looked at Ella.

"I was thinking, Ella, that you are right. That maybe we should just do this another night." Gone was the warm, light-hearted joke in his voice that Ella had grown used to over the course of the evening.

She didn't really know what to say, and now with the professor here about to ask who knows what, she almost didn't care at the moment that Ryan was leaving.

"Yeah, I understand. Maybe I'll see you around," she stammered, not really looking at him.

Ryan lingered for one moment without saying anything else. The professor said nothing as Ryan abruptly pushed past the man and went out into the rain. He was gone quickly, and Ella sighed.

"Is that your boyfriend?" The professor asked with a peculiar tone in his voice.

Ella looked at him. "That's none of your business, but no, he's not my boy-friend." The question bugged her more than it should have. Clearly her patience was running out with this man. *Or maybe*, she begrudgingly thought, *it hurts my feelings that Ryan has left so suddenly.*

"So what do you want that you felt the need to stalk me and freak me out?" Ella crossed her arms and leaned against the wall.

"I just was trying to find the best way to ask you about yourself, and I am afraid I didn't come up with more than just asking you." The professor fiddled with his glasses as he spoke. "I do think we should speak privately." He said it sincerely but apprehensively.

"I am not comfortable letting you up into my apartment," Ella said sharply. "I am not even comfortable with you being here."

The professor stared a her for a minute without saying anything.

"Ella you have a secret, don't you?" He said it flatly, un-accusingly.

"I don't know what you are talking about." She uncrossed her arms and crossed them again while shifting uncomfortably against the wall.

"I think you do know what I am talking about. I am simply here to help, if I can." After the professor said that, there was a sound of a door opening on a floor above them, and someone started to descend the stairs.

"I think we should talk privately," he put an emphasis on privately. Barely nodding, Ella began to go up the stairs to her own floor. The professor's foot-steps were deliberate and careful as they walked up.

Ella led him down the hall to her door, which, it appeared, Ryan had left open. She pushed open the door and automatically reached to turn on a light. It wasn't a bright light, but it was placed in a way that it would illuminate one of her paintings. Except the painting that was supposed to be there was gone.

"Where...? What...?" Ella wasn't entirely sure what had happened. She looked around the room as if it would magically appear from somewhere else. Of course, it did not.

"Ella, is something wrong?" The professor stepped into the apartment. "Oh my!" He sounded truly surprised. "This is breathtaking."

"Did someone follow you here? What are you doing here?" She was nearly yelling. "Where is my painting?" Frantically running around the room, she was so boiling hot she couldn't catch her breath.

The professor was looking at the walls and was not paying much attention to how upset she was. Running over to him, she grabbed his arm. He looked at her blankly.

"Where is my painting?" The shake in her voice was unmistakeable.

"Your painting? One is missing? I'm sorry, I was so awestruck by this room." His eyes wandered over her head to the next room.

"Professor..."

"Ella, that boy, you don't think he took it?" The professor focused on her again. He looked serious.

"Ryan? What? No, he walked right by us. He didn't have it..." She didn't sound entirely sure though. *Why would he take my painting? I would have just given him one.*

"Ryan, right, Ryan. Look, I'm sorry about your painting, but we should talk." He turned and noticed her blown-out window. "What happen to your window? Your curtains look wet. Did that happen tonight? Someone broke in?"

Ella glared at him. She stomped over to a chair and sat down.

"Would you please just tell me what you want." The light made her face look angrier than she really was. She was really just confused. But whatever he must have seen made the professor more nervous. He rubbed his hand through his hair over and over again, silent for a full minute. Ella said nothing, though on the inside she was trembling, shaken to the core. *What is going on?*

"Look, you obviously are very secretive, and that leads me to believe you could use some help." The professor's voice was tremulous.

Ella started to feel a bit bad for making him uncomfortable, *but still, what is he doing?* Outside it sounded as though the storm was kicking up again. The wind made the wood board in the window creak. The sound gave Ella a chill. She felt a jolt of pain in her neck and it caused her to wince. She sighed. All the relief from her joints appeared to be wearing off. *Really,* she thought ruefully, *the damn night couldn't get a whole lot worse, and doubtfully anymore complicated.*

The professor was watching her closely. She tried to keep a cross look on her face. She stared over his head at her painting of the planet Jupiter. It hung from the ceiling on a piece of rounded wood that she had painted on both sides. When it spun, its silvery lines appeared to flow across the planet.

He noticed her gaze had shifted and looked behind him.

"These paintings are quite remarkable," said the professor. "I really can't emphasize that enough." He turned around in time to see Ella rubbing her neck.

"You're in pain," he said matter-of-factly.

"So? Look, Professor, you said you had something so important to talk to me about, so talk. It's been a long night, and I wouldn't mind putting an end to it."

"Yes, well, I suspect that if I weren't a professor I might not have noticed that this particular substance," he said the words carefully, "is an unusual material, and if you can just tell me what it is, I will be on my way. Or you can tell me what it is, where you got it from, and we can figure out what to do together. Because my guess is that this material that was in the rainwater has something to do with the discomfort you seem to be suffering. I've tried having a look at it already, but my results were most certainly incorrect. Be that as it may, it was such an unusual result I really wanted to find you and talk with you. I don't know if this stuff is dangerous. As I said, I am not even sure I know exactly what it is yet. As for 'stalking you,'" he said this somewhat sarcastically, "all I had to do to find you was chat with a few people in the café where I encountered you. They pointed me to the club, where I learned a bit more, though not as much as I would have thought considering you've worked there a while now, from some of your co-workers. To be fair, they were cautious about giving me any information. I told them a little bit about how we met and then, well, the Internet, being the magical place that it is, filled in the blanks for me. And thus we now sit. So there is my explanation. You know my name and where I work. Oh, and where I prefer to get tea during the workday. I'd say we are relatively even in the information department."

Ella thought for a long while, staring off into space. She was tired. She was excited. There were suddenly many new things in her life. Some of them seemed to possibly be great, others seemed just horrible. She didn't know this man. She had no idea if she had a good sense of people at all. She did know that part of her really wanted to tell this man her secret. It was pretty irrational. She'd only ever told one other person and, as far as she knew, they had never betrayed her. The urge, she realized, was overwhelming. She chewed on her lip and felt tears spring to her eyes. *This feels like too much, too soon. But how could it be too soon?* Only one other person knew her secret and she had no idea where that person was. Leaning back in the chair, she kept staring off into space. She momentarily noticed that the professor, sitting in the chair across from her, was slightly ill at ease. But he stayed quiet nonetheless. Ella suspected he knew that this was very hard decision for her.

The wind was coming and going. There was lightning and a rumble of thunder, moving farther and farther into the distance. She wondered what time it was. She didn't have to work at the club tomorrow, but she wanted to put a lot of time into her art.

"Well," the professor said softly, "I don't need an answer right now." He got up and stood, looking down at Ella, who didn't meet his gaze. He strode over to the door and opened it.

"You know where to find me if you change your mind and want to talk. I really do think I can help you." He didn't sound angry. *Strangely, he sounds sorry.* He stepped out into the hall and the door swung closed. She heard the footsteps as he walked down the hall.

Quickly getting up, she ran across the living room, opened the door, poked her head out, and called out. "Professor!"

He was almost to the stairs, but he stopped and looked back at her in the garish light of the hallway. He looked odd in the light. *Not scary but oddly safe. Yeah, convince yourself you're about to do the smart thing.* Her voice of reason swallowed its pride and stomped off.

"Yes, Ella?" he said carefully.

"Professor, please come back in here." She stepped into the hall and held the door open with one arm.

The professor opened his mouth as if to say something to her, but seemed to think better of it. Instead he just walked back up the hall and briefly looked at her. She tried to smile but failed. She sucked in her breath, walked back in, and closed the door.

Walking across the living room and through the dining room, she went into the kitchen.

The professor followed her. "I can help you, Ella, I really do think, with whatever you have to tell me. I worked in the private sector for a long time. I have a wide field of experience."

While he was talking, Ella had gone to the sink and turned on the water.

She held her hands on the edge of the sink and looked at the water running into the drain.

"Why do you want to help me?" she asked him. Her tone was flat, showing no emotion towards the question one way or the other.

"Yes, I had thought you might ask me this," the professor responded. "And I thought about what my answer would be for quite a long time. I realized there are quite a few reasons."

"Well if you don't mind, I'd like to hear some of them." The rain had stopped now, and it was quiet in the dark outside. Ella felt sure that the whole world was listening to them.

"First, foremost, and honestly, I am curious. I am a scientist and a doctor. I look into what makes me curious. You, Ella, have made me curious. You also seem to be in pain. And truth be told, I was not sure if you were hurt in some way. But like I said, the results of the tests I've already performed were so confusing, I surmised you might not be as well-off as you could possibly be. As a doctor, if there is something I can do to alleviate some of your pain, I would like to do it. Additionally, I am an educator. I seek knowledge in which to share information with my students and, on a few rarer occasions, with the world. Now, of course, I am telling you this with the caveat that I will not share any information you do not want me to share. You are certainly a private person and have been for some time, I am guessing, and there needs to be trust between us if we are to work together at all. And, of course, you helped me. I apparently somehow put you in peril with that occurrence of my papers being pulled out of your hands. I still do not know what that was about, nor what that man was after. But I can promise you I will find out, and at the very least confront him on his incredibly ungentlemanly behavior," he finished with a grimace.

It made Ella wonder what was on those papers. *Even if it is not any of my business,* she reminded herself. *But the jerk did knock me on the ground.* That's when it hit her that perhaps that man was following her because she was talking to the professor. It very well could have nothing to do with her at all. All the same, that did not comfort her. Nobody should have to be intimidated by anyone else. Waiting for someone in a dark parking lot was pretty much never a nice thing to do unless you were asked to be there. There was not a whole lot that truly angered her, but someone else finding ways to try to intrude unwelcome in your life was something of which she had long since had enough.

"This is completely freaking me out," she told him. "I don't share much about my life, you're right. It's been a crazy couple of days. I think a man is following me."

She stopped to gauge his reaction. The professor pursed his lips and nodded his head.

"I guess I'm wondering if he is following me because of you?"

"Well, it's possible," the professor said it without hesitation.

"Do you think I'm in danger? Are you in danger?"

"I don't think so, Ella, but I do not know. I'm going out on limb here to say this. I'm pretty sure I have not been followed around before by strangers." He stopped for a moment when he saw the look on her face. "That limb part was a joke. I don't think I've been followed before."

"You don't seemed surprised to hear me tell this to you." Ella wanted more information. Private or not, she might be in danger. *People don't follow you around to give you flowers.*

"It's true, I'm not surprised. And I am assuming from this conversation you want to know more about why that would be. Normally I would not share that with you, but I did come here to ask you to tell me something. I will tell you, and you can decide for yourself if you think that my contribution to the facts we are acquiring about each other warrants a bit of trust."

"Fair enough. Though I also have to decide to believe you," Ella pointed out and turned the water off so he could talk.

"That is true. You can look at least some of the story up on the Internet if you choose."

Ella had no response to that because she would not have expected to hear those words. *Curiouser and curiouser.*

"Down the rabbit hole then," she motioned for him to continue.

"Indeed." He paused and smiled at the reference. "You are an odd girl. Anyway, I believe it is possible that I am being followed because of a former job. You see, I left education for some time to pursue an interest of study that teaching would not allow enough time for me to follow. Without getting into all the sordid details, because, well, you'll read some of them anyway and we can talk about them later, I went to work for one of the largest pharmaceutical companies in the world. The money was excellent, and the mission, or at least the supposed mission, was a noble one. I was given free rein to pursue whatever courses of testing I wished."

He stopped for a minute and rubbed his palm against his temple.

"Whatever courses of study you wished?" Ella leaned back against the counter. "I can only imagine what that could mean. These types of companies are not known in the world for being good guys."

"Again, you are correct. They are not known for being good guys, but believe me when I tell you I believed that if I went into the company and led the way, things would be better. Great, grand, excellent. There were, and are, plenty of good people who produce for pharmaceutical companies. But as all deals with the mixed righteous go, not everyone who worked there shared the same vision. There is always a catch, isn't there? I was told the truth, but only up to a certain point. I should add that everything I did was, in theory, information and work that belonged to the company. But at some point I felt that my morals and the morals of some others who worked for the company parted ways, and as such I broke my contract. I took information that I feel belongs to me, and left.

As you can probably see where I am going with this, my point of view on this matter is disagreed with by a few people. Powerful people. There is more to the story and, like I said, a lot of it is on the Internet. I believe it is possible that man works for someone at the company. I have no way to prove this to you or the police, but, hazarding a guess, I assume they are investigating everything about my life at this point. Especially since the path of action with which they chose to harass me failed. Which reminds me, did he break your window? I would not believe that someone would do that, but good grief, who knows?"

"No, it was just the storm," she said thoughtfully, weighing what he had told her and the fact that he kept saying she could look a lot of this up on the Internet. "That's quite a story professor."

"Yes."

"And there's more apparently."

"Yes there is more."

"This is not the type of thing you run into in real life."

"Certainly not, Ella. It is a mystery series to be sure. But you can also be sure things happen in the world that if the population in general knew, there could be a revolt against some very important people. Unfortunately the reality is that not all science is good science. And not all science, good or bad, is used in ways to help the world. I grew, and grow, ever more tired of its murky depths."

"Those are some pretty serious allegations, and it's a strange situation to have thrust upon me. But regardless, it seems this man is going to follow me. I have not actually spent time with you, yet he has appeared."

"He has appeared? How many times have you seen him, Ella?"

"Honestly, I'm not sure."

"What do you mean you're not sure?"

"Well, you're right about me being in pain, and I do occasionally take painkillers to alleviate some of it. But they mess with my head and my memory. I hate it. And anyway there may be two men."

"You should really let me help you, Ella."

"Maybe. I can look more of this up on the Internet, huh?"

"Oh, yes. My disgrace is all over the news." His tone was forcibly light. His face was not.

"Right," Ella said. "Here you go, then." Taking off her gloves and turning the faucet back on, she stuck her hands under the water. The professor stepped up next to her and looked into the sink. There was nothing out of the ordinary.

"Ella, I am not sure what I am supposed to be looking at here..." he started.

"Just wait a second," and, with that, her secret began to run down the drain.

"Oh my, what is that?" The professor stared, and then stuck his fingers into the sink. Ella just watched him as he mumbled, touched her hands, and rubbed the water between his fingers.

"What is it?" he asked again. Ella sighed and turned off the water. She walked over to a towel to dry her hands.

"I don't know. I am kind of hoping, Doctor, that you can tell me." She carefully folded the towel and set it on the counter.

The professor took out a glass vial and filled it with the silvery-blue liquid that had come off Ella's skin.

"Do you mind if I take this?" He held up the vial, and the liquid shimmered in the shadows.

"I don't know." She wrung her hands together. This idea of her secret being taken out of the apartment, and not by her, was worrying.

"I understand that this must be rather frightening for you, Ella, but the only way I can possibly start to tell you anything about this is to test it further. I tested the sample from the rainwater, but the results have made me wonder about the water it was mixed in. Rainwater is pretty dirty and that is probably why the results were so confusing. And I can't do it here," he looked around the apartment. "As beautiful as this space is, it's not made to be a lab." He tried to laugh jovially, but it fell in the still room.

"I don't know for sure if I can trust you," Ella said softly. "But if you really think you can help me figure out what is wrong with me, I'd be grateful."

"I'm certainly going to try my hardest. I've seen some unusual things in my time, but never have I seen someone secrete silvery-blue liquid from their skin."

"One thing," Ella said to him, as he carefully wrapped the vial in a cloth and placed it in his pocket. "You can't tell anyone about this. No one knows, and I'd like to keep it that way."

"I will not say a word to anyone." He held out his hand as if to shake hers. She just looked at him, not really sure what to do. A drop of the liquid was slowly absorbing into his skin. James noticed it as well, as it disappeared from sight.

"Extraordinary," he muttered.

"Do you feel anything?" Ella asked suddenly.

"Yes, a bit tingly and warm, not unpleasant at all." He rubbed his finger over the spot where the drop had been.

"I've wondered..." she whispered.

"Wondered?"

"I've accidentally gotten it on a few people over time. But I've always been able to cover it up with an explanation," she said quickly when she noticed the surprised look on his face.

"So no one at all knows that this comes out of your skin?" The professor took out a notepad and started to write things down.

"What are you writing?" Ella went back into the living room and sat down. She stood back up and picked up her crystal glass, still full of juice. She sipped reflectively. It was warm and flat. *Like my date.*

"I need to collect as much detail as possible. Any bit of information could be important in understanding." He went across the room and sat down. "You've never actually told anyone about this?"

"Um, no." Ella looked down in her lap.

"Are you sure? I mean, has this been happening your whole life?"

"Yes, for as long as I remember." She turned to look at the spot where her painting used to hang.

"So even as a child? What about your parents?" He wrote something down.

"I don't know a whole lot about my parents. They died when I was young." Her voice was sad and wistful.

"I'm sorry," the professor said. "I can ask you questions some other time. We can get together later this week if you like."

"No, it's fine. I am just not used to talking about my family, or lack thereof anyway. And sure, we can get together. Maybe after some of your tests or whatever."

"Your parents died when you were young. Do you have any siblings?"

"No, Professor, as far as I know I have no family. I was a ward of the state until I graduated from school and moved here."

"School? Where did you go to school?"

"I went to a private school up north. I was there my entire first seventeen years of life on scholarship. My grades were pretty good so I was allowed to attend. I guess I'm lucky that I was able to attend such a prestigious school, but, truth be told, I was terribly out of place. As you can probably guess, I didn't have a lot of friends."

The professor pursed his lips again. He looked as though he was suppressing a laugh.

"What?" Ella demanded.

"Well you don't make it easy to talk to you is all, young lady." He let out a little tee-hee.

She wanted to say something witty in retort, but he was right and she knew it.

"I feel like I have a good reason to keep people away."

"Maybe you do, Ella, maybe you don't. You have no idea why your body reacts this way. It doesn't make you a bad person."

"You know hardly anything about me, Doc. I could be an awful person."

"Awful people don't help strangers in pain in the dark," he replied.

She had nothing to say to this. She would like to think she was a nice person, but, truth be told, she had no idea. *Really, about anything.*

"Did you have more questions to ask me? I am tired. It's been a long night." Ella stood up.

"I am sure that I will have more questions soon. Do you have a number where I can easily reach you?"

Ella grimaced. She didn't want to give out her number.

The professor didn't hold back his chuckle this time.

"What's so funny?" she asked, sounding more than a little perplexed.

"I'd say it's safe to say that you don't have too many more secrets from me." He seemed to find this very funny. "So I don't know why you wouldn't give me your phone number."

Now she felt embarrassed. He was right. She wrote down the number and handed it to him.

He was about to leave when Ella motioned for him to stop.

"Dr. Reynolds, did you notice anyone following you?"

"No, I don't think I was followed tonight. Do you think that man took your painting? Is that why you ask? Are you sure it wasn't that boy that was here?"

The strange look on his face, the one that told her she was crazy, made her say, "Oh no, never mind, I'm just tired and clearly it's been a long night."

The professor looked at her for a moment longer, said good night, and left. The door closing echoed in her head and, with the wood on the window, left an odd sound of the air being sucked out.

Ella walked around the living room for a few moments, yawning and running her hand over things. The velvet of the couch, the soft, shimmery fabric of curtains, the smooth texture of the paint on the walls that left her with the usual tingle. She once again noticed that her joints were bothering her but not as much as they normally did. She hurt, but not debilitatingly so. Maybe her joints did hurt, but she was just distracted. By Ryan. Sighing loudly and more dramatically than was necessary, especially since she was alone, she decided to leave the dishes for tomorrow. Something she never did. She was pleased to allow herself this luxury.

She smiled at the space before turning out the light to go into the bedroom. *It has been some kind of night.* As she walked down the hall to the bedroom, she didn't notice the small streak of lightning in the pitch black revealing, if only for a second, the secret she thought she was imagining.

Carefully hanging up all her clothes and folding the gloves, Ella stretched out on the bed and looked at the patterns in the ceiling. The wood rattled in the next room and she thought about Ryan. She liked him and had a hard time believing he would take her painting. *Maybe the doctor took it. No, he wasn't alone in the apartment at all. It was just too bizarre. Of course, that did seem to be the theme to the evening.* The doctor sought her out, she had an art show, her window blew out, a boy was interested in her, her painting was stolen, and she was pretty sure she was being followed.

It was exhausting and she passed out into deep sleep.

The black melted into the water and the pressure was unbearable. There was no way to see what was around her. There was an orange flickering light above, and it made the water look as though it was glittering. Pulling what she thought was her hand in front of her face, she tried to make out any shape that she could. There was a phantom of a sight in her vision. Barely an image and she couldn't make it out. A pain in her chest was forcing her to swallow water in gasps. Something brushed against her leg. At least she thought it was her leg, though somehow that didn't seem right. *How could that not be right?* Whatever it was brushed against her again, harder this time. It scared her. The light above seemed to be fading and getting clearer at the same time. Desperately trying to keep her burning eyes open, she moved in a way she thought would take her up. Kicking with might she wasn't sure was hers, she pushed and pushed in hopes of breaking the surface of the water. Not making it wasn't an option. She would die. This was something she knew. *Out of the water,* was the only thought that was clear. *Out of the water.*

Harder and harder, her arms felt like they weren't going to move anymore.

Then there was no more water. Horrid stabbing in the muscles of her hands as she broke the surface. Heaving in agony, the air raced through her. The drips were clouding her eyesight and there was no way to dry them. Trying to reach with hands to wipe away water was impossible. As Ella sat at the surface of the water carefully treading in what seemed an eternal abyss, some of the surroundings came into focus. There was a burning mountain range in the distance. A terrible fire seemed to be raging up the sides of it. Something hard and sharp rubbed against her in the water. It glittered with the wetness. The fire was consuming everything in its path. There was a loud, screeching creak. It sounded like something was breaking in half. The loudest thud Ella could ever imagine hearing rang through the orange night. The ground shuddered and swayed under the weight of it. Ella could see the shore shake, and large pieces of rock and sand tumbled into the water from high above. The sight of it all was terrifying. She started to swim toward the shore, moving carefully through debris and trying to avoid it as more of the overhanging cliff face fell in around her.

As her head bobbed up and down, through the water she could vaguely make out what looked to be the silhouette of a person against the glowing light. It was hard to tell with all the smoke and water, but for some reason she hoped beyond hope that it was another person. Not knowing where she was nor how she had gotten in the water was disorienting. What happened had something to do with her, she could just feel it. Not having the energy to focus on more than one thing at a time, she pushed on toward the shore when she felt her leg catch on something.

Ella was jerked under the water and inhaled a deep breath that caused her to choke. Stuck and unable to get free of whatever her leg was caught on, panic started to set in.

The water weighed on her chest heavily. Reaching down, she pulled as hard as she could on her leg. Out of the corner of her vision something... *no, someone*... swam past.

The strong hands pulled on her and swiftly dragged her through the water. In no time at all, Ella was back at the surface and almost to shore. Her feet were grazing the ground. Drifting a little farther shoreward on a wave, she shakily walked onto the land and surveyed the destruction. It was humid and bleak, the wind blowing dust all around. Despite the heat, she could not make herself stop shivering. There was no longer anyone around, and the fire was growing. Turning to the water, she saw it sparkle with dangerous beauty in the chaos. Colossal, silver chunks of metal floated around and lay scattered on the beach.

Something splashed in the water, drawing her attention.

It was a dream. She was gripping her velvet blanket tightly when the rain woke her. She sat up, looked around the room, and wished the night had ended. *It seems destined to go on forever,* she thought grumpily. She wiped the moisture off her forehead with a towel folded on the nightstand. It wasn't the first time she woke up from the intensity, covered in sweat.

Standing up to get a glass of water, she noticed a light was still on in the living room. Walking down the hall to turn it off, she tried not to shake her grogginess. It would help her sleep.

She reached up under the shade to the switch, only to see that her painting was right back where it belonged.

Chapter 7

Ella was sitting in the living room, staring at her painting, not having any idea how to deal with this unsettling occurrence, when the phone rang. In the stillness of the night it seemed as though it could wake the dead. Numbly walking over to it and picking it up, she said nothing into the receiver

"Hello," a male voice hesitated on the other end.

"Ryan," Ella acknowledged hazily. "Ryan, it's so late. Why are you calling now? Is something wrong?"

"I know it's really late, and I'm super sorry. I hope I didn't wake you up. I took a chance you might stay up late because you work in a club." He sounded fearful.

"Yes, that's true. I normally do stay up late. But right now really is not a good time."

"Look, if I could just have a minute, I just wanted to apologize."

"For what?"

"I wanted to apologize for running off so suddenly. It seemed like you wanted to talk to that man who came to your house, and I didn't want to intrude."

Ella did not say anything for a minute.

"You know, Ryan, I kind of thought you might know the doctor, the way you acted when you saw him."

"Know him? No, I don't know him. I just get... strange around doctors. That's all. I've had to spend a lot of time around them, and I don't exactly like them, you might say."

"Really? Why is that?" He finally seemed like he might tell her something that mattered.

"I wanted to tell you some of this stuff, Ella, but the night got a touch hectic."

"Yes, I guess it did," she agreed, finding herself relaxing a bit. "To be honest it has not gotten any less strange."

"What do you mean?"

"You know, it's really late. I should let you go." She stood up from the chair to hang up the phone.

"No, wait... really, it's fine. I am a bit of a night owl anyway. In fact, this may seem super... forward, but do you want to get together right now?"

"What? You mean like now?" Ella stammered. "Uh no, I don't do that sort of thing."

"What? Oh wait, right." Ryan laughed. "That's not what I meant, Ella."

"Now I feel stupid."

"Don't. What else would you think? I suppose if I were a normal guy that's exactly why I'd be calling right now."

"So, you're not normal?"

"Not even a little bit. Does that mean you don't want to talk to me, now?"

"No, Ryan, honestly it's a bit of a relief, since I am such a weirdo."

"You don't seem that weird to me."

"That statement right there proves that you are, in fact, not a normal guy." And they both laughed. "Sure, if you want to come back over to the nuthouse, be my guest."

"Yes, I do. You can tell me what else has happened tonight. It's going to take me about 45 minutes to get there. Looking forward to it. Again," he quipped.

"Just buzz when you get here." They hung up, and Ella went to the bedroom to change out of her pajamas. She realized her heart was a bit... racy. She'd never had anyone over this late, and certainly not of the male persuasion.

She was antsy trying this again, especially after the whole day's events. While she was waiting, she decided that she would look up what she could find about the professor. Going to the computer and sitting down, she typed: Dr. James Reynolds.

The name got a lot of hits. It seemed the doctor had been a busy man before he became a professor. Maybe this information would let her know if she could really trust the doctor with her secrets. She started to scan the many, many articles. Quite a lot of them had to do with a scandal that seemed to have the doctor in the center of it.

Ella clicked on the top link and was sent to a news page explaining that the doctor had been an employee at a prestigious pharmaceutical company. In fact, the article stated, he was the star of the company. He created numerous drugs and procedures that had shown many promising outcomes, including claiming to be very close to a real cure for more than one type of cancer. There were links to article after article filled with praise and accolades for the doctor's work.

Then the accusations started leaking out to the press: rumors of unethical testing on patients. But the company stood by the doctor at first, dismissing the allegations out of hand and going as far as to hire a lawyer on his behalf. Then it seemed to Ella that two things happened at once. A story leaked out with both a hard-to-see but incriminating picture of the doctor putting something into an IV that looked as though it was in the arm of a very sick child, as well as the parent's claims of having no knowledge of what he was doing. At same time the company's owner, who was also the president, died. It was at this point that the new president stepped in and said that there was no room for someone who would do such horrible things to children. The doctor was fired in a exceptionally public way, complete with reporters, and was taken into custody by the police.

The article continued on to state that the doctor was ultimately freed and no charges were pressed, as there was no actual evidence of wrongdoing. The pharmaceutical company wouldn't release its test records, claiming property rights and privacy for its patients. The parent of the supposedly wronged child was nowhere to be found, and neither was the child. But the damage was done, and for a time it seemed the doctor couldn't find any employment. This was two years ago. Clearly, enough time had passed that the university had been willing to take him on as a professor.

She leaned back in the chair and closed her eyes for a minute. This was an unnerving story. She didn't like the idea of experimenting on kids. Not one bit. But the doctor had told her to look up these stories. He told her they could talk about all these things that had happened before he became a professor. It seemed that he was not trying to hide anything, so there had to be more to the story. At least she hoped. *Trusting someone with a secret I have kept mostly hidden my whole life is a pretty big deal.*

She sat back up and scrolled to the bottom of the page where she found a picture of the new president being welcomed in an office building. The new president was Alexandra's father! And in the background of the picture stood the headmistress and the man she thought was following her! She leaned as close as she could, thinking that maybe this was not who it was. Her shock forced her to hold her breath as she peered closely at the picture. *It is them. No doubt about it.*

Getting up and pacing again, she nearly forgot that she was having a late-night visitor. *One that was at least welcome this time,* she thought angrily. Stomping over to the stove, she put on water to make a pot of tea. Pouring the water, she stared into the clear glass teapot and watched the leaves of the jasmine flower fold out as the water seeped into them. Giving the doctor information about her life was oddly comforting, almost a relief, as she looked back on the conversation. She had a lot of questions about herself. Things that had always just been there and she had never bothered to try and sort out. She'd been told for so long as a child that she was simply an oddity. It was just a given, and because of it she kept everyone at arm's length. Except Alexandra.

Ella put the cup down and made a decision. She was going to find her friend. Maybe some of these new people, who had made their presence so obtrusive in her quiet life, could point her in the direction of resources. Like the doctor, who seemed to have no trouble finding her.

The day was still so clear. The woman's cold face as they led Alexandra away. The strange things Alex kept muttering to her. Ella trying to get close and being pushed away by the men who handled Alexandra as though she might break.

Looking around her desk, she rolled her hands over objects on it. Memories tied to each thing phased through her mind, so clear and so muted all at once. So many strange little pieces she had collected over the years, not even entirely sure where they all came from. The more ornate ones were things Alexandra had given her. Gifts from traveling, or tokens of love given to Ella after selling or returning something her father had sent her. Ella only ever met Alexandra's father once, and it was a tense and strained meeting. He was icy and distant toward his daughter. A contrast to the way he reacted when he saw the headmistress. Warm and inviting, like they were old lovers. A theory Alexandra herself had thrown about. They had no way to prove it, but as is the way of teenage girls, they spent a lot of time musing about it when they were alone. Alexandra was even convinced that the headmistress may have killed her mother to get to her father. An absolutely unproven statement, as Alexandra herself didn't even know if her mother was dead or alive. In fact, Ella realized she had no idea why Alex would think that, and it had not occurred to her how strange a statement that really was. Until now.

Ella Cerulean

As a teenager she never thought much about her friend's dramatic statements, but those statements frequently contained a bit of truth. But only a bit. Alex did not know much about her mother, only that she was gone. It was a subject Alexandra herself had broached many times to her father, only to find herself at a steel door, slammed shut and locked up tight. In the end, he sent her away to school so she couldn't seek answers where she wasn't welcome. A subject about which Ella had spent many hours listening to her friend's heartache and pain. Alex desperately wanted her father to love her. A longing Ella knew all too well, and possibly in an even more complex manner, never having known her own parents. A truth that hit harder than anything could be one Alex didn't know yet, and on occasion Ella herself had momentarily considered the possibility that maybe she was better off not knowing her own parents.

Sometimes when she meditated, she thought she could remember some things. But in reality she never knew for sure. The pictures felt so distant, and it seemed as though she might be confusing the time periods, which she assumed must have come from all the historical reading she did. She often imagined herself as a child, wearing sumptuous gowns and running in vast courtyards filled with lavish flowers and trees. There appeared to be many people around her at all times, and they were always paying careful attention to her every move.

She knew in her heart it was merely wishful thinking from a life of not knowing.

What kid who never knew their parents didn't imagine that they belonged to some grand lineage and were unconditionally loved?

No. The reality, Ella imagined, *is much harsher than that.* A reality she hadn't yet decided she was sure she wanted to know.

Can I live without the knowledge of where I came from? She suspected the more the doctor investigated her condition the more he might encourage her to delve into the past. Once again, she didn't know where to start. *Though, it would have to be at the school, right? In my entire life, where else have I ever been for sure?* Of all her memories, time there was the clearest. She couldn't do it tonight. Looking at the clock, she saw that Ryan would be over soon.

Needing some air, she walked out of the apartment and to the front of the building to wait in the small, dreary lobby for Ryan. Opening the door, she stuck her head out and took a deep breath of the misty rain air. It made her feel slightly less crazy. The street was silent, sans an occasional rustle in the night from the breeze.

I wonder where Ryan lives. She felt like this day, the last few days, had started a long time ago and were nowhere near ending. Glancing down, she noticed a glint of light coming from something. As she stared at it, she could swear that it moved closer to her.

"What in the world..."

She bent over to pick it up just as Ryan said, "Hey Ella."

Standing up quickly, she noticed he seemed so vivid in the black night.

"What are you doing out here, Ella?"

"Oh, I just wanted some air. And I thought, I saw..." her voice trailed off. She looked down toward where she had bent over to pick up whatever the object on the ground was, but she did not see it now. Ryan made a face in the shadowy light.

"Seriously, Ryan, I am pretty sure I'm losing my mind. You can cut your losses right now and go."

"You're a painter. You're supposed to be crazy, Ella."

She grimaced at him as he brushed past her. She couldn't help but notice how wonderful he smelled. Again. Because apparently she might like him and was pretty sure she should not like him. *Whatever. Blah.*

They went back upstairs to the door she had not bothered to lock this time. *Because clearly locking it DID NOT matter,* she thought quite sarcastically. Her mood was taking a downward swing and she did not want it to. *After all, I am having my first somewhat... tawdry?... encounter.* This was supposed to be an exciting night, not an aggravating one.

"So, does trying to go on dates always suck this much?" Ella asked with an obviously tragic tone of voice.

"Yep, pretty much," Ryan replied. "Though this one has been far more interesting than sushi and a movie."

"I've never been one for sushi. Other Japanese food, but not sushi."

"Well," Ryan said, "people seem to like it, and I try to like people. Not always successfully, however."

"Date much, do you?" she threw herself into a chair and figured she'd roll with the questions and see what happened.

"Um, first off, that seems like a trick question." He sat down, and Ella stuck her tongue out at him, making him smile. "But I have tried to go on dates and it's not the greatest sometimes. But I have made a few friends, which is also not the worst. How about you? You go on a lot of dates? Between doing all your art, going to garage sales, and working at the club?"

"You forgot fainting. Fainting takes up a lot of my time as well. And no, I do not go on dates much. I don't think I've been asked out on too many." She cocked her head to the side to think it through. "It's hard to know if someone is just hitting on you in a club, or if they are genuinely interested in you."

"But I met you at the club. Why did you agree to see me?"

"Well you tried to help me, right? Don't I owe you?" Her voice was comically innocent and deadpan, and Ryan could not tell if she was serious.

"What? First, you were doing fine on your own. And good grief, I hope that's not why you said yes." He stood up and looked down at her very sincerely.

"I'm kidding. I just said yes to get back at that girl." She met his eyes with a playful look that got him to sit back down. "Mostly I like your glowy clothes."

"My glowy clothes?" Ryan looked down at his black pants and silver top.

"Yeah, whatever that material is that you wear. It's really cool and sometimes looks like it's glowing."

He had no response to this, though he looked incredibly solemn.

"Ryan, I said yes for lot of reasons. You seem nice, we ran into each other again, you made a point to check on me again at the club, and, you know, other stuff."

"Mostly I'm curious about that 'other stuff' statement." He leaned back and folded his hands in his lap, as though waiting for her to explain.

"The other stuff you don't get to know yet without you telling me some things about yourself. Do you want something to drink? I made tea."

"Tea sounds great. What do you want to know?"

"Ryan, that is an annoying question. Begin at the beginning and go on till you come to the end: then stop."

"Alice."

"Yes." She went to the kitchen and poured tea. She brought the porcelain delft teacups to the living room, set them on the table, folded her legs under herself, tried not to groan at her complaining knees, and watched as he picked up the cup.

"So much blue. Blue everywhere. It suits you." Ryan sipped a bit of tea, and Ella continued to sit in silence.

"Okay, I am not used to talking about myself, I think. I don't tell people too much. I don't know that they would want to hear it."

"That's pretty judgmental," Ella pointed out.

"How so?"

"You assume people don't want to hear about you. Do you assume that they are that selfish? Or has each person actually said to you that they don't want to know anything about you?"

"No, it's not that. I don't think I've ever looked at it that way. I guess I just don't want to dump a tale of woe on someone."

"I asked for your tale of woe, so you can't assume any longer that I don't want to hear it."

"Fair enough. Let's see... I am not from here. I left home a few years ago because... well, let's just say that my relationship with my father was tumultuous, and I was tired of it. I felt like I was not getting anywhere with him. My mom is alright but she is so afraid of... a lot, that it got hard to tell her anything anymore."

"I occasionally take classes at the university, and I've taken a lot of online courses. Those I prefer because I like to study on my own. I am not entirely sure what I want to focus on in school, so that is something I struggle with, and it made my father decidedly displeased with me."

"I haven't gone to school at all," Ella told him. "I don't tell a lot of people that because, well, honestly I have no idea what to study. I like to paint, and sometimes I feel like people hold it against me, and I don't want them to."

"Why do you think that, Ella? Has anyone said that to you specifically?"

"Funny. Actually sometimes they just say sort of bitchy things."

"I guess I can understand that," he said. "My father did not take art seriously at all."

"What does your father do?"

"He's a businessman. He works for a big, fancy medical company. My mom used to write, but she hasn't in a long time and I wish she would. I feel like she misses it, but I think she gave it up for me."

"Yeah, well, I understand moms sometimes do things like that, and you shouldn't feel bad about it, Ryan."

"I don't feel bad about it. Exactly."

Ella frowned at him. "Yes you do."

"Fine, I do. But I don't know what I can do about it. Hey, you know you said the night had gotten even weirder than your broken window and strange doctor guy. What happened?"

"Is that your way of telling me you're done telling me stuff about yourself?"

"Not forever," Ryan told her.

"Fine. When I was downstairs talking to the doctor, we came back up here to talk more and one of my paintings was gone."

"Gone?" Ryan looked round the room. "It doesn't look like any of them are gone."

"Nope. Because that's the even more ridiculous part of this story. It was back when I woke up, which means someone was in here while I was asleep, and that does not amuse me in any way." She dropped her cup onto the saucer and it shook, splashing tea over the sides.

"No, I would imagine that is not amusing."

"It's been an alarming few days to say the least. I don't do much besides work and paint, and I'm often just fine with that being my life."

"Does it get lonely?"

"I guess it could if I let it. But I went to a private school full of girls, and everyone was always in everyone's business. It's nice to have my own space, and usually no one gets into my business. I do have one friend, whom I miss a lot." That surprised her. She didn't know why she told him that piece of information.

"Why don't you get back in touch with her?"

"It's not that simple."

"What do you mean? Is it because you're a weirdo? I'm sure she'd be happy to hear from you. You're alright." He said it lightly, but Ella's face darkened as he joked.

"It's. NOT. THAT. SIMPLE."

"I'm sorry, Ella. I was just kidding." He moved over to couch next to her and sat down stiffly. He put his hand over hers. "Tell me why it's not that simple."

"No."

"You should tell me. Have you told anyone?"

"No."

"You should tell me."

"Why?"

"Because, Ella, I care, and want to know about your life. Even the parts that suck. Maybe even especially those parts."

His hand was so warm she felt the heat creeping into her chest and into her cheeks. The heat was perplexing, and she pulled her hand out from under his.

"I'm sorry," he said. "I didn't mean to invade your space." He went back to the other couch.

"No, it's okay. I know you're just trying to be nice. It's just hard to even think about her, and I've talked so much about myself today I feel overwhelmed by it.

Sometimes I also talk about things from the past and I don't feel like I'm talking about my life. I guess that's a stupid thing to say, but it just feels so surreal sometimes. It's probably the painkillers that make my head swim."

"Why do you take painkillers?"

"I take them because I suffer from chronic pain in my joints, and no one seems to know why."

"I'm sorry. I would never have thought something like that because you are so young, and clearly you work a lot."

"Yes, and I can't let the pain control my life, can I? I try to avoid the pills as long as possible, but it's not always easy, and sometimes the agony is too much. It's one of the reasons why I want to get to know the doctor, I guess. He thinks he might be able to help me."

"He does? Huh."

"What?"

"What what?"

"Don't answer a question with a question, Ryan. You know what. You're making that face you made when you first saw the doctor. The one that makes me think you know him."

"I don't know him. Like I said, I don't necessarily trust doctors."

"I have nothing to lose at this point."

"Don't say that, Ella. You always have something to lose."

"What do you mean by that?"

"I mean be careful, Ella, that's all."

"Okay, now I'm positive there is something you're not telling me."

"There's lots I haven't told you yet, Ella."

"This is fun. These circular comments."

"I'm not trying to be evasive, Ella."

"Yes, you are. It's fine. We just met. I'm just wound up tight right now."

"I can go if you want."

"No. Actually it's nice to have the company, and I doubt after waking up and finding my painting back in the apartment that I am going to sleep much tonight, anyway."

"What would you like to do?"

"Let's just veg out. I'll put on a movie. Is that okay?"

"Yeah, that sounds great, actually. Talking, not great at it. Sitting and not talking, super great at it."

"Me too." Ella put in a movie and sat back on the sofa. Ryan sat on the opposite end.

The next thing she knew it was morning and the television was still on. Ryan had fallen asleep as well and was leaning on the arm, sleeping sitting up. He looked illuminated in the sunlight streaming through the window. His blonde hair was lustrous. She watched for a moment more and then put her hand on his arm. He stirred slightly.

"That was great a movie," he joked.

"Yes. I liked the three minutes I watched, as well. Do you want to go get some coffee?"

"Only if you promise to faint and make a scene," he sat up and ran his hands through his hair, fluffing it up in a way that made Ella, without thinking, reach up and smooth it down. She quickly jerked her hand away. Ryan smiled at her.

"Sorry. Geez, like I'm your mom." She moved to stand up, and Ryan grabbed her wrist, gently. She wanted to yank it away. *I am so bad at boys.*

"Thanks for letting me come over." His voice was soft and serious. Ella did not care for it.

"You're welcome," she said in an obnoxiously loud tone, and pulled away. "Let's get some caffeine before you regret being around me this early in the day." He chuckled and they started putting on their shoes to leave. She pulled on the gloves that she had taken off before going to bed.

"You're going to have to tell me where the gloves came from." He laced his boot and stood up, face-to-face with her.

"Do I? I'm not sure I need to tell you anything else until I get a little more background on this guy who slept on my couch. You have the dubious honor of being the first of the male species to spend the night in my apartment."

"I do not consider that a dubious honor," he said as she locked the door.

The sun was rising higher in the sky, and the streets were slowly coming awake with people getting on their way to work and school. The clouds were clearing out, and it was cool, but not so cool that it was uncomfortable. *It is quiet and normal feeling out in the world,* she thought, as they walked to the coffee shop. Neither of them were talking much but to point out flowers and funny things here and there. They got to the coffee shop and Ryan reached to open the door. As he did so, the blonde girl from a few nights ago was walking out.

"Hi, Ryan." She flipped her hair and walked up to him. "Thanks for holding the door open for me."

Her voice is impressively flirtatious for so early in the morning. I'm pretty sure I sound grumpy as hell. Ella wiggled her nose and cleared her throat.

"You're welcome, Megan. But I didn't really hold it open for you." Ryan turned in Ella's direction, much to her surprise. He was being super snarky and it made her twinge happily.

Megan glared at them both, "Whatever," and stomped off as much as she could in her precariously high heels.

"I told you she was annoying," Ryan said, and exaggeratedly bowed as Ella walked through the door. She shook her head at him.

"You're sort of ridiculous, you know that, Ryan?"

"Indeed, I do. Anyway, let's get some caffeine lest I see this beast that lives inside your 'mild-mannered painter' facade." He kept up with the silly formal tone and went to order them drinks. Ella went to sit in a booth and watched him from across the room.

For what felt like the thousandth time, she thought, *He is super cute and he seems so, so... I don't know what word to use. Shiny?* And thus she rolled her eyes at herself as Ryan came back over to the table.

"How could I possibly deserve an eye roll from all the way over there? I mean, maybe, my walk is pretty stuck up." He slid into the chair in front of her.

"Ha. The eye roll was for me. Because I am melodramatic and sort of, just..." she trailed off.

"Funny? Talented? Beautiful? Any of those the words you're looking for?" He sipped his coffee.

"Not quite," she tugged her sleeve down and picked up the coffee with black cotton-covered hands.

"I do like the gloves," he said.

"I started wearing them because I always have paint on my hands," she said. *Well, that wasn't completely untrue*

"Ah. Too busy to wash. I understand."

"It takes a lot of time to paint as much as I do, as you know. And of course, bar-tending is an art in and of itself that requires clean hands and a focused mind."

"True. I have had my fair share of the artistic cocktails at your fine establishment. Have you worked there a long time?"

"A couple of years. I graduated high school just after my seventeenth birthday. Though I wasn't at the actual school anymore. My, uh, condition made it hard for me to be in class regularly, so I finished by correspondence." *Also, mostly true.* She just left out the part about the headmistress pressuring her, and Alexandra's disappearance, and how the depression overwhelmed her and she didn't want to be around anyone anymore. *Yep, left those parts out.* Ryan did not need all this first thing in the morning. *I don't even need it.* She crumpled a napkin in exasperation.

"You were still so young," Ryan said in an admiring voice.

"I guess. I went to school in a place where there were a fair amount of girls who moved out of high school education much earlier than your average student. They had a lot of expectations on them to succeed. Not me, though. No expectations on me. Anyway, at least tell me how old you are, Ryan."

"I am twenty-two. I live about thirty-five minutes from you in a renovated loft space that is pretty cool. I like puppies, kittens, and conveniently my favorite color is blue."

"That *is* convenient. I happen to like blue as well. Tell me more about your family."

"Hmmmm... I am a tremendous disappointment to them," Ryan said it very casually.

"If I knew anything about my parents, I have no doubt I'd be a tremendous disappointment to them as well. So we have that in common, too."

"You don't know your parents at all?"

"Not even a little bit." She sipped coffee and averted her eyes. The doctor was at the counter, placing an order. He hadn't noticed them yet. *I wonder if Ryan will be crazy again if he comes over.*

"I'm sorry you don't know your parents. That sounds like a hard way to grow up."

"I guess. I don't really think about it anymore. I had a really great teacher at school who helped me a lot. And my friend Alexandra."

"Is she the one you mentioned last night? I'm just wondering. I don't want to upset you by bringing up something you don't want to talk about."

"It's okay. I'm sorry I'm so defensive about it. The truth is that I would like to find her, but I think part of my problem is that I don't know where to start."

"I would guess we could start with the Internet." Ryan pulled out his phone. "What is her name?"

"Wait? You're going to help me? And anyway, I've already searched the Internet. I haven't been able to find anything."

"You haven't searched the Internet the way I would."

"That's an odd statement, Ryan. What in the world does that mean?"

Before he could answer, the professor had spotted them and came over to the table, holding a cup that had steam rising from it.

"Hello, Ella. Nice to see you here again. It really is the only place around here I can get a decent cup of tea besides my office." The professor smiled at her.

"Hi, Dr. Reynolds. You remember Ryan?"

"Of course. Hello again."

Ryan didn't respond, just stared intently at his phone. Ella did not like that at all.

"How are you this morning, Professor?" She wasn't going to let Ryan's rudeness interfere with talking to her new friend.

"Actually, I am quite glad to have run into you this morning. I was hoping you could stop by my office again soon. Do you remember where it is?"

"Yes. Despite the pouring rain and the guy snatching your papers and the giant bruise on my tailbone, I haven't forgotten about your office."

"Yes, I suppose it made quite the impression. Are you free this afternoon, by any chance?"

"Um, yes, later I should be. I do need to go to the club to talk to my boss, but I could meet up with you after 4 or so?"

"Great. I'll see you then. Nice to see you again, Ryan." Ryan just looked up at the professor and said nothing. The professor shrugged his shoulders at Ella and left the coffee shop.

"You know, I realize you said you don't like doctors but he is also a person. You don't have to be rude." Ella felt herself getting a little mad. "Keep your secrets but don't take them out on people." She got up to leave.

"Ella, wait. I'm sorry. I am really sorry. You're right. Please sit back down."

"Why are you acting like that? You know, I don't know if I can try and hang out with someone who won't tell me about their life."

"Okay, I will tell you that I remember reading about the professor in the news. About him testing on kids without permission. That's horrible. I was a sick kid. I can't even think about the pain that must have caused those families."

"Those charges were never proven, Ryan."

"That doesn't mean it didn't happen."

"I don't think it did happen, Ryan."

"How well do you know him, Ella? You just met him."

"I did just meet him, and I think you shouldn't judge people until you get to know them. So if you have a real reason to not like him or trust him, I will listen to you. But if you do not, I am going to assume he *is* innocent of the charges of which he was proven innocent." She knew she sounded angry and sarcastic, but this really rubbed her the wrong way.

"Just be careful, Ella." He stood up. "I'm sorry I upset you. I'll see you around."

And he left abruptly. Again.

Chapter 8

After Ryan left her at the coffee shop, Ella decided to head to the club to talk to her boss about taking some time off to get ready for the show. She had never asked him for vacation time before and was really hoping it was not going to be a big issue.

She had no idea what to do about Ryan. It did not feel great that it seemed like things just went really badly between them. She did feel as though he was being unfair to the professor. She wanted to empathize with Ryan because of her physical problems, but not all the people who had tried to help her had failed. *It's not like they were doing it on purpose.*

Ryan seemed to think there was some sort of evil force behind all doctors. She certainly did not think it was fair for him to assume the doctor had done all those things of which he was accused. He hadn't tried to hide any of them. Still, something was not sitting right about Ryan. Something beyond feeling bad about the last twenty-four hours. All the things that happened, and now his behavior towards the professor, twice no less, being so odd. She was absolutely positive there was more to it. What she wasn't sure of was if she should worry about it at all. They had only just met, and their time together had been tumultuous.

She got to the club, which was closed since it was the middle of the day, and she had to dig out her key to get in. Going in through the side door and crossing the dance floor to get to the back where the employee lockers were, she noticed some of the chairs for the tables on the edge of the bar were turned over. Ella went over to pick them up and straighten the things that had been knocked over. It was very quiet in the normally loud environment. Her boss was usually there during the day making phone calls, restocking, and doing paper work. She wondered if she had come in on the one day he had taken off.

She went back to put her stuff in a locker and to look for a notebook she had left there the last time she worked.

"What in the world?" Ella walked around in disbelief. The locker room was destroyed. The lockers were tipped over, locks broken, and the contents spilling out all over the floor. Makeup was mashed on the floor, clothes were strewn everywhere, shoes were tossed in the trash. Forgetting about her stuff, she ran to the office looking for her boss. She found him unconscious on the floor.

"Oh my god!" Ella ran over to him and bent down to see if he was breathing. There was blood on the floor near his head. It looked like he had been hit with something.

"Are you okay? Wake up! Please wake up!" She nudged him gently. Not sure what to do she ran to the freezer for ice and grabbed a wet cloth.

She dabbed his wound carefully with the cloth and tried to hold the cool ice on the top of his chest. He started to stir a bit.

"Ella?" he managed to croak out. "What are you doing here?"

"What? Are you okay? What happened? I came to talk to you." She kept dabbing his head with the cloth as he tried to sit up. "What happened? The locker room is destroyed, and then I came in here to tell you and found you on the floor."

He pulled himself up with Ella's help and leaned against the desk.

"There were a couple of guys. They looked familiar to me but I'm not sure why yet. They came in here asking about you, Ella." He looked at her with a worried, fatherly look on his face. A look she was getting tired of seeing. *What is going on? Does this have anything to do with the professor?*

"They were asking what about me?"

"Ella, they were asking about strange things like where you came from. They wanted me to tell them about you. And, Ella, I didn't tell them anything."

"Yeah I kind of would've guessed you didn't, since they knocked you out."

"Why are they looking for you? Do you know who they are?"

"I don't know who they are or why they would want to know where I came from. That's a seriously creepy question."

"Ella, if you're in trouble and need help, you know I'll help you. Just tell me what to do. You said you came here to talk to me?" He struggled to his feet and sat in the desk chair.

"I came here to talk to you because I have good news. But that doesn't really seem important at the moment."

He started to laugh and it seemed so preposterous that Ella started to laugh. They laughed for a couple of minutes before catching their breath. *I am laughing like a maniac a lot lately. Better than crying I suppose.*

"I'm serious though, Ella. Are you in trouble?"

"I don't know why I could be. I have had a few strange encounters the last few days, but nothing I think would warrant someone trashing the club and kicking you in the head."

"To be fair, they used a bottle."

"Right. Nothing to warrant hitting you in the head with a bottle."

"Wait..." he blinked his eyes as if trying to clear a foggy memory of sorts. "Your strange encounters? I'm pretty sure one of the guys that came here was that guy that grabbed your arm and made the bottle fall on you a couple of days ago."

Ella dropped the cloth on the table and stared at him in shock.

"Uh, okay? That is super-duper creepifying. Why would he break into the club? Did I really make him that angry?"

"I don't know, but he's the one who hit me with the bottle. The guy in the suit is the one who kept asking me questions. Except..." his voice trailed off.

"Except what?"

"This is probably just the blow to the head talking, but it was like the guy in the suit kept disappearing."

"He kept disappearing?"

"Yes, he would ask me a question, and I would tell him where to stick it. And then he would be gone."

"He would be gone? I don't understand? Like he would leave the room?"

"No, not leave the room. Just be gone."

"I have no idea what to say to that. Would the other guy be 'gone' too?"

"No he was always there. Delightful fellow that one. Chewing on a toothpick and hitting people with bottles. You meet this friend of yours before?"

"Only a couple nights ago. And I have no idea who he is or why he would be assaulting you with your inventory. But the guy in the suit, he might be someone I've seen before."

"You've seen him before? Where have you seen him, Ella? These people are dangerous, whoever they are, and we should go to the police about them."

"I think he's been following me, and yeah, you should call the police about them breaking into the club. But I don't have any proof that he's been following me."

"Well, them asking questions about you is certainly a place to start. You said the locker room was trashed. Do you think they were looking in your stuff?"

"I didn't have much in there. A change of clothes, a toothbrush, my notebook." Realizing what she just said, she ran out of the office, her boss calling after her, and went into the locker room.

She tried to push the lockers up by herself until he followed her into the room and they lifted them up together. There was stuff scattered everywhere and she started to dig through it as quickly as she could. Her boss was picking up everything she discarded and making neat piles of it.

"I called the police and they are probably going to want to ask you questions."

"Fine. I don't have to be anywhere until later."

"Ella, what are you looking for?"

"I'm looking for my stuff. I found my gloves and my shoes, but I can't find my notebook or my other clothes."

He bent over to help her finish picking everything up from the floor and folding all the clothes.

Her clothes and notebook were most definitely gone.

"We'll have to report that to the police," he told her, as he reached for a broom to sweep up the broken containers.

Ella sat down hard on a bench and looked at her boss.

"This is so weird. This week has been so WEIRD."

"Ella, what's your good news?"

"How's your head?"

"I have a bit of a headache, but I'll be fine. Stop changing the subject. I want to hear your good news."

"I got an art show."

"For your painting? That is not good news. That is WONDERFUL news." He dropped the broom on the floor and pulled Ella up into a giant bear hug. She couldn't help but hug him back. "I'm so proud!"

She laughed. "I still have to pull it off."

He let her go and ruffled her hair. "You can absolutely do it. I will have to come to see it. I will bring the girls and the wife. She will be happy to hear it, too."

"I came to ask you if I could use some vacation days. I know it's really last minute, but I think I have some."

He held up his hand. "You have plenty, and you can use as many as you want to do your show. I do hope at some point you'll take a trip somewhere, but this is important, too."

"Thanks. I think the police are here. I heard a knock at the door."

"Let's go answer their questions."

"Are you going to tell them about the man disappearing?"

"Well, Ella, I suppose I could, and I suppose I could also have them take me to a funny farm. I'm sure I just imagined it. I was surprised and angry. Come on."

They went to the front of the club and let in the officers, who searched the building and around the grounds to see if they could find anything. They did not, and they kept Ella there until it was time for her to go see the professor. Luckily it was not a long walk. As she was leaving she could've sworn she saw the man in the suit standing across the street, but when she looked again he wasn't there.

Being beyond confused at this point was an understatement, and Ella knew even less what to do about it. *I certainly have some more questions for the professor,* she thought, as she reached the school and made her way to his office. He was speaking with a student when she arrived, so she waited outside as he finished up.

At the end of the long hallway of offices and classrooms that were starting to empty of students, she saw Ryan walking with the girl from her building. They were both laughing. *So much for her being annoying.*

The professor finished with his student, came out to the hall, and welcomed Ella in.

"Is something wrong, Ella?" He took off his glasses and rubbed them on his shirt.

"Quite possibly," she said, her mind on Ryan. *Which it SHOULD NOT BE.*

"Care to elaborate at all?" He sat down on his desk facing her. He crossed his arms and waited, not impatiently.

"So that man in the suit that might be following me, possibly because of you?"

"Yes?"

"It appears he has stepped up his insistence of introductions."

"What in the world do you mean by that?"

"I mean he broke into my workplace, and with the help of a friend of his–a really nice sort of guy who harassed me at work the other night before I even ran into you and made the highly questionable decision to tell you about my life–assaulted my boss and stole some of my things. And, oh yeah, there's a bunch of makeup that didn't survive the attack either."

"Oh my. Is your boss okay?"

"He's okay, kind of angry. He said they kept asking him where I came from?"

"Hmmm... It might be possible that it's not tied to me, Ella."

"How do you figure? No one else has told me they have deep, dark, albeit highly public secrets, complete with angry people wanting answers. Just you."

"I'm highly honored to be sure, but you said that one of the men was bothering you at work before you ran into me that night."

"Oh wait, you're right. That could just be coincidence. Why in the world would anyone be following me?"

The professor said nothing as he got up and closed the door to the classroom and then the door to the office.

He turned back to Ella. "You do seem to have a bit of an extraordinary secret."

"I guess, but no one really knows that, and I don't even know what that secret is, and neither do you. Isn't that why I'm here? So we can start figuring this out?"

"I haven't put much time into it yet, that is true. But I have put some time into it, and, of course, I have spent a lot of time researching the many things that can make people sick. I've started to form some theories."

"I see. What theories would those be, exactly?"

"Your body, for some reason, is producing an unknown compound."

"Right, I guess. I know this, but I wouldn't have necessarily put it that way."

"I am going to assume that the production of this compound is what causes your pain. Can you tell me a little bit more about it? Do you have to go anywhere for a bit?"

"As it happens I do not have to go anywhere for a bit. I took some time off to do an art show."

"Great. All great. Let's talk a little. Tell me about your pain."

"Excellent! Super-fun conversation topic."

"Ella, I need to know these things if we're going to move forward."

"I know, fine. My joints are the worst, and sometimes I feel as though I can't even move."

"Now, I wonder if the compound pools around your joints."

"Whatever it's doing, it hurts a lot, and then I can't sleep so I take painkillers, and then I feel like I'm disconnected from everything. I can't remember things correctly, and they give me intense dreams. People tried to help before, but they often thought I just might have some kind of undiagnosed disease. I've never had health insurance, so that hasn't really been a great help. Plus, I don't think anyone knows about the uh, the whatever... the compound."

"I imagine they would not know what it is. I don't yet, and I would not have thought to test the way that I did, except that you showed me that it came from your hands."

"I don't think it's just my hands. See, I wear dark colors all the time because I like them, yes. But also because if I get wet or sweat, you can um, tell... that I am not like other people. The compound is just different from my hands. More concentrated? I don't know if that's the right word, but I can use it and manipulate it."

"Manipulate it? That is very interesting. Have you done anything with it?"

"Yes." Ella looked off behind his head.

"Would you mind telling me what you've done with it?"

"I paint with it. Sometimes I don't even have to use brushes."

"You paint with it? That is very interesting, indeed. I didn't think it was so easy to manipulate."

"It's not always. I sort of found out by accident that I could paint. I mean who thinks to paint with anything that comes from their body? Seems sort of gross, right?" Ella looked at the professor.

"I don't know that it's gross, Ella. This is clearly not a regular body secretion," he said, and she made a face, "if you'll forgive the word. I know it seems odd to you, but my going theory at the moment is that you manufacture something. I don't know what or why, but that's what we are going to try and figure out."

"I manufacture something?"

"Yes. It's just a guess at this point, and I've barely begun to study you. I'll have to do a lot of tests, and to be completely upfront with you, they are not always going to be pleasant. There will be needles. Possibly sitting for a period of time hooked up to machines to monitor your heart rate, body temperature, things such as that."

"If there's a chance you can actually figure out what's wrong with me, I'll take it."

"There is a chance, but there is also the chance that I won't be able to. You have to know that as well."

"Fair enough. When can we start?"

"How about now?" He got up and opened another door which Ella hadn't previously noticed. "This my private lab."

"Do all teachers get a private lab?" She got up, crossed over to the door, and peeked inside. It was a very nice lab. White, clean, up-to-date equipment.

"No, not all the teachers get a private lab. You have to test history, dates, and verbs the old-fashioned way."

"Funny. But seriously, this is nice," she said as she stepped inside. "Nicer than most of the doctors' offices I've been in."

"Yes, well, I did make a lot of money at the company I worked for before I left." He busied himself turning on machines, and Ella thought there seemed to be a somewhat bitter note in his words.

"I read a bunch of articles like you suggested," she told him in a neutral voice.

"I'm surprised you still came to meet me." He looked at her directly.

"The charges were dropped, and I couldn't help but notice it was when the first owner wasn't around anymore that the accusations started."

"Believe me, Ella, when I tell you that is not by chance." He went back to turning things on and getting out tools. He handed her a folder that was filled with papers. "Fill out this medical history as best as you can, please."

"I don't know anything about my parents." She sat in a chair and started to look through them.

"Fill out whatever you can. Your situation is unique enough that we pretty much should start from scratch anyway. There may not be a case or another person anywhere that has characteristics like you."

"Awesome. I'm a freak. Not that I didn't already know that," she mumbled, more to herself than to him.

"Let's not say 'freak.' There are somewhere near seven billion people on this planet. There are bound to be things we don't know yet or haven't happened yet." He said that cheerfully, and she could not decide if she should be weirded out by that or comforted by his curiosity.

"My friend Ryan doesn't trust you. He keeps telling me to be careful."

"Your friend is just looking out for you, and he's right." He smiled at her. "Someone who really cares about you will always offer the advice of caution when caring for oneself."

"I guess I hadn't looked at it from that point of view. I'm sorry he was so rude to you. I think he's had some bad experiences with doctors." Ella held out her arm as he wrapped it to take her blood pressure.

"There are some bad doctors out there. Chances are good that he has had bad experiences. I feel terrible for him. He's so young." He took off the blood pressure wrap and wrote something down. "Your blood pressure is very low. That is good."

"I am pretty young." She arched an eyebrow at him.

"Sometimes when people are in chronic pain, it is my experience that they have high blood pressure," he explained as he listened to her heart. "The first thing we are going to do is eliminate all the negative things you could be suffering from. Such as irregular heartbeat, but that sounds good as well. I'm glad for these things, Ella. It can make our work easier. Now relax in that chair as much as you can."

For the next few hours he did a series of tests. Some she had before, such as reflexes, checking her eyes and ears, as well as drawing blood. But others no one had done before, such as stretching her joints, measuring them, and of course soaking her hands in warm water in order to produce the silvery-blue compound that started the entire inquiry. Ella and the doctor mostly did not speak as he worked, only to answer short questions here and there about how much pain she might feel and what medications she was taking. He had put on some classical music in the background, and as Ella waited in-between the testing and filling out more forms, she was lulled into a light sleep. She could hear the beeping of the monitor that was keeping track of her heart rate as she drifted off and the music faded into the distance.

The dream was of school again. It was the day they took Alexandra away. The headmistress told everyone Alex had a nervous breakdown under the stress of graduating, but Ella knew this was a lie. Something had been done to her friend. She knew it. But she couldn't prove it. Overnight Alex had gone from her gregarious, excitable self, who had all the grandest plans for revenge and fun, to a babbling, incoherent wreck that didn't even seem to recognize Ella. Ella was positive the headmistress had something to do with it. The entire school, it seemed, was out to watch as they took Alex away in a black van to who knows where. Ella was beyond angry. She didn't care anymore what the headmistress hung over her. After the van drove away, the woman came and put her hand on Ella's shoulder. She jerked away and turned to glare at the woman.

Angry tears ran down Ella's face as she confronted the frigid, hard woman in front of all the students.

"I know you did this," Ella screamed at her. The headmistress could have been a statue for how little she moved.

"Keep your voice down, Miss Cerulean," the headmistress turned to everyone in the halls watching. "The show is over. I suggest all of you get back to your classes now. Anyone caught discussing this event will be suspended." Everyone went back to their classrooms, student and teachers alike, except for Ella.

"What did you do to Alex?" Ella's tone had dropped a notch as she felt a rage simmering underneath her skin, desperately wanting to scream at this woman until she got some answers.

The headmistress walked to Ella and looked her straight in the eye.

"Miss Cerulean, I helped Alexandra. She has become a threat to this school and to herself."

The headmistress did not blink. She never blinked. She was inhuman.

"You don't help anyone but yourself, and I am going to find out what you did if it's the last thing I do." Ella gripped her hands in fists. Her anger was so close to boiling over. An incredibly irrational part of her wanted to slap the headmistress. Ella had never felt the urge to strike someone before.

"Be careful what you wish for, Miss Cerulean. Threats are not taken lightly in this school." She lowered her voice so only Ella could hear her, "I would think you would take your friend's expulsion as a warning. Think of all her family provided this school, and they couldn't protect her. You provide nothing but problems for this school. You have nothing to hide behind. Now I suggest you return to your room and clean yourself up, or I will suspend you and you can finish your classes during the summer break."

"Do you think I care if you suspend me? You already made sure I had no future in school, didn't you?" Ella's voice was rising again.

"You gave me no choice." The headmistress flicked an imaginary piece of dust off her pristine white clothing.

Ella was about to step closer to the woman when Miss Magritte stepped between them.

"Ella," the teacher said calmly to her. "Ella, look at me." Ella hesitated before acknowledging her friend and mentor.

"What?" Ella snapped.

"Ella, let's go to your room. You are understandably upset."

"This horrible woman did something to Alexandra."

"I know she did, Ella."

That got Ella's attention. She blinked at the teacher. "You don't think I'm crazy?"

"Of course not, I never have. But fighting with her is not going to fix anything. Come on, let's go to your room." She put her hand on Ella's tensed fist and tried to pull her away. It took a minute before Ella relented and started to pull back from the headmistress.

"Well, it's nice to see you doing your job for once, Miss Magritte," the headmistress snapped at her in a haughty tone. "I was starting to wonder what we paid you for."

The teacher dropped Ella's hand for a moment and turned to face the woman.

"You are not starting to wonder what you pay me for because you do not pay me. You think you can frighten me like you torture these poor kids? I am not afraid of you, you horrible, dreadful woman. I know you did something to that poor girl. I will find out what, and I will have no problem exposing you to the world for the monster you are and the awful things you use this school to do."

"Don't overstep your bounds. I can have you removed from teaching." The headmistress was so confident that Ella wanted to scream. *Who does these things?*

"Go ahead and try." The teacher turned away from the headmistress and led Ella down the hall to the stairs that led to the students' rooms. Ella did not want to go back to the room that she had shared with Alex. It would be so empty without her. But she let her teacher lead her there anyway. It was better than facing anyone in class.

When they got to Ella's room and Miss Magritte had shut the door, Ella sat on the bed and stared at the floor. She was only vaguely aware of the teacher wiping her face with a wet washcloth and handing her a glass of water to drink. She could not believe Alex was gone. She could not believe her father had let that woman take his daughter away.

"Why did she do this?" Ella finally managed to stammer out the words and felt the tears start down her face again.

"She did it because she is afraid of Alex. The headmistress only responds to those who threaten her. Alex must have found out something very important for the headmistress to have gone to these lengths to remove her credibility."

"Then we have to find out what it is that is so important. I know she drugged Alex or something. I have to find a way to prove it. Will you please help me?" Ella was ready to beg. She couldn't figure this out on her own.

"Yes, I will help you. I have about had it with the immoral behavior of that wretched woman." She sat down next to Ella. "But first you should rest. This is a terrible day for you and for me, and you look exhausted."

"I'm not tired," Ella argued, as her teacher stood up and helped her get out of her uniform and into a sleeping gown.

"I'm sure you're not." She smiled as Ella lay back on the bed.

"My head hurts from crying, but we have to start looking. Who knows how awful it is where they took Alex? It could be the worst place in the world. I can't bear the thought." Ella felt the tears coming again and took a deep breath to try to stop them.

"Rest for a while, Ella. I will start looking into it tonight. And then we'll continue together first thing tomorrow. It's the weekend, so you don't have any classes to worry about."

Tomorrow never came. When Ella woke the next day, Miss Magritte no longer worked at the school, and no one would tell her where the teacher went.

When she woke up the music was still playing softly in the background, and the professor was humming in time as he worked.

"Did I fall asleep?" Ella sat up.

"Only for a little while," he said to her, and smiled.

Feeling somewhat unsettled by the dream and her surroundings, she pulled herself to the edge of the seat.

"Do you need to ask me any more questions today, Doc? Because I think I'd just like to go home now. It must be getting pretty late."

"You've been asleep for about ninety minutes or so, which gave me some time to run a few tests. I really disagree with the heavy number of painkillers I am finding present in your bloodstream. You're too young for such things to be bogging down your system."

"I don't even take them as often as prescribed."

"Who prescribed them for you?"

"I don't know. One of the nurses at my school had it done a long time ago, and the prescription is renewed automatically without any work on my part."

The professor came over to her and unhooked her from the monitor.

"That is extremely unusual," he told her. "I think I have something I want you to try. I believe it will alleviate some of your pain, though not all of it. But the added benefit is that it won't make you groggy. You shouldn't feel that detachment you described to me. I will be up front with you and tell you that this is an experimental drug, something I've only begun testing, and there could be side-effects."

"There have been side-effects my whole life, and if you think it's better than the stuff I am taking, I don't see why I shouldn't give it a try."

"Very well, then." He went to work putting together a bottle for her. She gathered herself together and got ready to leave.

"There is one other thing, Ella. When you were asleep you said a name."

"Oh?" She felt her guard go up. She wanted to trust him, but she was not sure if she was ready to tell him all her secrets. *I don't even want to know them.*

"Yes. Who is Alexandra?" He handed her a bag and she looked away from him.

"She was a friend of mine." Fighting to keep the tears back, she swallowed the words hard.

"You seemed to be under a great deal of distress by whatever you were dreaming about. Do you want to tell me about it?"

"Not especially."

"It could be helpful. Stress can be a great indicator of the origins of illness."

"Can we do it next time? It's been a long day."

"Yes, fine. That sounds just fine. Take those twice a day at first. Come see me in two days and we'll see where to go from here."

"Thank you," said Ella, and started toward the door.

"Ella?"

"Yes?" She turned back around to him.

"You said 'was.' Is she not your friend anymore?"

Ella sighed heavily and felt all her hardened protection fall.

"She disappeared when I was in school. She supposedly had a nervous breakdown and was sent to a care facility, but I don't know where. I have never been able to get help finding her, and I miss her a great deal. She is the only person who knew about my condition. I mean the real condition. Not just thinking I was sick. She knew I could manipulate the compound."

"I'm sorry."

"It was a long time ago." She shifted from foot to foot uncomfortably. "I'm gonna go now." She turned and left.

The professor stood and stared at the closed door for a few minutes before he picked up the phone. "I need you to find someone for me. A woman. Disappeared when she was a teenager. Supposed nervous breakdown. Her name was Alexandra."

Chapter 9

Ella unlocked the front door to her building, stepped into the lobby, and heard a female voice cry out in pain. A subsequent thump followed from the floor above. She ran up the stairs as fast as she could and came face to face with the man in the suit standing in front of her apartment door and over Ryan's blonde friend, who was lying on the ground, her pretty face contorted in pain.

"What is going on?" Ella yelled, and the man in the suit pushed past her. She turned around just in time to see him disappear. Into the air. Gone. Just like Jack said, he wasn't there anymore.

Hearing a soft groan of misery, Ella turned her attention back to the body lying on the floor, slowly trying to move. This was the second person today she'd found hurt on the floor, and she was very unhappy about it.

"Are you okay? What are you doing up here? Let me call 911." Ella fumbled in her bag for her phone.

"No, I'm okay," the girl croaked out, and sat up carefully. "That creep was trying to break into your apartment. I came up here to bring you a piece of mail that was mistakenly put in my box, and that jerk clocked me."

"Do you want me to call anyone for you?" Ella dropped her stuff on the floor and looked closely at the girl's face. "You're going to have a bruise."

"Yeah, I figured. It's fine. I'll be fine. Are you okay? He was trying to break into your place, and I yelled that I was going to call the cops if he didn't get away from your door. That seemed to annoy him." She sounded genuinely concerned, and Ella suddenly felt badly for their negative interactions before now.

"I'm fine. I haven't been here all day. I don't know why he was trying to break into my apartment." She sat on the floor next to her and leaned against the hallway wall. "It's been a weird day. I'm Ella."

"I know. I'm Megan, but maybe you know that? Have you been with Ryan all day?" Megan asked, as she gingerly touched her face.

Ella wasn't sure what to say. She didn't want the snark to come back between them. When Ella didn't answer, Megan laughed a little bit.

"It's totally fine. I really don't mean to be a such a twit to you. I haven't had the best of luck making friends with other girls. Ryan's just my friend. I used to think we might be more, but he really is just my friend."

"I have not been with him all day." Ella tried to keep her voice neutral. She *did not* want to think about Ryan right now. "Today, my boss was attacked at the club where I work. I have no idea why I am telling you this, other than you should be careful. Everyone around me seems to be in danger for some reason, and I seriously cannot even began to guess why."

"Who knows why people do anything?" Megan joked. "All kidding aside, I think we should call the police. Did you see where the guy ran off to?" She had pulled out her phone and was starting to dial when Ella stopped her.

"I don't think we should bother with the police. They weren't much help at the club. There is someone I do want to talk to about this, but involving the police seems pointless. I guess that sounds stupid, but I didn't see where the guy went, and it doesn't look like he got into my apartment."

"Okay. I'm sure they can't do anything to help me, either." Megan paused. "You should call Ryan to come stay with you, Ella. Don't look so surprised. I would stay with you, but I have to study for a final. I'll be downstairs if you need me." She got up and slowly made her way to the stairs and back to her own apartment.

"Hey," Ella said to her as she walked away. Megan turned around to look at her. "Thank you."

Megan smiled and nodded her head before continuing.

Ella unlocked the door and felt a head-rush as she turned the knob. She stopped and put a hand to her temple. *The man in the suit. I have to find out who he is and what he wants. And how in the world does it seem like he's just disappearing? That's what Jack said. He was just gone.* And that is exactly what Ella just saw. Losing her mind, possibly, but she saw it nonetheless.

Things were definitely complicated. As she was wondering if she should call Ryan, her phone buzzed in her bag. Ella pulled it out and saw a text message from him.

"Megan called me. Do you want me to come over? I'd like to talk, anyway."

Ella didn't really want a bodyguard, but she did want to talk to him. She waited a few minutes before responding, trying to decide what to do.

"I have to work on my show stuff tonight. I would like to talk, too."

She hit send and set about looking to see if anything was out of place in the apartment. Ryan didn't respond, so she called the professor. Not getting an answer from him, she left a voicemail.

"Hello, this is Ella. Apparently the mystery man in the suit tried to break into my apartment. I'm not sure what to do about it, Professor. Give me a call when you get a chance. Thanks." Hanging up the phone, she checked her messages again, but Ryan still hadn't responded. Not wanting to think about any of this stuff anymore, Ella took out a notebook and began to make a list. Ideas had been forming in her head since Evan had asked for thoughts about what to do for the opening. Not knowing how to go about it, she had made up her mind to just write down ideas and take them to him. All he could do was say no at this point. She hoped he wouldn't back out of the show, but she was going to take him the ideas no matter how ridiculous that might come across to him.

No more saying no until you try, she lectured herself. Without noticing, she made notes and sketches for two hours as the apartment grew darker and darker. She flipped on a light and checked her phone again, but there was still no message from Ryan. *Well why did he offer to come over if he wasn't actually going to?*

As she was feeling that tiny bit of rejection she absolutely should not be feeling over someone she just met, there was a knock at the door. She looked at it quickly. Only someone who lived in the building could be there without having been buzzed in by a resident. Setting aside the papers and opening the door, she found Megan standing outside, looking distraught as she supported a Ryan with a very swollen eye.

"Remember how you mentioned everyone around you might be in danger?" Megan asked. She struggled to get Ryan through the door as Ella took his other arm around her neck and helped maneuver him to the couch. "I guess I did not take you too seriously until I went outside to take a walk and found this one laid out by his car."

The girls hoisted Ryan onto the couch and stood staring at him for a minute.

"I'll get some ice," Ella mumbled in a state of shock. Megan bent over Ryan and was saying his name over and over again, trying to get him to focus on her.

He was only somewhat responding, and she was getting louder as the moments passed.

Ella put a towel full of ice on his eye and leaned over him. As she held a hand to his forehead, the faint feeling she had felt on their date started to overcome her, and she stumbled back and forth.

"Are you okay?" Megan had panic in her voice, and dropped her attention from Ryan to grab Ella's arm and steady her. "Do you get faint at the sight of blood?" She helped Ella sit in a chair, as Ryan started to sound more and more coherent.

Ella smiled weakly at her. "What the hell is going on?"

"I was kind of hoping you would know." Megan looked over at Ryan, who sat up and looked around with a confused expression on his face.

"When did I get here? God, my head hurts." Finally noticing the girls, "What happened to your face, Megan? Ella are you okay? You don't look so great. Wait. Did you punch me, Megan?"

Megan glowered at his joke. "Don't flatter yourself." She moved back over to him. "You were on the ground by your car. Which, by the way, is not particularly helpful when I told you to come check on Ella."

"Right, I remember that I decided to come over after Ella texted me, and then you told me about that guy you saw outside the apartment, Megan, and that he hit you. So I wanted to see if you were okay, too. I remember driving over here and someone hitting me. That's it." He held the ice to his eye and looked over at Ella, who had her head resting on the back of the chair.

"What's wrong, Ella? Did you get attacked too? This is so nuts."

Megan went to Ella's fridge, pulled out drinks for all of them, and came to sit back down. Ella lifted her head up and looked right at Ryan.

"Ryan, first off, you look like you're glowing again, and second, I think you make me dizzy. Third, I did not get attacked this time, and I have only the slightest idea what might be going on." She said it flat-toned and matter-of-fact and waited for them to tell her she was insane.

No one said anything. Ella just waited. Ryan had something to tell her. She knew it.

"Tell her." Megan said it quietly but firmly.

"I don't think that's a good idea," he grumbled back at her. "She'll think I'm nuts."

"All of this is nuts," Megan snapped. "Tell. Her."

"Megan, I don't think I should drag her into it." Ryan sounded very unhappy.

"Uh? Hello?" Ella waved her hands in the air. "I'm sitting right here. I can hear you, in case you hadn't noticed, Ryan. I get that we have not known each other long, but you have to admit someone is certainly forcing us to bond over something. And besides, I feel like I'm the one who is nuts. I just said you glow and it's not the first time I've thought that, though it does seem more, more, I don't know... pronounced, today? So, yeah. Nuts."

Ryan still didn't say anything.

Megan looked at Ella. "I'll tell you what I know."

"Don't," Ryan growled.

"She should know what is going on." Megan was starting to sound genuinely angry.

"I will tell her, Megan. Just wait." Ryan got up from the couch, dropping the completely melted ice all over the floor, went to the bathroom, and slammed the door.

"Wow, that ice melted quickly." Ella used the towel to start mopping it up.

"Yeah, um, Ryan's body temp is a little wonky," Megan stuttered out.

Ryan came out of the bathroom and exchanged a look with Megan.

"I'm going to go home," she said to Ella. "But let's check on each other in the morning."

"That's a good idea." Ella leaned over and hugged Megan quickly, who hesitantly returned the gesture after a moment. "Thank you, Megan. I mean it."

"Sure. I'll see you in the morning. Don't be a jackass, Ryan." With that, she left.

Ella snorted a little bit, and Ryan raised his eyebrow at her.

"Why would she call you a jackass?"

"Megan is not one to keep her thoughts to herself. It's an admirable quality, but she can seem a bit harsh. Also, I can be a jackass." This made Ella laugh more, and she was glad that some of tension seemed to be easing. They had a lot to sort out.

"She seems to think we should talk." Ella felt a tad nervous, and she was not entirely sure why. *I guess secrets are a big deal.*

"Yes, well, she is right. We should talk. Let's go sit on your couch, which is becoming my home away from home. I am glad it is such a nice couch." He smiled and touched his hand to her back. The hand was shockingly warm.

"I'm not sure how to explain this," he started, as they settled back. Ella tried to seem like she was comfortable, but really felt like she might die at any moment. Or burp, or snort, or any number of gross, boy-repelling things. They were not far from each other on the cushions, and warmth seemed to be coming off of him in waves. She blinked, trying to focus on his face and his blue-green-yellow eyes. *I've never noticed all those colors before.*

"Do you want more ice for your eye?" she asked suddenly, and wanted to get away from him on the couch. The seconds seemed to be getting intolerable while he gathered his thoughts. She hopped up and started toward the kitchen, but Ryan grabbed her wrist and pulled her back down. Close to him. She pushed herself away. *Inches are like miles or whatever.* She smoothed her hair with a sweaty hand.

"Sorry," he said. "I don't want you to leave before I tell you. I am nervous."

"You're nervous?"

"Yes. I don't tell a lot of people what I'm going to tell you, and when I do tell them they tend to get... weird on me." He wrung his hands as he said it, and then looked her right in the eyes.

"Ella, I think you're great, and I am sorry we had a disagreement over your friend, the professor. Try as I might not to, I hate doctors. I don't want to, but I do. I have had too many bad memories attached to them."

He stopped then, seeming unable to know how to continue. This time Ella reached out and put her hand on his arm. Instantly, she felt her cheeks flush and body temperature rise. It made her pull away again.

Ryan sighed a heavy, sad sigh.

"You're getting really warm when you touch me because I give off radiation of a sort."

"What?" Ella's tone was disbelieving. "How is that even possible?"

"It's not that strange." Now he sounded a little defensive. "Some people have cancer treatments that cause them to carry radiation around with them."

The weight of the words he said hung in the air around them, and she felt a deafening silence fall over the room. Ryan started to fidget uncomfortably.

"See? I told you. People get weird. Maybe I should just go." This time he got up, and Ella grabbed his wrist.

"No, sit down. I'm just... I'm just sorry, and sad, and... wow, that is so much for one person to have to deal with, I understand why you might not like doctors. I'm guessing you've been around them an awful lot."

"My entire life." He hadn't sat back down, but he was holding her hand.

"Tell me more." Ella carefully extracted her hand because the heat from his body was becoming unbearable, but she was not going to say that to him.

"I've been sick as long as I can remember." He started to walk the length of the living room. "This never went over well with my father. I always felt like he thought it was my fault, or something. My mom took care of me, and so did our housekeeper. My father was usually working. He's a busy man. Very important." Ryan's tone had turned sour, and Ella's heart broke at the sound.

"See, no one is exactly sure what is wrong with me. Only that I am sick, and it's probably cancer. My father works in the medical industry. He's not a doctor, but he knows a lot of them, and they are always looking for something to sell. Anything that showed even the slightest bit of promise was tested on me growing up. And I now believe that those experiments made me even more sick than I already was, and it makes me angry. This man who seems to be harassing us could very well work for my father, since I pretty much ran away from home. Not that I am not old enough to leave home, but I did just leave and I didn't tell anyone where I was going. What's more, I am not sorry I did it."

"That's why you don't like the professor."

"He's just like the rest of them." Ryan paced up and down.

"I understand that you might feel that way, but I can't think that way, Ryan." Ella said it softly, hoping it wouldn't make him angry again.

"I know, and I'm sorry it frustrates me. But the thought of what I went through happening to someone else makes me so angry. Especially someone like you."

"Like me? I don't know what you mean by that?"

He stopped in front of her, and she stood up. The look in his eyes was hurt. Ella didn't want to see it but she could not look away either.

"Someone talented and beautiful," his voice was gruff, and his face moved ever so slightly closer to hers.

She cleared her throat and stepped to the side of him. "Thank you, Ryan, those are very sweet things to say."

He clenched his fists and took a deep breath.

"I think Megan is right," his tone was completely different, as if the last few minutes never happened. "We should stick together a bit more. Maybe we can catch this creep, or at least figure out who he might be or what he wants."

"That's all well and good," Ella said, busying herself so she didn't look at him again. "But I have to get ready for the art show. I took time off my job to get ready for it."

"I have a flexible schedule. I can help you. Just tell me what to do."

Ella thought about this for a few minutes, as Ryan took more ice out of the freezer to put on his face.

"I guess I could figure out some stuff for you to do. But, I mean, are we going to be around each other 24/7? How's that going to work? And for how long? We have no clue who this guy is or what he wants."

"Well, probably we should spend some time trying to figure that out. I am pretty good at researching things."

"That's good to hear. I kind of suck at it. Between my boss getting attacked, Megan getting hit, and now this, I'm really at a loss for what to do. This is certainly the most peculiar situation I've ever dealt with."

"You don't seem scared," Ryan said in an admiring tone.

"I guess I am a little scared, but mostly I am just annoyed. I mean, what gives? You just don't go around breaking into places and attacking people. It's really terrible manners," she joked. Things felt heavy again, and she was not going to be able to get anything done if she was worried about walking on eggshells the whole time.

"Megan has been great to me," Ella told Ryan, as she pulled canvas after canvas out of the closet.

"She's really not bad. I wasn't kidding about her being annoying, but clearly that feeling is mutual between us. I cannot believe how much stuff you have painted, Ella." He set down the ice and started to look at the pieces she had pulled out.

"I've been painting for a long time. I'm not super social, and I don't give them away, so the piles have grown a bit large. I'm pretty excited to go through them, actually. I don't remember the last time I really looked at them. I clean them up and keep them organized, but that's it."

She stopped for a moment and watched him as he went through the works.

"Ryan, I really need you to give the professor a chance. He's been okay so far, and completely upfront with me. I know you think this might be because of your father, that man following us, but he also suspects it could have something to do with him and a job he used to have. The one where he was accused of those things we um... argued about. And if he calls back soon, we should go and talk to him."

He didn't say anything right away, he just kept looking through her work. She started to wonder if he heard. *He is six feet away. Of course he heard me. Not* knowing what else to say, she went back to work. About a half-hour passed before he finally responded to her.

"You're right, Ella, and I'm sorry I didn't respond right away. Like I said, doctors rub me the wrong way big time, but we need to make sure that you're safe. The harassment certainly seems to be centered on you."

"Yes. I feel very special," she dead-panned, making him smile. "Alright, Ryan, your first job is to sort those by theme. Space, sea, flower, etc... Got it?"

"Yes ma'am."

They got to work and carried on late into the night again, until Ella decided to go to bed and set Ryan up to sleep on the couch. Before she headed into her room, she texted Megan, who texted her back immediately and said she was fine. Exhausted and overwhelmed, sleep came easily for once.

The next morning when Ella got up, Ryan was gone, but had left a note saying he would meet up with her soon. He'd gone to get his computer.

The professor still hadn't gotten back to her, which was making her apprehensive. It made her start to think that he might have been attacked too. When Ryan got back, they were going to go to the school to see if he was there. This turn of events had her on edge, and she worked hard on making notes for the art show to avoid thinking about it.

It seemed to be taking a long time for Ryan to get back. She decided to go down to Megan's apartment to ask her where he lived so she had a better idea of how long she should expect him to take. She went down one floor, knocked on the door, and Megan answered wearing workout clothes and with her blonde hair pulled back in a braid.

"Hey, Ella, what's up?" She held the door open so Ella could step into the apartment.

"I'm sorry to bug you, Megan, but I have to admit I'm glad you're okay. I was just wondering where Ryan lived. He went to get his computer, but I don't know how long he's been gone because he left while I was sleeping." Ella stopped and noticed the surroundings for the first time. "Oh, wow, Megan. You're a badass." Ella strode around the room in wonder as Megan laughed.

"Yeah, I guess it started off as a way to keep in shape and now it's more of a way I like to live." Megan went to the kitchen and put on water for tea.

The living room was set up as a yoga-studio-slash-martial-arts practice area, with bamboo screens and kanji scrolls. Filling one wall was a collection of Asian swords, and lining the windows were carefully kept bonsai trees. The dining room had mats on the floor and a Japanese table where one would sit on those mats instead of on chairs. The whole place was muted and serene, and it blew Ella away.

"Megan, this is amazing." Ella bent over to take off her shoes.

"It's okay. You can leave your shoes on if you want, but there are slippers over there I keep for guests." Megan pointed, and then proceeded to set out the tea. "And thanks for the compliment, but this place is nothing like your apartment. I didn't mention it last night, but it is the most beautiful place I have ever seen. You know, where a real person lives, not like a castle or whatever." They both laughed and sat down on the floor at the table, where Megan poured them tea.

"So Ryan lives about 45 minutes away or so. I just sent him a text, too. But if we don't hear from him soon, we can go to his place," Megan told her. They drank tea in silence for a few minutes, as Ella continued to marvel at Megan's space.

"So what do you do? Martial arts, yoga?"

"Both," Megan said. "It started as a few-times-a-week exercise regimen, but it made me feel so much better that I adapted more and more of it into my life. Honestly, that guy being able to hit me really surprised me. I don't get into altercations too often, but the few times I have, I've managed to get out of them just fine."

"This may seem strange, but I don't think we are dealing with a regular man. He definitely seems out of the ordinary in more ways than one."

"No, it's not strange. I've met Ryan's father. It was long time ago but he was not what you would call a nice man. If he is looking for Ryan, I would not put it past him to hire some sort of horrible person to track him down."

"Megan, can you tell me a little bit more about Ryan?" Ella asked hesitantly. "I have a hard time getting him to talk to me. I know we just met, but I feel like he is someone who is hard to get to open up at all."

"I understand," Megan said. "I've known him for a long time. I am friends with his cousin, who we don't really see anymore. After Ryan left home, the family that he reached out to sort of abandoned him. Ryan's father has a lot of money and control over most of them. I'd even go as far as to say that some of them are afraid of him. Ryan and I became friends easily. He never went out too much, except to visit his cousin, since he was always in pretty rough shape. I liked him, and I hated seeing him that way."

"What about his mom?" Ella wasn't sure what she should ask, only that she wanted to know more about him.

"His mom is a kind woman, though very timid. She dedicated her life to taking care of Ryan, which actually drove him crazy."

"Yes, he mentioned she used to be a writer."

"She was, but when Ryan got older and sicker he pretty much became her job, other than taking care of Ryan's father's personal business and the family home. Believe me when I say, taking care of that house and Ryan's father is a full time job."

Ella considered all this for minute, and as she tried to think of her next question, Megan's phone buzzed.

"Ryan says he's on his way back here and is stopping for coffee. Do you want any?" Megan asked her. Ella nodded her head, yes, and Megan texted a response.

"I'm gonna hop in the shower. I told Ryan we could all meet back at your apartment and figure out what to do next. If that's okay with you, Ella?"

"Sure. I'll go back upstairs and see you soon. Thanks for the tea and talking to me about the boy," Ella joked.

"You're welcome. I do wish Ryan liked me the way I've liked him, but at least he is showing interest in someone. He spends so much time alone, it's good to see him getting out. I'll warn you, he is not going to be an easy person to date." Megan pulled her hair out of the braid and shook her head. "But he's totally worth it."

Ella smiled and went back upstairs. Ryan was already waiting outside the door, laden down with a bag from the bakery, a coffee carrier, and blue and yellow roses.

He handed the roses to Ella. "The blue ones are for you, obviously," he smiled. "The yellow ones are for Megan. I also brought chocolate-like treats for you two nursing me last night."

"Thanks, I am really hungry. I went down to Megan's place. Boy, she is super awesome, huh?" Ella put all the coffee and bags on the counter, as Ryan pulled out his computer.

"Megan is my best friend, really," he said distractedly as he typed something onto the screen of the computer.

Ella pulled out a chocolate croissant and took a bite as Ryan worked.

"Megan is going to meet us up here," Ella said to him.

"Uh-huh," Ryan barely acknowledged her.

Giving up on his attention for the time being, she put the roses in water and checked the phone to see if there was any word from the professor. There wasn't. She frowned. She figured he was busy, but this was sort of important. Remembering that she needed to take the pills he gave her, she went and pulled them out of her bag. The rattle of the bottle got Ryan's attention.

"What are those?" He dropped the laptop on the couch and snatched the bottle out of her hand.

"Uh, my pills," she snatched the bottle back.

"Those are not in a regular pharmacy bottle." His voice was bordering on angry, and Ella felt herself get defensive.

"You know, Ryan, I don't have to tell you everything about my life." She crossed her arms and returned his glare. "And your eye looks terrible."

There was knock at the door, and Ella stomped past Ryan to let Megan in.

"Hey, what's wrong?" Megan noticed Ryan as she asked, "Should I leave you two alone? You look like you're in the middle of something." She only had one foot in the door and looked ready to turn and leave as quickly as possible.

"We're not in the middle of anything, Megan," Ella said in a loud, overly cheerful tone. *I sound kind of crazy.* Ella pulled Megan in, slammed the door shut, stomped back over to the coffee, and handed the bag of baked goods to Megan. "Here. Ryan brought us treats and roses for taking care of him last night." Trying for a more normal tone, she looked right at Ryan who wouldn't meet her eye.

"Thanks?" Megan glanced between them quickly. "I can come back later. It's totally fine "

"It's not totally fine," Ryan all but growled at them.

"What is your problem?" Ella demanded

"Yeah, Ryan, what she said," Megan said between bites of pastry.

"Ella is taking pills that are not from a pharmacy," Ryan said directly to Megan. "The bottle looks familiar, too."

"It's none of your business, Ryan," Ella snapped back. "I can take whatever pills I want."

"Wait. What? Are you sick, Ella?" Megan sounded so perplexed Ella suddenly felt sorry that she hadn't let her leave.

"I'm not sick exactly," she explained. "I just have problems with my joints, and the professor is trying to help me with them."

"Professor? What professor?" Megan's voice had a tone of urgency that took Ella by surprise.

"A man I met a few days ago. He's really nice. I helped him out, and he figured out that I have a condition. I met with him at his office yesterday, and then he gave me this treatment to try. I have been taking strong painkillers that I really hate, and I don't think they help me anyway, so I was willing to give these a shot. That's all. Then Ryan sort of melted down about it." Ella shrugged. "Why?"

"Well," Megan paused, "um, what Ryan is so very POORLY trying to express is that the professor may be involved with the people who experimented on him."

"Experimented? I thought we talked about this? The professor was cleared of those charges," Ella confusingly asked Ryan, who was standing stoically aside while Megan was clearly trying to figure the best way to continue to explain to Ella.

"Ryan, do you think it's the same people?" Megan nodded her head in his direction.

"I don't know, but I'm pretty freaked out, Megan. I didn't think we'd ever see those bottles again." He stuck his hands in the pockets of his jacket and started to aimlessly pace around the room.

"Your pacing is going to wear a hole in my floor, Ryan. Does this have to do with some of the things you told me earlier, Megan?" Ella was completely at a loss.

"Yeah it does, Ella," Megan continued, "I told you that when I met Ryan he was really sick?"

"Yes." Just as Megan was about to tell her more, Ella's phone buzzed. "Hold that thought, Megan. Hello? Yes, you got my message?"

Ella was listening to the professor, as Megan and Ryan moved closer together and started to speak to each other in hushed tones.

"Okay, yeah, we'll be over shortly." She hung up the call as those two looked at her expectantly.

"Look, I don't really know what you guys are trying to tell me, or why, but the professor just asked me to come over to his office at the university. I think we should all go and talk to him. Especially you, Ryan."

"I agree," Megan said after a minute. She turned to Ryan. "You could just ask him questions."

"When did those people ever give a straight answer?" Ryan sounded very bitter.

"Look, we have to start somewhere. We can't stay in the dark about why this guy is coming after Ella and you."

"Please, Ryan?" Ella went and stood right in front of him. "I really want you to come with me."

He wouldn't look at her at first, but then glanced up quickly before looking away. "Okay. Let's go."

As Ryan and Megan put on their shoes, Ella ran into the bathroom and took one of the pills the professor gave her. She felt a little weird hiding it from them, but she had no answers yet and only a small bit of hope that these were better than the other drugs.

They left to go to the university, and walked the way in silence. Ella was sure at any moment Ryan would turn around and leave them, but he didn't.

They followed her into the building and to the professor's office. The professor didn't say anything about Megan and Ryan being with Ella, but rather, led them into his back lab and motioned for them to sit down.

"I trust all of you are well this morning?" the professor directed the question at Ryan's bruised eye. "Though some of you look a little worse for the wear than others."

"Doctor, I was really worried about you," Ella started.

"I am fine and I am sorry you worried. I promise to stay in better contact with you, Ella. Especially while these strange events keep occurring. But you see, I went on a bit of a drive yesterday, and only just made it back when I called you. Where I went did not have much in the way of cell service, if you can believe that. However, where I went will interest you a great deal, Ella."

"Okay?" Ella shifted around in her chair as the professor picked some papers off the lab table.

"After you left the other day, I thought about what you told me about your friend."

"My friend? You mean Alexandra?"

"Yes, you said her name more than once when you were asleep, and you sounded so distraught that I felt just terrible for you. I know you don't have much in the way of friends and family. And well, I know my way around investigations, at least to a certain degree."

"No doubt," Ryan muttered, and Megan smacked him on the arm.

"I guess I'm not sure I entirely understand, Doctor. But that is my general state of being these days." Ella leaned back in the chair and looked pointedly at Ryan, who pretended not to notice. Megan had the tiniest smile on her face, which just added to the absurdity of the whole of the past twenty-four hours.

"I think I managed to find your old school, Ella, and I went there," the professor said.

"You went to my school?" Ella took a deep breath. That was pretty much the last thing she thought he was going to say.

"I did and I am afraid I didn't find much when I got there."

"I'm not surprised. The headmistress isn't the most forthcoming woman."

"No, you misunderstand me, Ella. There was no headmistress."

"She's gone? Wow, I guess she finally crossed the wrong person. I sort of can't believe that because she seemed to have so many powerful friends, and I think she had been working there for pretty much forever. The school has been open for over one hundred years. They really liked to talk about how old and prestigious they were. How only the best students got to go to school there," Ella turned to explain to Megan and Ryan. "It was such a crock of crap, though. It was just a lot of spoiled rich kids whose parents didn't want to deal with them. The only reason I got to go there is because I had really high test scores, and the state didn't want to deal with my 'emotional problems.' " Ella air quoted the last two words.

"Did you like it there at all?" Megan asked her.

"Yeah, I guess. The classes could be really interesting, and I had Alexandra. At least for a little while. And there were a few teachers I really liked. I hope they are all doing well." Ella turned back to the professor and waited for him to explain more. "Oh, and the building was really old and beautiful with amazing gardens. I did like that a lot." She smiled at the memory. "I hope those are still there, too."

"I really am sorry, Ella," the professor started again. "I really did not start this conversation right at all. When I said I didn't find much, what I meant is quite literally: I did not find much. The headmistress, the teachers, the school, they are all gone."

Chapter 10

Megan and Ryan were staring at Ella, who was sitting silently, mulling over what the professor just told her.

"I guess hundred-year-old schools just go out of business sometimes," she finally said, but for some reason she didn't feel so sure.

"I didn't think too much of it," the professor told her, "but then I did a little research, and that yielded some strange findings."

"Like what?" Ella had a demanding tone in her voice and couldn't help it.

"As far as I can tell, the school never really existed in the first place," he answered her quietly.

Ella closed her eyes and felt a smile creep to her lips, as she shook her head from side to side.

"Professor, that is one hundred percent incorrect. I am not making up my entire existence. I went to school, I remember school, I have notebooks upon notebooks of work and art I made in school, I have a diploma. I will bring them to show you."

"That is not necessary. I believe you, Ella. The bigger question here is, why did someone go through all the trouble to hide the existence of this school?" The professor shuffled around some papers, looking for something. "It is my experience that when someone tries to erase the presence of something, there is usually a very big, often not good, reason. I've been accused of it myself."

He found what he was looking for and handed the piece of paper to Ella. "I found this posted on a job site. It was buried in more than few pages of links. If the school didn't exist, why would someone have it as a reference of their previous employment? As you can see, Ella, I believe you," he assured her once more, as she looked over the piece of paper. Megan and Ryan had been sitting silently, listening to the exchange between them. Ella looked over to them and grimaced.

"I'm sorry," she told them. "This is not why we came here in the first place, is it? You guys are being really patient."

"No big deal, Ella. This is important," Ryan said quickly, and Megan agreed. "We'll go get some coffee while you guys talk. Why don't you meet us over there when you're done? That way none of us will be alone. It's not much of a walk, and there are plenty of people around." Ryan pulled Megan up from her seat before she could say anything, and they left the lab.

"Good grief, he is so weird," Ella said aloud.

"Truly," the professor replied. "But quite good looking, the two of them." He was trying to joke with her, but it didn't work.

No one is having much luck with me lately. Staring hard at the paper in hand, she thought there was something familiar about some of the references to experience on the resume. But the name was not one she recognized. Rubbing a hand hard against her temple and feeling an impending headache, all she wanted to do was go home and get ready for the show.

"We actually came here to try to see what we could figure out about this man who apparently keeps attacking us. Although my boss said there were two men who broke into the club." She handed the paper back to the professor. "I have no idea what to say about the school at the moment. It's a lot to process, and really, I just want to get ready for my art show and not think about any of this. Except I don't I have that choice at the moment."

"What show is that?"

"I am going to have an art show at a gallery. Did I not tell you? I thought I mentioned it. I have a lot of work to do for it, too. But this guy knocked Ryan out cold and hit Megan when she was trying to stop him from getting into my apartment. He was in the hall when I got to my building. When I saw him, I yelled for him to get away from Megan, but it's like he just disappeared."

"What do you mean by disappeared?" The professor wiped his glasses on a shirt sleeve.

"I mean he was there one minute being menacing, you know like he is supposed to as a creepy guy following us, and the next he was not there."

"As in, he ran out of the building?"

"Nope." Ella massaged her temples some more.

"He did not run out of the building? Into another apartment then?"

"No, Professor. He vanished into thin air, as they say."

"Like your school?"

That comment annoyed her the tiniest bit, but she held her tongue.

"Yes, I guess like my school. But my boss said the same thing, so all the things you could possibly be considering that I am imagining are incorrect, Professor." Ella knew it came out snippy. *So be it.*

"I said I don't think you're imagining things. No need to be defensive, young lady." His voice took on a teacher-like tone.

"Sorry," she said sheepishly.

"It's alright, Ella. I know this is unnerving to say the least, and as it is, I don't have much in the way of answers. I don't know why, if they are following me, they are so focused on you. Nor do I have any guesses why it seems someone is deliberately trying to discredit you."

"Discredit me?"

"Yes. Does it not seem, there being no trace of your school nor of the man who has attacked you and your friends, as though you are being quite purposely made to look a bit unstable. You, yourself, have confessed to feeling disjointed from your painkillers."

"Why in the world would anyone care about making me seem anything?" She was incredulous. *No one cared I was alive until about five minutes ago.*

"If I were to hazard a guess, I would think it has something to do with your condition." He paused. "Did you take a pill yet?"

"I did. But wow, did it not go over well," she confided.

"What do you mean by that?" He went back to shuffling papers and making a stack of them separate from the rest on the table.

"Ryan had a meltdown over the bottle you gave me."

"The bottle? Those are left from my previous job. I suppose I could've recycled them, but I just didn't have anything else to put your pills in. Speaking of which, how do you feel?"

"Normal, I guess, except I'm getting a headache." She sat down in a chair and looked up at him. "It is actually getting a bit worse."

"I was afraid of that. It could be a side-effect for twenty-four hours, and I am sorry for that. But I think that if you can get through it, the treatment will help you."

"What exactly is it going to do?"

"I am hoping it will relieve the pressure around your joints, and thus some of your pain, without the aid of narcotics. I really do think you are too young to be using those things. As far as I can tell, you are otherwise healthy, so I'd rather we figure out something less addictive for you to take." He handed her a glass of water. "I think you should go meet up with your friends quickly and head home to rest. Keep your feet above your head when you lie down. Elevate them like you would if you had a sprain. We can talk about more of this stuff tomorrow. I will come to check on you and spend the night doing more research. Maybe it will yield something."

She almost couldn't hear him. There was a dull buzzing sound rising in the back of her mind and it seemed as though it was filling her ears. So she just nodded and got up to leave, nearly stumbling on the way out.

The coffee shop, I have to get to the coffee shop. Her vision was starting to blur. *What did he give me? I guess I should've listened to Ryan.*

Making her way to the coffee shop, she was relieved to spot the two of them sitting at a table outside. Megan waved her over, but her face quickly changed when Ella went over to them.

"Are you okay, Ella?" Megan stood up and wrapped an arm around her.

"I just have a headache." Ella did not want to tell Ryan why she had a headache. "I was hoping to lie down for a little while at home before we do research."

"We can get started on it," Megan volunteered. "I have to turn in some work at school, but then I'll get to it. Ryan, why don't you take Ella home?"

"Okay," he said, and as Ella turned with him to head home, there was a blinding flash of light in the sky.

She rubbed her eyes hard and looked up. Ryan and Megan were gone. Looking at her surroundings, she momentarily forgot how she had gotten here, but remembered she had been wanting to come. *I really do not trust my mind these days,* she thought, and started to wander in the grass.

The path to the office was one that stuck in her mind well. The grounds were remarkably quiet, and no one seemed to be around anywhere. It was summertime, so regular classes were not in session. Most of the students would be off on lavish vacations, something Ella had never experienced.

The school seemed to be mostly as she remembered, though something about it definitely felt off. Not able to figure out what that was, Ella reached for an old ornate handle on the heavy wooden door and pulled it open. A creak echoed in the great hall, and there was no other sound but a gentle whistle of air and a clock ticking somewhere off in the distance of the building. As she stepped inside, the door fell shut with a noise that seemed so loud it made her jump and caused goosebumps to run up and down her arms, even in the hot air.

Feeling herself warm up in the darkened halls as her heart started to pound as though it might burst through, she took a step.

"One foot in front of the other, old girl," her voice carrying down the hall to no one. She looked in the windows of closed doors while making her way through the dim school. It smelled strangely like a hospital to Ella. Odd, considering there was so much old wood all around. The chemical smell grew stronger as the walk led her to the doors of the office that was such a frightening and uncomfortable memory. As she stood still and listened to the tiniest of distant sounds, old fears and tensions ran across Ella's neck. The days of uncontrollable nightmares, depression, and sickness flooded over her, and the persuasive thought of leaving as soon as possible swam in her mind. The weight of the questions and not knowing hung heavier in the ether.

"Maybe I don't want to know. Maybe it's better." The astringent smell started to burn slightly in her nostrils and proceeded to tear up her eyes. A headache would soon follow, so making a choice to continue searching or to leave was becoming paramount. Sometimes the headaches left her helpless and in pain for days.

She pushed on the door without consciously making a decision, and it swung open easily, much to her surprise. Everything was as she remembered, with the exception of a heavy, metal door she was not able to recall. It didn't match most of the rest of the historic, restored building. But there were a few modern updates throughout the school, so it didn't really seem out of the ordinary. Taking a deep breath and going around the counter to the etched glass door leading to the headmistress' office, Ella pulled the door handle. It wasn't locked either. *Now this seems questionable.* A sudden loud noise in the distance made her hurry in and close the door, hoping no one had heard the sounds. *Why in the world did I think no one would be here? That was really dumb.* She moved as quickly as possible around the desk and cabinets trying to open doors, most of which were locked. It was looking to be a dead end until she spotted a key that seemed like it could fit the filing cabinet. It worked.

The school's files were in perfect order. Easy to find by year, though a randomly picked one that she opened and flipped through had almost no information. *Maybe everything was computerized?* There was no computer in the room, nor, she realized, was there one in the front waiting area. These files were almost too perfect and too easy to find, except that it appeared as though a few students' records were missing, like Ella's. *I suppose I was a problem student.*

But Ella was no longer in school here, and Ein wasn't the headmistress anymore. *Ein. Yes, that is what we called her.* Ella had forgotten for so long. It really didn't make a whole lot of sense that Ein would be gone, nor that Ella's file would be.

She went through them again, more slowly this time, and the entire class was accounted for. Except her. *And Alexandra,* she realized suddenly. *Why didn't I notice that the first time?*

She felt a twinge of guilt when she admitted to herself at that moment that she had been so caught up in the desire to find out more about her own past that she had forgotten about the promise she made to find Alexandra. Anger washed over the guilt while she once again remembered the painful day that turned out to be the last time she saw Alexandra.

Alexandra had been forced to take a sedative because she had resisted leaving by locking herself in the dorm room and threatening to jump out the window. The doctors had come out of nowhere. Ella still wondered how Ein had managed to convince Alexandra's father to lock her up. Ella knew he often ignored his daughter, but he never seemed to bear her ill will. Ein's sway over the man had to be bigger than Ella could have imagined. She wondered if finding out what it was would make a difference in helping her friend. Ella was convinced Alexandra was somewhere she didn't want to be, even now, years later.

Ella looked through a couple more of the drawers, with their perfectly ordered class records, before closing all of the cabinets in frustration.

The room was different from when Ein was here. Warmer. The new headmistress had changed the room somewhat. Though Ella recognized at least one of the filing cabinets. It still had the symbol Alexandra had carved into it when she had snuck in to bother Ella as she was doing the weekly office-cleaning rotation. Ella walked over to the cabinet and ran a finger over the indentation.

The indentation, she remembered, that was shaped like Alexandra's signature flower: a rose.

Ella caught her breath at that moment. What was it her friend had said to her on that last day before she was taken away?

"Something about the roses," Ella mumbled to herself.

The roses. What roses? What did it mean? Did she mean drawings? Did she mean the roses outside, or was she just drugged and out of her mind when they had taken her away? Something in Ella nagged at her to reject that last thought. Ella trusted her friend with all her heart. If Alexandra said something about roses, then

Ella was going to look into all of the rose bushes in the state to find what she meant.

She left the office quietly, soundlessly shutting the door behind her. Her shoes made soft, thudding sounds as she walked down the hall toward the front entrance. There was a rose garden outside. *How is that supposed to help? I can't dig up every bush.* Going toward the door, she passed some pictures of the teachers and faculty. Stopping to look at them, none of the faces seemed familiar to her anymore. There was another loud sound, and it made Ella stop lingering. She walked out the door and further from the building, past the trees where some of the grounds were out of sight of the school.

Alexandra had loved the rose garden. She was obsessed with roses. She always had them fresh in her room. She volunteered her time to care for the gardens at school. She had jewelry and paintings. A lot of her spending money was dedicated to roses in some form. Her friend had always planned her home to be full of the "biggest, most luscious roses in the world." Ella believed her, too. Alexandra knew more about the fragrant flower than most anyone at school knew about anything. The International Rose Society had even named a hybrid plant after her because she had supported them so much, even as a young schoolgirl.

Ella had always suspected Alexandra also liked the rose garden because it afforded a certain amount of privacy. It was out of sight of the school, and Ein had little interest in the outdoors. On top of that, the teachers were far too busy with students to have much time to tend them during school hours. Ella had once asked her friend if she had chosen the rose garden for privacy. Alexandra had merely smiled and said, "I didn't choose them, they chose me."

At the time, Ella had rolled her eyes because Alex was prone to dramatics. But now, Ella couldn't help but wonder what that meant. Sometimes it felt as though Alex knew more than she was letting on. Always protective of Ella, being the younger of the two, her friend had, on occasion, kept her out of a few things. Which used to make Ella feel terribly left out. But now she couldn't help but wonder if it was a good thing. Who knows what Alex had planned for graduation day? It must have been something really big for Ein to have reacted so harshly. The woman was cold. Ella knew that through and through. But she hadn't seen her be irrationally vindictive. At least not as far as she knew, she supposed. A voice in her head nagged with the thought, "How just is it to send a high school student to who knows where?" *And of course,* Ella reminded herself, *not even let her closest friend know where that is.*

Ein had done her best to keep a tight lid on whatever it was that took place. She told Ella it was to "respect the family's privacy." At seventeen, with no money and no family of her own to help her, Ella had to take what the woman said as law.

"Well, I'm no longer seventeen," Ella said aloud as she walked through the woods on the path to the garden.

Upon reaching it, she gasped. The garden was bigger than she ever remembered it being. She walked aimlessly through, taking in all the beautiful flowers that were in abundance on the plants. They were breathtaking with their deep-colored petals and rich fragrance. She noticed that the air had a lighter, cleaner feel than that inside the school. The plants were arranged in neat rows, with stone steps laid in the ground between each row so that the earth, where the roots of the flowers grew, was undisturbed. There were stone statues placed in with a few of the plants. One of the goddess Artemis, another of the goddess Athena.

As Ella continued walking along the row of the richest red-colored flowers, she saw that they rounded at the end on all sides of the field, and in the middle stood a fountain that was not here when she was a student. It was a large, stone fountain with a carved woman in a gown made of roses. The water ran down the gown and trickled off into a stone pool carved with more of the flowers. The woman was carefully created, Ella could see, with an attention to detail that was unusual for a stone carving. Strangely, the woman looked vaguely familiar to her. She stood watching the light glint off the water as it ran into a stone pool with a mosaic of roses on the bottom. In the last few years, someone had put a lot of work into her friend's girlhood hobby. Ella didn't know what to make of it. But it was stunning.

She wandered over to a stone bench that sat between the rows of flowers and the fountain, and sat down facing the flowers. Taking a deep breath to fill her lungs with the intoxicating scent, she relaxed a bit and closed her eyes. The warmth of the light was on her skin, and Ella pictured her friend's face.

Alex was so happy when she tending to the roses, and it was the only time her normally perfect outer facade would be in disarray. She was always perfectly and fashionably dressed, with matching in-style accessories and incredibly well-kept hair and nails. But when she worked in the rose garden, she didn't worry about her appearance at all, frequently having wind-blown hair and dirt on her hands and clothing. Upon returning each day, she would be perfect again in no time, but while outside, it was as if she allowed herself some freedom from all the eyes that often watched every move.

With her friend gone, Ella had wondered what would become of the flowers, assuming that, being so far out of sight, they might fall into disarray. As one could imagine, many of the girls at the elite boarding school had no interest in something as menial as gardening.

"Hello, miss," said a soft female voice that pulled Ella out of her reflections.

Ella turned to the sound and saw a young girl standing in front of her in an apron and holding a bucket in her hands.

"Hello," replied Ella.

"You mustn't go to school here," she said. Shifting the bucket from both hands to one.

"What makes you say that?" Ella smiled.

"You're too fashionably dressed," said the girl. This made Ella laugh. She never considered herself the least bit fashionable. Most of her clothes came from thrift stores.

"You are right about me not going to school here. I graduated from here a few years ago."

"Welcome back," the girl said pleasantly. "What brings you back to the grounds on this day?" She set the bucket down and removed gardening gloves, putting them into a pocket as she walked over to Ella and extended a hand.

"I'm Julia," she smiled.

"Ella." Shaking her hand and standing up.

"Ella?"

"Yes."

"Are you the Ella who created all those paintings in the hall on the second floor, of the grounds and building?"

"Yes, those are my paintings. Wow, I can't believe they're still up." Ella put a hand up to shield her eyes as the sun slipped from behind some clouds momentarily. She heard the girl take a quick breath.

Ella looked at her. "Is something wrong?"

"No, no, not at all. Just the silver in your hair which looks deep blue surprised me."

"Um," Ella shifted uncomfortably, "yeah, its a little weird. It grows that way." She said almost apologetically.

Julia smiled a big smile again, "It's gorgeous." She sounded so cheerful. Ella felt herself warming up to the girl, and if she was this friendly, maybe she'd tell her who created this garden.

"Julia, can I ask you a question?"

"Sure, what's that?" Julia walked over to the fountain and leaned over, sticking her hands into the water. "The water feels so nice," she said. Her long brown hair seemed to shimmer in the sunlight.

In fact, everything around us seems to be shimmering. It must be the headache messing with my vision.

"My friend used to tend to the rose garden when we went to school here. Who does it now? It's so perfect, and much larger than it used to be."

"I take care of them two times a week," Julia said, standing up and shaking water off her hands, "But mostly the patient with the white hair takes care of them."

"Patient? You mean student?"

"No," Julia said with a smile on her face, as if Ella was a child who didn't understand their conversation. "I mean patient. Her hair is really unbelievably white. Sometimes she gets big packages delivered, filled with things to plant and decorate the gardens. Like all the fancy birdbaths." Julia gestured around them and made Ella take notice that there was a rather large collection of blown-glass birdbaths and stone statues carefully decorating the landscape around them.

"We're all patients, Ella. School is only part of it so they can see."

"I'm sorry, I don't think I understand what that means." Ella was starting to think that this girl was a little off. *Why does the school seem to be shimmering in waves?* "That's weird."

"What's weird, Ella?" Julia started to skip around the water fountain.

"The school, it's... wavy or something." Ella looked at Julia, who was now carefully smelling roses and humming softly. "Never mind. I don't understand why you are saying the school is only part of it. Can you explain that? Has the school changed? Is it not just a school anymore?"

"Ella, silly," Julia turned and looked at her with the kindest, childlike expression, "it's not changed. You just don't remember."

"What..." Ella trailed off as she heard her name being called somewhere off toward the horizon, where the school seemed to be fading more and more into the sky. "I don't understand, Julia." She turned back to the girl, who was no longer there. And the garden wilted into dead plants and dried, cracked cement all around the grounds, as if they hadn't been touched for a long time.

Ella walked around, bewildered by the change, and started to follow the sound of her name being shouted. *Whoever is calling to me must be a long way away,* she thought, and started to walk toward the dark woods.

"Ella, wake up," said an accented voice. "Ella, can you hear me?"

"Maybe we should take her to the hospital," said another terse, male voice.

"Hey, you guys," said a female. "She's waking up, I think."

Ella slowly opened her eyes and blinked as they adjusted, to see Megan, Ryan, and the professor standing over what seemed to be her bed.

"Why are all of you here?" Confused, Ella sat up quickly and a rush of pain shot to her head. She groaned aloud. Megan sat next to her and pressed a cool, wet cloth to her forehead. "Thanks," she said. Her throat felt like sandpaper. Taking a glass of water from Ryan, she saw the professor looking at his watch and writing in a book. "I don't understand. Why are all of you here? I've only been asleep for a little while."

"No, you haven't, Ella," the professor replied, putting his book into a satchel. "You've been out for almost a full day, and we all became very worried. I didn't anticipate this happening. I thought you'd have a mild headache, not this. I've adjusted the dose of medication I gave you. This shouldn't happen again."

"How did you guys get here?" Ella felt uneasy with everyone being in her very private bedroom.

"You don't remember?" Megan asked, the worry in her voice clear. "You came to the coffee shop, and Ryan was bringing you back here after you started to get a headache. Then you didn't move for hours. We came to check on you, but after about ten hours your breathing was so shallow we dug through your things to find the professor. I ended up going to the school to get him here to help you. I'm so glad you're awake."

"I think I hate that coffee shop," Ella said grumpily, making Ryan laugh.

"It's not been a great place for you the last couple of days," he agreed.

"How do you feel now?" The professor took her pulse.

"I feel fine, I think." She stretched a little. There was almost no pain in her joints. "I don't feel any pain."

"Something good should come out of those meds," Ryan snapped directly at the professor.

"Ryan. Stop." Megan sounded even but firm.

"Young man, if you have something to say you should just say it." The professor looked straight at Ryan and arched an eyebrow whilst crossing his arms. "I am trying to help our friend, and your attitude is certainly not adding anything to these increasing number of encounters."

"You used to work for that pharmaceutical company," Ryan said accusingly.

"That is not a secret, sir." The professor didn't flinch at all.

"I don't trust you," Ryan continued.

"I don't need your trust. I am not here for you."

"Okay!" Ella pulled herself out of bed and looked down at the pajamas that seemed to have made their way onto her. *I am not thinking about that right now.* "The two of you stop." Ella stepped between them. "This is stupid. I am an adult, Ryan. I can take whatever pills I want. And professor, please don't engage in confrontations in my bedroom. I appreciate all of you coming over. I do. But maybe most of you should leave. Except Megan."

"But, Ella," Ryan started to protest, and Ella put a hand up.

"I don't want to hear it. Don't you think we have enough problems right now? With all of us getting assaulted and harassed? Because I do. And the truth is, until we figure what is going on, we have to trust each other."

"I agree." Megan stood up next to Ella. "We need to find out what's going on, and fighting about other stuff right now isn't going to help anything." With that, both Megan and Ella left the bedroom and marched into the kitchen. Ryan and James had no choice but to follow them.

They both sat on the couch and began to talk between themselves, pointedly ignoring the guys.

"You ladies are right, of course." The professor crossed the room and sat in the big blue velvet chair. All three of them turned and looked at Ryan.

"I agree, under protest." Ryan sat in a chair at the dining room table that looked over to the living room, but was far enough away to make a point.

Megan rolled her eyes.

"Fine," Ella said. "Since I've lost a day, can you tell me what happened? Has anyone found anything new?"

"Well," James said, "I have sent email messages on the employment website where we found that resume. So far I've heard nothing. How are you feeling? I'm so sorry you suffered so much. I only thought you'd have a passing headache. Maybe two." His face was lined with concern and apology.

"I feel better now. Let's not dwell on it. Thank you for coming over to check on me and adjusting the dose. I still want to try to get off those other painkillers." Ella turned to Ryan and Megan. "Did either of you find anything out? Has anyone bothered you?"

"I've been trying to find out more about the school," Ryan said quietly. "But I'm not having any luck."

Ella nodded and looked at Megan. "Have you been okay? Has anyone tried to bother you?"

"Nope. I've just been here and home. Ryan and I traded shifts, though it was hard to convince him to leave," Megan said with a soft smile. "We've been worried about you." Megan put a more-than-subtle emphasis on "we." Ella patted her hand and looked between the three of them.

"I wish I hadn't been out for the last day. I wanted to hel...," she stopped before finishing.

"What is it, Ella?" The professor leaned forward and looked at her creased face.

"I think, I think maybe I remembered something," she stammered.

"Oh? Just now? What was that?"

Everyone waited for her to say something.

"No, I think I remembered something when I was asleep. Is that even a possibility?" Ella looked at the professor questioningly.

"It most certainly is. As confusing as dreams may seem, they often can contain a lot of information. What do you think you remember?"

"I think I wasn't in a school." Ella's voice was leaden.

"What do you mean? Where were you?" the professor asked.

Megan frowned and held Ella's hand.

"You don't have to tell us, Ella." Megan squeezed her fingers gently.

"No. It's okay. I'm just... gathering my thoughts, I guess. I don't think I've had them in a few years," she joked weakly.

"Take your time," Megan told her.

"I think I was in an institution."

Chapter 11

"This is good," said James.

"What?" Ella hadn't thought he'd say that. She looked at Megan and Ryan. Neither of them said much, and their expressions were unreadable. "If you guys don't want to hang around now, I totally get it." She hoped her voice sounded like she didn't care. She hoped.

"Don't be weird," Megan said, then got up and went to the kitchen. "If I stopped being friends with people because they were crazy, I wouldn't know anyone."

Ella laughed a bit out of relief. She had a friend. It was nice.

"I said this is good, Ella, because now we have more information that could help us find out things we did not know before." The professor stood and went to the door. "I need to get back to work for now. All of you stay in touch, especially if Ella has any more problems."

"I'm fine," Ella told him. "Actually, seriously, I feel much better than I have in a while."

Ryan still hadn't said anything but had started typing away on his keyboard. *His communication skills are going to take some getting used to, but at least he didn't leave.*

"I have been doing some digging around," Ryan said, without turning from his computer. "My father is one of the people who tried prosecuting the professor. Uh, I mean, James. He said we should call him James while you were sleeping. It's a little strange, but whatever."

"Ryan." With a warning in her tone, Megan came back in the room and handed Ella a mug of tea.

"No, it's okay, Megan. Maybe we should hear this. The professor thought people were after him, and Ryan's father, it seems, worked for the company that started the accusations against him. And Ryan thought maybe his father was looking for him, right?" Ella looked at Ryan, who finally looked up from the screen and nodded his head. "So they're both connected to the same company. Plus, I think I found something."

"What did you find?" Megan sat in the lotus position on the floor with great ease.

"I wish I could do that," Ella smiled at her. "It hurts too much."

"I'll teach you. Step by step, you'll get stronger. My roommate is moving out soon, so I'll have even more free space."

"What did you find, Ella?" Ryan interrupted them, somewhat impatiently.

"I saw a picture on the Internet when I was looking up the professor. I think my friend's father was in it. I think. It was hard to tell. But still, I thought it was him."

"So possibly there are three of us with a connection to this company? That is very interesting." Ryan started to turn around, but Ella stopped him.

"There's more."

"Okay?"

"I used to have this woman we knew as The Headmistress. I thought it was because she was in charge of the school. We used to call her Ein, which means 'one.' We called her that because she only cared about herself. And besides that, she only cared about being number one."

"Okay? But, Ella, I don't see what this has to do with the company?"

"I think she was in the picture, too. And so was the man who is following me."

"Ella, why didn't you tell us?" Megan asked.

"Honestly, with everything, I haven't given it much thought, and remembering that woman isn't something I like to do." Ella was defensive, but she felt bad. She wasn't trying to endanger anyone. Then Ella smacked her hand to her forehead. "I'm such an idiot!"

"Forgetting things doesn't make you an idiot," Ryan told her kindly.

"Really? That guy in the suit! He 'ran' into me at the store a couple of days ago. I swear, it's like what the professor gave me started taking lids off jars of memories."

"Maybe it did."

"What does that mean, Ryan?" Megan sipped off a mug of tea.

"Well, think about it. Something is messing with Ella's memories. Maybe her painkillers. Maybe she repressed it herself. Doctors use therapy and drug treatments to regress into memories. Maybe that is what is happening."

"I repressed it myself?"

"You did just say you don't like remembering Ein," he pointed out.

"Fair enough, and I don't. That woman was a terrifying monster to me when I was a teenager. You're always afraid of your principal to a certain degree, I suppose, but this was different. She always threatened to tell people I was a freak, and pressured me to turn on my friend."

"Wow, she sounds awesome," Megan said sarcastically.

"Like I said, she only cared about herself."

"Someone who should definitely be in charge of other people," Ryan said. "But you did call her 'headmistress' so there must've been some school there? Not just an institution."

"Yes, I have clear memories of classes and of a few teachers. And I know I took art classes."

"This is all bizarre, but it gives more pieces to the previously almost empty puzzle." Ryan typed notes into his laptop. "What was your friend's name?"

"Alexandra Francis." Ella hesitated. "Ryan, she was the one I had a hard time talking about."

"I remember," he said. He stopped typing and smiled at her. "It's okay, I understand."

"This is a lot to take in, Ella. I'm glad you're telling us this stuff. It's so personal and, well, we were just kind of thrown together," Megan added.

"I want to know more about you guys. I am gonna go put on some clothes, and then let's talk more. And I really need to get my art show together. I don't have a lot of time. It's happening kind of fast." Ella pretended to tear her hair out and they all laughed.

Once she was dressed, they worked through the afternoon, looking for information. Not having much in the way of success, Megan left to do errands, and Ryan went for a walk and to stop at the library. Ella had the apartment back to herself. She looked around and couldn't believe that she didn't have the usual uncontrollable urges to put everything back in its right place and lock the door so no one could get in again. It turned out she liked the company.

In fact, rather than cleaning up the various messes around her apartment, she began to add to them by hauling out boxes, folders, and piles of paintings, drawings, and art supplies. She put together frames and notes to show Evan.

She worked for hours, stopping only to stretch and to marvel at how little pain she felt.

Ryan came back with piles of books. They didn't talk much. They both just worked, and worked some more. Eventually they stopped to take a break and eat something, and Ryan asked Ella if she needed any help. Ella set him to work putting pieces into frames and laying some with glass.

Ryan fell asleep in the wee hours of the morning on the couch, but Ella was not tired and kept working all night.

In the morning, Ryan got up and found her still working.

"Do you want some coffee?" he asked, trying to stifle a yawn.

"I do, but I am not going to that coffee shop," Ella told him, without looking up from her pile of work. *Irrational, yes, but the place feels like a jinx.*

"Fair enough. I'll make some of the stuff I bought." He went into the kitchen and banged around, looking for what was needed. After about a half-hour, he set a plate of food in front of Ella, and a steaming cup of coffee, which she accepted gratefully.

"Can I help you more?" He sat down and started to eat.

Finally stopping for a few minutes, Ella started to eat as well.

"Don't you have things to work on? What *have* you been working on? Can I ask?"

"Sure. Mostly I've set up automatic searches that are scouring the 'net for any of the names you mentioned and anything about my dad or the professor. I haven't found anything we haven't already seen. It took a bit of work to build the searches, but really the hard part is waiting for anything to show up. I also did some work for a programming job I have. Gotta pay the bills," he said with a smile, but did not actually sound like he was joking. *Always guarded. I wonder if I'll be able to crack through the wall.*

They finished eating in silence.

"I want to take my ideas to the gallery curator and see if he's into what I've come up with." Ella picked up the dishes and put them in the sink. "It's actually not super far away, so I could walk."

"I'll go with you. We need to be careful. I think possibly you more than the rest of us," he told her, his tone matter-of-fact.

"You don't have to follow me around." It somewhat annoyed her that she had a bodyguard now.

"I promise I won't get in the way. Besides, until we know what's going on, I'd prefer not to get punched out again, myself. So let's go."

With no further discussion, they gathered everything together they needed and left for the gallery. They closed the door just as the computer returned a result they hadn't yet seen. They also missed someone coming into Ella's apartment and erasing the evidence of it being found.

When they got to the gallery, the door was open and the only person working was Evan. He was on the phone and gestured for Ella to come in. Ryan stayed out in the hall.

Ella wandered around his office, taking in the pieces hanging on the walls while he finished talking.

"What can I do for you today, Ella?" he asked her when he hung up.

"I thought about what you said for ideas for my opening, and I came up with a few if you would like to see them?" She nervously held out a folder.

"Sure," he took them and started to flip through the pages. After about five very long minutes, Evan looked up and set the folder down. "It's a lot of work for such short notice."

"I know, I just thought..." he held up a hand and cut her off before she could finish.

"I didn't say we wouldn't do it, but I need you to get your pieces here as soon as possible. I can close the gallery down and not let the staff be distracted by anything but getting ready for your show. Which, by the way, that phone call was me inviting some of the press."

"Press?" It had never occurred to her that someone might write about her work or take pictures of it.

"Yep, that's how we fill the gallery," he teased her. "Do you want me to help you move stuff here?" As Evan asked the question, he came over to Ella and stood very close to her. And she once again had that feeling that he was not exactly being kind.

"I have help," she stepped back and motioned at the door for Ryan to come in. He had been watching the exchange closely.

"Yes, I'll help bring the pieces in," Ryan told Evan, with no humor in his tone whatsoever.

"Great. Bring me some today." Evan was all business, like the moment didn't happen, and indicated that they should leave.

Which Ella was happy to do.

"You know," Ella started, "I really want to have a show more than anything right now, but is it just me, or does he seem a little..."

"Like a creep?" Ryan volunteered helpfully.

"Yes, like a creep." She stopped walking and stepped in front of Ryan. "Thank you for helping me."

"Of course." He seemed about to say something more when a long, dark, town car pulled up in front of the gallery. "Fancy place." He cleared his throat and moved down the sidewalk away from Ella.

She watched as a driver got out the car and held open the door for someone whose face she could not see. All she thought she saw was a glint of gold on dark hair.

Ryan kept walking, and Ella ran a bit to catch up to him.

When they got home and Ella was about to unlock the door, she remembered she had seen a shimmer of something shiny down in in the plants. She bent over to look for it, but was pretty sure it was nothing. Ryan bent over, too.

"What are you looking for Ella? Did you drop your key?"

"No I thought I saw... A-ha! Look!" She held a gold-colored stone and showed him.

"That's cool." He stood and looked at her like she was completely off her rocker.

"I like rocks." Not saying another word, she quite happily put it in a pocket and unlocked the door.

When they went upstairs, they found Ella's door was unlocked. Stopping just outside the crack, Ella whispered, "My door is open. We did not leave it unlocked."

Ella pushed the door open carefully, and Ryan moved quietly behind her. Despite better judgment she was very aware of him being so close to her.

"Be careful," he whispered in her ear, and the warmth of his breath sent a tingle down her spine. They stepped into the room and saw Megan looking through Ella's work. Ella let out a sigh of relief.

"It's just you."

"It's just me, but the door was unlocked," Megan said. "These are awesome, Ella." She held up a drawing of a futuristic building. "Really cool. Ryan, I checked your searches. It's not coming up with anything so far, so what is the next step?"

Ella went to take a pill while they started to chat.

She came back to the room and they both stopped talking.

"What? Do I have something on my face? My fly down?" Ella was wearing a dress.

"We think we should go to your school," Megan told her.

Ryan shuffled uncomfortably.

"Okay," Ella shrugged.

"Okay?" He was disbelieving.

"We haven't found anything here, have we? And now that I'm starting to remember all these bits and pieces, I wouldn't mind knowing what is real and what isn't."

Megan looked close to laughing and barely stopped with a small snort. "Ryan was sure you'd say no."

"Last week I mostly certainly would have, but will you guys go with me?"

"Of course," Ryan said gruffly, and Megan nodded in agreement.

"Can we do it in a few days, after my show?"

"Sure. I'll need to go get time off work, anyway. How far away is this place?" Megan asked her, and set Ella's drawing back down.

"About four-ish hours I'd say. It's been a long time, and I took the bus from there when I left. But I think I went back once. I think." Ella was hoping the therapy from James was going to keep making things clearer in her mind. Even if it was hard.

"Great! We have a plan? Should we tell the professor?" Megan asked them.

Ella wasn't entirely sure why, but she said, "No, Megan, let's wait until we get back."

Ryan looked at her with surprise.

"What?" Ella returned his look. "What are we going to tell him? We don't know anything yet."

"Right," he shrugged, and set back to work.

Most of the next week they all fell into a routine. The professor would stop by to check Ella's vitals and monitor her progress on the therapy. Ryan would work. Ella would work. They would check on Megan, who was getting her room-mate out of the apartment and setting up more workout space. They shared dinner together nearly every night and would take turns going in pairs to the store, and to see the professor at his lab to pick up things he was giving Ella for her care. Ryan and Megan helped Ella move everything that was to be set up for the show into the gallery. The gallery itself was a hustle of activity. Evan didn't say much to Ella beyond hello when they dropped things off. One of the workers at the gallery did comment that they had never seen Evan go to such great lengths to set up a show, nor had they seen one put together this quickly.

"Not that your work isn't great," the female employee told her. "I'm just surprised. These are usually scheduled out months in advance."

"I'm not surprised by it," Ryan informed Ella when they left the gallery that day.

"Why not?"

"I read the last few shows there haven't gone well, and it's clear that Evan thinks you're very talented." It was the nicest thing he said to her all week.

Despite the time they had been spending together, he still hadn't revealed much about himself, and the only thing they didn't do together was go to Ryan's place. He went by himself. He always brought her something and would ask her if she needed anything at all when she called him, but he still never invited her to come. Ella tried not to be bugged by it. She had too much to think about, and every time it started to sneak into her brain, it was all she could do to force the curiosity and the little bit of hurt out. Best of all, though, pain had been minimal and when she made time to sleep, it was restful and there were no dreams. She couldn't remember the last time she didn't dream, and it was a relief, to say the least.

The sudden friendship with Megan was a comfort. She was warm, helpful, funny, and for a few minutes a day, she was teaching Ella new meditation techniques that were helping her focus more than ever before. Ella greatly admired Megan's physical condition, and made her new friend swear to help her get into equally good shape.

"I'd love to, Ella. Really, I love teaching people."

They were busy with about a million things up until the night before the show. Ella's heart raced at the thought of the opening as she tried on a million different outfits, with Megan giving advice, before finally deciding on something.

No one noticed at all that they were being watched very closely.

Chapter 12

It's tonight! The show had been all she could think about for days, now. The time since meeting Evan, taking her pieces there, and tonight's opening had gone by so quickly. Her mind had needed a break from all the stressful things of the past that seemed to be haunting her lately.

What should I wear? Megan had picked something out the night before, but now she was second-guessing everything, rifling through the closet and throwing piece after piece onto the bed, after looking it over carefully and then rejecting it. It had to be special. Something she did not wear all the time. Something that was creative and projected an artist statement. She grimaced to herself. The melodrama was absolutely getting the better of her at the moment. Tossing a jacket onto the pile, she decided she was allowed to be as crazy as she wanted to be, today. Tonight was about her. The work. And the plan was to completely and totally enjoy it. Especially since she had no idea if she would ever get this chance again. Evan had said to dress up, and dress up she would. Having perused vintage stores and second-hand clothing boutiques for years, she certainly had plenty of things from which to choose, all of them dark. Black, blue, purple, and here and there, a silver accessory.

I guess I have a look. She closely examined a dark-blue velvet blazer. Then she put on what Megan had picked out the night before. *Who would, no doubt, laugh at me.*

On second thought... Ella decided the blazer had a lot of potential. She hung it on the door and continued to dig when her cellphone rang.

It was the professor.

Grabbing it, she answered, slightly out of breath.

"Ella?" His now familiar accent came over the speaker. "Are you okay? You sound out of breath?"

"Oh, I'm just making a complete disaster of my bedroom looking for something to wear to my show tonight." She plopped down on the bed next to the pile and flung herself backward, stretching luxuriously until her back cracked a bit. The new treatments the professor had given her were definitely helping.

"Show? What do you mean, show? Are you performing in something? I have to admit I am surprised, since you are so private."

Ella laughed. "Performing? No way. I'm having a gallery opening. My first one. I didn't tell you?"

"No, you didn't mention it." If Ella didn't know better she'd think he sounded sort of hurt. *I am sure I mentioned it. I really need to get my head straight.*

"That is because my head has been firmly up my butt, and of course I would love it if you wanted to come. Truth be told, I'm not sure I'm going to know a lot of people there, so it would really be doing me a huge favor."

"Really? I wouldn't miss it, then. You can tell me where it is and what time in a minute. I wanted to know how you were feeling with the new treatment? Do you feel any relief from the build-up?"

"Actually, I was just thinking I feel better than I have in a while. So, yes, I'd say that they are helping."

"That is good to hear. I still want to be very careful with them, and possibly adjust them more as we go. They are only a temporary fix. We need to figure out what is actually happening and how to heal you, not just put a Band-Aid on the problem, so to speak."

"Does that mean more tests?"

"Yes, I'm sorry it does. Your condition is so unusual, I don't even have a control for the basis of my testing. This is a one-of-a-kind situation. But look at it this way, if there are other people like you, what we find out may help them, too."

"Do you really think, Professor, that there are other people like me?"

"A couple of weeks ago I would not have even guessed you would exist, yet here we are. It seems unlikely, with as large as the world is, that you are the only person out there who might need help with this issue."

She was silent for a moment, and wondered for about the hundredth time if there was something about Ryan's illness that made it different. She just always felt so drained around him. Not emotionally, but physically. But he was even more secretive than she was. He seemed to want nothing to do with the professor at all, and she still had no idea why.

"Ella? Are you still there?"

"Yes, I am. Sorry. My brain is full of insanity today."

"Hmmm... okay, well, what should I wear to your show this evening?"

"I suppose whatever you want. I don't even know what I'm going to wear yet."

"Well give me the details, since you are being so unhelpful in the clothing department."

She tittered, told him where and when, and hung up. She thought for a minute about the fact that Ryan knew about the show but she had no idea if he was going to come, as he had been so awkward toward her since the first night they hung out together. The other times they'd seen each other, he just didn't seem as comfortable around her as he had been that first night. She knew part of it was because of the professor, but there was more. It sat between them like the proverbial elephant in the room. In fact, the more she thought about it, the more she wondered why he even bothered to stay in touch at all. He really seemed like he wasn't interested in her at all. She realized that, other than the first time, she had been the one to ask if he wanted to do things, and he had agreed reluctantly. He had only been to the club once since they met. Her mood was darkening.

She shook her head. *No. I am not doing this tonight. I am going to enjoy myself. Who cares about Ryan? The professor is trying to help me.* It was a bit strange that the professor was so hyper-focused on the treatments, but of course, as he had pointed out, he had never seen anything like her condition before. And she did feel better. *Whatever.* She couldn't make Ryan do anything he didn't want to do, no matter how much she wanted to see him. She did actually like him.

"BLAH," she yelled. She went back to digging in her clothes and tore off what Megan had picked out. After another thirty minutes, she finally decided on a long, form-fitting black dress with a mandarin collar and a silver tree painted all down the front, with the dark-blue velvet blazer over it. She put on vintage, black velvet gloves, and pulled her hair up in a loose bun. A pair of small silver moon earrings completed the look. She studied herself in the mirror for far too long in order to avoid thinking about how incredibly anxious she was getting.

It was finally time to go. She skipped eating dinner because she thought it would probably just upset her stomach even more.

Evan had told her to come about an hour early so she could decide if she liked the placement of her pieces. He had promised to set each room up with the themes that she had organized ahead of time. He had seemed impressed with the ideas, and she felt so pleased when he mentioned her dedication to the presentation. He was used to dealing with artists who did their work, but not much beyond that. Ella had never dared hope she might have a show, and she wasn't going to miss any more opportunities.

In between visits with the professor and whatever was happening with Ryan, she had spent every spare minute planning for the opening and the experience she wanted people to have when they looked at her work. It had also been an eye-opening experience for her, never having realized how much work she actually had. Hundreds of pieces filled the apartment. Paintings of every type. She had painted boxes, furniture, drapes, vases, even some of her clothing. But she never thought much about it until she started to plan the show. It was just what she did. How she wanted to spend her time. And being someone who was on her own a lot, she had spent a lot of time creating.

The other possibility she hadn't even considered was selling any of the art. Evan had brought up pricing the pieces, and it somewhat shocked her. The idea that someone might like something she had made enough to take it home, that just blew her mind. *Don't get ahead of yourself,* she told herself on the way out to the car. *Absolutely no one could show up and absolutely everyone could hate your work. Just be ready for that, too.*

When she arrived at the gallery, the front entryway had been set up with seats, and a few people were milling about, filling glasses of wine and trays full of pastries, fruits, and cheeses. The light shades had been carefully directed to the ceiling to give the room a warmer, welcoming feel instead of the bright white lights that normally shone in the front of the space. The tables were covered with silver cloth and the glasses had been etched with the name of the show, her name. Running a finger across the etching, she couldn't suppress a smile.

"Make sure you take at least one home with you." Evan came around the wall that blocked off the rest of gallery. "Do you want to see your show, Ella?"

Nodding her head excitedly, she followed him down the hall that had been painted with her name and the date of the event in dark blue paint. Under her name was one long, midnight-blue rose with a black stem. A copy of one of her images.

"This is so amazing." Ella stopped in the hall and stared at her name.

"This is just the entry, Ella," he laughed. "You haven't even seen the show yet. Come on." He pulled her by the elbow out of the hall and into the first area.

Ella had requested that there be separate rooms to accommodate the exhibit. Each room would be set up with her work, and arranged as if it were a particular place.

The first room was the garden room. It was filled with her large, blue, flower garden paintings interspersed with the blue and silver tree paintings that stretched from floor to ceiling. In the middle stood a black pedestal with one of the large glass vases she had painted with the most delicate orchid winding around it. In the vases were paper flowers she had made at the last minute out of sky-blue origami paper. The lights were carefully placed on the silver trees and lit low enough to give them a shimmer, with additional small lights above each individual flower painting. The room was completed with large, painted, paper butterflies hung from the ceiling at varying heights. Ella had painted these with the most delicate of silver skeletons outlining the shape of each wing. The effect was moody and ethereal.

"Oh, my!" She walked around and around, not believing that these were her creations.

"Yes." He pulled her by the arm again, leading her into the next room. Here the ceiling had been covered with a carefully rounded material and painted a dark azure color to create a dome overhead. The walls were filled with paintings of caves from her imagination. Large geodes and rocks she had collected over the years sat on corner shelves. She had decorated them with tiny imaginary creatures. Fairies, goblins, bat-like mini-monsters. There was a carefully timed sound of dripping water to complete the idea of being in a cave filled with underground wonders.

As she was reading the small placards with black script that Evan had created for each piece, one of his assistants came into the room to get his help.

"Ella, I'm gonna go deal with whatever this supposed emergency is, but you should keep looking at the rooms. There are three more set up like you requested. What do you think so far?"

"Evan..." She turned, walked over to him, and hugged him as hard as she could.

Very surprised by this, he stiffly patted her back, and then extracted himself from her embrace. She smiled at him, probably the biggest smile she could ever form, and he turned and walked away.

While he was dealing with whatever crisis, Ella continued to walk around the rooms. With complete and overwhelming happiness, she examined the way the gallery was decorated with her art and laid out in the elaborate style she had described to Evan, but was not entirely sure he would go for. But he had. He had clearly spent a lot of time, and probably a lot of money, setting up this exhibit, and it made her hope that she could sell something so he could get some of the money back.

"Did you look at the other three rooms?" Evan came back around the corner as Ella was straightening, ever so slightly, one of the last paintings in the exhibit.

"I did. And it's far more perfect than I imagined. You did an amazing job, and I don't know how to say thank you."

"The work was already done when you brought your portfolio here. And you made the plan for the rooms. It was an interesting challenge. I've never set up a show here like this before. But like I told you when you came in, I'm always looking for new work and new ideas. I have a few last-minute things to make sure are ready. Get comfortable, have some food. I got more positive responses to attend this show than ever before. It's going to be a long, but hopefully not unpleasant, evening." Evan left her again, and Ella went to the restroom.

She leaned in close over the sink and examined her face. She did not look like someone who could think up things like this art show, nor did she quite believe she had actually done it. *Yet, here it is.*

She ran the satin gloves over her hair to smooth it down, straightened her dress, and fussed with the blazer. Starting to hear more and more voices outside the door, indicating the gallery had opened the show, she nervously looked in the mirror one last time and went back into the fray.

Much to her surprise, there were already a lot of people gathered in the rooms, ooh-ing and ahh-ing over her pieces. Ella quietly wove her way to the front and picked up a bottle of water.

"Ella, please come over here." Evan gestured to her from across the room. He was standing with a group of people. She had no idea who they were.

"Ella, this is Jessica, a writer for the arts section of the paper, and her photographer, Michael. They want to interview you and take some photos of you with your work. How do you feel about that?"

"Terribly nervous," Ella said, and everyone laughed. "Oh. I'm completely not kidding."

"I know you're not kidding, Ella, but based on what I've seen in just the last half-hour, you should get used to the attention."

"Maybe. But I'm not sure I'll ever get used to any attention. Especially not this much."

"Attention is highly overrated," a smooth, deep, slightly accented voice said over the noise in the room.

Everyone turned at the same time, and behind Ella stood a tall man with deep, amber eyes.

"But it can also be useful. Hello, Evan. The show seems to be going well."

"Yes, it is. This is Armand El Dorado, the owner of the building, an investor in the gallery, and a declarer of dramatic statements."

"Truth tends to be dramatic, my friend." He shook Evan's hand. "Who are all these lovely people?" He said it to the group, but his eyes did not leave Ella's face. She shifted from side to side but held his gaze. She wanted this to go well, and being intimidated was not going to help her in any way, even though she was still unsure, at this point, what she wanted to achieve tonight. *Or any night.* Evan introduced each person in the group beyond them before he turned back to Ella.

"And of course, Armand, this is Ella Cerulean." Armand took her outward-stretched hand delicately and inclined his head ever so slightly.

"It is lovely to meet you, Miss Cerulean. Your work is outstanding, and I am very impressed with the setup and turnout to this presentation."

"Thank you so much for giving me the opportunity," she said, hoping her voice did not betray her nerves. *Fake it till you make it.* She almost laughed at that silly thought.

"It really is our pleasure." He held her hand a moment longer than he should before he let go. Breaking eye contact with her, he turned to Evan and asked how many people were in attendance.

"I'd say at least 200," Evan replied, "and I'm expecting that after tonight it will be a steady flow of people and press. Speaking of which, this woman wanted to ask Ella some questions for the paper." He motioned to Jessica, who seemed to have forgotten Ella and wanted only to engage Armand's attention.

Ella stepped back for a minute and took a look at him. He was well-dressed, obviously not an American, he had dark hair that seemed to have a gold shimmer to it, his complexion was warm, and his accent indicated to Ella that he might be possibly South American. He was also wearing gloves. Something about seeing that made Ella feel a little happy.

"So you're the owner?" Jessica stepped in front of Ella to make sure Armand had to look at her. Ella smiled to herself and left them, as Evan went off to talk to other attendees.

As she walked through the rooms, she was stopped by people who were figuring out this was her show. They had nothing but complimentary things to say to her. She couldn't believe it.

"I'd say this is turning into a success." Ryan stopped next to her, as she looked at a group of people seemingly engaged in a conversation about her work.

"I wasn't sure you would come," she said.

"I wouldn't have missed it," he replied. He reached out to her, and she turned and hugged him. It took a minute before he hugged her back. Reluctantly, she let go of him. The initial pleasant warmth she felt when she touched him was dulled, but she still felt it come over her. She made up her mind to tell the professor about it. It's not just that she liked Ryan. *Wait... I like Ryan.* Ella stood there for a minute letting the revelation wash over her. *I do not have time for this. Or whatever. Especially since he's been so weird the last week or so.*

"Blah."

"Blah?" Ryan looked at her with a confused expression.

"Oh nothing. I'm just my own worst enemy." Ella smiled at him and put her hand on his arm. "Thank you so much for coming, Ryan. It means a lot to me."

"I wasn't going to miss it. I have seen your work. I knew it was amazing, but this show is unbelievable. This room is so fragile feeling. And the last two rooms, those are my favorite. I don't know if I could pick between them, but they are so cool. Astonishing. They did such a good job with the lights, too." He stopped abruptly. "Ella, I think I'm still a little nervous being around you."

She didn't say anything to him. She turned to look at the room where they were standing, surrounded by the gauzy paper fans Ella had painted with animals and landscapes in all different shades of blue. Large fans hung on the walls, and smaller ones hung from the ceiling with the pictures facing down, placed intermittently between paper parasols, the tops of which she had painted with characters of different languages from all around the world. She stopped in front of the folding rice-paper screen standing in the corner of the room. It had a Chinese dragon, painted midnight blue with silver scales, running across the three panels. It had been funny to her to pull this screen out of her closet. She'd all but forgotten about it. *It's lovely.* She was glad she had not put it up for sale. Sighing, she turned back around to face him.

"Honestly, Ryan, I don't know why you are nervous around me, but it has been hard to know if you want to even see me. You come over and help me when I ask, but you have not really asked, yourself, since the first night. And you act so strangely, I have no idea if you even like me. But yet you keep coming to see me, so... You could say you make me nervous, too, but I'm not sure why. I'm pretty confused, and to be totally up-front, I really feel that you don't like me that much at all."

Ryan came over to her, took both her gloved hands in his, and looked her in the eye. "Ella, I like you a lot. You are smart, talented, and weird."

"I'm not sure that last one is a compliment."

"It is, I promise." He said it so seriously that Ella had to resist the urge to pull away from him.

"Ella, it's just... there are some things about me that I want to tell you, but..." People started to come into the room. Ryan dropped her hands and stepped away. "Ella, I like you. Just know that, and we can talk after your show. Enjoy this. It's a really cool opportunity."

"I was hoping I could speak to you about your show, Miss Cerulean." Armand's smooth, accented voice cut through the growing din in the room as he entered, followed by the reporter, the photographer, and Evan.

"Yeah, Ella, you sure can disappear," Jessica, the reporter, said, with a not-very-well-hidden hint in her voice.

"Evan, you wouldn't mind showing this reporter and photographer around while I speak to Ella alone." Armand said it pointedly, without looking at any of them, and never breaking his eye contact with Ella.

"I'll find you later," Ryan said, but not before he leaned in and kissed her cheek, surprising her almost half to death. *But not in a bad way.*

"Sure, Mr. El Dorado, I'd love to tell you about my show. You'll have to tell me about that very unusual last name of yours."

"You don't know who he is?" Jessica, the reporter, said, in a voice that indicated Ella was, in fact, quite ridiculously stupid.

"Evan, if you don't mind." Armand still didn't look at the ever-preening reporter, who gave Evan a very irritated look, as he held his arm out to her to move her out of the room.

Ella had to smile. *The whole scene is so INSANE.*

"I'm sorry, Mr. El Dorado, I don't know who you are." Ella said it sincerely, and felt slightly concerned that, since he did own the gallery, maybe she should have bothered to find out who he was. *And Evan, for that matter.*

"Was that your boyfriend, Miss Cerulean? And please call me Armand, and know that I am delighted that you do not know who I am. In fact, it seems to me, by looking at the amount of work here in the gallery, that you don't waste too much time. Something that I admire a great deal."

"I try not to waste time, but trust me, I stare off into space plenty when I am trying to paint. And if I am going to call you Armand, you have to call me Ella."

"Agreed. Now let's start in the back room and make our way to the front. The back room may very well be my favorite of all the rooms."

"Oh, you've seen them all already? I thought you had only arrived when we met up front."

"I've been in and out all week while you've been bringing things and the exhibit was being set up. My work schedule keeps me plenty busy, but Evan promised me a unique show, and I have to say he, and you, Ella, delivered quite astonishingly for our little space." He took her gloved hand in his, looked at it a second, smiled, wove it through the crook of his arm, and led her to the back room.

They spent the rest of the evening talking. People would come, ask questions, congratulate Ella on a job well done, and express how impressed they were with the unique qualities of the whole exhibit, but mostly they talked, uninterrupted. A lot of people tried to expressly talk to Armand. He was polite, but dismissive. He seemed only interested in Ella.They spent two hours just in the back room of the show, while Ella explained why she wanted the room set up to feel as though they were in a planetarium. Paintings of planets, nebulae, and stars covered the walls. A grouping of individual paintings were hung in the shape of the Orion constellation.

"The detail in the work is astonishing. Especially since the color palette, at first glance, seems so limited. But it's not, once you take the time to examine the pieces closely." Armand was leaning in close to a particular painting, mulling it over.

As he was looking at it, Ella wandered into the room where she had, thus far, spent the least amount of time. She was pleased to find the professor starring intently at a floor-to-ceiling, as-wide-as-the-wall painting of a coral reef. It was one of her favorites, and she had spent a long time creating the piece. Even now, looking at it, she thought there were things she could still add. She had put it up for sale for quite a lot of money with the idea no one would buy it.

"Hello," she said to him, as he was bent over, muttering to himself. *He is such a funny person. Like an imaginary doctor.*

"Thank you for coming to my show, Professor."

He straightened up and smiled at her. "I wouldn't have missed it. It's remarkable all on its own, but, as we both know, for other reasons as well. And the setup of the exhibit is so unique and even somewhat peculiar."

"Thanks, I guess," she laughed a little. He was not wrong. It was strange, but she liked it. She loved it, actually, and she smiled as Armand walked into the room. *He is really handsome,* she noticed for the first time. He had been so kind to her tonight and had asked so many questions. It had been a great deal of fun to find herself sorting through her thoughts about her work by talking aloud with someone, coming up with more answers than she knew possible. She was unaccustomed to so many people being interested in her life in any way. If she was being totally honest with herself, she really was enjoying making new friends. The reflection brought a sad moment, as she once again speculated about finding Alexandra. She was going to try and find out where Miss Magritte had gone as well. *I wish I'd thought of that before. Maybe she could help me find Alexandra. We are going to the school. There must be some leads there. Well maybe not school,* she corrected herself. It didn't please her to remember she had been in an institution, but at least, for once, it seemed like a clear memory.

"This room has a grand quality to it," Armand declared, bringing Ella back to the moment. "It feels larger than it is because of the size of your pieces." The room only contained a handful of them. They were very large and filled the space. A light that shimmered like waves of water covered the ceiling. The music was low and ambient.

"It took me the most time to create these few pieces," Ella told him. "I still look at the reef and think of things I'd like to add."

"A lot of artists feel their work is rarely done," Armand replied. "I think it is a sign of growth. If you are always content with what you create, how will it ever change or improve?"

The professor finally seemed to notice there was someone else in the room. Ella realized the show must be coming to an end, as it seemed the noise of the party had faded quite a bit. She wondered where Evan was, and how he thought it went.

"Armand, this is my friend, James Reynolds." She stood between them as she made the introduction.

"Actually, Ella, Armand and I know each other." The doctor put his hands in his pockets and looked at the two of them. "Is this your gallery, Armand?"

"The building is mine, and only part of the gallery, Doctor. It is good to see you." They were being formal with each other, and it occurred to Ella that she still did not know much about Armand. He had spent the last few hours focused on her and never directed the conversation towards himself.

"How do you know each other?" she asked, wondering why the doctor would assume the gallery belonged to Armand. *People seem to know a lot about him. I'm always late to the party.*

"Armand's company is a major contributor to the university where I teach. He helps fund my work, Ella."

"You have a company?" She was astonished. *He can't be that much older than me.*

"A company?" The professor laughed. "No, Ella, Armand has a multi-national corporation that has its hands in a considerable part of the entire world's business. That explanation is not nearly enough, but alas, I am going to continue to look at your work, Ella. I saw your apartment, yes, but this is another thing entirely." The professor strolled off slowly and hummed to himself.

Ella looked at Armand. "I guess that explains why so many women want your attention. Because you're not married, I take it."

"No, Ella, I am not married."

Her world was getting odder by the minute with all these people.

"Do you want to tell me about your company, or would you rather talk about something else? Maybe your last name? It's so different. I like it, though."

"It's just an old family name with a myth attached to it, as you know, Ella." Armand was forthright in the way he looked at her, always watching her face and rarely breaking eye contact, except to look at her work. If she were not so comfortable around him already, she'd find it unsettling. *It is an unusual amount of confidence for someone in their twenties to have. Assuming he is in his twenties.* Obviously, she was fairly clueless. But she did feel remarkably comfortable around him.

"Well, like I said earlier, I don't know who you are, or anything about your company. I don't pay much attention to business, to be completely honest."

"Ella, I doubt most people know much about my business. I would imagine most of them get their supposed information about me from gossip magazines. As a single male with a famous company, and, well, a fair amount of scandal attached to my family name, papers like to write about me. Whether it's true or not. So you can read what you like, or I can just tell you more about it another time."

"Another time?"

"Yes, another time. Maybe during, say, a dinner another time."

"Are you asking me out on a date?" Ella thought of Ryan and wondered what he would think of that, only to remember he was the one who had been acting so aloof. And they most certainly were not dating in any way. Armand had been so attentive to her, and interested in her, and he was certainly good looking.

Yeah, I want to go on a date with him, so no point in pretending.

"Did I say something funny, Ella?" He tilted his head at her as if puzzled.

"No, Armand, I am just a strange person. Going to dinner sounds great. When would you like to go?"

"I like that you are strange. Would you be free tomorrow night?"

"I am free. When should I be..." She was interrupted by the professor calling her name from the next room. She walked quickly over to where he was standing, leaning very close into a painting of the Cat's Eye Nebula.

"What is it, Dr. Reynolds?"

He leaned back so Ella could have a look at what had caught his attention. The painting that had previously covered the entire piece of canvas now contained a handprint. A handprint that appeared as if it had removed that section of paint like an eraser. It looked as though it had never been painted. Which it most certainly had been.

"How in the hell...?" She stared at the spot, as if expecting someone would appear and put the missing piece of the painting back.

"That's not good. And how in the world did that happen?" Evan had come in behind her, as well as Armand. "It's shaped like a handprint. Could bleach do that? I'm so sorry one of your pieces sustained damage during the show. I'm positive this did not happen during install, Ella."

"I know it didn't, Evan, and I'm sure it did not happen until a few hours ago, because I was in here for a long time talking with Armand, and I don't even remotely remember someone trying to touch my work."

"Nor do I," added Armand.

"I'll have to contact the person who bought the piece and let them know what happened. We'll have to issue a refund." Evan looked through a notebook he was carrying as he said that.

"I sold a painting?" Ella was so surprised, and despite the fact that a refund would be given, and the painting probably didn't have a new home after all, it was still exciting to hear that someone liked something enough to buy it.

"Oh yeah, it sold. Everything did." He continued going through his notes nonchalantly.

Ella laughed. *This can't be true.* "Are you serious? Everything sold?"

"Yeah, first time it's ever happened. We usually sell a few pieces from a show opening night, and often quite a bit more through the time of the exhibit. But this is the first time we've sold everything, and, well... don't look so shocked. Your work is incredible, and everyone thinks so." Evan found what he was looking for and went to the front of the building.

"Oh my. Congratulations, Ella. You do deserve it. I mean, look at these rooms." The professor moved as if to shake her hand, but she grabbed him and hugged him. It took a moment before he relaxed and hugged her back, but when he did, she felt even happier. If that was even possible.

"Thank you, Professor, for helping me so much these last few days. You have made me feel a lot better."

"You're welcome. But remember what I said, we still have a lot to look into." Stepping back from each other, Ella turned to Armand.

"Thank you, Armand, for letting me have a show here. I just can't tell you how grateful I am to Evan. He's been so helpful and open to my ideas."

"I'm glad to hear that, Ella. He is a good partner. It seems dinner is going to be of a celebratory nature."

"You two are going to dinner?" the professor asked. Funny enough, if Ella didn't know better, she would think his tone to his question sounded almost disapproving. *But obviously that can't be, and maybe his accent always made him sound a little judgmental,* she thought snarkily.

"Yes, Doctor. Do you mind if I take our talented friend out for dinner to celebrate her great success?" Armand said it without a trace of sarcasm, but with a bit of questioning.

"No, of course not. I was just surprised. Ella is a bit on the introverted side," the professor backpedaled.

Ella looked between the two of them and made a decision to try to find out what this was all about. Every day was bringing her more things to investigate. *Look out, Veronica Mars.*

"ANYWAY," Ella said it loudly, and hoped to make the point that it was her decision to make, "dinner sounds wonderful, and I am so pleased and happy you both are here. Now, I'll give you my number, Armand. Call me. We will figure out our plans. I am going to go say goodnight to Evan and head home."

She handed Armand one of the hand-drawn business cards she had thrown together at the last minute this morning, and walked through the rooms that were now empty of people. Some of the lights had been turned off, and there were spots littered with empty wine glasses, napkins, and plates. The ambient music from the ocean room was still on, and it could be heard through the entire building now that it was quiet. The effect was somewhat eerie.

She went into Evan's office, where he was packing up things to leave.

"I called the guy who bought the painting and told him about the damage."

"Should I call him, too? Did you give him his refund?" Ella sat down in a chair, and it hit her that she was pretty tired.

"Actually, he said he still wanted the painting."

"Really?" Ella started. "I would not expect to hear that. I wonder if I could fix it."

"He said it didn't matter. He loved the painting and even asked if he could pick it up tomorrow. I told him that he could not, unless you said so. Normally, I would not even allow that exception because, sold or not, the show stays up for the full run of dates. But this is a special case. He is being really cool about the damage, and I didn't know if you would want a damaged piece to stay up the duration."

"You know, Evan, the more I think about it, the more I think I could fix it. Is it weird to ask if I could see who the buyer is? I'd like to talk to him about it, and see what he thought about me fixing it."

"Sure, that's no problem." He shuffled through some papers and handed one to her.

Looking at the slip she saw a familiar name on the receipt.

Ryan had bought her painting.

Chapter 13

Ryan and Megan were waiting for Ella at a late-night cafe. She was glad to have a chance to see Megan. It had been so busy at the show she missed her completely. They were sitting out on a deck of the cafe with tea, cupcakes, and more blue roses. They both clapped when they saw Ella, and it made her so happy. She was sure she had never felt this happy in her entire life.

"I'm so sorry I didn't get to talk to you at the gallery, Megan." Ella settled in next to them and hugged her. Then she clasped Ryan's hand. "Thank you for buying one of my paintings, and I think I can absolutely fix the damage to it."

Ryan smiled as Megan asked, "What damage?"

"It's the strangest thing. It looks like someone used a bleach pen or something to make the paint come off in the shape of a hand," she said, shrugging her shoulders and reaching for a cupcake.

"That is weird," Megan frowned. "But tell me, who was that gorgeous man you were talking to for so long?"

Ella couldn't help but notice a gloomy look cross Ryan's face. "Oh, him? His name is Armand. He owns part of the gallery. He's very nice, actually. Not at all what you might expect from someone like him."

"Like him?"

"You and I, Megan, might be the only people who don't know who he is," Ella told her, licking frosting off the wrapper. "Good grief these are really good. Thank you for the flowers, you guys."

"They're from Ryan." Megan grabbed a cupcake and started licking frosting too. "Be careful not to get frosting on your gloves, Ella."

"MmmMM, yeah, it's fine," she mumbled between bites. She was starving.

After a very un-polite few minutes of cupcakes and tea, she looked right at Ryan. "Thank you for all the roses, and the help you gave me to get ready. I know the circumstances that kept you around are not great, but you helped me a lot. Thank you."

Ryan blushed. Both of the girls glanced at each other in surprise, and Megan tried not to laugh by grabbing another cupcake.

"You're welcome," he said shyly, without his usual aloof, distant tone. "I was glad to help you, and I would love it if you could fix the painting."

"Absolutely. I felt tired at the gallery, but now I'm full of adrenaline. Or sugar. Not sure which. Let's go to Alchemy! I am always working, so I never actually get to dance there. I would love to tell my boss how the show went."

"That sounds fun. Let's totally go. Ryan?" Megan waited for him to answer. He stared off into space for a minute, and Ella noticed something she hadn't noticed tonight. He was giving off that strange light that she saw only around him. *Maybe I'm turning into someone who can read auras. Or whatever. Maybe I am just a loon with bad vision.*

"Hellloooo." Megan snapped her fingers in front of his face. "Earth to Ryan. Let's go dancing."

"Yeah, sure." He absentmindedly started cleaning off their table, and Megan looked at Ella. "I have no idea what is going on with that boy ninety-five percent of the time."

"If you never know after all this time. How will I know?"

"His mystery is part of his charm, maybe?"

Ella laughed at Megan's joke, pulled her to the sidewalk, and they went to the club. All the while, Ella kept glancing at Ryan and noticing the light that seemed to be emanating from him. He was especially cute tonight, and she was a little warm. She stepped a bit closer to him as they walked, with Megan up ahead, saying hello to every guy that walked by.

"Hey," Ella said softly, "are you okay?"

Ryan smiled back. "Yeah, just a little tired. Let's go celebrate your success." And then Ryan took her hand in his. Ella had the most ridiculous urge to squeal with delight, but decided not to do anything but smile.

Megan stopped up at a corner and turned back to them, "It's about time, Ryan." And whistled loudly, making Ryan finally laugh.

Megan's energetic, good mood was washing over them both, and they ran to catch up with her, Ryan's silver-lined suit glimmering in the street lights. The nice weather had brought out lots of people. The sidewalk was filled with goth girls and boys, smoking cloves and chatting on the patio. The guard let them pass the line outside, and Megan went straight to the dance floor, leaving Ryan and Ella on their own.

"Hey, I want to go say hi to my boss and tell him how my show went," Ella told Ryan.

"Sure. I'll just be wandering around." He bent over and kissed her on the cheek before disappearing into the crowd.

Ella felt flush and giddy over his sudden turn of behavior toward her. The show and her friends, definitely one of the best nights she'd had in a long time. And on top of that, she still felt good physically. Making a note to herself to thank the professor for helping, she went and asked her co-worker where their manager was hiding out. She headed toward his office, where Jack was sitting behind his desk. It had been cleaned up, with no evidence of there having been a break-in. He had the remnants of a bruise on his face, but a smile that lit up the room when he saw Ella. Without a word, he got up and engulfed her in a big bear hug.

"I'm sorry, sweetie, I couldn't make it to opening night. But the wife and I will head over there tomorrow to look at your work."

"It's okay," she disentangled herself with a smile. "I figured someone had to run the club. It's so busy tonight and the office looks back to normal. Please tell me no one else has bothered you."

"No one, darling, has bothered me, and even if they had, you should not be worrying about it." He heaved his large frame back into the chair. "Tell me how it went."

For the next twenty minutes, Ella launched into a description of the show, people, the setup, and then she told him, "And I sold every piece! I can't believe it!"

"You sold every piece! I'm so proud of you. Oh, and I scheduled more days off. You have too many saved up, so enjoy the time off. Now, go have fun. I know you never get to hang out." He shooed her out of the room, and she went off in search of Megan.

The club was packed to capacity, and the music was pulsing. Everywhere she turned, there was another lavishly-dressed person moving to the music.

A touch on her arm made her stop and turn around, thinking it might be Megan or Ryan, but it was neither of them. It was Armand, his golden eyes intent on her and a solemn expression on his face.

"Hello again." Despite the loud noise Ella could hear him just fine. As clearly as if it were silent in the room, in fact. "I'm glad to see you, Ella. I am looking forward to our dinner."

Ella had almost forgotten, she'd been so caught up in the moments following the show. Ryan's seemingly sudden change of heart made her wonder if she should still go to dinner with Armand.

"By the look on your face, it does not seem as if that feeling is mutual." He guided her carefully through the crowd to a private table. Several men and women were sitting at it and when they saw the two of them, they stood up to leave.

"It's funny..." She slid down onto a velvet chair. "It's so loud in here, and I can hear everything you're saying perfectly." He leaned in close to her after sitting on the couch. He smelled fantastic, sophisticated and smoky. It made her head swim the tiniest bit.

"I can hear you as well. I am very pleased to see you again, and I do mean it when I say I am looking forward to our dinner."

Armand was the gallery owner and had probably put a lot into her show. Having dinner with him would be a nice thing to do, especially since he offered it as a way to celebrate. It did not have to be anything but that, despite the fact that she had to admit her heartbeat seemed to be going a little faster with him sitting so close.

"I am looking forward to it as well. Thank you for everything tonight. It really was one of the best nights of my life."

"I'm glad. I hope I can add to the list of best nights of your life." He offered a glass of champagne, which she declined. Not knowing what would happen with the meds, she didn't drink much, if at all.

"Water would be just fine for me," she told him, and Armand motioned for the server who smiled a hello at Ella.

"It's strange for me to be here not working," Ella said, as she tried to move slightly away from Armand without him noticing. "Especially to be sitting in the fancy section."

"If you are uncomfortable, I am glad to move." He moved to stand, and Ella shook her head no.

"It's fine. Don't give up your table on my account." Trying to look for Megan and Ryan without seeming like she was looking, she asked Armand if he had been to the club before because he seemed familiar to her. "I didn't realize it until I left the gallery, but honestly, not to sound too weird, but your eyes seem especially familiar. I swear I just notice details. I'm not a nut. Well, not a dangerous nut."

Armand smiled that dark, mysterious smile at her again. "All great artists have to be a touch crazy. The point of view they possess must be unique. But I am not sure why I would seem familiar to you. Perhaps you have seen something with a picture of me in it. Irritatingly enough, my picture gets taken more than I care for it to be." He took a sip of champagne with a black gloved hand. Ella looked down at her gloves. *They hide a secret. Do his?*

"Why do people take your picture so much?" She tried to relax since she wanted to have fun, and Armand was, in fact, kind and very handsome, and for some reason interested in talking to her. There was no shortage of female and male attention being tossed his way. He seemed not the slightest bit interested in any of it. "You mentioned family scandal earlier. Is that why?"

"It's a big part of it, yes. I won't pretend I haven't made a few, very public, mistakes. But I learned my lesson and try to avoid the spotlight now. I do not have much success when I am in the city. It's easier when I am out in the country, or at my home."

"Your home? Is it far from here?" *Why are my nerves getting the better of me now?*

He leaned in close and she could feel his breath. The lilt on his words from the accent on her ear sent a thrill down her spine. "Would you like to dance, Ella?" He held his hand out, and without a second to spare in-between her rapidly accelerating heartbeats, Armand pulled her to her feet and to the dance floor.

The floor was overflowing, the lights dimmed, creating dancing shadows over the mist-filled room. His arm was around her waist. Never having danced so intimately with someone, Ella lost track of the world around them. His scent washed over her completely, his self-assurance dominated the dance floor as the music slowed. The lush voice of PJ Harvey, slow and seductive, spilled out from the speakers. A weightless feeling of belonging there, almost déjà-vu-like in quality, settled over them.

Looking up at Armand, whose intensity was evident when he returned her gaze, she knew he felt the same been-here-before, belong-here-now feeling that she did, and the smallest fear slid into the moment. Nearly jerking back, she caught herself when she became aware of how strong he was, and tried to relax by leaning into his shoulder. Armand was taller than her, but close enough in height that they were matched well in the slow motion of the movements. Ella felt the breathtaking desire to stay in his arms for as long as possible. Nothing else existed for eternity. Just them. Eyes closed, and swaying without a space between them, neither of them noticed that the music had long since picked up tempo, and the circle that had cleared around them was filling again.

"Ella," Megan intoned over the loud music with a cheerful, sing-song voice.

Ella slowly reawakened to the fact that they were at the club she worked in. Megan was standing next to Armand, staring wide-eyed at Ella, with Ryan right behind. Suddenly feeling a bit self-conscious of everyone looking at them, Ella reluctantly disentangled from Armand, who also seemed unwilling to let go.

Gathering thoughts, and hopefully intelligible words, she turned to her friends, "Hi guys, I was looking for you."

Ella moved off to the side of the dance floor, and Armand seemed to bow slightly to her, with a ghost of a smile playing about his lips as he stepped back to the private table. Ella knew he was watching every move, and could not fathom why she felt connected to someone she had just met.

"You didn't seem to be looking too hard," Megan cracked, and swatted Ella on the arm.

"Well, I was," Ella fumbled for words and looked at Ryan. He returned the scrutiny, unflinching. Hands in the pockets of the smooth, silver-lined suit, he simply turned and walked off to the other side of the club.

"I think maybe someone might be kind of jealous." Megan motioned her head towards the tall, blonde silhouette that seemed to leave a flickering trail of glowing dust in its wake.

"Jealous? What? Why?" Ella stared at his back until it was no longer visible, and then bent closer to Megan.

"I told you I think he likes you. But I know he is absolutely the worst about feelings. Like a wall would absolutely tell you more about how it felt. But seriously, Armand? YUM! Good grief, he is ridiculously good looking." Megan clutched her arm. "Introduce a lady, would you?"

"Don't you think we should go find Ryan?"

"Nope, I say let him stew. Maybe he'll stop being so weird for once in his life." Megan, not taking no for an answer, stepped over to Armand's table and introduced herself. Ella had to laugh, wishing once again for a tad bit more confidence.

"Armand," Ella tried to sound more settled outwardly than she felt inwardly, "this is my friend, Megan."

Armand stood and shook Megan's hand warmly. "Any friend of Ella's is a friend of mine." He offered a glass of champagne, which she took.

For the next couple of hours, Armand was attentive and funny to both of them, making Ella feel glad she had stayed with him. He flirtatiously deflected Megan's advances without offending her, and made sure to share a glance here and there that only Ella would notice. All the while, the sense of knowing him now and before lingered. After some time, he asked to be excused for the evening.

"I've had a wonderful time this evening. Thank you, ladies, for the company, and Ella, I shall be in touch tomorrow about dinner. Don't stay out too late and be too tired to see me." His teasing tone added to the charm of the accent. *Stereotypes be damned, accents are sexy.* "Please stay at the table as long as you like. My treat." And with the final flourish of actually kissing both their hands, but with a knowing twinkle in his eye of the cheesy factor, he left them.

"Be still my heart!" Megan flung herself back dramatically onto the couch. "What a babe! And that accent. I don't care what anyone says, they are hot." Megan poked Ella in the side. "He most certainly likes you. If I didn't like you, I would be completely jealous. Did you have fun? You seem distracted."

"I'm okay. It's just been a crazy, great, unusual night on top of a crazy, great, unusual week. I am afloat in feelings of all kinds," she joked.

"Speaking of feelings, shall we go find a certain handsome, pouty blonde?" Megan asked, as she finished off the champagne.

They got up in search of Ryan, who had seemingly left them at the club, the idea of which infuriated Megan.

"Not that I need his help! But we're supposed to be sticking together. I am going to give him a piece of my mind," she declared. Linking arms with Ella, she swayed a bit to the left. "Let's go home. I'm a teensy bit tipsy, so you have to be my walking stick." She hiccuped and then giggled.

Ella waved good-bye to her boss and thanked her co-workers as they headed out. As they made their way to the door, Megan was more of a handful than Ella was expecting. She was relieved when she saw Ryan had not actually left, but was outside, leaning against the wall of the club, waiting for them.

"I thought you left," Ella said softly as Megan, wobbly-like, flirted with some boys on the sidewalk.

"No, just needed some air," his tone was neutral. He pointed to Megan and said, "Need some help?"

"That would be great, but be warned, she drank about a gallon of champagne, and she also thought you abandoned us."

"I don't think I could, Ella, even if I wanted to."

They both stood together, waiting for Megan to finish exchanging numbers with one of the guys. When she turned and saw Ryan, her mouth opened as if to yell at him, but it closed just as abruptly. They turned to see what had shut Megan up, and the professor was standing behind them.

"I'm sorry to interrupt your good time. Congratulations on your successful show, Ella." He said it hurriedly.

"Thanks, James. What are you doing here? Are you okay? You're all sweaty."

"I just went back to my lab and found out that someone had tried to break in while I was gone. They didn't get in because we have good security at the university. But I think it might have something to do with what I think I found out today. I was waiting to tell you until after tonight, but it seems time might be of the essence." His voice had dropped to a whisper. Megan was all but sleeping in Ryan's arms.

"We should probably go somewhere to talk," he continued. He looked at Megan and Ryan. "I don't mind if your friends come, if you don't mind, but she doesn't look ready for much of anything." He pointed at Megan.

"Go with him, Ella. I'll take Megan home and come and meet you."

"Are you sure you can get her home?"

Ryan smiled. "It's not the first time Megan has been a handful. For as small as she is, you'd think she didn't weigh much, but she is solid muscle." He laughed and heaved her over his shoulder, fireman style. He touched Ella's cheek. "Go. I'll meet you guys at the lab. That work for you, Professor?'

"Yes. Great. Let's go." James moved quickly down the street.

Ella looked at Ryan taking Megan, and then followed the professor. *Never a dull moment lately.*

Hurrying as fast as she could in her dress, she was breathless when she caught up to him as he crossed the parking lot to the school building.

"Professor? What is so wrong? What did you find?"

"Let's talk inside, Ella." They got to the door, where the security guard let them in and locked it behind them.

"Professor, the police are circling the building and checking in regularly. Anyone bother you, sir?" The security guard tipped his hat at Ella.

"I'm fine, Jerry. Thank you so much. I'll be in my lab if you need me."

"Have a good night, Professor. Miss." He smiled and wandered down the hall to check in the windows of other classrooms.

James hastily unlocked his door, ushered Ella in, and locked it behind them. The door had an extra lock on it Ella didn't remember seeing the last time she was here. *What is going on?*

Finally in the lab, he started pulling things out and putting them onto the counter. His clear anxiety was starting to rub off on her, and she caught herself wringing her hands.

"Please tell me what is going on, James???"

"I will, but I have to set these up so you'll understand what I found. If I just tell you, it might seem like I am off my rocker."

"Well, I feel that way all the time," she said, stepping away from him for a minute so he could get everything out. She wondered when Ryan would be getting here, and found amusement thinking what dealing with Megan was like right now.

"Okay, Ella, I've been running tests on your blood, tissue samples, and the substance from your hands." He paused and Ella thought she was going to die of the anticipation.

"What did you find? Please tell me?"

"I wasn't sure at first. The results were so confusing, and I ran test after test until I realized I might have to broaden my horizons, so to speak. When I was at the pharmaceutical company, we continuously searched for anomalies in patients that would set them apart in treatments. Why did some people get better? Or not sick at all? A constant quest. Further, if they were somehow different, could that difference be replicated for others? This is an important question in the constant search for cures. For anything. Your anomaly is obvious. The question is, what is it? Or so I thought."

The phone in the lab rang, startling them both. The professor answered it. After a moment he put his hand over the receiver, "Your friend Ryan is here. Do you want him to be here? Do you trust him? What I am about to tell you is going to change a lot, I believe."

"I trust him," the answer true and automatic. Ella did not doubt Ryan's trustworthiness.

James told the guard to let Ryan in, and they waited for his knock. Ella went and unlocked the door.

"Did I miss the big reveal?" he joked.

"Nope. I don't know what type of freak I am yet."

"Hey," Ryan tilted her chin up to meet his eyes. "You're the great kind. Like me." It made her smile, and they went back to the lab, where the professor was pacing up and down the room.

"Okay, back to it. So, looking at anomalies in medical history, I couldn't find anything similar to yours. Until I had the tissue samples done and something clicked." He shuffled some papers around and handed them to Ella. Ryan looked over them as well.

"I don't really understand what these say, James." Ella handed them back to him.

"They are the numbers that I ran. I had them run through a dozen times, and the result came back the same every time, until there was no question that they are correct results."

"But what are the results?" Ella rubbed her forehead. *What a long day.*

"The numbers coming back the way they did made me consider that perhaps you didn't *have* an anomaly, but that you *are* an anomaly."

"Um... Okay? Can you explain the numbers to me?"

"Yes, of course. I'm sorry. I'm just getting ahead of myself. My mind is racing with a thousand thoughts. The numbers are how old you are, undoubtedly."

"Why would you be testing for that?" Ryan asked. "It's pretty obvious how old Ella is."

"So you would think. And I wasn't testing for that. It's just part of the result. But it was so wrong that, like I said, I tested it again and again."

"Well, then how old am I? twenty-two, not twenty? What?"

"No, Ella, you are over one hundred years old."

"Yep, you're right. You've lost your mind."

"There is no doubt. You are over one hundred years old. What's more, the material that exists within your being is even older. I don't have any idea how this is possible, but there is no question, I promise you."

"What is it??"

"It's cobalt, Ella. Your entire body is filled with it. You are producing it. It's what comes from your hands, and I am sure it's what pools around your joints, causing pain from the build-up because something seems to be keeping you from manufacturing it in a manageable way."

"I shouldn't be producing it at all!" she cried out. *Cobalt! What do I know about cobalt? Only bad things. Poison, toxic, the color blue.*

"Well, all human beings have cobalt in their bodies in this day and age. It's also part of vitamin B12, so it's used to treat certain medical problems. It's just when there's too much exposure that it becomes a problem."

"Wait, if I'm manufacturing it, am I exposing people to it? Oh god, am I hurting anyone?" It was too much, and she gripped the table. Ryan put a hand on her back and the spot instantly heated.

"I do not believe anyone is suffering from this except you, Ella," James told her. "Sincerely," he added when she looked at him like she didn't believe him. "You are made to be doing this. I know how that sounds, but I am pretty sure this is the case."

All the years she wanted to know, apparently even more years than she ever knew, she had been waiting to hear what was wrong with her. *How could anyone have guessed that this was it?*

"Am I human?" she stammered out, not even believing she had just asked anyone that question.

The professor stopped everything at this point and walked over to her. He waited until she looked at him with the silvery-blue tears that she had hidden her whole life now running fully down her face for everyone to see.

"You are human, Ella. You are a very special human. That is what you should be absolutely sure of. No doubts. No questions."

Ryan and James let Ella gather herself together before anyone said anything else.

"James?"

"Yes, Ella?"

"Do you think there's anyone else like me?"

"I don't know, but I hope so."

Chapter 14

Megan opened the door to the apartment, cleared her throat in a loud way, and woke Ella, who was fast asleep on the blue velvet couch with Ryan's arms around her.

"And I thought I had a long night. You look awful, Ella," Megan said, as she handed over a cup of coffee from the shop's carrying tray. "Hey, Boy Wonder," she nudged Ryan's foot to wake him, "take your coffee." Ella sipped hers, set it down, and looked at Megan.

"I feel like absolute crap," Megan declared, and plopped down next to them on the couch. "You, however, look like you've been crying. And you have blue make up all over your face. What happened? Did Ryan do something, I swear to god..." The look on Ella's face stopped her. "Ella, sweetie, what's wrong?"

"Thanks for assuming it was me," Ryan croaked out. He took a long swig off the coffee and got up to wash his face.

"It wasn't him. He was great. He took your drunk butt home," Ella informed her.

"Well, then, what happened?"

Ella gave her the Cliffs Notes, and Megan's disbelief grew with each passing revelation.

"So, wait, you paint all of this with your hands?"

"Yes, but I mean you always paint with your hands."

"Har har. You know what I mean, the paint comes from your hands?"

"It's not paint, it's cobalt. I make paint with it. Using mineral oil and the like."

"And you make this stuff, in your body." Megan pointed to Ella's chest.

"Yes, I guess so."

"And you're older than you thought?"

"Yes."

"A lot older?"

"Um, somewhat."

"Are you going to tell me or do I have to guess?"

"It's not polite to ask a lady her age."

"It's a good thing you're not a lady. Good grief, out with it already. My headache wants food."

"Well," she started, as Ryan came back into the room, "the professor seems to think that I am over a hundred years old."

"What the crap?"

"Nice French, Megan."

"Bite me, Ryan. Are you serious, Ella? That's... That's... That's... You look great," she finally finished. "Is that possible? I mean maybe he's a total nut, Ella. I mean, you met the guy in the dark."

"I don't have any reason not to believe him, at this point,"

"What about you? Do you believe him Ryan? You automatically didn't trust him."

"I know, but he really does seem like he wants to help Ella. I don't know, Megan. I've learned to distrust all doctors and researchers..."

"And everyone," Megan added helpfully.

"I trust both of you," Ella interjected into the conversation.

"I'm glad you do," said Megan.

"Me too." Ryan put a hand on her shoulder. It grew very warm. Warmer than ever before.

"Ryan, whenever you touch me I get so hot," Ella said.

"Uh, maybe I should go," Megan quipped.

"Not like that." Ella stopped when she saw the slightly injured look on his face. "I mean, like actually hot." She sighed. "Ryan, I think you're hot. Can we just not talk about it right now?"

"Fair enough," but his face was notably happier.

Megan made a face at them as if to say they were boring her.

"I actually get physically warmer when you are around me, and especially when you touch me. Do you think it has anything to do with your, um, condition?"

"It might," Ryan said thoughtfully. "I think some cancer radiation treatments use cobalt in them." He went to his computer and started to type away.

"Wait, like you can absorb radiation, too? AWESOME! OW! No yelling." Megan stuck her head under a pillow. "So, I'm not gonna yell anymore."

"I don't know what else I can do, but it's weird that I feel so strange around Ryan."

"You've been painting a long time, Ella." Megan sat up and looked at her with sad eyes. "You've kept this a secret a long time, haven't you? By yourself?"

"Mostly. My friend in school knew, and I can't help but think who might've known at school, or wherever I was. I wish I could remember better. Although that does remind me that I haven't taken my treatment for a while. I think it's possible it was dulling my reaction to you, because I positively felt like I was going to pass out from the heat the first few times I was with you, Ryan. I would feel almost sick. I just figured it was me, but now I wonder if there was some reaction taking place between us leftover from your treatments. I don't know. There is so much more to figure out, now. One answer gives me a million more questions."

"Can you answer a question for me?" Megan was dead serious.

"Of course, what do you want to know?"

"Can we please go get some food? So I do not die from this hangover."

"We wouldn't want that to happen, but I have to wash all this off my face, first. A lot of people seem to know a lot about me, all of a sudden, but I'd prefer not to let the whole world know I'm a freak."

"Stop calling yourself that," Ryan said from the table. "You're just different. Am I a freak because I'm sick? I thought I was most of my life."

"Of course not."

"Then stop calling yourself that," he said staunchly.

"Or you're both freaks, and soon I'll be the dead friend of two freaks. Feeeeeed meeee..." Megan made sounds as if she was taking her last breath and Ella laughed.

"I just told you I am a hundred-year-old human who makes cobalt, and all you're worried about is my starving you to death."

"A hundred-year-old human who makes cobalt and might absorb radiation. I think, sweet, she's a superhero. Who might starve me to death. Not very superhero-like behavior. Bad friend. Now go get washed up. And change your dress. You look like you shacked up at a stranger's house and did the walk of shame home."

"I most definitely did not do that," Ella chuckled, and went to change.

Though I did make dinner plans with a handsome stranger. Who I feel like I've known my whole life. The connection between them was undeniable. "How did I go from no boys to two boys?" she said aloud, thinking no one was listening.

Megan laughed behind her. "Because life is annoying, and nothing is ever easy," her friend said, and threw a short, black dress at her. "Hurry up, Ella. Even Ryan is ready to go, for once."

"Right, right, right," she said, pulling off her clothes from last night and slipping the clean dress on. She washed her face and pulled her hair back up into a knot. It shone in the sunlight pouring in through the window. Today it looked cobalt blue to her, the silver shimmered in the mirror.

They left to grab food at a nearby diner, which saved Megan's life, according to what she told the server.

"How is it that you can be hungover and dying one minute and flirting with our server the next?"

"You're not the only one with superpowers, Ella." Megan winked at her and drank her thousandth cup of coffee.

"Did you find anything else out, Ryan?" Ella turned away from the quite impressive show Megan was putting on.

"I don't know how much of it would relate to you. There's lots of information out there about cobalt, but I don't think it all relates to, you know, human cobalt."

"Hey," Megan said, as if she just remembered she had come there with friends and not the cute server, "you know, I was thinking, in between dying of course, that if you can't remember who knows about you when you were growing up for, like, forever, or whatever, is it possible people do know about you and that they're looking for you? Like that creep trying to break into your apartment."

"I started to wonder that as well," Ryan said quietly. "I just don't see it being a coincidence. Neither do I think it's coincidence that three of us have a connection to that company. We need to go to your school."

"Let's go today," Megan volunteered. "I'm off the next few days, no work, no classes."

"Okay," Ryan agreed with her.

"I can't go today."

"Why can't you go today, Ella?"

"Because I am going out to dinner with Armand." She did not dare look at Ryan when she said it.

"Oh, you lucky duck," Megan said enviously, then glanced at Ryan out of the corner of her eye. "I mean gross, why, Ella? He's so hideous. And that accent, belch."

"Thanks, Megan," Ryan said sarcastically. "No, you should go to dinner with him to celebrate your show. The success of last night got lost after we left the club. I'm sure he put a lot of money and work into your presentation, and if you sold everything, he'll make money. You should go, and we'll go to your school tomorrow. I can drive and plan out the route and find us a place to stay overnight, if you guys want."

Both of the girls sat in stunned silence.

"What," Ryan asked, "do I have something on my face?"

"Uh, no," Ella managed to get on board with the new and improved Ryan. "Thank you for taking on all that. That would be really great. I've never been on a road trip."

"Really? Well we'll have to make it special, then," he said nonchalantly. Megan was still looking at him with an eyebrow arched so high it looked like it might reach her hair.

"What are you up to?" Megan poked him with her foot.

"I'm not up to anything. I'm trying to be helpful. And to be totally honest, I'm pretty curious about all this, and about Ella's life. I'm sorry, is it weird for me to feel that way, Ella?"

"No. No, it's totally fine, I'm curious about my life, too," she joked.

"You don't meet people with superpowers everyday."

"They're not superpowers, Ryan."

"They might be, Ella."

"I agree," Megan piped in.

"Can we not call it that until we have actual information? Besides, if I can't fly, I don't know that I want any of this nonsense, anyway."

"True," Megan said, "flying would be awesome. I mean you're just an insanely talented painter who had her first, wildly successful show and is going to dinner with the handsomest... er... second handsomest man I've ever laid eyes on. No big."

"Exactly. No big," Ella agreed.

"I think you're kind of a big deal," Ryan shrugged.

"Thanks. Kind of," Ella replied. That made Ryan laugh. Megan signaled the server for their check. And also got his number.

"You got someone else's number last night."

"I know I did, Miss Thing. I like to have options."

Ella laughed at Megan, who sure didn't seem to be terribly affected by too much champagne anymore.

"I can't believe you ate like a total pig and you're in such good shape." Ella admired Megan's legs as they walked back to their building. Ryan had headed home to rest and make plans.

"I exercise a lot, and I don't eat like that too often," Megan pointed out. "I need a nap like nobody's business. Will you be okay if I just crash out at my place for a while?"

"Oh yeah, I'm fine. Not to jinx myself, but no one's bothered us in days. Maybe they gave up," Ella said hopefully, but didn't actually believe the words as she said them. "Besides, I need a nap, a shower, and I still don't actually know what my plans are with Armand."

"I can't wait to hear about it. Don't get me wrong, I love Ryan, but until he gets it together, you should absolutely go on dates with that gorgeous human." She pretended to swoon and fan herself as she let herself into the apartment.

"I'll call you later," Ella giggled.

Ella went upstairs as the phone rang. "Hello," she answered, as she fumbled with it and keys at the same time.

"Hello, Ella. It's Armand," the warm voice filled the phone, and he did not have to say who it was. She knew as soon as he said her name.

"Hello, Armand." Getting in the door and taking off her shoes, she went and lay on the bed to talk to him.

"Would you still be able to join me this evening?"

"Yes, I would love to." *I hope that didn't sound too eager.* Although she had to admit she was eager.

"Wonderful. I'll shall be around to pick you up at 8." He said good-bye, and hung up before she could give him her address.

Not thinking too much about it, she set an alarm and fell asleep.

It's a dream, was her first thought. *Yes, a dream. Or was it a memory.* She wandered the burning land, and saw things dying all around. The life cycle was over.

The land shifted. People walked in long lines, carrying baskets filled with a glowing substance that splashed over their bodies, their bones weary from the weight of whatever it was they were carrying. Ella tried to look in a basket and was chased away by a man wearing an old-fashioned explorer hat and carrying a hunting rifle. The terrain changed again, and there was a strong smell of rubber burning. Overpowered, she started to choke, gasping for air. She felt her hands gripping something soft, as a man with deep brown and gold eyes leaned over her to breathe air into her suffocating lungs.

The alarm was going off, and Ella woke from her nap, clutching the black velvet blanket on the bed. *So much for the dreams being gone. Or were they dreams? Nope, not going to go through this right now.*

Not having much time, she groaned at the mess she had left in the bedroom while looking for clothes last night. In fact, in her world, the whole apartment was in disarray. Not something she was used to at all. Getting washed and dressed as quickly as possible, she settled on a silver-blue, velvet, backless, 1920's-style dress with black tights, heels, and gloves. She let her hair stay down tonight and slipped in a pair of art-deco, dangling earrings. They picked up the blue in her hair. As she was dabbing some ginger oil behind her ear, the front buzzer sounded.

"I'll be down in just a minute," she said into the intercom.

As she grabbed a silver-mesh evening bag, she saw Ryan had left his laptop on the dining table. He'd be missing it. She'd have to remember to tell him it was here.

She went downstairs and opened the front door. Armand stood just outside in an impeccably tailored, black suit with gold threads discreetly woven through the fabric. He wore an ascot with a tiny, golden rose pin stuck in it. He looked amazing, to say the least.

He held out a silver-blue orchid. "It would look very beautiful in your hair. May I?"

"Oh, sure." She smiled as he adjusted the flower behind her ear, taking care to only brush it ever so slightly.

"You look stunning, Ella."

"You don't look so bad, yourself."

"Please," he held out an arm to her and led her down to a black-as-night town car, where a driver held the door open and waited for Ella to get in before Armand settled in on the other side. There was a full bar, but also sparkling water, just like she drank last night at Alchemy.

"Thank you for picking me up," Ella said to him, as he gave instructions to the driver. "Where are we going for dinner?"

"If you don't mind, I'd like to take you to my apartment overlooking the river. We can watch the sunset from the balcony as we have dinner. As much as I love my home in the country, the sunsets over the city can be quite astonishing."

"Um, I guess that's fine," not sure if she did think it was fine.

"If you're worried, I can promise at least two other people will be present. I procured a chef for the evening to cook for us, since I had to attend to business all day and had no time to do it myself. And of course, my housekeeper. She will not let me mistreat you, I can promise you that, Ella."

Ella laughed a little and decided she would let her guard down. "That sounds great."

"It's also a selfish move on my part," he confessed. "I don't want anyone to bother us tonight, and if I show up to dinner with such a lovely companion, I fear the press won't leave us alone."

"I have definitely had enough attention for a while," she told him, and settled into the seat as the car wound its way through the streets.

"You should really get used to the attention if you want to be in the art world. Your work is extraordinary, and your show got a very complimentary write-up. I think you will be hearing from other galleries soon."

"I don't know what to say to that," Ella told him, feeling rather shy. "I am new to the whole being a part of the world. I think, anyway."

"You think?" He smiled quizzically at her. "Do you not know what part of the world you belong in?"

"Not exactly." She looked out the window. "A lot of things in my life changed rather suddenly over the last couple of weeks. I don't know that I was ready for any of them. What's more, each change brings another wave of new people and occurrences with them. I'm not sure I'm handling it right."

"I imagine we handle it the best we can. We don't always know what the right choice is to make. Unfortunately it's with hindsight that we wish for better decision making. I know I feel that way about some choices, myself. Besides, life changes quickly. It is the only constant we can count on, and you do not seem to me to be doing too terribly, Ella."

The tone of his voice had softened and had that strangely familiar comfort about it that she had felt last night. As she turned to him and studied his face for a moment, a reassurance of trust wrapped her, a connection.

"I don't know why I am telling you any of this, Armand."

"I am glad that you are, Ella." A quiet moment passed between them as the car stopped.

"We are here, Ella." Armand got out of the car before the driver did, and opened the door for her. The golden hour before sunset was coloring the landscape in twilight tones, and the water in the distance was twinkling. Stepping out of the car as he waited, she couldn't help but stop right in front of him, their faces inches apart.

"Thank you," Ella said, and broke away quickly. He closed the door and ran his gloved hand through his hair in a nervous way. *I know that gesture. Why is everything about him in my mind? More mysteries, always mystery.*

The apartment was, not surprisingly, quite large, but also elegant, filled with old European antiques and pieces of art that belonged in museums. Ella spent a long time admiring them. One entire side of the space, which sat at the top of the mid-rise building, was floor-to-ceiling windows that looked out over the river. The sun was starting to set, changing the rippling water into a rainbow of oranges and reds. There was a small, elaborately set, wrought-iron table on the patio that overlooked the city, river, and sunset. The patio itself was filled with every imaginable variety of orchid, all carefully kept and artfully arranged. Armand waited patiently while Ella made her way around, observing details, drinking in every magnificent piece, and carefully running her gloved hands over the woods, marbles, and what she was fairly sure were real gemstones and gold in some places. When she finished, a pretty, older woman in a fifties-style dress handed her a glass of amber liquid.

"Ella, this is my friend, housekeeper, and overall ruler of the realm, Elsa. Elsa, this is Ella."

"It is so nice to meet you, Ella. I have heard many things about you, and I was becoming very curious," the woman said as she offered to take Ella's purse, and then carefully hung it on an exquisitely crafted hook by the door. "Armand doesn't talk much about other people. I've known him his whole life, so I pay attention. Your dress is beautiful. Welcome to our home."

"Thank you. I am surprised he is talking about me. We haven't spent much time together, as yet."

"That may be, but the quality of the time has quite clearly made an impression on him," she said in a motherly manner that was tinged with humor. "Please enjoy yourself. I'll be around if you need anything. Either of you." She winked at Ella and left the room.

"Ella, that's not alcohol, it's Elderflower juice. I thought you might like it," Armand told her.

"Thank you, it's lovely. This whole place is amazing. Your art collection is gorgeous. Thank you for inviting me over."

"I am glad that you like it, and I have to admit that if you like it here, then I can't wait for you to visit my old family home, just a few hours away. We have had many of these things in our family for generations. Quite a few members of the El Dorado clan have been artists. Part of the reason I have such an affinity for painters."

"Are you an artist?"

"I am not. I am not gifted with the brush or clay or wood. I have a head for business."

"Well, I would not be able to run a gallery, so I appreciate you being one of the people who attends to those things," Ella said, genuinely feeling grateful. "And Elsa is great."

"Yes, she is very great, actually. I don't know what I would do without her. I really don't deserve her most of the time." In spite of how serious he sounded when he said it, Ella laughed.

"What's so funny?"

"You. My life. Mostly everything, really."

"Alright then. Shall we have some dinner outside?" he slid open the glass door and a balmy air filled the room.

"I would love to."

For the next couple of hours, they talked about everything from art to business to music, as gourmet dish after gourmet dish was set in front of them, each carefully constructed and superbly served. Mushrooms, fruits, and vegetables Ella had never eaten before, laden in the lightest of sauces and flavors. Every sense of pleasurable eating.

"I had no idea vegetables could taste this way," she kidded him.

"Neither did I, trust me." He took a bite and dramatically made melting sounds in his throat.

Ella smiled. "You are far less serious alone than you seem out there," gesturing toward the darkened horizon to indicate the rest of the world.

"I suppose that's true. I am not always trusting of people, to be completely up front with you. In business you have to be careful whom you call friend, and even more careful what confidence you place in them."

"That's not just the business world," she said, somewhat sadly. "Though I have been getting some lessons in trusting, lately. I have become friends with some good people." Ella looked at him thoughtfully. "Of course, there are the feelings you give me."

"Oh? Do tell, my dear," Armand said it with a tease, but stopped when he saw the seriousness of her expression. "Really, Ella. Tell me what you mean. Please?"

"I am not sure how to put this without sounding very strange."

"We are both strange people." Armand leaned back and glanced over the dark water. His voice took on a distant tone as he said, "It took me a long time to come to terms with being an odd man out." *Even the most common of words sound wonderful with his accent.* Ella blushed at the thought, and was glad for the dim lights. She was not used to any males getting the better of her, and it seemed it had happened a few times lately. Megan would, no doubt, laugh at her.

I wonder what she is up to? And Ryan?

"I think it's hard to understand you can't fit in a certain mold," he continued. "What I am trying to say is, do not feel uncomfortable telling me the truth of your thoughts and feelings."

As he looked back at her, the candlelight bounced over the gold in his dark eyes, giving him an almost otherworldly look. It was angelic and intimidating all at the same time. The time passing between them was unearthly. It was the only word Ella could think of to describe it. *Not that you're prone to dramatics.*

"Okay, well, I feel like you are someone I know. I feel like we're meant to be talking. Or even more, I mean, that we have before. It is disconcerting yet comforting. I feel a connection to you that seems old and new all at the same time. I told you you seemed familiar to me, but it's more than that. I am unsure how to describe it to you."

"No, you don't have to, Ella. I feel it too."

They said nothing for a while, just listened to the water, the breeze, and the occasional clink of a dish or glass. It was not awkward or uncomfortable.

As they finally finished the extensive dinner and dessert, talking about lighter subjects, happier and at ease, Armand stood up.

"I have something for you, Ella."

He went into the apartment and opened an antique, roll-top, Chinese desk. Quite easily the most magnificent desk Ella had ever seen. She saw him remove a small box. He came back onto the deck.

"You have something for me? After you helped put on my show and had me over for dinner. Really, it's too much."

"We sold everything in your show. You helped keep our gallery afloat, and we are getting rave reviews for the way you planned out the setup. It's just a small thank-you gift, and I would be remiss not to give you one, as the artist." He put a small, blue-velvet box in front of her. "Really, a small thank you."

Picking up the box, Ella flipped open the lid. Inside was an antique book locket with a rose etched on it. Carefully placed at the center was a sapphire.

"It's... It's... It's... gorgeous." Removing a glove and running a finger over the rose, she flipped it over to see a calligraphic "B" engraved on the back. There used to be other letters, but time had worn them away. "I wonder who it used to belong to."

As she pulled it carefully out the box, Armand held out a hand as an offer to fasten it around her neck. She shook her head, wanting to hold it longer.

"The sapphire set in the rose reminded me a great deal of your work when I saw it today, and I knew it had to belong to you." He sat back into his chair. "I really do hope you like it."

"I love it." She reached back and fastened it around her neck after taking off the other glove. With a rarely bared hand, Ella reached across the table and covered the black glove he wore. "Thank you. I mean it. For listening, your generosity, bringing me to your home."

Armand seemed ill at ease as she touched him. He broke away from her gaze and looked at her hand.

"I like your silvery-blue nail polish." Changing the mood was obviously what he wanted to do. It was also a reminder to Ella that she was, in fact, not wearing silvery-blue nail polish.

"Um, yes, thank you. It's a long-time favorite," nervously sipping the Elderflower juice. Elsa came out to see how they were doing.

"If you don't need anything else from us, I'll send the chef home, and go to bed myself," Elsa told them.

"Please tell the chef the food was amazing. I loved every bite and I don't think I'll ever eat again." Ella stood and hugged Elsa, who returned the hug warmly.

"I hope you'll reconsider the eating because we do so love to have dinner parties, and we don't get to do it enough," the woman told her. She said goodnight to Armand and left them alone again.

"Shall I take you home?"

"Not yet, I just want to stay a little longer," Ella told him, and looked out onto the water.

"You shall get no argument from me." He wandered over to the half-wall of the deck, and the breeze gently ruffled his hair. Ella went and stood next to him. She felt bold and stood very close.

"Armand," Ella started. He moved ever so slightly. As he did, there was a deafening crash of thunder and the wind whipped up furiously. "Oh," was all she got out as they grabbed a few things about to blow away and ducked rapidly into the apartment.

Armand slid the door shut, as the abrupt and unexpected storm crashed down on the night.

Ella didn't realize she had been holding her breath. The fear of getting wet accidentally was one that always held dominance over her life. The fear of betraying the secret. She was so tired of it.

As they stood watching, the clouds gathering at an alarming rate and the wind raucously beating upon the plants, Ella almost blurted out everything that had happened in the last twenty-four hours. Something about the look on Armand's face stopped the words. He was no longer here with her. He looked almost angry.

"I should get you home, Ella." His manner became business-like as he called for the car and helped gather her things. In fact, Armand seemed very much in a hurry to get her home. The reason for the sudden changed eluded her.

As they walked down to the entrance of the building together, the mood of the evening was all but gone.

"Armand, did I do something or say something to upset you?"

Stopping in the middle of the golden, gilded lobby, his face softened.

"No, not at all. I just remembered something I need to take care of, and I had almost forgotten about it. I apologize for my rude behavior. I had a wonderful evening, and I would be most grateful and happy to spend time with you again in the near future." Without seeming to think about it, he ran a gloved finger across the side of her face.

"Alright, then. Thank you for dinner and for the perfect necklace." Wanting to say more, but not sure what it would be, she leaned over, kissed his cheek and went out to the waiting car. The driver opened the door for her as Armand watched. Ella couldn't help but notice his expression darken to almost frightening. As they drove away, the rain and wind started to subside.

Riding home in silence, she checked her phone for messages from Megan, Ryan, or James, and was surprised there were none. She wondered again what they were doing.

Arriving on the street where Ella lived, they found it blocked off by fire trucks and police cars. There were people milling about the sidewalks and going in and out of the building.

She thanked the driver, and as she approached the building, she grabbed the arm of an officer standing outside the door. "What happened?"

"Turns out nothing," the officer flipped a notebook closed. "There was a bomb threat on the block. Cleared everyone out, searched everywhere, there's nothing. We're clearing out now. Do you live here?"

Ella nodded.

"You can go back in. Just be careful to stay out of the way."

"Thank you, Officer."

She stepped carefully over some plastic and boxes, stopping to text Megan, who immediately answered back with, "On my way."

Ella went upstairs to her apartment. Or at least where it used to be. The door was off the hinges and there was no one on this floor. Having no idea what to do, she went inside to find that the living room, dining room, and kitchen had been completely and utterly destroyed. What's more, everything was gone. Her paintings, furniture, books, art supplies, everything. There were huge chunks gauged out of the walls where the murals had lived for the last few years. In shocked disbelief, she stumbled through to the bedroom. It was pretty much in the same shape with the exception of most of her clothes still hanging in the closet. All the clothes she had taken out and tried on were gone, though. As were the bed, velvet blanket, jewelry box. The golden rock she had found outside the other day lay in the middle of the room. Absentmindedly picking it up and looking around, numbness set in. Ella stood, doing nothing but mourning the loss of the sanctuary she had created to be home.

She was pulled out of her reverie by a shocked squeal from Megan, who came running to the bedroom.

"What happened???" Megan grabbed Ella and threw her arms around her neck when she saw the expression on her face.

"I have no idea. I got back here from dinner and the police said there was a bomb threat. But it turned out to be nothing. Everything was fine and I came up here. Everything is gone. My work, my things, everything." Now the tears came.

"Let's get out of here. Come on." Megan grabbed a bag that remained in the closet and stuffed everything that could fit into it. Ella stood watching.

"Where is Ryan?" Her voice trembled. Her throat ached.

"I don't know." Megan found another bag and crammed everything left on the racks into it. "I've been trying to get ahold of him all evening. Have you not heard from him at all?"

"No. I was at dinner all night. I didn't check my phone until afterwards, and I didn't have any messages."

Ella blindly followed Megan out of the room and out of the apartment. They went down the stairs to Megan's apartment, which, like the rest of them, was untouched.

Megan settled Ella onto some cushions, took her shoes off, and went to make her tea. Ella continued to stare at the golden rock.

"What is that?" Megan sat down with a tea tray and pointed to the stone.

"I found it outside my building the other day. It was sitting in the middle of my bedroom where the bed used to be. That is not where I left it. Of course, nothing is where I left it."

Megan's phone buzzed.

"It's Ryan. Apparently he's been asleep this whole time. Do you want me to tell him to come over?"

"Yes. I should call James." She dialed the professor.

Not knowing where to start, the words tumbled out fast and furious.

"Your apartment has been robbed?"

"Yes, but also destroyed. The walls that I painted, they're all but gone." Her voice cracked as she explained, and Megan took the phone from her.

"Hey, Doc. Um... Ella's pretty upset. Yeah, Yeah. Of course. Sure." Megan hung up the phone. "When Ryan gets here we are going to go to the university and meet with the professor," she said to Ella.

"I know this probably isn't a great time to ask, but maybe a distraction is a good idea. How was dinner?" Megan said it tentatively, as she poured out the tea service, and made Ella take a cup after taking the rock from her.

Finally coming back to the present, Ella felt a slight smile come to her face.

"That good, huh?" Megan smiled back.

"No, it was really wonderful. We had this amazing meal, his apartment was filled with unbelievable art, and he gave me this." Ella leaned over and held the locket out from her neck for Megan to see. "It's a thank-you for my show. He said it made a lot of money."

"Wow, that's gorgeous."

"Yeah, it was great. Except..."

"Except what?"

"At one point, a storm started, and then it was like Armand was gone. He seemed almost angry."

"Meh. Guys." Megan shrugged.

"Yeah, I guess. But I got the weirdest feeling it had something to do with the storm. Which obviously makes no sense."

"Did you ask what was wrong?"

"I did. He just said he had forgotten about something that he needed to deal with."

"Well, that's probably it. I mean he does run like a super-giant empire, and whatever."

"Yeah, I suppose." Ella fingered the locket. "I'm glad he gave it to me tonight, and not at the show. It would be gone, too." The sadness set in again.

"Hey, don't cry. We'll totally find out what happened. We'll find you a better place to live. I'm ready to move, too." Megan wrapped an arm around Ella's shoulders. "We could get a place together."

"Really?" Ella asked through the tears.

"Yes." Megan dabbed the silvery-blue streaks from her friend's face. "Don't make a mess of that beautiful dress."

Ella sniffed and mumbled an agreement as Megan's phone buzzed.

"It's Ryan. Let's get out of here. I've got the creeps, big time."

"Yeah, me too," Ella agreed as they left. Then went back to put the golden rock into her pocket.

Chapter 15

Ryan was sitting in his car when Megan and Ella came out to meet him.

"Would you clean out your car once in a while?" Megan said as she opened the door for Ella.

"Do you want to give me cleaning advice or get out of here?" he snapped back.

"What's your problem?" Megan asked.

"My problem is..." Ryan started.

"Can you guys not fight right now?" Ella said defeatedly.

Ryan looked back at her in the mirror.

"I'm sorry, Ella. I really am." He sounded sincere as they drove the short distance to the school. "If I can do anything to help you, please tell me."

"Thanks, Ryan. Let's just get to the professor."

"Of course."

Ella's phone buzzed as they were parking.

It was Armand.

"Thinking of you.-A"

"What made you smile like that at this particular, miserable time?" Megan asked her.

"Nothing." She stuck the phone back in her bag and caught Ryan looking at her in the mirror, but he looked away quickly.

James was waiting for them outside. Megan and Ella filled both of them in about everything they had seen at the building.

"So I guess I don't have a place to stay, nor do I have any idea who destroyed my apartment."

"You can stay with me," Megan volunteered. "I don't think you should be alone."

"I don't think either of you should stay in that building," the professor informed them. "Both of you will stay with me. I have plenty of space." He turned to Ryan. "You are welcome as well."

"Did you call the police?" James asked them, as they went inside to his office so he could gather up some things. "Ella, I am going to bring some treatments for you, as well. How have you been feeling?"

"Uh, fine, mostly."

"Mostly? Are you not feeling better? You should tell me. I can't help you otherwise."

"No, I feel better. I'm sorry, I'm really distracted."

"It's understandable."

Megan was wandering the lab, and Ryan came over to Ella.

"I am really sorry, Ella."

"Thanks. But you don't have to keep saying that. It's not your fault."

"Ella, I need to tell you..." Ryan started.

"Let's go," James interrupted. Megan took a box from the professor, who smiled at her gratefully.

"You look like you could use a hand, Doc."

"I'm fine," he said, but he clearly was in pain.

"All of us are a disaster," Ella said as they left the school.

"I'm not," Megan said, clearly offended.

"Tell me, what did they take?" the professor asked as they loaded boxes and files into his car.

"They took everything. Except a lot of my clothes, for some reason. I mean, they literally took my walls. Honestly, who does that? How crazy is this?"

"Very," Megan chirped up helpfully.

"Well," the professor said, closing his trunk, "you guys should follow me back to my house."

"I can't come," Ryan said. "I can't drive you guys over there."

"Where are you going that's so important?" Megan asked him.

"I just have a few things to do."

"Like what?"

"Like things. Mind your business, Megan." Ryan got in his car, slammed the door and drove off.

"That was fun," Megan put her hands up.

"I hope he's okay," Ella said quietly, and buckled herself into the car.

They drove to the professor's house in silence.

"Nice place you got here, Doc," Megan said as they drove up.

It was a nice place. A huge, two-story, red-brick house stood in the middle of a well-kept yard.

"Being a professor pays pretty well, I'd say," Megan joked as they got out the car.

"No, working for a giant pharmaceutical company pays well," James told her.

They unloaded everything, and James showed them each a room on the second floor.

"Please make yourselves at home while we figure out what to do to next. You are welcome to stay as long as you'd like. I could use the company in this big, empty house. I'll be in my study for a bit, getting settled. I moved every possible bit of information related to you, Ella, off school grounds. Someone is clearly after your secret, and until we know who and why, we must be more careful than ever." He left the girls to settle into their rooms.

"I need to go back to my place and get some stuff," Megan said, sitting on the bed in Ella's room as she hung up what was left of the clothes from the apartment. "Will you go with me?"

"Yes. No way we are going back over there alone." Ella sat down on the bed next to Megan. "I'm so sorry you were dragged into this mess. If I had any idea that things like this were going to happen, I never would've..." she trailed off.

"Never would've what? Been my friend?"

Ella didn't respond.

"You didn't do this. You're not attacking people and breaking into people's homes. Besides, I'm glad you're my friend." Megan got up. "I'm gonna go find some food. Want to come?"

"I'll be down in a minute. I'm going to put away the rest of this stuff." Megan left Ella, who leaned back on the bed, trying to make sense of the last 48 hours.

She took out her phone and considered texting Armand back, but had no idea what she should say to him. *What about Ryan? Where did he go?* He seemed about to tell her something back at the school. *He apologized, but for what?*

We have to decide on our next move. It has to be to go to my school. Institution, she corrected. *Or, you know, whatever it was.* Ella wondered if her mind would ever be clear. If things would ever make sense.

Getting up to go find Megan, Ella realized how big the house they were in really was. Trying to find the stairs back down to the main floor took a few minutes, and while looking, Ella passed no fewer than six bedrooms. After about ten minutes, Ella came upon Megan with her head in the refrigerator.

"Hey," Ella said, and Megan jumped a mile.

"Good grief, sneak about much?" Megan pulled some bread out and set it on the counter. "This house is huge, and I'm pretty sure there is a wine cellar."

"There *is* a wine cellar," James said, coming into the kitchen, "and you can have what you like, except for the bottles in the locked case."

"Thanks, Doc." Megan crammed a carrot in her mouth and offered one to Ella.

"I'm not hungry. This night actually started off really well, and dinner was amazing," Ella said.

"Did you do something special tonight, Ella?" James asked her.

"I had dinner with Armand El Dorado."

This statement seemed to bother the professor, but he hid it well. It almost wasn't noticeable. Almost.

"Oh, I see. Why did you have dinner with him?"

"He had me over to his place by the river to celebrate my art show's success."

"It was quite the show." James was very distracted now. "I need to make some calls, and then we should figure out what needs to happen next." He started to leave but turned back to Ella. "Be careful with that man."

"What? Who? Armand?"

"Yes."

"Why? Do you know something about him that I should know? Besides, it was just dinner. I doubt I'll see him again," Ella said the words, not believing them at all. She wanted to see him.

"Just be careful with him." James left them again.

"Well that was ominous," Megan said. "What in the world do you think he meant by that?"

"I don't know," Ella told her, "but when I was there tonight, everything was really great. Until it rained."

"It rained? It didn't rain over here." Megan was making sandwiches with cheese and veggies.

"I seriously cannot believe how much you eat." Ella had to smile at Megan.

"I'm stress eating." Megan crammed a piece of cheese into her mouth and made a funny face. "Do you want to see Armand again?"

"I guess. He just seemed so angry and distant all of a sudden. You know, when the storm started."

"Distant? What do you mean by that? And it didn't rain by us," she repeated.

"You'll think I'm crazy if I tell you."

"Ella, I already think you're crazy, so talk away."

"Thanks. Anyway, Armand is..."

"Handsome? Gorgeous?" Megan said helpfully.

"Yes, he is those things, too. But, well, I feel like I've known him my whole life. It's so easy to be around him and talk to him. I feel drawn to him."

"Hello! Handsome, gorgeous... We're all drawn to him."

"I'm serious."

"I know, I'm just kidding." Megan went to a cabinet and pulled out a glass. "Ella, I just realized you're not wearing your gloves."

""Yeah, I took them off upstairs. I figured I didn't have to hide around you and James. It's pretty nice for once."

"I'm glad. And no, I don't want you to hide. I'm so sorry that you've had to hide before." Megan paused. "Also, can you believe the size of this place? What do you suppose is behind all those doors upstairs?"

"I don't know and I don't care. It's really nice of the professor to let us stay here."

Megan's phone buzzed before she could respond.

"It's Ryan. Apparently he's done with his secret errands." Megan was annoyed.

"Megan, he seemed like he was trying to tell me something before at the university. Do you have any idea what it was?"

"Nope. Who knows with him? I swear. Anyway, what should I tell him?"

"Let's ask the professor if we can borrow a car and go get your stuff. Then tell Ryan to meet us at the building."

Ella drove them back to the apartments, and all the while could not shake the feeling someone was following them. Being as late as it was, there were hardly any cars on the road so it was easy to see there was no one behind them most of the way. Yet the feeling lingered.

Ryan was pacing back and forth in front of the door when they arrived.

"Hey," Ryan said to Ella.

"Hey."

"Why are you pacing?" Megan asked. "What's wrong? You're being really strange, even for you."

"I'm just worried about you guys," he said hastily.

"Well, chill out. We're fine, and you're making things suck," Megan told him, and opened the door.

She went in and started packing up clothes and things. "How long do you think I should pack for?"

"I honestly have no idea. I took everything I had left. I am not coming back here after tonight if I don't have to," Ella said, her voice cracking up just a bit. "Not that I have any idea what I am going to do."

Ryan wrapped an arm around her, and without thinking, she snuggled into his side. His chest was warm and muscular. Ella felt her cheeks flush ever so slightly. And she thought he may have kissed the top of her head when Megan had her back turned.

"Okay," Megan said, after a few minutes of furiously cramming things into a bunch of bags. She stopped in the living room and pulled a katana off the wall.

"What's that for?" Ella looked at her incredulously.

"I know how to use it. That's all I am going to say." Megan pointed them out the door with it, and Ryan picked up a bunch of the bags.

"I'll take these to the car," he told them, and left.

"I'll bring the rest. Meet you upstairs?" Megan asked Ella, who nodded and went up to her former living space.

"What are you doing here?" The words were out of her mouth before she thought about it.

Armand, in head-to-toe black, was standing in middle of what used to be a living room, looking around.

"Ella," he took three long strides and embraced her tightly. The fierceness of his hold was surprising, and without a thought she returned it.

"What are you doing here?" She repeated the words and extracted herself ever so slightly from the embrace so that she could see his face. He was so close to her.

"I heard on the news that there was bomb threat here, and I was very worried. The door was open out front when I arrived," his voice was hoarse. *He seems far more upset than he should be.* "I am so glad you are okay. This is your apartment?"

Ella pulled out of his hold, and he quite reluctantly let go.

"It was my home," arms crossed and voice terse. "It's not anymore. Everything but some of my clothes has been taken. Even the walls, as you can see. I had painted them. They were my art. I spent many, many hours painting them." She was starting to feel angry. Very angry.

"Someone took your walls?"

"Yeah, rather unbelievable, isn't it?" Ella started stomping around the broken bits of sheet rock and nails, looking to see if anything was left. Anything at all.

"What's he doing here?" Ryan's voice cut through Ella's noise. He and Megan were standing in the doorway. Megan looked both like she wanted to laugh and run away from them.

Ryan walked closer to Ella, who was now between the two guys, but touching neither of them. She looked at each of them in turn and stepped away. *I am so not in the mood for this.*

"He came to see if Ella was okay," Armand said condescendingly to Ryan. His accent made him sound all the more superior. "What are you doing here?" he said, authoritarian but softened. "Hello, Megan, it's so lovely to see you again." Armand walked over and hugged a stunned, blonde Megan, who was holding a sword. She awkwardly patted him on the back.

"It's, uh... nice to see you too, Armand."

"I am Ella's friend," Ryan snapped back. "I am making sure she is safe."

"Good job so far," Armand said sarcastically as he looked around the room.

"This is not his fault, Armand," Ella defended Ryan.

"I don't care what he thinks, Ella. Do you need me to do anything for you?" Ryan asked her.

"I don't think there is anything to do." Ella rubbed the gold stone she had put in her pocket. *Maybe it's my worry stone now.*

"Ella, you are welcome to take my apartment. I will go stay in my house. Elsa would be delighted for you to stay there. You made quite an impression on her." Armand took Ella's hand in his. "Anything I can do to help."

In spite of herself, she felt good, and strangely safe, that he offered for her to stay there. *There is that familiar feeling again.*

"Thank you for the offer, Armand, but Megan and I are staying with James Reynolds."

"Ah," Armand let go of her hand, disappointment evident on his face. "That is very kind of him. He is a good man. I never regret funding his research."

"I bet," Ryan said sullenly, as he moved pieces of broken wood out of the way.

"Ryan," Megan said warningly.

Ella sighed and pulled the stone out.

"Well, isn't that funny," Armand said, looking at the gold object in her hand.

"What's that?" Ella asked, and held up the stone. "Do you mean this?"

"Yes. I realize it's just a stone, but strangely it's shaped just like one I had on my desk at the gallery."

"I found it outside the building," Ella told him. "Here. If it's yours, you should take it." She held it out to him.

"I doubt that it's mine. How would it have gotten here? And even if it is mine, you are more than welcome to it. What is mine is yours." Armand's voice had dropped and taken on that serious tone again. As if what he said was only for her to hear.

After a few minutes of quiet, Megan cleared her throat.

"We should probably figure out what to do next," she said.

"Megan's right," Ella agreed. "We need to decide what to do. I can't take this anymore. I want to find out who is doing this, and why."

"We know why..." Megan said cautiously.

"Megan," this time Ryan cut her off, "maybe we shouldn't talk about this with him here." Ryan jerked his head in Armand's direction.

"I am glad to give you privacy if that is what you wish, Ella. But please know that I am glad to help you with anything."

"There's a lot you don't know..." Ella started.

"Ella," Ryan interrupted, "I don't think you should tell him. I don't trust him."

"You don't trust anyone," Ella snapped, tired of his attitude. "What is your problem? What were you trying to apologize about earlier? You were acting like this was somehow your fault, or something." A heavy silence fell on the room, and Ryan shifted uncomfortably.

"What were you trying to tell me?" Ella repeated, growing more impatient.

"Nothing. Never mind. Tell Armand whatever you want. I don't care." He stormed into the back room of the apartment, leaving them all staring after him.

"I'll go try to talk to him." Megan left Armand and Ella alone.

"Ella, I can go." Armand's careful speech was perfect to her. It was confusing.

"No, I don't want you to go. I am going to trust you. I do trust you. I have no reason not to trust you." She said it with James' warning echoing in her head. She didn't care.

"The thing is, Armand, I am tired of hiding."

"I hope that you don't feel as though you have to hide from me..." he started, but she held up her hand.

"Please let me get this out before I lose my nerve."

"Of course." He didn't say anything more and waited calmly for her to start again.

"We have only just met, and I have not known James, Megan, or Ryan much longer than you. I think they have come to me at a good point in my life. At least I hope they have, despite this mess. I am someone who has spent much of my life alone. I have tried to be shut off from the world. I have been afraid of it."

She stopped for a moment to gather her thoughts and then, taking a deep breath, continued.

"See, I felt like I had to keep everyone away from me because I have secrets. I don't even know what they are, these secrets, but I have them. Now they are coming out. Now other people are learning about them, and they are not reacting to them the way that I always feared. At least not these people," she pointed to the back room, where the door was partially closed. "I am becoming less afraid, but I am not completely sure. I still don't know what I am." She stopped, not sure if she could say more yet.

"May I say something?" Armand asked her.

"Please."

"I know what you are, Ella. You are special. I know it."

"Not in the way that you think." She leaned against a counter for balance, feeling light-headed. *Confessions can take a lot out of you.* Making a decision, she went to her sink. *Am I really going to do this again?* Yes, she was.

"Armand, come here."

"Yes, Ella." He came and stood next to her as she turned the water on and let it run.

The water turned silvery-blue quickly, and Ella felt the release of pressure that always came when the cobalt left her hands.

"Extraordinary." He breathed the word so close she felt it on her cheek.

"That's all you have to say?" Turning off the water, she moved away from him because it seemed to be the only way she could keep a level head.

"Do you know what it is, Ella?"

"I do now. I only learned what it was very recently. Like, a day ago, recently."

"Will you tell me what it is?"

"It's cobalt."

"Extraordinary."

"I guess."

"No, it is. I promise you. And this is why you think people are harassing you?"

"Possibly. None of us can really think of another reason, except maybe James and the company he used to work for, but there seems to be a focus on me for sure. Everything that has happened has been connected to me."

"What else has happened?"

She told him about the assaults on everyone, the man following her, how he disappeared, the picture on the internet that connected the three of them.

"How does Megan fit in?" he asked her.

"She is my friend, who has ended up in the middle of this and has been absolutely amazing to me."

"She does seem pretty great," he said lost in thought. "What's the next step, then?"

"We have to decide that, but I think we need to go back to the school I grew up in. Or something." She hadn't told him that she was over one hundred years old, that James thought the cobalt was older, that she seemed to possibly have powers. "Except it may not be a school. I think... I can't remember it well, but it's possibly an institution. I bet you do not want to talk to me now."

"Quite the contrary, Ella. Please do not let that thought cross your mind again."

"Thank you for listening, Armand. And for being here."

"Always." He was about to say something else when Megan and Ryan came back into the room.

"What's the plan?" Megan asked.

"I think we should get out to the institute and see if we can find anything."

"I agree," Ryan said. He looked at Ella. "I planned out the trip there, and we can go as soon as you're ready."

"Alright. Let's go now."

"Are you sure? It's so late and..."

"I have no reason not to get there as soon as possible."

"Yeah, let's go," Megan chimed in.

"I guess this is where we part ways," Ella said to Armand.

"I would prefer to come and help you," he said.

"You don't have to help me."

"I know I don't have to. I want to help you. All of you." Armand looked right at Ryan when he said it. "How far away is the school? We can take my car."

"I didn't see your car out front," Ella said questioningly.

"I did not come in the town car. I drove myself here."

"We don't need you to drive. I can drive," Ryan said abruptly.

"I have a sedan. It'll be very comfortable," Armand offered.

"Ryan?" Ella moved over to him. "I think Armand driving is a good idea. You planned the trip so you can navigate and get us there. How does that sound?"

"Alright, Ella. I'll do it for you."

"Thank you, Ryan. Are we ready? Megan, do you have everything?"

"I've got a sword. I'm ready to go."

Megan and Armand started for the door, but Ryan hung back.

"Are you going to come? You went through so much trouble to plan the drive," Ella said to him.

"I want to tell you something."

"Okay?"

"Ella, I am the one who dropped that rock outside the building. I took it from Armand's desk."

"What? Why?"

"I just don't trust him."

"It was in the middle of my floor when I came up here after the building had been broken into."

"I don't know how it got there." He said it quickly, and Ella realized she didn't believe him.

"Wait. I found that rock before my show. So you went to the gallery before then?"

"Yes."

"Why?"

"Because I am pretty sure Armand owns the pharmaceutical company."

Ella inhaled sharply.

"What? Are you sure?"

"No, I am not sure. I am trying to find proof, but I think we need to watch him closely."

"How long have you known?"

"I don't know anything yet. But I've suspected it for a while. Before you and I became... became, um... friends."

"Are you guys coming?" Megan yelled from the hall.

"Just a minute," Ryan hollered back.

"I would say that we can't back out of him coming now. It would be too weird. If he is connected to the company and the people following us, maybe it's better we keep him close," Ella said.

"Did you tell him your secret, Ella?"

"I showed him, yes."

"That worries me. I am worried for your safety," Ryan told her. His face was marred with concern, fear, and something Ella couldn't put a finger on.

"I appreciate that, but honestly, I trust Armand. Until I have reason not to trust him. I am glad you told me this stuff, Ryan, and yes, we should be careful, but I can't turn back what I've said and done now."

"Ella, I don't think..." He stopped when she held up a hand.

"Ryan, you don't actually know if he owns the company. We have to go to the institute. I have a feeling there might be answers there, and really, I don't have too many other ideas. I promise we'll be careful. I'll be careful."

"Alright. Ella, I couldn't stand it if anything happened to you. I am sorry I am not good at this, but I care about you."

"I care about you too, Ryan. And I know you're trying to help. So let's go."

"Alright." He flipped open his bag to pull out a phone, and that's when Ella noticed his laptop was in there. The laptop that had been on the table when she left the apartment.

Chapter 16

Ella got into Armand's jet-black sedan next to Ryan. Megan was in the passenger seat, flipping between radio stations. Armand watched Ella in the mirror.

"Are you alright?" he asked her. His tone seemed cautious, as if he thought she was going to be angry at him.

"I'm fine," she said brightly. It must've been too brightly because Megan turned around. Ella gave her a look to tell her, "Not now." *How can I tell her I think Ryan was in the apartment when it was robbed? Maybe he even stole from me and destroyed my work.* It made her stomach ache. What's more, she had absolutely no idea why. In order to avoid a meltdown, she spent the next few hours reading on her phone. Armand and Megan kept up a steady stream of chatter in the front, punctuated by directions from Ryan, who mostly worked on his laptop. Every time Ella glanced at it out of the corner of her eye, she couldn't decide whether to cry or to smash it. Opting for neither, she just stayed quiet.

Megan eventually drifted off to sleep, and the only noises were the sound of Ryan's typing and the low purr of the car. Armand was lost in thought, but Ella caught him looking at her in the mirror more than once.

"I think we are close," Ryan spoke up in the darkness. Armand had slowed down considerably and the roads were less well kept.

"I wish it was daylight so I could see the area," Ella said.

"Turn here," Ryan told Armand, who slowed and turned onto a gravel road.

"Were the roads always like this?" Armand asked Ella.

"It's pretty secluded. There were some important people's kids here. I don't think they wanted it to be easy to find us. Especially, if I am starting to remember correctly, since it's not really a school."

The headlights passed over a sign that they nearly missed. In broken letters and dilapidated brick it said, "The Lavoisier Institute of Higher Learning."

"Nothing creepy about that," Megan said in a sleepy voice. Ella felt a rush of grateful emotion that she was with them. She reached out and squeezed Megan's arm.

They drove a little further in silence, each of them looking at nothing, really. There were few lights, as if they were on simply because someone had forgotten to turn them off.

The entire place, or what she could see of it, anyway, as the car lights passed over the graveled road, looked abandoned and neglected. Trees were fallen, and at one point Ryan and Armand got out to move one so they could get through. There was even a broken-down car rusting out on the side of the road. A tree had fallen on it.

"A tree fell on that car." Megan pointed, as they slowed down again to avoid hitting it.

"No, look at the way the tree is dented on the side," Armand said. "That car hit the tree."

"Why would someone just abandon their car? You could get a service to help you get it out."

"I don't know, Megan." They came to a complete stop just before the wreck. For some reason, Ella got out of the car.

"Where are you going?" Ryan asked her.

"I just want to look at it for a minute." She closed the sedan's door and climbed over some displaced rocks and fallen branches to get to it.

The door to the destroyed car was hanging open. Armand put the bright headlights on so she could see. They all got out of the car and came over to where Ella was leaning over the driver's seat. There was no blood on anything, much to her relief.

"What are you looking for?" Megan asked her.

"I don't really know. I just wanted to take a look. It just seems so strange that this car was left here, this close to the main building. None of this makes any sense."

"It's strange for sure. But let's get up to the main building. This is giving me the total creeps."

"Sure. Just give me another minute." As she said that, some practically unnoticeable, black, metal pieces caught her eye. They were all over the seat and floor. Some were even sprinkled on the passenger seat, but the majority were on the driver's side. She looked around the front end of the car to see if they had come from something, but she couldn't discern any possible source. Pulling a tissue from her bag, Ella wrapped up some of them to keep.

Ryan seemed intent on the back of the car while Megan and Armand were inspecting the tree and hood.

"Are you guys finding anything?" Ella called out.

"What should we be looking for?" Armand asked her.

"I don't really know, I guess. Maybe we should just get up to the Institute."

Nodding in agreement, the three of them headed back to the car while Ryan continued to poke around. After about five minutes, he finally came over and got back into the car.

"Did you find anything?" Ella watched his face carefully. She didn't trust him anymore. She didn't know how he got the laptop back, but he definitely had been to her place not too long before it was destroyed. *Or maybe during.*

"No. Not really," he responded absentmindedly, already pulling out the computer.

"Right." She folded her arms and leaned back as they slowly continued up the drive.

It didn't take too much longer to reach the main building. There were a few lights on, but it, like everything else they could make out, looked completely and totally run down.

"This is so confusing." Ella got out, shaking her head. "This place looks like it's been closed down for a hundred years!"

"The weather has been crazy. Maybe it was affected more than normal," Megan offered, though her voice was doubtful.

They picked their way carefully through debris and branches. The door was shut with a padlock and chain.

"How are we going to get in?" Ella asked no one in particular. There was a sound of breaking glass, and the three of them saw Megan knocking shards off the window frame.

"Oops," she said sheepishly, as everyone watched. "When a door is closed, break open a window. Isn't that the saying?"

"Sure," Ella said, and followed the blonde through the dark hole into the building. Ella jumped down to the sound of glass crunching under her shoes. Megan still had the katana in hand, and Ella nearly laughed. *What in the world are we doing?*

Armand and Ryan got through the window with a little more work, as they didn't fit quite as easily as the two girls. Ella found herself jumping at every sound they made, afraid of being found out. By whom, she didn't know, because it did not appear that anyone had been in the crumbling building in a very long time. Except that her mind told her she had been here only a few years ago.

"Now what?" Megan looked unsure, but seemed ready for a bit of adventure.

Ella, on the other hand, was getting more and more nervous.

"I hadn't really thought that far ahead," she told them. "I didn't expect the Institute to be in this shape, and I thought there might be someone here to talk to. I'm not sure what to do, other than to look around and see if we can find anything. Like why the buildings and grounds are in this condition, or where everyone went."

"We should split up. We can cover more ground that way," Ryan pointed out, and took a flashlight out of his bag.

"I don't know if that is a good idea," Ella said. "I didn't think the school and buildings would be so decrepit and damaged. It's as if the place has been closed for decades, not just a few years. It might be dangerous."

"All of this is dangerous," Armand pointed out. "There are people breaking into your home and destroying it by using bomb threats. We are into dangerous territory already. I agree with Ryan, we should split up and meet back here in about an hour. What do you all think?"

"No time like the present," Megan chirped. "Armand and I will go this way. Ella, you and Ryan should try to find your headmistress' office, or dungeon, or coffin, or wherever it is mean headmistresses hang out."

"Alright," Ella said, though she wasn't thrilled at the idea of being left alone with Ryan. "Follow me," she told him. Taking a few steps and then turning back to her friends, "Be careful, please. I can't stand the thought of anything else happening to anyone because of me."

"We'll be fine, Ella," Armand said. "And none of this is your fault." He held an elbow out to Megan. "Shall we, my lady?" He bowed gallantly, and Megan giggled like a schoolgirl. Ella was glad at least someone was having fun.

"I guess that leaves us." Ryan shifted his bag from one shoulder to the other. In the dim light, Ella thought he seemed more pallid than normal.

"Yeah, I guess. Let's go." Ella went in the opposite direction of Armand and Megan, Ryan following behind.

Shining the flashlight on the rotted wooden floor, they stepped carefully, as pieces of it seemed to be missing, and others were falling down to the floor below. Every now and again Ella would stop to look at an old classroom or painting, all of which were disintegrating in one way or another. The building smelled of mold and decaying plants.

Ella was feeling more than a little distressed.

"What is it?" Ryan asked, so close it was whispered in her ear.

"I just don't understand," making a point to move away from him. Her voice felt as though it was loud in the quiet hall.

"What?"

"All of this. I remember being here just a few years ago. Are all my memories completely wrong? I thought they were becoming clearer, but now I don't know again."

"I think..." There was a loud noise not too far from them. "What was that? Ella, did you hear that?"

"I did," she whispered. "Do you think it was Megan and Armand?"

"Unless the way they went loops back around, they should be at the opposite end from us. At least according to the blueprints I could find. They didn't make a lot of sense."

"It doesn't loop around, if that memory is even right."

They moved into a corner and turned off the flashlight, waiting for another sound. Ryan put his hand on Ella's waist, and it took every once of will power for her to not pull away. They waited in the dark for a few minutes and heard nothing but a bit of wind and creaking as the building settled further into decay.

She disentangled herself from him and continued on without saying anything. He flicked the light back on just as she almost put her foot through a hole in the floor boards.

"Ella! Be careful."

"I'm fine," she snapped.

"Did I do something to upset you?"

"Nope." She kept going and tried to move faster, though the conditions around them kept her from ever getting too far from him.

After about twenty minutes, Ella stopped abruptly in front of the door to the office. She didn't hesitate to open it, and as it swung open, the glass in the frame fell out and shattered all over, making a tremendously loud noise.

"Crap," she swore.

Ryan grabbed her and pulled her into the office and behind the counter. That's when she heard voices, and they were not their friends.

"I'm telling you I heard something," a slightly exaggerated, New Jersey-style accent said. The voice was one she had heard before, but could not recall where.

The door creaked open and the footsteps grew closer to them. Ryan held a finger up to Ella to indicate they should be as quiet as possible. *Like I don't know that.* Her anger flared. But she didn't have time to think about it, as another set of footsteps followed the first.

"I didn't hear anything. Have you been drinking again?" said an angry man's voice.

Ella was positive it was the disappearing man in the suit. *What are they doing here?* It left no doubt in her mind that they were after her for some reason. None of the four of them except her had ever been here before today.

"There's no one in here. Come on. We have things to do," said the man in the suit's voice.

The sound of footsteps retreated, and Ella finally exhaled. They waited a minute longer, then stood up, cracking their foreheads together.

"Ow," Ella yelped, and took a glove off to rub the spot.

"Sorry." Ryan turned the flashlight back on and moved it over the room.

Ella thought the usual luminescence she saw around him was starting to grow in the darkness, or her eyes were finally adjusting. One way or the other, his color was quite bright.

"Focus on the task at hand," she said aloud and brushed cobwebs off her clothes.

"What?"

"Nothing," she smiled weakly. "Just pep-talking myself."

"Good, because we're gonna need it. Come over here and look at these papers." He waved a light over a mess in the dark. "You remembered right, Ella, This wasn't a school. These people were patients, and that means you were, too."

Ella looked at the papers that Ryan was rifling through. "These don't make sense to me. All these tests. I've never heard of any of them before, and is it just me, or does this," she pointed to a number, "seem like an awful lot of blood to be drawing from a person?"

"I know this company." Ryan's voice was grim as he pointed to the header on a memo.

"TriChem. Life. Science. Advancement. That's the company the professor worked for, I think."

"It is, Ella. If they were here and doing these experiments, that's bad."

"Experiments. One might think they shouldn't be experimenting at all. It's so awful to think about. So awful." Ella kept digging through papers and found another stack. "I don't understand why all this stuff isn't computerized."

"It's not on a computer because they don't want anyone to have access to it. This cabinet was locked, but the lock was mostly rusted so it broke away pretty easily. I would guess they wouldn't think anyone would come here. I mean, look at the place. It's a disaster. And if we weren't looking for these papers, we wouldn't have found them. Plus those men are here, and I'm guessing it's not for a picnic."

"Hello," said a voice behind them.

Ella and Ryan both whirled around in terror to see an older man with long hair standing in the room.

"Who are you?" Ryan demanded.

"Jeremiah. Who are you?" His accent was similar to Armand's but not exactly the same. He was wearing causal traveling clothes and carrying a woven bag.

"I, uh... used to be a student here," Ella blurted out the first thing that came to mind.

"That's interesting," said Jeremiah, "because I didn't think this was a school. I am sorry if you used to be a student here. I imagine terrible things happened here."

"Why would you say that?" Ella asked, completely taken aback by the comment.

"It does not feel like a good place." Jeremiah said it matter-of-factly, like they all knew that. "You still did not tell me who you are. Are you afraid of me? I am not with those men."

"What men?" Ella played dumb.

"The big, angry one and the one in the suit."

"Do you know who they are?" Ryan asked him, still standing in a defensive position.

"I have a suspicion."

"Can you tell me what it is?" Ella asked him.

"I might. You look like someone I used to know a long time ago. Her name was Bleu. She had the brightest blue eyes and dark black hair that shone blue in the sun. I cannot see in this light what color your eyes are but what I can see of you, you look quite a bit like her. But of course, you're very young. She would not be anymore."

Ella did not say anything, wondering how old this Bleu would be now. *Over a hundred years old?*

"I'm Ella. This is Ryan." She held out her hand.

"This is not a good idea," Ryan said, and stepped in front of her outstretched hand.

"Move, Ryan," the anger from earlier returning again.

When he didn't move she stepped around him and closer to the stranger. She offered her hand to him again. Jeremiah stepped forward and shook it. He studied her in the dark room, as much as he could.

"It is quite remarkable that you look so much like Bleu."

"Everyone's got a twin," Ella tried to joke, but it fell flat. There was an uncomfortable silence. *Well, I am uncomfortable, Jeremiah seems completely fine.*

"You said you went to school here." Jeremiah set his bag on the counter and pulled some things out of it.

"Ella, we shouldn't tell him anything else, and we don't have much time until we have to leave. We should keep digging."

"Ryan is right. I have to see if I can find anything." For some reason Ella didn't think Jeremiah would stop them.

"I did not mean to stop you. I am looking for answers myself," he said kindly. "Where I live is being destroyed, and all of my searching for a way to stop it led me here. I do not know why."

"Where you live is being destroyed?" Ella felt her heart go out to the man. "Where do you live?"

"Far from here. The other side of the world. But do not worry about me," he told her. "Find what you need. I will not get in your way."

Ella turned her attention back to the papers and started pulling open more drawers. Some were locked, but could be easily broken apart. She could not recall it being this easy to get around in the headmistress' office. *Of course, I was never trying to find out who I was back then. I thought I knew.* She shuffled another pile, hoping to see anything with her name on it. She didn't recognize many of the names that she came across. As far as she could tell, many of these people didn't stay here long. They seemed to be given one particular test, and if they failed it, it appeared they were sent somewhere else.

"You said your name was Ella?" Jeremiah suddenly asked aloud. He had been going through the papers while Ryan and Ella were digging elsewhere.

"It is."

"Then this is for you." He held out a large sealed packet. "It was in that box, there." Jeremiah pointed to a solid metal lockbox that he had clearly broken open.

"Thank you so much." Ella took them gratefully and tore off the seal. "Ryan, can you come over here with the light?"

Ryan came and held the light over Ella's shoulder as she pulled out old photos. Very old photos.

One of them drifted to the floor. Jeremiah leaned over and picked it up. He looked closely at the photo in the tiniest beam of light.

"I know these people," Jeremiah said.

"How could that be? These photos are old. They look like antiques." Ryan was looking closely at a stack, as well. He seemed just as confused as Ella.

"I really don't understand why these are in here," Ella told them. "I don't know who these people..." She stopped and stared intently at someone in a picture.

"What are you looking at?" Ryan asked, as he took the photo gently from Ella's hand. "Wow. She really looks like you."

"I find it unlikely that you look like two different people," Jeremiah said. "May I?"

Ryan hesitantly handed him the photo, then put his arm around Ella, who pulled away without thinking.

"Sorry," he mumbled, and took the light away to another corner of the room.

Ella didn't care. She was in shock. The girl in the picture was her. She knew it. She didn't know why she knew, but she did.

Jeremiah gave her back the picture without saying anything. They could barely see each other, since Ryan had moved away with the flashlight. Ella dug out her phone and turned on the camera light. Jeremiah was looking at her when it came on.

"Your name is Ella? And you went to school here?"

"I think we all now know that this isn't a school. No, it appears I was locked up here, and yeah, my name is Ella. I already told you that, so don't ask me again." Her mood was darkening with each passing minute. *What the hell is going on?*

"How old are you, Ella?"

"Hey man, mind your business." Ryan came over to them.

"I don't need you to defend me, Ryan," Ella growled at him.

"I'm just trying to help."

"Why did you ask me my age?" She directed the light in Jeremiah's direction. He was calmly watching the two of them.

"Because I think I might know you. Though I don't know how to prove that to you. I also do not understand why you would be so young. Do you know who your mother or grandmother might be?"

"I don't know who my family is at all. I guess I came here to hopefully find some answers to those questions."

"I might be able to give them to you."

"How could that be? Who are you? Why should I trust you?"

"I have thus far given you no reason not to trust me."

"Fair enough, but trusting strangers hasn't been working out too well for me lately."

"If you are who I think you are, I will need your help. I stand to lose more in this situation than you do." Jeremiah told her this with grief in his voice. Ella was struck again with empathy for him.

They heard the voices and footsteps return.

"We need to be careful," Ryan told them in a whisper. "Those men are here, so let's get on with this quick. We have to meet our friends soon."

"Who do you think I am?" Ella asked Jeremiah.

"I am looking for people. A fair number of them, but it is difficult because I believe they are hiding around the world. I think many of them are in danger. I think you are clearly in danger, as well."

"Yes, things are not going especially great."

"I think you might be one of the people I am looking for, but I expected something different. I expected you'd be older, and that you would know who your family was. At least some of them, anyway."

"Why do you think I'd be older?"

"Because," he picked up the picture they had looked at, "I think you are her. Bleu. It was her nickname. Her real name was Elliana. You are over one hundred years old, and I would think you would've grown into a woman, but you seem to be too young to be her. This concerns me a great deal."

"Why?"

"Because I believe it means someone has tampered with your health, your well-being, and most likely your mind. And it could mean others have been put at risk too."

"By who? And why?"

"I only have theories at this point. I have no proof, but I will get it. I may need your help."

"Can you please tell me why I would be this person? Why do you think that?"

There was a long silence. Ryan had not moved since they started talking, and was carefully keeping watch out of the broken window. Ella glanced over at him. He was nearly dark now, no light coming off of him. *Can Jeremiah see it too?*

"Let's look further through these papers. Then I think your friend is right. Maybe we should leave and possibly come back when it is daytime."

"Fine."

She started to dig through everything that was left. Ryan came over to help. Jeremiah moved over to cabinets they hadn't yet reached, and Ella saw him putting files into his bag.

"She does look just like you, Ella. She must be an ancestor. It's further proof of who your family might be, and it's easy to see the resemblance to the man who could be your great-great-great-grandfather. Wait... Was that enough greats?" Ryan smiled, but she was too distracted to notice. *The girl in the picture does look just like me.* It was most unsettling.

"I just don't understand who these people are," she said quietly. "On one hand it says they were a great European family. On the other hand it says the father was a monster. What does that even mean?" She looked up at Ryan, not even sure what she expected to hear from him.

"Look, there is a lot of stuff to go through," he gestured around the room, "and if someone in your family was in charge of the town or country, there is always someone to criticize those in charge. Just don't jump to any conclusions yet, okay?" Ryan put his hand on her shoulder, and she felt her cheeks start to warm. "Besides," he said as he moved over to look through a stack of photos, "we all have parts of our family history we wish we didn't."

Ella looked at Ryan's back. *If somehow he is saying that he has things he doesn't want to think about...*

"I'm not even sure where to start in here." Ella picked up a box and and tried to pry the lid open. It was most certainly stuck. "Hey, look at this box." She held it under the light so Ryan could see. "It has some really unusual markings on it."

He took the box and ran his fingers over the engravings.

"It's weird," he said absently, as he looked at the box, "but these marking seem sort of familiar to me."

"Really?" Ella took the box out of his hands and touched the symbols. "Familiar how? Is there a place maybe you think you've seen them? On another box maybe?"

"I'm not sure." He sat down in a chair and leaned his head back. "You know how something is sitting just off the edge of your memory, and you just can't quite reach it?"

"Sure." Ella didn't want to say that she felt that way all the time.

"That's how I feel about those symbols. Like, I know what they are, but I cannot quite grab the information." He had his eyes closed, Ella realized. The flashlights they had were starting to dim. Just like he had.

"Are you feeling okay?" She walked over to the chair, with the box in her hand, to stand in front of him.

"I'm just fine," he whispered cheerfully. Too cheerfully. She thought he sounded like he was trying too hard. "I'm just tired. I've been up too late reading and researching. I have a minor headache is all. Clearly, I haven't had enough caffeine. I mean, really, can you ever have enough?" He got out of the chair and was face to face with her. "I had taken some painkillers earlier for my headache, and I guess they could be wearing off." He took a pill out of a pouch he had pulled from his pocket and popped it into his mouth.

"Don't you need water?" Ella stepped back from how very, very close he was. She was angry, but did not want to be angry at him at all.

"Nah," he smiled in that fake voice again. "I have to take things all the time."

Ella frowned. "Like what things?" She set the box on the desk and crossed her arms to look at him.

"Just vitamins and migraine meds sometimes. Nothing big." He rifled through some more papers and was clearly trying to brush the question aside.

"What gives you migraines?"

"Oh they," he air quoted the word "they" in a light-hearted tone, "don't really know what causes them. There are a lot of theories. Air pressure changes, dehydration, you know, the usual." He looked at her for a minute. "Don't you think that all these things around us are a lot more interesting than my headaches and iron deficiency? This stuff might be your family's."

"No, it's not that. I'm interested in this stuff." This time she sat in the chair. "I'm just also interested in you, I guess."

"You guess?" That made him laugh.

"I mean I am." Now she was miffed.

"You don't sound very sure."

"I'm sure." She crossed her legs, making sure her boot made a stomping sound. A sure sound. And a hollow sound. She looked down at the floor.

"Ryan, did you hear that? Jeremiah, come over here." Jeremiah had been silently digging through papers.

"I sure did." Ryan came back over to the chair. "Do it again."

Ella stomped her foot on the same spot on the floor, and there was a sound like a piece of something breaking and falling.

"You should stand up," he said. "The floorboard goes under the chair."

"You're gonna have to step back." She was looking up at him standing so close. *Again.*

"Sorry." He said it with a smile that didn't sound sorry at all. Ella stood up and both of them pushed the chair back. The noise it made on the wood seemed to echo under the floor. Jeremiah knelt down to examine the bits of light that seeped through.

"I wish we had more light," Ella said, looking around to find anything. "Although, I suppose we're trying not to attract too much attention."

"There is certainly a room under here," Jeremiah told them. "We should try to get into it."

"I want to go in there, but we don't have time. We have to meet our friends, otherwise they'll get worried." As she said it, all the lights came on.

"I don't think you'll have to worry about that, Ella, dear. So nice to see you. It's been too long."

Standing in the doorway at gunpoint were Megan and Armand. The creep who was at Alchemy wearing the long gold chain was holding a gun, and so was the man in the suit.

Neither of them registered with Ella because standing in front of all of them was Ein.

Chapter 17

"I should have known you were behind this," Jeremiah said to Ein.

"Probably. But you never could keep up, could you, Jeremiah." Ein walked over to Ella and pulled the photos from her hands. "I see you've made your way here. Have your memories come back? I told that pathetic excuse of a scientist that he should just wipe your entire brain. Humans." She strode over to Ryan. "Nice to see you." She smiled a cold smile at him. Ryan stared right in her eyes, unwavering.

Ella could not believe the scene in front of her.

"All of you know who this woman is?"

"I don't," Megan cracked, and warily looked at the gun pointed at her.

"Of course they know who I am, Ella, darling. Everyone keeps secrets from you. Haven't you guessed that yet? You were always a little slow, though. That human body of yours is holding you back."

"Her body is holding her back because of the terrible things you did and, I have no doubt, continue to do." Jeremiah, for the first time, sounded angry. "And stop saying 'humans' as if you are not one of us. We are each part of this race."

"Not for much longer, if I can help it." Ein turned to her men. "Bring them downstairs."

"We're not going anywhere." Ella crossed her arms and planted her boots into the filthy floor.

Ein stopped and turned around. That glittering, cold smile had not changed.

"Oh, you're not? Well I guess I'll shoot your friend." She waved her hand, and the man in the suit cocked his weapon.

Megan didn't flinch. But Ella cried out, "Stop!"

"So you'll come, then? Without further trouble?"

"Fine."

Ella ran to her friend and they embraced. Armand put his hand on Ella's back, and she hugged him, too. Ryan watched from across the room. Ella noticed and glared at him.

"How could you, Ryan?" Ella was about to freak out, but kept it together. *The only way we're going to get out of this is if we all stay calm.*

"Ella, I can explain..." he started.

"No, you can't," she retorted, and turned around.

"This is all very touching," Ein said sarcastically. "Now move."

Without further discussion, they followed Ein to a stainless-steel door. She touched the surface with the palm of her hand, and it opened to reveal a huge elevator. The man in the suit shoved Ella, and Armand stepped between them.

"Do not do that again." Armand stood much taller than the man.

"I'm the one with the gun. I tell you what to do."

Armand did not say another word, but got into the elevator with them. Ella took his hand and he clasped hers tightly.

The elevator started a fast descent that lasted a few minutes. Ella could not guess how far down they had gone.

"Keep her," Ein pointed at Ella, "separate from everyone else. Ryan, you come with me."

Ryan looked at Ella with pleading in his eyes. She turned away from him.

The large man with the iron grip grabbed Ella's arm and dragged her away from Megan and Armand. He led her down a long hall until they reached a cell made of material Ella couldn't identify. He pushed her in, and the door slid shut.

"Behave yourself for once, little girl," he said in that exaggerated Jersey accent. "If you stopped giving Ein trouble in the first place, you might know who you are." He left, and Ella had no idea what in the world he was talking about.

Looking around the barren room, she wondered how many of her former "classmates" had been locked up here. *Had Alexandra been brought here?*

There was a sound of two people coming down the hall. It was Ein and a man wearing a lab coat whom she had not seen yet.

"Dr. Smith, it seems we have our patient back," Ein said in a bored tone.

"Indeed." The man had greasy, slicked-back hair and beady, squinty eyes. *Of course he has to look creepy, or this wouldn't be totally horrible.* "Do you remember me, young lady?"

"Nope."

"Do you know why you were here before?"

"Nope."

Ella leaned against the furthest wall away from them. *Not far enough.* She wondered where Megan and Armand were. Begrudgingly, she also wondered where Ryan was.

"As usual, you're useless, Ella, dear," Ein said. "If we can't get her power from her, I see no reason to keep her around anymore, Dr. Smith. It seems to be mutating, anyway. Although when I sent people to that professor's lab they didn't find any research on her. What do you think you can find out? And how fast?" Ein's impatience was clear.

"One, not all your efforts have been fruitless. That young man has helped us a great deal. We know that there is a reaction between the two of them, and he got us all her work and artifacts that have yielded a great many samples for testing. She seems capable of manipulating the cobalt to a certain degree. She has altered it to use as paint, which means it has other uses. We thought your powers had mutated and were going to kill you, until we realized what happened when you made contact with Ryan," the creepy doctor was now telling Ella. "You seem to have developed the ability to absorb uranium. An unknown possibility until this point. Even though it temporarily poisons you, we imagine we can find a way to control it," Dr. Smith said, somewhat excitedly.

Ein laughed. "Control it? Why bother? Her power *has* mutated, and if it's going to kill her, it's all part of the natural process. I knew she was useless. All those stupid paintings."

"YOU!" Ella choked out. "You took all my paintings and broke into my apartment."

"Yes, I did. With some help from your friend, Ryan. Now, granted, it took some convincing to get him to do it, but I can be very persuasive." She said it suggestively. Ella considered puking on her shoes.

"You're a vile woman," Ella said, more calmly than she had expected her voice could be at this moment.

"Yes, I know you've always had a special place in your heart for me. I tried to make peace with you all those years ago. Don't you remember? Your birthday night? Your father had that grand party. He always did put on the best events. I did so enjoy them and your house, especially once he got rid of all your mother's paintings. Dreadful woman."

"I think you are insane. I have no idea what you are talking about. Seriously, Doctor, you should examine her head."

"It's not *my* head that needs work, Ella," Ein said sarcastically. "You don't remember things that I don't want you to remember. So keep being funny and you'll never know who you are."

"I know who I am. Maybe I don't remember my past, but maybe I'm starting to not care, if you're in it."

"Oh you'll care, or you'll never know where you fit. Maybe we should just get rid of you, if you're so indifferent."

"Now, Ein, she's not useless because I am a gifted scientist who can make her useful. At least parts of her. Why kill her when a long life of scientific exploration can be so much more, how should I put this, satisfying?" Dr. Smith looked at her expectantly.

"Oh, fine! But we have to find the others. They are our priority!" She stormed out of the room.

Others? What does that mean? Does she mean the other patients? Or does she mean the same group of people Jeremiah was looking for? How are they connected?

The doctor looked at her through the glass and smiled lasciviously. "I don't have time for you now, pretty one, but I promise you, we'll do great things together."

"Charming. Can't wait. Don't you have a monster to go electrify?"

He stared at her. "You're funny. I like it." The doctor left without another word.

"No wonder Ryan hates doctors." Her voice echoed a tiny bit in the empty room.

Now that she was alone, she stood up, took off the gloves, and began to feel the walls of the cell, hoping to find some sort of indentation, button, key, magic portal.

Her mind was racing. *Where is Ryan now? Does Ein have him? Who are the "others" Ein mentioned? What did they mean, her powers have mutated? So many questions...*

Her hands slid across the dark gray pads. What were those for? The room seemed to be tightly sealed. Nothing was getting through. She hit the wall behind her in frustration. Something flashed behind her eyes, an image. Sharp and blurred all at the same time. Putting her hands flat on the wall, she slid them slowly across, trying to find an edge of the material. A couple of minutes later, she was about to stop and try the floor, when it hit her again. The image lasted longer this time. A girl. She moved her hand slowly back. Then the full force of the picture hit her and caused the blinding pain that came with it. She took deep breaths and tried to focus all her energy on the image so it might come through more clearly.

There was a girl with her back turned, pulling at the padding of the cell. She turned her head, and Ella saw her face. There were heavy bags and dark circles around her red, bloodshot eyes. She was frail and gaunt and looked like she would fall apart at the slightest touch. Ella felt hot tears streaming down her face. The girl was Alexandra.

Her arms and neck were black and blue with bruises, and there was a medical bracelet on her wrist with nothing on it except the numbers 8 and 7. Concentrating on the bracelet, Ella noticed a small piece of paper in her friend's hand. Trying to still her rage, Ella let the rest of the scene flow over her. Alexandra glanced around furtively before carefully removing a section of the gray padding and placing the piece of paper behind it. She dropped the padding at the sound of footsteps.

A man in a black uniform appeared in front of the clear cell door, as Alexandra finished scrambling around to put the piece of padding back. The man unlocked the cell, stepped in, and yanked Alexandra's arm. Her friend put up no resistance. As the picture faded, the look of dejection on her face forced Ella to the ground in tears and absolute furor. She had been right all along, Ein had taken Alexandra. *Why? To punish her for all her misbehaving at school?* Ella didn't know.

Wiping her face and standing up, she started pulling at the pad. It was not a surprise that it didn't budge, as she had no idea how long ago that image could've been from. She tried anyway, an inch at a time. Ella didn't really know how much time was passing. After what felt like twenty minutes, a piece finally gave way, much to her shock. She gently pulled it away, but it stirred up a lot of dust and almost made Ella cough. Tucked carefully away was a yellowed piece of paper. She pulled it out and unfolded it. The only words scrawled across it were "de los cristales."

Ella had very little time to contemplate what this could mean because at that moment Ryan showed up outside the cell and opened the door.

"Hurry," he whispered urgently.

"Why should I go anywhere with you?"

"Because you can trust me."

"No, I really can't."

"Look." He stepped into the cell, backing her against the wall. It forced her to look up at him, and the lights glared behind his head. The yellow shimmer was apparent and not at all subtle. "I didn't want to betray you. I didn't want any of this, except to find out what was wrong with me. Ein forced me to lie to you, to help them break into your place."

"Forced you? Whatever." Ella pushed on his chest with both hands but he didn't budge.

"Ella, she took my mother. Ein was going to have her killed if I didn't help them. I didn't want to do it, but I couldn't figure out how to save my mom."

"Oh," Ella let her hands drop to the side. "You should've told me. I've been telling you my secrets."

"Ella, I know. I'm sorry. But look, we have to go. Come on."

"Fine. We have to find the others."

"I know where Ein had them locked up. Follow me."

Ella grabbed her gloves and stuffed the paper into her pocket as they left the cell. "I still don't trust you, Ryan."

"Don't trust me. But also, don't trust Armand."

"He hasn't done anything to deserve distrust."

They rounded a corner, then pulled back quickly upon spotting a guard. The halls were lined with many cells, but it didn't seem that any of them were occupied.

"When I was first here..." he said, out of breath as they raced down a different hallway. It was the first time Ella noticed that he didn't look too healthy. "I swear I saw Armand here. It was only for a moment, and my view was blocked, but I am sure it was him." Ryan held out a hand to stop Ella from running into him.

"Why are you sure?" She peeked around him and gasped. The hall opened up into a huge facility. It was filled with machines, guards, and what appeared to be a handful of scientists, some of whom were closely inspecting large metal cylinders.

"Because I am."

"Great. Everyone knows everything except for me. Ein even said everyone was keeping secrets from me. Good god, it enrages me when that woman is right."

"Shhh..." Ryan held up a finger as a heavily armed guard came awfully close to them. Ella was positive he could hear her breathing. Her heart all but stopped.

"Hey," Ella whispered hoarsely, "how did you get a key?"

"How do you think? I stole it. Ein got what she wanted from me and then sent me on my merry way."

"Isn't she afraid you're gonna turn her in?"

This time Ryan stopped and looked back at Ella.

"And who exactly could we turn Ein in to? We have no proof that she has done anything, except for this place. And how could we possibly get someone to come to this place? I have a feeling Ein has powerful buddies."

Ella frowned, knowing he was right. *What could we do?* Not knowing what was going on wasn't helping her cause. They had to get Megan and Armand, and then see if Jeremiah could give them any more information.

"Hello, you two." For the second time that night, Jeremiah snuck up behind them without making a sound.

"How did you get away from Ein?" Ella asked in disbelief. *Is he some sort of ninja? But with hippie hair.*

"It is not the first time she has locked me up. She is not as good at it as she thinks."

It made Ella smile, despite the circumstances.

"We have to find our friends," Ella said, starting to feel frantic. *Poor Megan! What about Armand? Gah!*

"Yes. I know where they are. Let's go to them." Jeremiah eyed Ryan suspiciously, but said nothing.

"Fine. But after this, you talk. For real." Ella was determined to get some answers, no matter how preposterous. *It's becoming my middle name, after all.*

"Yes, I will tell you what I can." That's all he said before moving silently down the hall. If Ella couldn't see him, she would never have known he was there.

She sighed and followed him, with Ryan coming up behind to fill out their weird trio.

They went the rest of the way silently, trying to avoid video cameras and guards. *Ryan seems to know his way around pretty well.* That thought did not make her very happy.

What did make her happy, however, was seeing Megan's face light up when they reached her cell. Where she was sitting in the lotus position, meditating.

"Are you really meditating?" Ella asked her, aghast.

"Sure, what else should I do? I already did sit-ups and some yoga."

"You are something else." Ella clutched Megan in relief, once Ryan let her out.

"I am glad you are okay. Who is that hippie?" Megan pointed to Jeremiah.

"Um, that's Jeremiah. Keeper of the knowledge, or whatever."

"Ladies," came Armand's smoky voice, "I am pleased to see you both happily reunited, but would you be so kind?" He motioned to the lock on his cell door. Ryan stood off, watching Armand as if trying to decide if he deserved to be let out.

"Unlock his door," Megan said. Ryan didn't move.

"What are you doing?" Ella said to Ryan, but walked over to Armand. Without thinking, she put a hand on the window between them. Armand smiled faintly and returned the gesture.

Megan cleared her throat and snickered. Ryan stormed over and unlocked the door. His anger was quite obvious.

"Thank you, my friend," Armand said to him.

"I'm not your friend." Ryan walked over to Jeremiah. "What's your story? Can you help us get out of here?"

"We shall help each other get out of here." Jeremiah took out a small box. "I am going to leave this here. In a few minutes it will release a gas that will be detected as being poisonous. It is not toxic, but it should cause enough of a distraction for us to get outside. Presuming someone knows the way to the surface."

No one said anything.

"No one knows how to get out?" Megan asked.

"I might," said Armand. "I would just be guessing, though."

"Sure you would," said Ryan. Armand gave him a strange look, but said nothing.

"Let me try," Armand said it only to Ella, once again making her feel like they were the only ones there.

"Of course." Ella looked at everyone else. "Let's get this carnival on the road."

"You're the clown," Megan joked.

"Nope. Pretty sure you are." The two girls clasped hands and looked at Jeremiah. "Ready when you are, Sir," Ella told him.

Jeremiah set the box down and cranked what appeared to be a miniature timer. "We have about seven minutes before they figure out it's not toxic, so let's be quick about it." His accent was very pronounced at that moment. Ella wondered again where he had come from and what was happening to his home.

"Okay, move!" Ryan was on look-out as Armand led them down a service tunnel. They were not more than five feet in when an alarm went off. The girls looked at each other.

"RUN!" Ella shouted, and took off after Ryan and Armand. Megan got ahead of her pretty quickly, and Jeremiah had disappeared again. Ella stopped in confusion, looking for him.

"Ella, come on!" Megan waved for her to hurry.

The tunnels were getting darker and it was increasingly difficult to see, but Ella did not want to leave anyone behind.

"I can't see Jeremiah," she shouted to Megan. Who she also could not see anymore, she realized.

In the dark, a small breeze brushed by her ear. "I am here, Ella." Jeremiah sounded as if he had sighed, not spoken. It was unnerving. "Catch up to Megan. I am right behind you."

Ella decided not to hesitate any longer and took off running, hoping upon hope that she didn't run into any walls or trip over any pipes. Then she stumbled, and as she started to fall, someone yanked her up roughly.

"Where do you think you are going?" The pseudo-gangster accent oozed over her. The cretin from the bar had her, and once again she didn't think she could pull away.

"Fine, fine, creep face, I'll come with you. Just stop yanking on my arm. You are four-hundred times my size." As soon as he let go, Ella aimed as best she could and kicked with all her might. He actually groaned, which really surprised her.

Running as fast as was humanly possible, she came across an area of the tunnel that had a dim light. But no one was anywhere to be found. Biting her lip to keep from panicking, she had to make a choice as to which way she should go.

"Ella!" Armand yelled her name, but she didn't seem him anywhere. "Ella!"

Looking furiously around, but still not seeing him, she felt something graze the top of her head. Armand was above her, holding out an arm. He was dangling from a metal ladder that appeared to lead up to the grounds.

"I thought you were gone," as he pulled her up to the ladder. For a moment she was face to face with him.

"Never again," was all he said, before he motioned for her to move. He didn't have to ask twice, as shouting voices and stomping boots encouraged her to climb the ladder as if she were in good shape. Which, as she fell to the ground after Megan helped pull her out of the hole, she had to reconcile with the fact that she was fairly sure she was going to have a heart attack on the spot.

"I am in terrible shape," Ella moaned, and tried to stand up. Megan wasn't the slightest bit winded.

"Meh. You're an artist," Megan helped her up and started brushing leaves and dirt off both of them.

Armand got out, and in the dim light looked as if he wasn't disheveled in the least.

"Where are Ryan and Jeremiah?" Ella choked out between gasps of air. Megan patted her back sympathetically.

"They went to get the car. We are going to meet them by the road. I think I know the way. We sort of had to guess, but the sun is starting to come up, so that's helping."

"I don't understand. How did we get to the surface so quickly? Ella asked Armand. "It felt like we were down really far."

"I think," he said, brushing an imaginary piece of dirt off his impeccable top, "that we were taken to the bottom floor, but the building is a rotunda. As you move through it, you move further up to the surface. I suspect it's to confuse people trying to escape whatever is going on down there."

Ella didn't respond. Armand seemed to know an awful lot about this place. And knowing that Alexandra had been locked underground like some sort of prisoner, it was almost more than she could stand to think about.

"You can't hear anything," Megan pointed out. "That alarm was deafening, and nothing. All you can see is the main building down that path." The building was about a half a mile away.

"I imagine that it has very good sound-proofing. If I had to guess, I would say that Ein woman isn't doing anything she wants anyone to know about," Armand surmised.

"Yeah. She's super," Megan said sarcastically. "I can't believe you had to live under that horrible woman, Ella."

Ryan and Jeremiah arrived, with the sedan purring quietly in the dim morning. The three of them climbed into the back, and in the dark, Armand took Ella's hand.

Ryan started back down the road as soon as the door was closed.

"Where should we go?" He looked in the mirror at Ella.

"We should get to the professor's house. I am starting to feel a lot of pain and I need my treatment. And when we get there I am sure hoping, Jeremiah, that you tell me who I am."

"I will do my best." Those were the last words anyone said as they drove back to the city with the sun rising high into the morning sky.

Chapter 18

The professor opened the front door of his house with mussed hair and wrinkled clothes.

"ELLA! I have been frantic all night. What happened to you and Megan? I went to the apartment building to find you both, but no one was there. Goodness, what a mess!"

The door was wide open and they were all standing on the immaculate porch. Ella looked at her friends. They all looked terrible, except for Armand. But even he looked tired.

"Um, James, can we come in?" Ella asked in an exhausted voice.

"Yes, oh my, yes. I'm sorry. I was very worried." He stepped to the side. "Your party has grown, Miss Cerulean. Hello, Armand, I certainly did not expect to see you this morning."

They all shuffled in, and Megan went straight for the stairs.

"I'm going to take a shower," she declared. "And in order for me to maintain my cheerful disposition, I suggest someone make a big-ass pot of coffee."

"On it," Ella told her, and went into the kitchen, leaving all the males to deal with meeting one another.

The professor padded into the kitchen right after, however.

"Who is the other gentleman with you?" He handed Ella coffee beans and started pulling out various breakfast foods.

Meanwhile, the rest of them had come into the kitchen and tiredly sat down in chairs.

"James Reynolds, this is Jeremiah... well, I don't know what his full name is." Ella turned on the coffee maker and sat down.

"My full name is complicated. We can address it later. I'm more concerned with figuring out why, Ein… Is that what you called her? … is after you, and what she is doing in that facility."

"Jeremiah, you seem to think you know who I am and where I come from. Certainly more than I do. So please, share what you know."

"Ein?" James looked confused.

"My former headmistress. It appears she is in charge of some clandestine, disturbing-looking facility. Very Frankenstein's lab meets secret military installation. All underneath my old school. Which isn't a school, obviously. She locked me in a cell. It was fun."

"Good lord! You all had a terrible night." James was cooking, and the kitchen was starting to smell pleasant.

"Don't be silly. I didn't have to bartend for a bunch of drunk frat boys." Ella got up and starting pouring coffee. "I've had worse nights."

"I was in a fraternity," said James, peering over the rim of his glasses at her.

"So was I," said Armand, and Ryan snorted.

"Okay, okay. Fine. Frats are the best. I was just kidding. I did not love being locked in a cell. I'd prefer it not happen again, nor that I ever see the ice queen again. I always have the overwhelming urge to dump wine or grape juice on her white clothes. She wears white constantly. It's so WEIRD." Ella slammed a mug on the table, and coffee sloshed onto the surface. Megan came up behind her in a robe and with wet hair, and wiped up the mess.

"You smell infinitely better than I do," Ella told her.

"You do smell like a foot." Megan flopped in a chair, and James put a plate of pancakes piled with strawberries in front of her.

"Olfactory is a fascinating subject, but perhaps we can save it for another time. I do believe Jeremiah was going to regale us with a yarn of your history." James put food in front of everyone, and they started to eat, muttering thanks to him. He sat down with them, as Jeremiah pulled Ella's file out of his bag.

"I didn't know you took that." Ella took a sip of coffee as Jeremiah handed her the papers.

"I did. I felt it was important."

"Your accent," James said, "I can't quite place it."

"It is one I developed living many years in what is currently known as the Democratic Republic of the Congo."

"You are far from home, Sir."

"I am further away from home than you might guess," he replied. Jeremiah sorted through the many pictures and notes in Ella's file, as she continued to examine her school records.

"You sure got good grades in the classes you took, you nerd." Megan was looking at Ella's report card.

"Did I not see your name on the dean's list last quarter, Miss McCourt?" James asked her.

"Who's the nerd now?" Ella put down the papers and waited for Jeremiah to talk. If she wasn't so tired, her impatience might have gotten the better of her.

Armand was leaning back into a chair with his eyes closed, and Ryan was on his computer. Again.

"What are you always doing on there?" Ella asked him.

"Mostly making notes."

Ella watched him for minute, trying to decide what to feel about him. A myriad of emotions ran through her. Anger, empathy, even more anger. He betrayed her. Whatever the reason, she couldn't trust him. She had no idea what he had told Ein.

"I am here, as I told Ella earlier, because the village where I live is suffering great destruction. It has resulted in the death of my son." Jeremiah, for the first time, showed an emotion, and it was heavy grief.

Ella stood up and took his hand, "I'm so sorry." Her gloves were wet so she took them off and set them on the table. Jeremiah reached for her again.

"Your hands give you away, Ella." He pulled her hand up close to his face and nodded. "You are most certainly Bleu. Eliana. You are over one hundred years old, are you not?" He let go of her hand, and Armand's eyes were no longer closed. They were on Ella.

"There's no point in lying to any of you. Yes, I am over a hundred years old. A fact I only recently discovered thanks to James."

"But that number is not conclusive, is it, Professor?" Jeremiah directed the question to James.

"That is correct, Jeremiah. There are parts of Ella's DNA that seem to indicate she is older than that. Much, much older."

"Ella is over one hundred years old. That is correct. However, I suspect Ein did something to you that has kept you from growing into an adult. You should not still be in the late teens or early twenties of human development at this point. You should be closer to forty, I believe." Jeremiah lined up the photos from her file on the table. Everyone was paying close attention. Even Ryan had shut his computer.

"So, why am I not the right... uh... human age? Am I not human?"

"No, Ella, you are human. Just a different human." Jeremiah stopped and looked into the distance as if searching for the right words to explain. "Rather, you are a human body version of a piece of the world."

"Like a tree-person," Megan said helpfully. No one laughed when they all turned to look at her. "Geez, tough room. It's just getting very serious in here."

"Megan, you must be sick to death of all this stuff," Ella said sympathetically. "I totally understand if you want to go to bed. I can fill you in later."

"That woman took my sword and locked me in a cell, too. I am not going anywhere. Your drama is my drama." She crossed her arms and straightened her posture.

"I'm sorry you lost your sword. It's my fault."

"No, it's not," Megan insisted.

"Besides," Armand interrupted, "she stabbed the man in the suit with it before he took it from her." Armand laughed when he finished the sentence.

"Did you really?" Ella laughed, too.

"Yeah, well. He's a jerk and he hit me, remember?"

"I remember."

"But that reminds me," she said thoughtfully, "when I stabbed him in the shoulder, something weird happened. He didn't bleed. He sort of emitted some kind of... I guess it was gas, or air, or something. No blood, though. He pushed me into the cell, shut the door, and disappeared again. Just like you said he did."

"Any thoughts on that, Jeremiah?" Ella was bone-weary, tired, and anxious.

"I have one, yes."

"Care to share? Please start with who Ein is."

"I am about to tell you some important information, all of which should remain in your care and be guarded carefully. I cannot be more serious. We do not know who all our enemies are, at this point. I do mean all of us. Do you all agree?"

There was moment of consideration and then collective agreement, though part of Ella wanted to make Ryan leave.

"Very well. Ein, as she seems to call herself here, is an extraordinarily powerful being. She and I, and you, Ella, belong to the Naturals, as we are known to our people."

"Wait? What? I thought you said I was human?"

"You are human, but you are the human version of a piece of this particular universe. I should start by adding that there are many more worlds out there than this planet knows of, and Ella, you have been on a great deal of them. Not as you are now, but in your other forms."

Megan and Ryan were looking at her in awe, James was nodding and mumbling about how this made more sense than anything he had come up with yet. Only Armand looked unsurprised. He looked like he knew this already.

"You know what I am, then?"

"I didn't at first. But now that I have seen your hands, yes. You are cobalt. A very important element. It is a big part of this world. You have a connection to every living thing on this planet. You may not know this yet, but you have the ability to be in communication with all living things here."

"No."

"Yes. I'm sorry, but it is true."

"I mean, no, I know what you mean, I guess."

"Oh?"

"I wear the gloves because when my hands get wet, or I sweat too much, I seem to create this cobalt. But also, something else happens. I always thought I was just losing my mind. But now that you are here, it makes more sense, and honestly is a bit of a relief."

"What happens?"

"I get flashes. Images. They can be so real, as if I have done things, or felt things myself. But I have no personal recollection of them."

"You are an empathic element. It is a power that Ein covets immensely."

"How does she know what I can do? I barely know."

"Ein, being who she is, has been around much longer than you. You are not one of the young Naturals any more, but you are among the younger."

"I can't control this, this... whatever, power. How could she?"

"It is not her power, first of all. Something that she resents. Her anger seems to have only grown over the many, many long years. She has many abilities. An elder of the Naturals, in fact, she used to be one of our most revered leaders, if not the one held in the highest of esteem."

"You said 'used to be?'"

"I did. We do not know yet how long this was happening. It could have been over many millions of Earth's years. That is the best way to explain for everyone. As we already know, you, Ein, and I age much differently. She began to question the order of things. That was not a problem, until some of us learned that with her questioning, she was performing secret experiments on other Naturals, as well as our own population. An utterly forbidden and unforgivable offense."

"Yeah, humans definitely don't like that," Megan said.

"It has not been just humans," Jeremiah explained to her. "It has been since we left our first home. On many planets, to many races. We thought we had settled into peace with her, until we were on our way here. That was when those of us in opposition to her thought process learned she had many allies and we had many enemies. Something that, up until then, was unfathomable to the Naturals, as we were always meant to work as one. Different purposes, but the same goals. Somewhere along the way, Ein became unsatisfied with this. I still do not know why. Not for all the years I spent searching for answers. I think your school," he continued, turning back to Ella, "where we were this past night, is a place where she is doing this again. And I am afraid you are one of her victims."

"It's not just me."

"What do you mean?"

"Tonight Ryan and I found records, lots of them. Of people, students, being tested on and then sent away."

"Her treachery runs very deep. For all her power, she has no kindness left in her being."

"What does she want from these experiments?" James asked.

"She wants more power. She seeks to take the characteristics of the other Naturals in order to eliminate them and control all the pieces."

"To what end?"

"That answer, James, is still a mystery to me." Jeremiah sat back and looked around the table. "I fear you are all in great danger." His eyes lingered the longest on Armand.

"My powers are not that great," Ella said. "I am pretty much in pain constantly, and I don't know how to use them. I get blinding headaches and suffer from constant swelling in my joints."

Armand put a gloved hand over Ella's uncovered one. Ella couldn't help but look at Ryan and saw him look away ashamedly.

"I am sorry you are suffering. The power you carry here, something is wrong. You are not the first Natural to be sick. My son was one of us. His power became corrupted and killed him. Very few of us die. It is of great importance that we live our full cycle each place we go. Our cycles are multiple lifetimes long, but they grow ever-shorter in this world. Another answer I do not have."

Ella felt both like a great weight had been lifted off her, and a new, heavier one had been placed just above her head. Waiting to crash down any minute.

"I have so many questions, Jeremiah," she started.

"I know you do, and I will answer more of them as best as I possibly can. I am, my child, very happy to have found you. But please forgive me if I beg a leave of rest from all of you. I have come a long way for a great while to find any hint of another Natural. To find two, I am both pleased and worried. Ein is a formidable opponent, and yet we are not supposed to be at odds. I do not know what to do at this point. May I please ask a space of you to rest, James?"

"Of course, I have lots of rooms." He left to get one ready.

"Ella, look through the files I brought with us. Read them, gather your questions. I am sure many answers may be found in them. Ein was always very adept at collecting information. Even if she wasn't supposed to have it." Jeremiah stood up and ran a hand over Ella's hair. He smiled kindly at her before leaving the kitchen.

The remaining four stared blankly at each other.

"Well, there ya go," Megan finally said. "I told you you were a superhero."

"You are extremely optimistic, human," Ella joked in a tired robot voice.

"Do you want me to help you go through these papers?" Megan picked some up and fanned through them.

Ella looked at her friend. She was freshly showered, but obviously completely worn out.

"No, I'm fine. Go get some rest. We need to figure out what to do in a few hours."

Megan got up and kissed Ella on the top of her head. As she left the room, she glanced back with a worried look to Ella, who was still sitting with Ryan and Armand.

"I'm fine," Ella reassured her, and Megan went up the stairs.

Ryan reached over to pick up some of the papers and Ella snatched them away.

"I think maybe you should just let me go through these."

"But Ella..." he stopped when she held up her hand.

"Not now, Ryan."

"Ella, I really am so..." he started again and she shook her head vigorously.

"I think you should rest, Ryan."

"I'm not tired."

"Ryan, I need you to leave me be for now." Ella was unwavering. *I just can't do this with him right now.*

Without another word, he got up and stormed out of the kitchen. For as big as the house was, Ella could still hear him slam a door upstairs.

"Would you like me to go upstairs as well?" Armand had sat patiently, waiting.

Ella didn't want him to leave. Yet there was something off that she couldn't quite put her finger on.

"No, stay with me for now. Do you think we can at least get these in chronological order? Maybe that will help us make sense of some of this information. I don't know where else to start."

"I think that is a good idea."

They worked for several hours, sorting, with no interruption except James bringing Ella a round of her treatment.

"Do you still feel okay?" he asked her.

"Barring the whole, I'm a human, sort of, stuff? Yeah, I'm fine. I do think this is helping me. When we have time, I would like you to explain it to me more."

"Of course. And like I said, this is not a permanent solution. But we will find one," James said, and went up to sleep for a while.

Ella went back to reading a document.

"Armand, this sheet here, it seems to say that, if I am this Bleu person, my father was a leader in Belgium."

Armand moved closer to her, and Ella was forced to ignore the fact that, even though they had run through tunnels and climbed metal ladders, he somehow still smelled wonderful. *Focus, Cerulean. It's pretty clear that boys are nothing but trouble.*

"His name," she continued, swallowing hard, "is blacked out, though."

"Let me have a look." He took the sheet from her, his gloved fingers brushing her hand.

"Armand?" She studied his face while he read the paper.

"Yes, Ella?"

"Take off your gloves."

Armand set the paper down and looked straight at her. He pulled one glove off, folding it carefully onto the table, did the same with the second, and held his hands out for her to look. She might've been shocked a day or two ago, but not anymore.

"You're a Natural."

"So it would seem." He leaned away, appearing to be on edge, as if expecting her to be angry.

"How long have you known?"

"I have known my whole life, but in many ways, I know only as much as you."

"How old are you?"

"I am about six or seven years older than you in our human form. Just as you do not know exactly how old you are, I do not know how old I am, either."

"What do you mean, you only know as much as me?"

"I do not know why we are here. I do not know where the others are, or what Ein wants. I do not know why there seems to be something wrong with you, or what happened to Jeremiah's son. I, like Jeremiah, have been looking for answers for a long time, and have come up with very little."

Ella contemplated this for a few moments.

"Did you know who I was when I had my show at the gallery?"

"Not yet, no. I had my suspicions, but it didn't matter, Ella, because your art and you, well, I would not and do not care if you are a Natural."

"I see."

"Ella, are you angry with me? I could not stand the thought of you being angry with me."

"No. I am not angry. I am confused, bewildered, overwhelmed, relieved, and even happy. But no I am not angry. I am not even really angry at Ryan."

"He did help us escape," Armand pointed out.

"He doesn't trust you."

"That is fine. I do not trust him, but to be fair, I do not trust many people."

"He thinks he saw you at Ein's monster lab."

"Indeed."

Ella waited to see if Armand would elaborate, but he didn't. He went back to reading the papers in front of them and did not put his gloves back on. Ella watched his hands as they moved.

"Does anyone else know about you, Armand?"

"A few trusted confidants, but mostly no."

"Your housekeeper knows."

"Yes, she does, and she wanted me to tell you immediately. She is a good judge of people, and I trust her every instinct."

"Why didn't you tell me?"

"Really, when have I had a moment? We've been on our unexpected adventure since our dinner date."

"True. Are you going to tell the others?"

"Not yet, Ella. Let me keep my secret, except from you. Let us see how this plays out. I am wary of what will happen to you. And if I do not give away my advantage, I might be able to help you if you need it."

Ella didn't like the idea of hiding something from James and Megan, but she agreed nonetheless. It was not her secret to share. They still didn't know who Jeremiah really was, and Ryan definitely could not be trusted.

"I'm worried about what Ryan told Ein about me."

"Do not be worried. We are gaining ground on her, and we will find out what she wants. Let's go through more papers, as I think I've put these in the right order." He showed her the forms and old pictures that were lined up on the table.

She stood up and stepped back from the table. There was a lot to look at. It was her life. Ein had tried to steal it from her.

"I lied," Ella said, as she examined pictures of a little girl from another century.

"What about?" Armand put his hand on her lower back, but Ella stepped away.

"I *am* angry. I am angry at Ein. She has been haunting me my whole life. Maybe even more than my whole life. Look."

Ella held out a picture that was her, another woman, who looked a lot like her teacher at the institute, a man in full military uniform, and Ein in a long evening gown, that cold glittering smile unchanged over the last hundred years.

"There is no doubt, then. You are Bleu. Eliana, I mean." His voice sounded hoarse.

"Yeah, sure. Why not? Look, I need to rest a bit. You should, too. I am going to go upstairs to my room for a couple of hours. There's a big couch in the front room."

"Thank you, I will investigate." He was not really paying attention to her anymore.

Ella was starting to walk away when, out of the corner of her eye, she saw Armand take a sheet of paper from the stack, crumple it, and put it in his pocket.

Chapter 19

A few hours later, when Ella came back to the kitchen, Armand was not there. Both Ryan and Megan were at the table, talking quietly and eating.

"Hey," Ella said. "Sorry, I didn't mean to scare you."

"You didn't, you just got in here like a ninja." Megan got up and handed her a cup of coffee.

"Where's Armand?" Ella slid into a chair next to Ryan.

"Asleep in the living room, looking dreamy as ever." Megan sat across from her and held out a photo. "This is supposed to be you, right?"

"Yeah, I think that's the rumor. Dreamy as ever? Were you watching him sleep, weirdo?"

"Do you know who that man is? And only for a minute, Miss Judgy."

"Nope."

"I do."

"How do you know who he is?"

"European history class. Why are you in a picture with him?"

"Dunno." Ella took a piece of toast off a pile and messily stuffed it in her mouth. "Is there a point in which you give me something useful in this conversation, or do you just keep asking me questions?"

"Look who got up on the wrong side of the bed."

"Sorry," Ella grumbled, and ate another piece of toast. "I slept like total crud."

"He was the King of Belgium. He was not what you would call a great guy."

"Why is that?"

"His legacy was to pretty much destroy the Congo. He is responsible for the deaths of millions of people. He created the rubber trade, and while doing so, raped the land and let his soldiers and businesspeople run havoc in that part of Africa."

"Sounds like a swell guy. Why am I hanging out with him? Of course, maybe I've always been a bad judge of character."

"She had my mother, Ella," Ryan said miserably.

"You should have told me, Ryan."

"What is done is done," Megan told them sternly. "You both are my friends, and we have to get through this, whatever this is, anyway."

"Thank you," said Ryan.

"Don't thank me, Ryan. I am mad as all hell at you, but I am trying to believe you thought you had no other choice. I think Ella ought to kick you right in the head, but since I doubt she is going to do that, you can put up with her being angry for as long as she is angry. However, we don't have time for that now, do we?"

"No," both Ryan and Ella mumbled.

"So call a truce, and let me finish."

"You'll make a good teacher, if you decide to be," Ella said.

"I'm good at everything," Megan reminded her.

"Yes, it's annoying." Ella smiled at the pretty blonde and almost laughed to think that, not all that long ago, she couldn't even imagine them being friends.

"What concerns me about this photo, Ella," she continued, "is not only are you in it with him, and we don't yet know why, but Ein is in this photo. Close to you, and with Leopold. If she was involved with him, she probably has more money and power than we could ever guess. Combine that with her space powers, or whatever... I'm not sure what we should do. She is very dangerous," Megan finished, perplexed.

"She is very dangerous." Jeremiah came into the kitchen. He looked much more rested, but no less worried.

"Speaking of ninjas," Megan said.

"Ninjas?" The man looked at her, confused.

"Nothing."

"I have been meditating on what to do next."

"You meditate?" Megan's voice was enthusiastic.

"Yes, I do, child. Do you know how, as well?"

"I do. I love it, it helps me so much. I want to teach her to do it," Megan pointed to Ella.

"That is a good idea, Megan." Jeremiah sat down, his silver-gray hair tangled in knots. "The Naturals could use all the help they can get to find balance in this world."

"But where are the Naturals?" Ella asked him.

"I do not know. I wish that I did. But we will get to that. I heard what Megan was saying about Leopold. Ella, he is your father."

"WHAT?!?!?"

"ELLA!" Armand came tearing into the kitchen, his hair actually somewhat a mess. "Are you okay?"

"I'm sorry. I'm fine, except apparently I'm related to a mass murderer."

"What?'

"Have a seat, Armand. Let's hear more about my horrible family history." Ella sounded dejected.

"You are not responsible for what he did, Ella," Jeremiah told her gently. "Most of the world did not know you were his daughter. He had another family, a human family that lived far from you and the home you lived in with your mother."

"You knew my mother?"

"I did. She was a lovely woman. Kind, smart, talented. One of the finest Naturals. She was always trying to make peace between Ein and the rest of the Naturals, who were at odds. You look a lot like her. Ein was her best friend for many years. They grew up together, traveling, and sharing the responsibilities beset upon us."

"What happened to her?"

"There was an accident, Ella. She died. Many of the Naturals blamed Ein."

"She died," Ella let this roll over her. Of all the news, this carried the heaviest weight yet. Part of her had always dreamed her mother was still out there. Lost and looking for her, but out there nonetheless. To find out that wasn't true took some of Ella's hope away.

"Your power comes from her."

"Cobalt?"

"Yes. Each of the older Naturals passes their power to their children at a point in their life cycle. We do not always know when it will happen, nor on which planet it will take place, but we do."

"What happens to the power if they die? Like your son?" Ryan asked. "I'm sorry," he added quickly, noticing Jeremiah's face.

"It is okay. You do not mean offense. It is a good question, and Ella should know what I can tell her. The power goes back to the parent, if they are still alive. It is a tremendous burden, as it carries the life-cycle memories of the child. Or so I have learned. As far as I know, I am the only Natural whose child has died. As of yet, I do not know the full extent of the consequences."

"You said you came here from the Congo?"

"Yes, Ella, I did, after a while. It took some time to find any hint of where Ein might be. Each previous piece of information turned out to be a false lead."

"Did you know this man? This father of mine?"

"Only briefly. I tried to work with him, but I was forced to leave when I questioned too much of what his advisers were telling him to do."

"Was he human? Not human like us. I mean, like, Earth-human."

"Ella you are a part of the human race. I know it's hard to understand, but do not trouble yourself with feeling as though you do not belong, because that is the wrong idea of what you should feel. You belong here. You are part of this world. You are this world. We all are. And yes, he was human. Your mother was the Natural, and she loved him very much. I do not think, however, he could ever handle the fact that he felt he was less than her. He saw her as a deity, to a degree, and his ego, being what it was, drove him to anger and, I'm afraid, away from you. It is a shame that her peaceful nature could not quell his troubled heart."

Megan handed Ella a tissue, and it was only then she realized that the tears that had been on the verge time and time again the last few days, the angry tears, the sad tears, the frustrated tears, all poured down her face. In a silvery-blue wave.

"I can get you a canvas, and you can cry on that. Then we'll go sell it at Armand's gallery." Megan ran her hand over Ella's hair.

Ella hiccuped out a laugh and mopped up her face.

"I am sorry. I feel as though I have ladened you with nothing but bad news," Jeremiah said sadly.

"I'm the one who wanted the truth. Be careful what you wish for. It's not like I've never seen a Disney movie."

"What we should be doing now," Ryan interrupted, "is figuring out what to do next. I would imagine Ein is not going to let us get away with knowing where her secret cave of misery is located."

"Ryan is right," Armand said. "We should decide what to do next."

James came into the kitchen and saw Ella's tear-streaked face, Megan's pile of food, and Armand's messy hair. "Good morning, everyone. What'd I miss?"

"Oh nothing," Megan said cheerfully. "Ella's father is the King of Belgium, you know the great guy who razed the Congo. Her mother died. Jeremiah has his son's power but isn't supposed to. And Ein is probably after us. Now we have to figure out what to do next. Thoughts?"

"Not until I have some tea." James put on a pot of water.

"I think I know where Ella and I have to go." Jeremiah's voice was deadly serious.

"Just us?"

"Yes, I believe so."

"Ella is not going anywhere without me," Armand said in a commanding tone. It was then Ella remembered the paper he put in his pocket and noticed the gloves were back on his hands.

"Me either," piped up Megan.

James looked at Jeremiah and said, "I imagine I can speak for Ryan when I say that is true of us as well. We started this together. We will finish it together." Ryan nodded in agreement.

"I can tell you now, if it is an end you seek, there is not one in the immediate future. If you join us now, you will have to continue on with us for many, many years." Jeremiah folded his hands into his lap, as if to give them time to reconsider.

"I'm pretty sure we all just gave you our answer," Armand spoke for them.

Ella looked at them all, wide-eyed.

"None of you have to do this. Ein is after me."

"You know that is not going to stay that way," James said. "We all have something she wants, or knowledge she doesn't want us to have."

"Megan?"

"Don't look at me like that. I am not afraid of her. I stabbed someone. With a sword. Remember?"

James looked quite shocked at that statement, but let it slide.

"I do not mean to seem as though I underestimate any of you," Jeremiah started again.

"Just tell us what we have to do," Ryan insisted.

"Tell me," Ella said.

"Long before you and I were as we are now," Jeremiah sounded like a dramatic storyteller, causing Megan to giggle. James waved a no-no finger at her.

"Long before we took on our human bodies. Being born and growing. We came here to grow with the planet. It is what we always do when we go to a new place. We are with it when it is born, and watch it progress until it reaches the point in the process where we can join in to the evolution. We wait and acquire knowledge. Some of us leave before others to join in the growth, as more of us wait for our turn."

"Is this why I seem to remember things I couldn't possibly remember? Such as watching dinosaurs out of a window?" Ella asked.

"Yes. You did watch dinosaurs form and grow. You watched them rule the world, and watched the time of their end."

"THAT IS SO AWESOME." Megan couldn't contain herself at this point.

"It really is awesome," Ella agreed with her. "It's beyond the most ludicrous thing I've ever heard, but hey, why not? There's a man with long, silver hair from the Congo telling us this stuff so it must be true."

"You were not Ella, yet, but you were Cobalt. You were your mother first. Now you are you. You are also your father," he added quietly.

"Did I have a name?"

"Your name has changed for each place we have gone, but your mind has always been drawn to words that represent something to you. A color, your element. They way they are 'spoken' or 'pronounced' can be different, but they always carry a similar meaning."

"I have other memories," Ella told him. "They are terrible and frightening. I feel like I am suffocating in some of them."

"I am sorry your memories are not clear anymore. As I said before, I suspect this is because of Ein. Your empathic powers, your connections to this planet, make your memories far more real than many of us."

"But what are they? They are not of the world around me, Jeremiah. They are me drowning, unable to breathe. I cannot even begin to tell you how many nights I haven't slept because of them."

"We come, then, to the point in the story that I have never told any of the Naturals, though I imagine many of them figured it out over time."

Jeremiah closed his eyes and took several deep breaths. A clock ticked in the far room, and Ella thought everyone could hear her heart. He opened his eyes, and Ella could see a sorrow she had not seen ever before in her life.

"We were set to arrive here, as always, when the planet was being born, and to prepare for our entrance into its growth. The ship we came in from our home was not far from the ever-growing surface of Earth. Waiting for the time to land when some of the winds, which would have been devastating to any living thing, had come to a survivable point.

"The Naturals are many things but we are not invincible, and as with all things in nature, we have a part to play." Jeremiah sipped some tea before continuing. "What happened next must have been set in motion before we left home."

"Where is your home?" Megan asked, absolutely enthralled with the story.

"That, lovely child, is not something that matters anymore."

Ella felt her hope fall further with that statement, but kept silent, willing him to go on.

"Before the weather had stabilized into any survivable measure for us, which I might add would not be weather in which humans, as they are now, could live, there was an explosion on the ship. Many of the Naturals were in a state of stasis for our long journey. Those of us who could live in space as part of the environment, or at least in a flux around it, moved the vehicles to our destination points. It is our duty to make sure the others reach their new homes safely and move them into their responsibilities. We had always been prepared for emergencies. For attacks from other races, star explosions, black holes, even a malfunctioning engine or other part of the ship. But we had never prepared for someone in our ranks to sabotage us. It never even occurred to us that this would happen."

"Even with being at odds with Ein?" Armand asked.

"Even then. And like I said, we thought we had reached an accord. Before we left for this mission I believed, as did many of the other elder Naturals, that we had brokered peace, and Ein herself was acting as though none of it had ever happened. Deception is not part of our culture. We have one mission together as a planet. There is no need for secrets."

"What happened? You survived, so the other Naturals must have." Ella felt a sadness she couldn't explain. She did not know them, yet they were her family.

"The memories of drowning come from your mother. Within each element are the memories of the last form it had. It is why I have my son's memories. We always knew that our memories passed to our children, and it was important for us to fill those memories with what they needed to know to complete their tasks. The Earth-born Naturals are the first to have suffering such as this in their memories. Assuming any more of us had children and passed on the element to them, they will remember the crash and the many years of pain that came after, as we worked to survive. At least those of us that were with me."

"Not all the Naturals were with you?" This time Ryan asked the question. He had said nothing for the entire time, but this question seemed especially important to him.

Jeremiah regarded him with great consideration.

"There is something about you, Ryan," Jeremiah said it as if noticing him for the first time, "that is known to me. But to answer your question, no not all the Naturals were with me. The ship broke apart as it entered into what little of Earth's atmosphere had formed, and parts of it were pushed into the far reaches of a young and ever-changing planet. The Naturals were kept in different parts of the ship, as we did not always know how each of them would react to the new environment. That was one of the many tasks that lay before us each time we came to a new place. Simply, find what works and what doesn't, keep each other safe, and above all, keep the inhabitants of the world safe. Particularly from us."

"What works and what doesn't?" James was as enraptured as Megan.

"Not all Naturals have powers or purposes where we go. We do not know this until the planet reaches what we call it's Golden Age."

"I'm not sure I understand." James cleaned his glasses on a towel quickly, as if taking them off would cause him to miss part of the story.

"Let me see if I can explain. Here we know the inhabitants need air to breathe. As such, the elements that are needed use their properties to manufacture air with the environment. Oxygen for example, is a cornerstone of life here, a need. But other places we have been, oxygen is a poison, and thus is rendered inert until such time as it is needed again. Not to say that the Natural does not get to live out a life cycle. It most certainly does, as the Naturals who are at work in each place need the support of the full network of us from home. We have many tasks everywhere we go. Or I should say we did."

"You've, several times now, said things that make it sound as though the Naturals no longer have the jobs they were sent here to do. Why is that?" Armand had a very commanding way of speaking, Ella realized. She wondered if he was a leader among the Naturals.

"With the destruction of the ship and the loss of the other Naturals, we have no way to get home. Our purpose is now void."

"What is our purpose?" Ella asked. She had to know. Even if she couldn't do it.

"Our purpose is to preserve and grow the greatest parts of every life-form we encounter."

"That seems a little... a little..." Ella was searching for the right word.

"That seems to be a little general of a purpose," Armand finished for her.

"But that is what our purpose is. We are the guardians of all the great creations of each race of beings. We make sure that every race can continue."

"I think I wanted to say that seems like a big job," Ella said. "Like maybe it would take a really long time?"

"Indeed. That is why we are here at the start of all creation and move through the evolutionary process of each place." As the last word left Jeremiah's mouth, an ear-piercing siren went off.

"What is that?" Megan jumped out of her seat.

"I never turned the motion detectors off from last night. Someone is in the house. We need to get out of here." James pulled Megan to a door that led out of the kitchen. They all ran into a spacious garage, and James tossed Armand a set of keys.

"I'm sure your home is exceedingly safe, Armand. I will take Ryan and Megan one way. You take Ella and Jeremiah. I'll meet you there."

Without further discussion they all got into separate cars and sped off.

Chapter 20

"I don't remember going this way to your place," Ella said, staring out the window. The city streets had turned into wide expanses of land between buildings, until there were miles between houses.

"We are going to my family's home, not my apartment. James is right. It is safe. You will be safe there." Armand's eyes were fixed on the road.

"All of us need to be safe," Ella replied, "even you."

Jeremiah had been quiet for the first part of the trip out of the city, but now Ella turned to him. As she did, the locket Armand gave her swung out from under her top.

"I know that locket." Jeremiah brushed over the rose with a finger. "How did you get it? I mean, it does belong to you. I only thought that you knew nothing of your past."

Ella's brow furrowed.

"Armand gave it to me." Both Ella and Jeremiah looked at Armand for an explanation.

"What? I took it from my family's heirlooms. I did not know where it came from. My family has a ton of pieces. This one seemed to suit you."

"That is an extraordinary coincidence," Jeremiah said, pleased.

"I doubt it was a coincidence." Ella was mad. "I thought you said you didn't know who I was?"

"I didn't know for sure, but what difference does it make? I wanted to give it to you regardless."

"What are you two talking about? Why would Armand know who you are? And by that, I am assuming that you mean that you are a Natural." Jeremiah looked between the two of them, confused.

"I think Armand should tell you." Ella crossed her arms and leaned back in her seat.

"Why would you know that Ella was anyone but Ella?" Jeremiah sounded distraught. "No one should know about us at this point. Not like this, anyway. Everything has gone wrong."

"We can discuss this later. Let's get to my house so Jeremiah can tell us what the next step we need to take is. And where. Because I doubt it's hanging out at my pool."

"Whatever," said Ella.

"Is there a problem we should address?" Jeremiah asked Ella.

"It's fine," she snapped.

"Ella, I was going to give it to you, no matter what," Armand insisted again. "That's not really the point, is it?"

James, Megan, and Ryan were waiting outside the gate when they arrived.

"James must drive very fast for him to have beaten us here," Armand observed.

"This is your family home? I think it's more of a castle fort," Ella said. If she had thought James' house was big, it was nothing compared to the partially hidden from street-view estate laid out before them as Armand opened the large iron gates.

"It's been in my family for a long time, and some members have made additions. I'm the only one who keeps it now, though. They've all moved on to other places."

The cars ambled slowly up an extensive stone driveway that was surrounded by majestic gardens.

"It's like something out of a movie," Ella said, taking in the fields of beautiful flowers and ripe fruit trees.

"You are more than welcome to stay here if you do not want to stay with James. You will have more than enough privacy." Armand's voice, Ella thought, sounded shy. Which made no sense, as he exhibited nothing but confidence all of the time.

He pulled the car up under a covered port and parked next to three very expensive-looking, black town cars of various makes. Megan hopped out of the other vehicle and walked to Ella's door.

"Well, this place is a dump," she declared as she yanked opened the door. "What's with Ryan? He's being super moody. What should we do about him? I've known him for so long, Ella, but I can't believe what he did to you."

"I don't know, Megan. He told me that Ein threatened his mother. How can I be angry about that?"

"She did? She really is the worst. Like, completely the worst. Still, though, he should have told us."

"I agree, but I don't know what to do about it right now." They stood in contemplation for a moment, and then Ryan called their names.

"Are you two coming, or what?"

"You're so charming, Ryan," Megan yelled back. "We should be careful around him. I don't know why I think this, Ella, but something is still not right with him." Ella followed her as she started up toward the house.

Megan went inside, but Ella stayed outside by herself, drinking in the sunlight, taking deep breaths. There was so much to think about and, apparently, so much to do.

"Ella." Ryan came outside and stood beside her, and she could feel waves of heat radiating off his body. "Ella, I am so sorry." His voice sounded broken and helpless. "I really did not know what to do. I've been really sick off and on these last few months. These are not excuses, but I just want you to know that I never, ever meant for you to get hurt. My mother is not great at helping herself, and my father... well, I think my father works with Ein."

"I understand why you did what you did Ryan," Ella responded. She really did. Ein threatened his mom, and all he had to do was give up Ella's apartment, her secret. Ryan didn't owe her anything at that point. They didn't know each other that well. She didn't have to tell him her secret. She just wanted to so much. She had wanted to trust someone so much. But now she didn't. And as much as she hated herself for feeling that way, Ella was going to be on her guard from here on out.

"I understand, Ryan, and really it's not that my apartment was destroyed, or all my things were taken, or that I've been followed and harassed. It's that I thought you were my friend. Just because of me. No other reason. But it wasn't why, and that's what hurts most of all."

"I am your friend," he said miserably. "I always have been."

"No. You became my friend under false pretenses, and now I can't ever believe again that it was a good thing, or that you actually liked me." With that, she went inside where everyone was waiting for them.

It took her a few minutes to figure out where they were, as the house was huge. It was as perfectly kept as any museum Ella had ever been in, and filled with just as many wondrous pieces of art and furniture from all over the world.

She couldn't believe a family could have all this and not live in the home. *Where did they live? Versailles?*

She finally came across Megan lounging comfortably on the biggest sofa Ella had ever laid eyes on. Ella sat at the end, and Megan could still stretch all the way out.

"Comfortable?" Ella swatted her feet, and Megan nodded dreamily.

"Shhhh! I'm having a moment." Megan closed her eyes and massaged her temples.

"Should I leave you alone with yourself?" Ella laughed at her.

"I think we should not get too comfortable." James came into the room followed by Jeremiah and Armand. "Where is Ryan?'

"I'm right here." He slunk into the room, his face looking sickly, jaundiced.

"You don't look so well, Ryan," James said to him. He put a hand on his forehead. "You're burning up." Ryan jerked away from the professor.

"I'm fine," he snarled. "Just a headache. I just took something."

"You get headaches a lot," Ella said without thinking.

"What do you care?" He threw himself into a large, overstuffed chair, and glowered.

"Before we talk about what we have to do next," Ella said to Jeremiah, "you said you had a theory about who the man in the suit is? But we haven't had a chance to get to that yet. So who is he? Is he a Natural too?"

"No, I do not believe he is." Jeremiah sat down. "There were rumors for many years about Ein's experiments. We never truly had proof of many of them. There were some of the Naturals who insisted we never knew the depth of Ein's treachery. In hindsight, I believe they are right. But so many of us were eager for peace, I think we turned a blind eye to much of what was happening."

"Is he human?" Ella felt uneasy about this conversation, but she wanted more answers.

"No, he is not human. I am unsure what he is, or who he is, Ella, but I think he is one of the UnNaturals."

"UnNaturals?"

"That was the name given to some of the rumored experiments. Ein wanted more power, and she could not take it from other Naturals, so she started experimenting to create her own Naturals. It was suggested that, using combinations of elements and DNA from all sorts of lifeforms, she had created a group of highly unstable, terribly dangerous beings. The UnNaturals. They are strong, violent, and can only endure for very short periods of time. That is why I think we were never able to prove they actually existed."

"That would explain why it seems like he disappears," Megan pointed out. She poked Ella with a toe. "See, lady? You're not totally crazy."

"No, I guess I'm not. But I am starting to think it might be better that I was, rather than that this stuff is happening. I don't understand what Ein wants here."

"Neither do I," Jeremiah said to her. "At another time, I only thought we all wanted the same things: To complete our tasks and return home until the next world was given to us to grow with and live in. She lost her way, and now that we can't get home, I cannot guess what she hopes to accomplish. It does not seem as though she is trying to find a way home."

"What are these tasks?" James asked. "You've referenced them a few times now. You have jobs? To enter our evolutionary process and to be a part of the growth of the planet. But if that was all, you would not need to be in human form."

"As I said earlier, we are here to preserve the best of life. To lead Earth through its Golden Age. We have done it in many places, at many points in time. We are collecting the best of all existence."

"But why?" Armand stood across the room where he had been keeping watch over the grounds from an enormous window.

"It is what we do."

"That did not answer my question."

"Because sometime in the distant future, the idea is to bring together all the collection into one unique world. All the beings, all the work, all the best of each planet's creation living together. So nothing that matters is ever lost."

"That is what we are doing?" Ella said uncertainly. "How is that even possible?"

"Now it may not be possible," Jeremiah told her. "Your legacy has been stolen from you. The opportunity to watch what humanity has created, and will create, is being destroyed as we speak. And without the ability to get back to our home, preservation is not possible. As the Earth began in pieces, it may well end in pieces. Our mission, our purpose, is gone. All we can do now is protect ourselves and what we can of the planet and its people."

"Protect its people?"

"I fear, Ella, that Ein is no longer the only Natural who is corrupt and power-hungry. For the ship to have been sabotaged, it would have taken much help.

Since we do not know where any of the others are, we do not know what they are doing, or with which side they may have aligned, even before we left home."

"At least you have a family," Megan said helpfully, "and they are just as screwed up as everyone's family."

"Yeah, great," Ella grumbled. "So what next?"

"What we have to do is simple," Jeremiah began to explain. "We have to get to the part of the ship that I crashed in. Cobalt was in my care. There are the pieces of your element there. They will help you gain full use of your powers and maybe help you feel healthier. I am not completely sure of what will happen, as you should have had the pieces already, and you should not be sick. But it's the best idea I have at the moment"

"Pieces?" Ella asked. "I thought I was cobalt?"

"You are, but there are older parts of cobalt that contain more characteristics that you need to fully develop as a Natural. Pieces that contain things learned and gained on other planets. Knowledge and traits that can help you. I hid what I could after we finally were able to leave the ship, but I have not been back to them in an unimaginable amount of time. I do not think Ein knows where my part of the ship is hidden. I barely know where it is myself."

"You don't know where it is?" Armand was frustrated. "That isn't going to get Ella what she needs." He got up, opened a decanter, and poured a brown liquid into a glass. He took a long swig and then offered the rest of them a glass.

"I have an idea where it is," Jeremiah told him. "It has been thousands of years since I've been there. I had no reason to go back. Not until now, anyway. I did not think I would ever need to return. And it did occur to me that if we had enemies among us who would risk all of our lives, or maybe even kill some of us, that it might be better if I didn't actually know where it was, so they could not extract the information from me."

"That's what you think is simple," Megan said dubiously. "Maybe simple means something different in the Congo?"

"What's your idea?" Ryan asked. Ella noticed he seemed somewhat better. Despite herself, she felt relief. She didn't want him to suffer; it was horrible to see.

"The ship is in Mexico. With the changing land, we can assume it is absolutely underground. Probably deep into the terrain."

"So, in a cave?" asked Ryan. He started to type on his laptop.

"Yes, in a cave. I definitely made my way out of the ship and onto land by going through caves."

"There are a lot of caves in Mexico," Ryan declared dejectedly. "We need more ways to eliminate which ones it's not in."

"Wait," Ella dug in her pocket, "I had completely forgotten about this until just now." She pulled out the crumpled piece of paper that had Alexandra's handwriting on it. "Ryan, see if this means anything." Armand looked over her shoulder.

"I know that name," he told her. "That word means 'crystals.'" He had reached around her so that she had to move in closer to him. It was nice, and it somewhat irked her.

She went over to Ryan while he searched for the name.

"Find anything?"

"Maybe," he said. "I'm just trying to double-check some of these sites. They're not always accurate. According to what I can find, this is the name of a cave in Naica, Chihuahua, Mexico. Apparently a smaller cave sits atop a bigger cave that was only discovered more recently. As in the year 2000, recently. The Cave of Swords, the smaller one, was discovered in about 1910."

"There is no way to know if this is the right place, I'm guessing?" Ella directed the question at Jeremiah, who had come over to look at the computer screen.

"Actually, see what it says about the crystal formations being perfect? That they've been undisturbed for about 500,000 years? I think the ship is under them."

"Why?"

"Because the ship is organic, and it would create a perfect environment for such things. It's happened before, on other planets. Nothing like this, however." Jeremiah tried to examine the photos posted on the website more closely. "The crystals are unlike anything I've ever seen before."

"A Cave of Swords, huh? Maybe I can get a new katana." Megan had joined them. In fact, all of them were now crowded around Ryan, each trying to get a better look at the pictures.

"It is extraordinarily warm right in this area," James said suddenly, and stepped back.

"Yeah, it is." Megan ran a hand over her brow. "It's really hot. How can you stand sitting there, Ryan?"

"I'm fine," he shrugged.

"That is odd. The house has precise temperature control. I'll have to have it checked," Armand said. "If you are uncomfortable, Ryan, please feel free to move anywhere you like."

"I said I'm fine."

Ella watched as he worked out mapping how to get to the cave. It was far away, to be sure.

"I don't know anything about spelunking? Is that even the right word?" Ella told them. "Plus it's in Mexico, and that's pretty far away. We can't exactly drive there in a timely manner."

"We should try to get there as soon as possible," Jeremiah said. "I think it would be best to try to find your pieces before Ein catches on to what we are doing. And if there are any others there, we should move them. They've been sitting in one place for far too long."

"Were all the pieces stored together?" Ella asked.

"No, we kept them separate. As with you and the rest of the Naturals, we did not always know how they would react in each new environment that was growing. It is a great gift and miracle to watch the birth of a planet. But it can also be quite harrowing, no matter how well prepared you are, or where you fit in its make-up."

"Right, well, we need to get there, I guess. Should we buy plane tickets?"

"We can take my plane." Armand's accented voice cut through Megan chatting with Ryan about the crystals.

"Of course you have a plane." Ryan was venomous.

"I do. It's safer to travel on my own, with people I trust, than it is to travel in public airports. Some members of my family have made many enemies, and they often do not bother to discern who is who, out of the El Dorado clan."

"Grand," Ella said, "we'll take your plane. But what about supplies? This doesn't look like an easy place to get to, or through."

"I imagine we can find what we need here, or in Mexico. I have had many hobbies," Armand joked. "I'm going to go ask my staff to get the plane ready, and we'll leave in a few hours."

"There's staff here? I haven't heard anyone?"

"The perks of a castle fort. Help yourself to anything you like, all of you." Armand left them.

"Where's the kitchen?" Megan pointed left and right down the hall.

"I am starved," Ella said, following her.

"This place is astonishing." Megan started opening up closed doors. They were ornately carved wooden pieces, heavy and old. She opened one, and then quickly closed it.

"What?"

"Nothing. Come on." Megan started to walk faster down the hall.

"Megan, what is in the room, you nut?" Ella went to turn the knob, and Megan grabbed her hand.

"Don't freak out, Ella."

"About what?" Ella pushed her friend out of the way and opened the door. Every piece of her art from the gallery filled the room. Much of it wasn't hung yet, but the room appeared to be laid out in order to be set up the same way Ella had Evan set up the gallery.

"Why is all my stuff here? What happened to the show? I know everything sold. I guess I hadn't considered it all sold to Armand."

Megan and Ella were walking around the room. Ella picked up paintings and vases. It felt like a million years ago, now, that she had the show, and it had only been a few days.

"I had it all sent here after I saw what happened to your apartment, Ella." Armand's accented voice had a touch of pain in it. "I did not want all your work lost. It is so lovely."

"Are you upset?" Megan asked her tentatively. "I mean it's a little strange, I guess."

"I don't think it's strange." Ella strode over to Armand. "Thank you for keeping these pieces safe. It means a lot to me. I have never loved anything as much as I love painting, and I thought all of my life's work was gone." She hugged him tightly, and he returned the embrace, full force. They held onto each other for a while, as Megan busied herself about the room.

"Okay, you guys, I'm starving, and nobody's dying, so let go." She poked Ella in the arm.

Armand smiled at her and led them to the kitchen.

"We'll be ready to go in a few hours. I asked that all the outdoor gear I have stored here be put on the plane and sorted by person. I guessed at your sizes. I hope I did well with that. Let's eat something, and then I have a few things to do before we leave. I don't know how long we'll be gone, and I should have the company in order before we go."

He pulled out food from the biggest fridge on the planet. After setting it all out and putting together platters of every cheese, chocolate, and fruit known to man, he left the two of them and went down the hall to an office.

"I'll be in there if you need me. Ryan is resting, and Jeremiah and James are looking over maps." Heavy mahogany doors closed behind him.

"He is so hot." Megan was pulling her favorite chocolates off the platter.

"Yeah, so you mentioned."

"Do you not think so? You'd be wrong, but you don't seem so head over heels as you did even a few hours ago."

"Ryan has caused me to have some trust issues."

"Even about me?" The blonde looked crestfallen.

"Absolutely not about you," Ella smiled. "You might be the only one I trust completely. Armand stuck a paper in his pocket that I have no idea what it said. Plus, I am fairly sure he sought me out somehow. Ryan told Ein who knows what. Jeremiah is mostly a mystery telling the most fantastic of tales. And James has helped me, yes, but… and maybe this is just Ryan putting this into my head… he did work for TriChem, the company that I am pretty sure was running Ein's monster lab. So yeah, Megan, pretty much Girl Power."

"Crap, you're right. We may not be able to trust any of them. How come we're going to Mexico, then?"

"Do you have any better ideas?"

"Hawaii?"

"I have a feeling Ein might be able to find us there. Besides, if there's something that witch wants that I can keep from her, maybe I can use it to find Alexandra."

"Once we get your pieces, Ella, I'll help you find Alexandra."

"I know you will. Now I am probably going to eat this entire plate of cheese, so if you expect any, you should probably take it."

Megan laughed and snatched a few pieces off the platter. They ate until they were sick, and then Megan decided to explore the house more.

"This place is amazing, and I want to see as much of it as I can. Are you coming?"

"I think I am going to talk to Armand first, but I'll catch up with you after."

"K." Megan grabbed another handful of chocolate and went up a staircase at the back of the kitchen.

Ella went down the hall to the doors Armand had gone through an hour before and was about to knock when she heard his voice. The doors were slightly ajar, and she leaned in to listen.

"That was not our agreement. I told you to sell that company a long time ago. Why do we still own it?"

There was a long silence as he seemed to listen to a response.

"No, I do not understand. This is wrong. I will not have you putting her in jeopardy." Armand sounded livid, and Ella heard him slam down something, presumably the phone.

She thought better about knocking, but ended up accidentally pushing on the door.

"Ella? Ella, you can come in." Armand was sitting in a chair behind his desk, but he got up and pulled the door all the way open.

"I'm sorry. I heard you talking on the phone and didn't mean to interrupt you."

"You didn't interrupt anything. Come in. Have a seat, if you like." He was clearly angry, and trying to seem as if he wasn't.

"May I look at your books?" The office had floor-to-ceiling bookshelves on three walls, filled with antique books.

"By all means."

"I love to read," Ella told him. "Old books are so wonderful. Have you read all of these?" She pulled a red, cloth-bound poetry book off a shelf and opened it.

"Yes, I have read the majority of them." He seemed calmer now and was seated back at his desk, watching her.

"Amazing. I wish I could say the same," her voice cracked. Armand came over to her.

"Ella, what's wrong?"

"Nothing, gah, everything, I don't know," she sniffed. "I really hate crying. I hate it, and I've done it more the last two days than in my entire life, which makes me mad."

Armand smiled at her.

"Yes, it's crazy."

"No, it's not. It's been a roller-coaster ride for all of us. You, the most." He handed her a silky handkerchief, and she dabbed her face with it.

"It's just, there's so much I don't remember. I've been in human form for over a hundred years, but I only remember a handful of them. It makes me angry and frustrated."

"Don't be frustrated," he pleaded. "I will help you get this all sorted out. I swear."

"Armand, did you know me? Before?"

"Before?" He looked at her questioningly. "I don't understand what you mean."

"When I was in Belgium. Did you know me then?"

"I did."

"Did you know who I was right away?"

"No, I did not. Like I told you before, I wasn't sure. But yes, I was starting to look for you."

"Is that why you seem so familiar to me? Because I knew you so long ago?"

"Maybe." He was absently tucking her hair behind her ears. "My name was different then. My family changed it as we grew older than everyone around us but never aged. My name was Dorran."

The name sat in the far reaches of Ella's mind as she walked around the office. She pulled more books out and flipped through them. A slip of paper fell out of one. It was covered in symbols.

"I know these symbols." Ella picked the paper up off the floor. "They are on a box I saw at the institute. They are also on a slip of paper in my file."

"I haven't seen that sheet of paper in many years, but I do remember it being in that book." Armand looked at the book Ella had set on the desk. "My father brought me this volume from a trip he took to Europe."

"What are the symbols? Why do they keep showing up?" She stopped and looked at Armand. "Why is one of them on me?"

"What?"

"Look." She pulled the collar of her top to the side, so Armand could see the symbol on her upper chest.

"Maybe Jeremiah knows what they are." Armand said while examining the mark on Ella. "I don't have one of those, I don't think. But my body is not unmarked."

"What do you mean unmarked?"

"Similar to my hands, the evidence of my other-worldly existence is evident in many veins and lines through out my body."

"Is that why you always seem to be fully dressed?"

"It's one reason," he smiled. "I do also just like to dress nicely, Ella."

There was a beep on Armand's phone. "Sir, the plane is ready."

"Thank you. We should get the others. Our adventure awaits."

Chapter 21

Ryan eyed the sleek little jet skeptically.

"Does this seem like a terrible idea to anyone else?" He dropped his bag on the ground and held his hands out to them. "Anybody?"

"I am a good pilot," Armand said smoothly. He had changed into black, as had the rest of them. Armand's staff had dug up all-weather suits for them. Ella couldn't quite believe someone had this stuff laying around. *But there you go.*

"That suit looks fabulous on you," Ella said, as Megan came out, looking about as beautiful and tough as a fictional spy.

"I was completely meant to be a secret agent."

"Good, then I can count on you to keep an eye on Ryan."

"I always keep an eye on Ryan." Megan made a face. "I don't want to have feelings for him anymore, but I still do, Ella. I know it seems like he's a terrible person, but I promise you, he's not."

"I don't think that he is, Megan. I think he was scared for his mother. I swear I am trying to trust him, but it's hard. My whole world has changed in a matter of days, and I don't know who wants what from me."

"I mostly just want you to not be a cow." Megan stuck her tongue out at her.

"Thanks. Does that mean you think I look fat in this suit?" Ella spun around ridiculously, as if wearing a tutu.

"Nope. Annoyingly enough, you also look like a hot super-spy. Come on." Megan linked arms with her, and they walked from the tiny car that had brought them out to Armand's family's private hangar. "Can you imagine having so much money you have your own mini-airport?"

"No, I cannot imagine it. I was pretty happy with my job at Alchemy and painting all the time. I guess I was lonely, though."

"But you were a princess, or whatever. I've seen the pictures."

"Illegitimate princess of a horrible man. Besides, I barely remember, and I definitely don't remember being treated like a princess."

"Maybe you were a crappy princess, so you had to be punished all the time, or something."

Ella laughed. "Yeah, maybe."

Several men had been loading gear onto the plane, and when they were done, one went over to Armand and handed him a box.

Jeremiah came up to the girls.

"The flight is fairly long, Ella. I'd like to talk to you more about your family."

"Will you tell me more about my father? Also, I have to ask you about something, myself." Ella had tucked the sheet of paper with the symbols on it into her bag. She was going to ask Jeremiah if he knew what they meant, or why she had one on her chest. She had a lot of questions. *Always. Always.* She sighed and hauled her bag over to the steps in front of the plane.

"The suit looks nice on you Ella," Ryan said shyly. "You and Megan both look like Russian spies from James Bond."

"You don't look so bad, yourself." She handed him the bag, as he had stretched out his arm to take it from her and offered a hand for climbing the steps. She hesitated only a moment before taking it and smiling at him. A look of relief crossed his face, and she felt a pang of guilt. She couldn't forgive him. Maybe someday, but not yet. *But you can be nice to him.* Megan wasn't the only one still harboring feelings for Ryan.

"Don't you need a co-pilot?" Ryan asked, as he strapped himself into a seat.

"That's what I'm for," James said.

"You know how to fly a plane, too?"

"Who do you think taught him?" Armand said, as he walked up to the cockpit. "Everyone get ready to take off. Once we are at a cruising altitude you can move around the plane."

"Where's your sexy, flight attendant uniform? Can I come sit on your lap and get wings?" Megan cracked.

"Maybe later, darling." Armand winked at her in an obnoxious way that made Ella giggle.

"We are headed to Mexico to find a spaceship, and you two are flirting," Ella chided her.

"Um, excuse me, but some of us didn't get to go to Mexico for spring break." Megan snapped a seat belt over her lap and pretended to call for a cocktail. "I intend to be on spring break as of right now."

"I have a feeling none of us went to Mexico for spring break," Ryan said nervously.

"Is something wrong?" Ella asked him.

"I am just not the biggest fan of flying."

"Neither am I," Jeremiah told him, and put a reassuring hand on Ryan's shoulder.

Ella saw him look down at his hand, and was pretty sure that Jeremiah had noticed the luminescence that had returned to Ryan's person. She could see it again clearly, too.

"Didn't you fly a spaceship here? Through the Big Bang or whatever?" Megan was pulling headphones out of a bag. And more chocolates.

Ella grabbed one from her.

"I did, Megan, and you'll recall it crashed. That's the sort of thing that makes one skeptical of flight." Jeremiah smiled at her.

"Yeah, I guess it would. But now you've beaten the odds. No more crashing," Megan snorted. "Wake me when we get there." She stuck in the earbuds and went to sleep before the plane was even ready to take off.

"I wish I had her attitude," Ella said wistfully.

"I think you're doing pretty well," Ryan told her. "I broke your trust, you found out about your parents, that you're not exactly human, that you had some great destiny but now you don't, some crazy woman is chasing you and has probably experimented on you... Should I go on?"

"No, please don't. I might puke on your shoes."

"Please don't puke on the plane," Armand's voice said over the intercom. "We're about to take off, so everyone get strapped in please. James, if you would be so kind as to come take your seat with me, we'll be off."

Ella closed her eyes as the plane picked up speed. She had not been in a plane in recent memory, but also did not know if she had ever been in one. Her mind wandered back to the task in front of them. To finally see where she came from boggled her mind. She had always assumed she might be able to find adoption papers. Going to find her origins in a cave was most assuredly not something that she had even imagined.

Ryan was right, she was doing pretty good for such a mess. She thought of a question that hadn't crossed her mind until now.

"Jeremiah," she said loudly, over the plane lifting off the ground.

"Yes, Ella?"

"What Natural is Ein?"

"She is Hydrogen, Ella. Like I said, an important and powerful element."

"No kidding. Hydrogen is everywhere. What power could she want besides that?"

"All of them, Ella."

The plane continued up. Ella felt the weightless feeling in her stomach and looked over at Megan who hadn't budged at all. Glancing at Ryan, she saw that he seemed somewhat less ill-at-ease, now that the plane was starting to level out. The sun washed his hair in light, reminding Ella why she had thought he was so handsome in the first place.

"If you need to get up, you can move around now," James said over the intercom. "Our Captain informs me that we should not have too much of a rough ride." His voice indicated that he seemed to be enjoying himself a great deal.

Jeremiah unbuckled his seat belt and moved to a seat closer to Ella.

"Let's talk more about your family."

"Wait." Ella reached into her bag and pulled out the paper with the symbols on it. "Do you know what these are? And why one of them is on my chest?"

"I do," Jeremiah said as he examined them. "Where did you get this?"

"I found it in a book in Armand's library. He said the book was one his father brought back from Europe. What are they?"

"They are Earth's Naturals' identifying markers. One has formed on you so that other Naturals would know who you are. They react to each other, as well, once you have your pieces. Each place we go they are different, and these are an entirely new set, though not a full set. They don't form until Naturals are in what would be the teenage years of whatever race we are with. Naturals are expected to grow up as any of the young lifeforms would wherever they are. They are not given their responsibilities until they are old enough and the aging process has transformed to keep them from aging too quickly, or in some cases too slowly. It, of course, also depends on where the Natural enters into the growth process of the planet." Jeremiah started to count them.

"So wait, they don't form until the teenage years? Does that mean..."

"It means that whoever drew these has been in contact with at least 20 other Naturals. We need to find out where this book came from after we get to the ship. This means others survived the crash and are in the world somewhere."

"Did anyone survive with us, Jeremiah?"

"A few did, yes. But so many got lost in the chaos. I had a very hard time just keeping track of myself and what I could of the ship, trying to hide it and making sure what was left of the pieces were not in danger, and weren't a danger to the planet. I was also injured, and I did not think I was going to survive. I lay in pain for an unknown amount of time, sometimes wishing death would come."

"That is horrible."

"It was long time ago, now. What matters is protecting you."

"You saved my life already," Ella realized as she said it.

"I endangered your life in my cowardice to stand up to Ein. I was one of the many who wished for peace and helped push forward commuting any punishment she would have received. I cannot abide disharmony."

"I don't think this is your fault, Jeremiah."

"I share part of the blame, Ella. I was blind to her because of my feelings."

It took Ella a moment to realize what he just confessed. "It's not wrong to love someone, Jeremiah. No matter what mistakes they make. Some would say that's when they need it the most, when they deserve it the least."

"You are younger than me, but far wiser. Your empathy is a trait that has helped many a civilization work together. I only wish you could have your full purpose now. There is much of Earth that needs empathy."

The plane bounced around a few moments from turbulence. Ella wondered what it would be like to have a goal for her life. She wasn't sure what hers was now.

"Ella, I want to talk with you about your abilities. I know it's new information to you, to hear that you have these powers. And they are not developed much yet, but you still have them. Your connection to all the cobalt in the world is potent and crucial to the development of the environment. It has helped many times, with other races, in making choices about how to lead."

"I have no idea how to do much of anything with cobalt."

"Take off your gloves. It's where we should start."

Ryan asked Ella if she would mind if he listened to what they were doing.

"Well, Ryan, we are up in the sky in this teeny plane. I'm not sure I could tell you no."

"I could put on headphones or something."

"It's fine," she told him, and took off the gloves that were tailored to the suit she was wearing.

They all had gloves now for climbing. They only had a bit of an idea as to what they should expect in the caves. From what they had learned, it was not the easiest place to explore. Most people could only make it ten minutes at a time. But, Megan had reminded them, they weren't most people.

Ella held out her bare hands to Jeremiah. He took them into his hands. They were worn with age and more gentle than anything Ella had ever felt. He told her to take three deep breaths and to focus her mind only on the sound of her own breathing.

"Try to push the plane, me, Ryan, everyone, and everything out of your thoughts for even just a moment."

Ella nodded, as she had been trying to do this for years during yoga. She had a faint grasp on meditation and was really looking forward to any advice Megan could give her about the practice. The plane hit a rough patch of air and Ella's eyes flew open.

The intercom flipped on.

"We are going over some storms, so be careful if you get up," Armand said. "Ella, when you have a moment, please come up here. No hurry."

"I wonder what he wants," she said to Jeremiah.

"Don't go yet. Let's try to do this, as I would like to prepare you, even a little, for taking on your pieces. They are filled with memory, and they will flood you with lifetimes of experiences. It will be overwhelming, to say the least, and you've had no training."

"I'm nervous."

"Understandably so. It is difficult to sort out our feelings as it is, never mind adding so many others. Now close your eyes and breathe."

Ella did as she was told. Surprisingly, it came much more easily to her than she anticipated, to relax and to take each breath moment by moment. Jeremiah held on to her hands, and while they sat there, short glimpses started to flow over her. Slowly, and in many broken parts at first, but with each minute that passed, they grew in length and cohesiveness. Ella started to see bits of a village filled with people working. A young man being educated. Traveling through many cities and walking around a spacecraft. Looking down, she saw a silvery-blue metal held in a titanium container. Ella opened her eyes just as a hand reached down to pick it up.

"What is it, Ella?" Jeremiah asked her calmly. "Tell me what you saw."

"I think I saw you pick me up. I saw you pick Cobalt up."

"Yes, in traveling I would have been caring for you. What else did you see?"

"I saw your village and its people. I saw you traveling here to find me." She stopped suddenly. "I saw your son."

Jeremiah released her hands and leaned back.

"I'm sorry. I shouldn't have told you."

"No, Ella, it's okay. He is my son, in my memories. Of course you would see him. I have simply not processed my grief over losing him."

"What happened to him?"

"He became ill from the poisoned land and water where we were living."

"What made it poisonous?"

"It was made poisonous by greed. The land is being over-mined for resources. The people are paid to work with no protection and no healthcare. It has been happening for many, many years."

"What are they mining?"

"Many things, such as uranium and cobalt."

"Oh my god!" She jerked back in horror. "Cobalt?"

"Yes, but it is not your fault. Not at all, so do not even think it."

"Can I do something to stop it?"

"I do not know." He paused for a minute, as if trying to decide whether to tell her something. "You were there once."

"I was where?"

"You came to the Congo. You were supposed to come with your father. He backed out at the last minute, but you and your teacher were already on your way there. So you continued on, and lived there for a short time."

"Were you there when I was living there?"

"I was not in the village you were in, no. I only heard stories of a girl living with her teacher, teaching people to read and to do mathematics."

"Why did I leave?"

"You did not leave, Ella. You disappeared. Many assumed you were taken by the leaders of warring tribes to get revenge on your father. Very little could be done to find you, as the terrain of the interior of Africa, the Congo, is unforgiving. But I suspect, now, that Ein had you kidnapped."

"It seems she knew my father."

"Yes, she did, and no doubt could manipulate him quite well. She has always been dangerously charming and exquisitely beautiful. She and the country of Belgium grew rich off the Congo. The rubber trade, in particular, proved to be quite lucrative. Interestingly, your father never set foot in the Congo, despite claiming it as his own."

"This is horrible. I cannot believe that this is my father. I don't think I can take hearing any more right now."

Ella unbuckled the seat belt and went up to the cockpit. She knocked softly on the door, and James opened it. Armand smiled up at her and stood.

"Don't you have to fly this thing?" Ella asked him.

"Quite a lot of the hard work is done by brilliant machines made by brilliant humans. I can get up once in a while."

He came out, sat in a seat in a nook, and motioned for her to sit next to him.

"I want to give you something."

"Okay?"

Armand opened a compartment next to the seat and pulled out the box one of his staff had given him before they took off.

"I gave this to you once before, but it ended up back in my father's possession. I do not know how. I only clearly remember that it belongs to you."

He set the box in her lap, and Ella flipped it open. Nestled inside was a delicate tiara.

"Um, I am not sure this is going to be particularly helpful climbing around in caves."

"Everything is not as it seems."

Armand took it out of the box and touched one of the seemingly precious stones on the top point. The tiara folded itself into a dagger.

"Oh my!" Ella held the carefully crafted blade up to the light.

"Keep it a secret. I made it for you many, many years ago. For your birthday."

"When we are back from Mexico, and, you know, maybe not being chased by a murderous psychopath, you are going to tell me what you know of our relationship. It is not fair that you can recall everything, but I cannot."

"I do not recall everything, Ella. I have been unwell, too, at times. But I do remember quite a lot, and I will tell you everything that I can. I think you should hide the dagger. Keep it close, as we know not what we get ourselves into." Quickly brushing her cheek with his lips, he went back into the cockpit and shut the door.

Ella made her way back to the seat, having stashed the dagger into the suit.

"Is everything okay?" Ryan asked.

"Everything's fine," she responded absentmindedly. "You seem better?"

"I feel better, thanks. Are you guys going to try more work on your abilities?"

"I would like Ella to try more with me, yes."

Jeremiah sat back up and held his hands out to her. She stuck hers out to him, and he surprised her by moving them over to a metal panel of the plane.

"Am I going to read the plane's mind?" she joked.

"Planes contain cobalt. See if you can find it." That was all he said and sat back.

For the next couple of hours, Ella put her hands on any metal plates that she could find exposed in the fuselage. She stepped around the small, luxury jet, finding spots to sit, crowding into corners, and meditating as best as she could, trying to repeat the success she had seeing the images in Jeremiah's mind. She looked over to the silver-haired man and saw that he was asleep. Determined to do this before he woke up, she went to the tail end of the craft and sat on the floor. She tried to sit in a lotus position like Megan but she didn't quite fit.

"How's it going?"

Ella popped an eye open to see Ryan towering above the not-so-sacred spot on the floor of the plane.

"Mostly just feeling like an idiot."

Ryan held out his hand, which she took and pulled herself up.

"You're not an idiot," he said, trying to lean back so as not to be right in her face. "Besides, I'm sure the plane has enjoyed being massaged." He snickered, and she couldn't help but laugh a little.

"I must look pretty silly." She went over to the drink bar and took out a bottle of water.

"Okay, you're not an idiot, but you do look a bit crazy."

Ryan stepped to the bar just as the plane hit another random patch of rough air. Ella grabbed on to him as they slipped against the wall. Her hand was bracing them, and that's when she had a flash. Jumping suddenly, Ryan quickly moved back.

"I'm sorry, Ella, I didn't mean to."

She shook a hand at him. "It's okay. I know it was an accident. I just felt something."

"What? I mean, I feel something for you to, but we really shouldn't talk about this now, should we?" He looked confused and distressed.

"Not about us, doofus. I felt the plane, I think. Maybe some of the cobalt in it."

"Oh," his voice sounded relieved. More relieved than she cared for, but she definitely wasn't getting into relationship stuff and all that right now. She would rather go climb into the depths of a cave looking for a spaceship. *Yep.*

Touching the same spot again, but not getting anything, she smacked it in frustration.

"Nothing this time?" Ryan opened a bottle of water for himself.

Ella noticed again that he looked... different. Stronger. Then she had an idea.

"Give me your hand," she demanded.

"What?"

"Just give me your hand."

He bashfully took her hand as she leaned into the wall again. She felt her body temperature rise and the wave of Ryan's heat wash over her. She felt the mark on her chest get hot. She was about to pull away from the plane when she started to feel the movements. Fragments of silvery-blue were moving through the plane in streams. There were microscopic pieces stacked upon one another, working in confluence to create the metal. She made out the length of the plane, the outline of the seats, the inner workings stood out. She could make out the bags, the storage, the cockpit door.

Leaning into the machine and trying to concentrate more, she noticed something was out of place. Squeezing Ryan's hand hard and breathing in deeply, she held the breath for as long as she could stand it, and let it out a bit at a time. Focusing only on that, shutting out the noise of the plane, the heat, the slightly painful sensation from the mark on her chest. Still, she was unable to make out what the box was, but her instinct told her it wasn't supposed to be there.

"Ryan." Ella poked him in the side with her free hand.

"Yes." He was holding her hand and absently caressing it with his finger.

"Ryan, you can let go now."

"Sorry."

"Yep. Is there a way to get down to our gear?"

"I don't know, maybe. Why?"

"I just have a strange feeling about something."

"Okay? I guess let's look around for a latch or something."

"You'd think, after the last couple of hours, I'd know where everything was." Ella started to feel around again.

"Hang on, I think I found the hatch." Ryan pulled up on a handle, and a small door slipped up to reveal a way to crawl down into the storage area.

"Can we get down there?" Ella looked over his shoulder into the darkened area.

"I think there's enough space for us to get down there, yes."

He started to climb into the opening, his long frame seeming to take a while to get all the way down. Ella felt the anxiety growing and didn't really understand why. Turbulence made it hard to get down into the space, and she hit her head more than once climbing down.

"What exactly are we looking for?" called Ryan. His voice was muffled, between the noise of the plane and the smallness of the space.

"It's some sort of box, I guess." *What are we looking for?*

Feeling around for anything that matched what she had seen, *or thought I saw. In my brain. Great. I am imagining things again.*

"ELLA! I think we have a problem." Ella could not get up next to Ryan. There were too many bags in the way. The turbulence was getting rougher, and she heard Armand tell them to buckle in again.

"RYAN! I CAN'T GET UP TO YOU! WHAT DID YOU FIND?"

"I THINK IT MIGHT BE A BOMB!"

"HOLY..." She didn't finish the response, as her head smacked into the ceiling of the space. "RYAN, I NEED TO GO BACK UP. I THINK MY HEAD IS BLEEDING. GET UP HERE. WE HAVE TO TELL THE OTHERS." A drop of something wet fell in her eye. *Not something. My blood.* She tried to inch backwards. It was hard to see where the ladder was. *Why did we bring so much stuff?!?*

Finally her foot bumped into what felt like the end rung. Ella squeezed around to shimmy up the bars as fast as she could. Sticking out her head, she saw that Megan was awake and looking around worriedly.

"ELLA! What are you doing? Where is Ryan?" Megan unfastened the seat belt and pulled Ella up. Ryan hauled himself out.

"Ella, what's wrong?" Jeremiah was moving to get up. "Your head is bleeding."

"Jeremiah, don't get up. It's not safe." They were all knocked to the side of the plane.

Armand's voice came over the intercom. "Are you guys not strapped in? You really need to sit down. The air is very turbulent." His accented, normally soothing voice sounded agitated.

"You guys sit down. I have to talk to him."

Ella braced on the backs of seats, made her way to the cockpit, and pounded on the door. "ARMAND! JAMES! There's a bomb on the plane."

The door flew open, nearly hitting her.

"What?!?!" Armand grabbed her. "Where is it?"

"It's in the luggage compartment with all of our gear."

Ryan had worked his way up to them as cautiously as possible in the bumpy air. "I think it's set to go off when we're landing. The timing is such that it would break the plane apart, and it would just look like we had an accident bringing the plane in. If we could land sooner than that, I think we might be able to get it off the plane. It's not attached to anything, except to be affixed so as not to slide around."

"I'll try to find a place to put us down," Armand told him.

"Are we far from the caves?" Ella fell into Armand, who caught her without a problem.

"Not so far that we can't make it there today. Now please go fasten yourselves in. It's going to be dangerous to make this happen, and you've already hurt yourself." His fingers tenderly brushed the spot that was bleeding.

"Ow. Fine, I'll sit. No need to torture me."

"I'll get us on the ground," Armand told them, and went back into the cockpit.

Ryan and Ella bumped around getting back to the seats and buckled themselves in.

"Care to tell me what my nap is being disturbed by?" Megan was sitting up and looking distraught. *For once.* That worried Ella.

"Don't freak out, but there's a bomb on the plane."

"I'm pretty sure those are not words that are supposed to follow 'don't freak out.' What are we going to do?" Megan gripped the armrest as the plane dipped dramatically.

"Armand is going to put us down as soon as he can."

The intercom clicked on.

"Okay, everyone, I found an abandoned spot where I think we can put the plane down. It's only about twenty or so miles from our original landing spot. Hold on. THIS IS GOING TO BE ROUGH."

With that, the plane dropped faster and faster. Ella clutched onto the chair for dear life.

Chapter 22

The plane hit the ground with a thump that jarred Ella's entire body. It seemed to hop about, tossing everything inside around the fuselage. Trees, dirt, and other debris flew past the windows, when Ella dared open her eyes. More than a few things hit her in the head. *Again. At this rate getting memories back is going to be pointless.* She heard Megan cry out, as a particularly hard turn forced the plane to skid to a stop. The sounds of a whole lot of everything crashed and settled down around them. Ella kept her head down, before daring to look up.

"Is everyone okay?" Armand came tripping through the mess with James close behind him. "Megan? Ella? Are you okay? Jeremiah, Ryan? Somebody answer me."

It wasn't until then that Ella realized he couldn't see them.

Megan leaned out to check on Ella. The blonde's hair was tangled in every direction, and her lip was bleeding, but she looked no worse for the wear. She stuck a hand up in the air, and Ella heard Armand cry out.

"Megan! Can you see Ella?"

"I can see her. She looks like she got the world's worst blue tattoo on her face, but she seems fine. Are you okay?" Megan started to try to wiggle out of the restraints.

Ella clicked the button on the chair's belt and fell forward.

"I'm fine," she choked out. The inside of her cheek was bleeding, and her head hurt like nobody's business, but nothing seemed to be broken.

Megan got herself upright and looked straight at Armand.

"Worst. Spring break. EVER."

Armand and James started to laugh. There was a hysteria to it that caused Ella and Megan to laugh as well.

It went on for a couple minutes before Ella said, "Wait, where are Ryan and Jeremiah?"

James coughed and wheezed.

"James, are you okay?" Ella got up and managed to find a bottle of water in the mess to give to him.

"I'm fine," he coughed out, and took the water gratefully.

There was a wind kicking up, and they could feel it coming into the plane.

"Damn. I was hoping we didn't breech the side." Armand climbed over, past Ella, to where the hatch was, and tried to look down. "The cargo door is open," he shouted. "I think they went out of it."

"We should get out of here. What about the bomb?"

Ryan pulled the door open from the outside.

"Jeremiah and I ran the bomb as fast as we could, a ways down from the plane, but we should get clear as far as we can. Hurry, we only have a few minutes. Come on." Ryan grabbed gear and threw it to the ground.

Everyone else sprang into action, throwing bags to each other, and jumping over the mess. They all got out in a matter of minutes.

"Come on!" Ryan stood to the side like a coach encouraging his students.

Ella ran as hard as she ever had in her life, carrying what she could and watching out for her friends. Megan stumbled once, and Ella ran back to pull her up. They both ran together. James fell the furthest behind. Ella started back to him, but Ryan stopped her.

"Keep going. I'll get him." Ryan made it to the professor and took him by the shoulder.

A rumble started in the distance.

"GET DOWN!" Ryan screamed at them.

He dove behind some rocks with James. Ella yanked Megan down just as rubble started to fly by them. The rumbling was followed by a roaring explosion. Rocks and sand rained from the sky. Everything started to settle down, and Ella popped up to find everyone.

"Where is everybody? Are you guys okay?" She could hear Megan coughing but couldn't see her. Jeremiah was dusting himself off. Ryan and James were struggling to stand up, using the rocks to support themselves. Ryan had thrown himself over James and was covered in dirt. "Where is Armand? Armand?"

"I'm over here," he sounded strained.

Ella, still not being able to see him, ran around until she came across him lying behind an especially large pile of boulders. His suit was torn open, and she could see what he meant about the markings on his body. He was struggling to sit up while trying to cover up the exposed spot. Ella bowed over to lend him a hand.

"Are you hurt?" She braced on a rock to lean in and pull him up.

"I'm fine, I think. Knocked the wind out of me is all. I only hope the plane survived. Otherwise getting home might be complicated."

Megan crawled over the rock Ella was on and choked out some dust.

"Armand, you plan terrible vacations," she said, as Ella pulled a stick out of her tangled knot of blonde hair. Both of them giggled in a maniacal way, as Armand sat up against the rock and smiled.

"I'm glad everyone seems to be enjoying themselves."

"Seriously, though," Ella told him, "this is the worst."

They all gathered a moment to get their bearings. They had managed to keep most of the gear they needed. Armand pulled out a compass, and amazingly enough, Ryan still had his phone.

"We need a plan," Armand said. "There is an expedition entrance to the caves, but I doubt we can get in that way without being spotted. How are we going to explain what we are doing there? We're about ten miles away, and I have no idea if anyone is going to come and investigate the explosion, so we might not want to stand around too long,"

"Jeremiah, what do you think?" Ella asked him, as he surveyed their surroundings.

"I think I can get us there," he told her. "The ship is organic, as I said earlier, and each of us who have grown with it over the many long years are attuned to finding it if we become separated. Even after this long. The terrain is different, Ella, but in many ways it is also the same."

"So, I guess, follow Jeremiah?" She started picking up the bags strewn about on the ground.

They all followed suit. Before long, they had covered a great deal of the territory between the crash site and the cave, and stopped only once for water.

"Ryan seems to be doing really well," Megan said to Ella as they rested. "Better than the rest of us, for once. Maybe it's being on adventure. Are you guys getting along okay?"

"I guess. I don't really know what to do. Ein threatened his mother. Granted I don't have a mother, but I imagine I would want to protect her, too. It's just hard to know about trusting him." They watched as Ryan checked on James and picked up lots of bags. He noticed them and saluted in a dramatic way. "But, yeah, he seems good, and I'm glad for that, at least."

"Hey, how are you feeling?" They started hiking again.

"I feel pretty good, actually. You know, considering bomb, plane crash, et cetera... I guess danger is good for the soul." She stuck her tongue out at Megan.

They continued on for what Ella could only guess was another couple of hours or so before Jeremiah called to them to stop.

"We are close, and I need a minute to figure out what to do." He dropped all his packs and disappeared into the jutting caverns and cliffs.

There were plenty of places for them to hide from sight, which was good, considering there seemed to be a few people staffing the area, including an armed guard. He was back before too long.

"There is a very small but workable opening on the back side of the large opening. It also seems to be unguarded. Follow me."

They went to the back, carefully picking their way through rocks, holes, and some formidable looking plants. Ella had never spent much time in the desert and didn't even want to think about the fact that there might be snakes. *I won't bother them, they won't bother me. Hopefully.* She gritted her teeth and kept going.

"This is a workable opening?" James was dubious, and Ella could see why. The opening was really more of a crack. Smaller than the hatch on the cargo port of the plane. And there were huge boulders and certainly unmovable bedrock.

"I think we can get through if we work to move some of the rock fragments," Jeremiah was completely calm. "Ella, I meant to ask you, did you find the bomb using your abilities?"

"Yes, I think I did. Ryan helped me."

"Very good." He smiled. "I am not surprised to hear that Ryan helped you. I think Ryan is going to be a great help many times over his life." Jeremiah returned his attention to the opening and deliberately set about moving chunks out of the way.

Ella did not understand that statement about Ryan, but wondered if, like herself, Jeremiah was having some suspicions about his state of being.

Speaking of which, look at him go. Ryan was clearing away the blockage quickly and as if these giant stones weighed nothing.

"Wow, somebody had their Wheaties this morning." Megan tossed a pile of brush to the side.

"Yeah, I don't know what's with me," Ryan told them. "I feel great today. But hey, look. There's enough space for us to get in now." He was right. He'd cleared the opening, and they could fit through easily, gear and all.

They all started pulling out flashlights and gloves. Armand showed them how to tie their ropes and harnesses together.

"Everyone ready?" he asked, and started to climb into the opening.

"No time like the present." Megan smoothly hopped down into the dark.

Jeremiah and James followed, then Ella, and behind them all came Ryan.

It took a few minutes for Ella's eyes to adjust in the dark, and she felt the rope being tugged.

"Follow my voice carefully. One foot in front of the other," Armand said quietly, his accent echoing gently in the space. "There's a tunnel we are in, and from what I can tell, it opens up in about 10 meters or so. Use your hands to feel the wall and ceiling of the space to avoid hitting your head."

All Ella could hear was the muffled sound of their footsteps. As her eyes adjusted more and more to the dark, she could more accurately make out the area around the flashlight. One by one, they moved into the open space, and she heard Megan exclaim.

"This is AMAZING!"

Ella felt the rope tug as each one them stopped in the opening. She and Ryan finally made it in. Light seemed to be streaming up from below them. Shining her flashlight above them, she could see overhanging formations growing out of the walls. But looking down is what blew her away. As far as they could all see, there were colossal white and silver crystals growing in a labyrinth into the depths of the cavern. It was as if someone had buried the Fortress of Solitude. Upside-down. The air around them was humid and nearing unbearable, but they had only just begun their descent. *So complaining about it is probably not going to do any good.*

"That is where we are going," Jeremiah said.

"We're going down there?" James eyed it cautiously.

"Are you going to be able to do it?" Jeremiah said to him. "It is okay, my friend, if you want to rest here. We can come back for you."

"I am going to feel terrible one way or another," the professor told him. "I want to come with you, if you don't mind."

"Of course we don't," Ella told him. "Besides, who knows if I can make it either?"

James smiled gratefully at her as Armand found a place to put stakes into the bedrock. He had Ryan hammer them down as he tested point after point.

"This place is incredible," Megan said wondrously. "I cannot believe it." She squealed the tiniest bit, and Ella could not help but find the enthusiasm contagious.

"It is pretty marvelous." She took off one of her gloves to touch a crystal, and a vibration rang through her body. Then she heard a buzzing. It was faint in the deep, but it was there.

"Do any of you hear that?" She ran a hand along the crystal. The vibrations continued, and the buzz was still audible.

"I do," Ryan said. "It's coming from down there." He pointed into the opening.

"Maybe it's the ship," Jeremiah said mysteriously.

"Right. Would you mind explaining what that means?" Ella, fascinated with the whole excursion and even feeling something like déjà vu, wanted to know everything she could.

"I told you, we are attuned to the ship," he said simply.

"I thought you only meant yourself."

"No, Ella, all the Naturals. We are connected. To each other, to everything. You'll see more soon."

"Okay, we're ready." Armand got up. "I'll go down first, see what kind of landing there is, and see if I can map out something of a path down. Ryan is going to anchor everyone. Ready?" He smiled at them and climbed down.

They waited and watched as much they could, hearing his occasional hammering echo in the chamber.

"Okay," he called back up. "I've got a place to start bringing everyone down. Send Megan down first."

Megan, barely able to contain the excitement, jumped down and rappelled with great skill. It took her much less time to reach the landing.

"Come on, Ella! You won't believe it down here!" Megan's happy chirp rang the crystals like bells.

"You're gonna be just fine," Ryan told Ella, taking her hand and holding it while she felt around for the foothold. Finding the spot, she smiled at Ryan and carefully moved around to find the next indentation to hold. Slowly, but surely, she made it down to the landing.

"I'm sorry it took so long," she told Armand and Megan, who were balancing carefully on a crystal as big as a building lying on its side. Everywhere she looked, crystals jutted out at all angles.

Jeremiah, James, and Ryan made it down in the same amount of time it took just Ella to get down. She made a silent promise to move faster, though her nerves were about as rattled as they could possibly get.

As they ohh-ed and ahh-ed over the wonderland into which they were descending, the humidity was making it harder and harder to catch a grip on anything. Time and again, Ella had to shake her gloves free of condensation.

"I feel as though I am in a Jules Verne novel," James told them, his delight evident with each passing level. "If only he could have seen such a place!"

"How is it that these crystals could get so big?" Megan asked the professor. "They seem as though no one has ever touched them before."

"Probably no one has touched them before. I read about the conditions needed to create such a place, and it included no humans interfering with its development. It appears as though no one has been this far down. Of course, the harder it gets to breathe, and the more humid, it could make most climbing expeditions impossible. I barely feel as though I can make it, but I am determined. It doesn't hurt that the equipment we have is state of the art."

Armand and Ryan were carefully tying rope to the formations that seemed to be the most steady.

"My family is full of spoiled explorers," Armand explained. Ella might've laughed if he didn't sound so irked by it.

"My father is responsible for the deaths of millions, apparently," Ella said. "You don't have to feel bad." She smiled at him. "This stuff isn't our fault, remember?"

"Yes, I remember. Alright. Down we go." Armand effortlessly rappelled down to the next crystal landing. "This one is bigger and it feels stronger than the last. Everybody down," he called up.

One by one they went down again. *We seem to be getting the hang of it.* And as soon as the thought was there, Ella lost her footing and fell. Megan screamed her name, and as quickly as possible, grabbed the rope. The free-falling halted with a jolt. Smashing into an overhanging crystal, she cried out in pain as it sliced through her suit.

"Ella." James and Jeremiah were leaning over the ledge looking down at her as she swung between the protruding points. "Ella, hold on," James wheezed breathlessly, and Ella couldn't help but worry about him.

"I think I'm okay. I cut my leg open and it is bleeding a lot. Take a break, James. I'm worried about you. Anyway, I think I can actually see something that looks like the bottom."

She could hear drops of water and make out what looked like a crystalline forest beneath them. The pain in her leg was getting intense, but the beauty of the space was still utterly breathtaking.

"Ella." Armand's accent echoed in the chamber in a way that made her dizzy. *Or maybe it was the non-stop swinging.* She shook her head furiously. The heat was making her light-headed. "Ella, listen. Ryan and I are going to lower you down as much as we can, okay? Try to find a place to stop and pull on the rope twice in case we can't hear you call up. Then the rest of us will climb down and meet you. Hold on, okay?"

"Okay, go ahead!"

They slowly lowered her down, and she kept a foot out to maneuver away from any more sharp points. It didn't take long before she found the footing she needed. Tugging on the rope twice, she also called, "I'm okay! It's not so far down!" Ella investigated, cautiously, where she had stopped.

Armand made it to her first, and Ella had to pull herself out of his bone crushing hug.

"I'm fine," she said. "Get everybody else down here without killing them."

They were together again in no time, and Ella showed them what she thought they could do.

The crystal they were standing on was the widest one yet and seemed to end on solid ground.

"We could put a spike in here," she pointed to a wall, "and create a controlled slide."

"I think that might work." Ryan was trying to gauge how far they had to go. "It seems to be about six to seven more stories down. If we slid down, it would take the risk out of climbing. Most of the crystal is indented far enough in the middle, we may not even have to worry about plummeting to certain death."

"Hooray," Megan's sarcasm dripped as much as her sweaty face. "Could it be anymore humid? This place is awesome, but the weather is quite awful."

Jeremiah bandaged Ella's leg with a tourniquet, and the bleeding seemed to slow.

"It's sort of ironic," she told them.

"What's that?" asked James.

"That I spent all this time not crying in public, wearing gloves, black clothes, only to bleed cobalt all over the place." Ella looked at their faces. None of them knew what to say to her. "It's fine." She threw up her hands. "Let's slide!"

"I'm ready on this end," Ryan said.

"I wish I could get a running start." Megan wisecracked, "I'm sweaty enough that I could be my own water slide."

"Gross. You go last," Ella poked her and jumped feet-first onto the crystal, not expecting to slide fast. But the crystal was as smooth as perfectly ground glass.

Ella torpedoed down as each person joined on. It was less than a minute before they heard the rock shatter above them, and the peg tore out of the seam above, sending them plummeting down the slide at break-neck speed. Ella hit the bottom and rolled into a wall. Megan shot past her and cracked into a crystal. Of the males, Ryan hit first and struck a wall with a thump that seemed to shake the room. Armand, James, and Jeremiah landed in a pile atop one another. Ella groaned and rolled on to her side. Tangled in the ropes, she wiggled out the dagger Armand had given her and cut herself free.

Megan flung her arms to her sides like a snow angel. "THAT WAS AWE-SOME!"

"The buzzing! It's coming from the other side of that wall," Ella exclaimed, standing up and feeling absolutely every part of her aching in a way she could not put into words.

There was light coming from somewhere, but she couldn't locate the source. Flipping on the flashlight again, she realized that pieces of the walls were glowing.

"Fluorescent minerals in the wall," James said. "But where are they getting the UV reaction?"

"More importantly," Ella interrupted, "how are we going to get out of here? This is a dead end. The buzzing is so loud. Can you hear it?"

"I can, yes," Jeremiah answered. "The ship is not far, but she's right. How do we get out of here?"

"Look," Megan pointed. "There's light coming through a crack on the left wall."

She climbed up a pile of stones and crystals.

"It looks like these are covering a tunnel or something. Maybe if we move more we can see better."

She jumped down and started to pick away at the pile. Ryan came up behind her. Megan glanced at him and did a double-take.

"The fluorescent minerals are completely making you look glow-in-the-dark."

"Yeah, maybe," he mumbled, and pushed away rocks and boulders that had to weigh tons.

"How in the world did you do that?" Megan asked, shocked.

They were all looking at him.

"I don't really know. I feel strong. Super strong, in a way I've never felt before. There's something here that is helping me feel better, I guess." He stood for a minute, staring back at them, and then turned back to the opening. "Hey look! We can talk about me later. I believe this is what we came for?"

The ship was broken in parts. The crash was evident, as was the erosion from the surrounding environment. Even though it wasn't complete, the pieces were massive. Ella could say she had never seen anything so big in her entire life. Crystals had grown through parts of the walls. Everywhere they looked, crystals shown in brilliant, lucid colors.

"The ship being organic," said Jeremiah, "the crystals grew around it, and so did those flowers." He pointed to a cluster of plants that were so extraordinary in color and shape it was hard to believe they were real. Some of them were as big as the crystals, which Ella guessed were fifteen and twenty feet high.

They had no leaves, but long, wing-shaped branches with gossamer coloring that they could see through. The colors shimmered as Ryan walked underneath them slowly, gently, the space around him lighting up. Ella followed him carefully. Looking up as she walked, she noticed dotted patterns on them.

"Oh!" she proclaimed, grabbing Ryan's arm. "The constellations are on them."

Ryan had stopped and was looking at her face. Ella didn't notice at first, but realized her hand was warm and dropped it quickly. Ryan turned his back to her and walked further ahead.

"They grew that way," said Jeremiah. He kept trudging through the cavern.

Ella could not see how far it went. It seemed endless.

Without the ship, the cavern would have still been a place to behold. Ella could feel the ancient age of the Earth here. The buzzing was immense in her ears now, like in her dreams, but she knew it had a purpose. She still didn't know what, but it felt as if it were a beacon of some sort, calling her to somewhere she needed to be. The heat that was intense at first had settled around her, as if her body had adjusted to the environment, and her skin absorbed the energy.

What was the energy, though? Is this all my imagination? She was astounded to learn who her parents were, what she might be able to do, but this... this was beyond human imagination.

As she made her way through the uneven terrain in the dim glow, she had to balance herself by putting her hands on rocks jutting out of the walls and ground. Sometimes they would be hot to the touch, nearly burning her skin until it felt as though her senses kicked in and evened the temperature.

She couldn't see Armand, Megan, James, or Jeremiah anymore, and even Ryan was moving out of her sight. But she had to move more slowly and take this all in. Her dreams were here, the window where she had stood and watched dinosaurs roam was in here. She was positive it was the same one. She put a hand on it, and it felt hard but flexible. She pushed a little bit and there was a slight, but firm, give. Not being able to see what was on the other side of it now because the years seemed to have filled in the walls around the window, she ran her hand along the edges and felt impressions in different shapes. The shape of them reminded her of something, but at the moment she couldn't recall what.

Wishing she had some more light than the tiny beam that was now reaching her, she reluctantly drew her hand away and began to catch up to everyone. The mark on her chest flared to life, not exactly stinging, but tingling. *The symbols on the window! They were the same symbols drawn on the sheet of paper.*

"Jeremiah," she hissed. "Jeremiah? Where are you? Come back this way. Someone's been here, I think."

She followed something of a pathway made from metal parts.

"Jeremiah! The symbols on the paper! Someone's been here. They are scraped into the window..."

Ella found her friends in what appeared to be the main room of the ship. They all had their backs to her, and no one was moving.

"What are you guys doing?"

Seemingly very reluctantly, Ryan slowly turned to the side, and now Ella could see what they were doing.

Ein was standing in front of them with her two henchmen. All three had guns.

And they were pointed right at Ella.

Chapter 23

"Nice of you to finally join us, Miss Cerulean." Ein actually sounded somewhat gleeful.

"Well, with you trying to blow up the plane, it was bound to take a little longer," Megan snapped.

"Careful, human, I don't need you at all." Ein redirected the gun at Megan. "Besides, I don't know what you are talking about. I needed you to get here, so it would not make much sense for me to blow up what I needed, would it? But humans are not particularly good at solving puzzles. They are very good at causing me problems, though. Miss Cerulean, move up here so I can see you. NOW."

Ella wound her way up toward Ein, and stood between the gun and Megan.

"What do you want now, you psycho?" Ella did not want that gun pointed at her friend.

"Did I not teach you to respect me? Or at least have TriChem program some respect into that useless mind of yours?"

"So you did tamper with my memories."

"For all the good it did me. Yes. I tampered with your memories as well as many others." Ein strode over to Armand. "I really should thank you, Armand. Your family's fortune has continually kept my research going over these long, miserable, Earth years."

"Not by my choice," he spat at her.

"Now, now. That wasn't always true, Armand." Ein chucked him under the chin with her golden revolver. Ein was in a sparkling white suit, and the gun's handle matched it.

"What is she talking about, Armand?" Ella turned to face him, and he looked away with agony on his face.

"Really, dear, you don't know?" Ein looked between their two faces and laughed in a way that only a wicked witch in a cartoon would laugh. "Armand is one of the Naturals. Now, look at that face," she pointed to Jeremiah. "You didn't know that, did you, lover?"

"Ella, I was going to tell you," Armand started, the anger coloring his cheeks. "I am sorry you have to hear this now. My family owned, I mean owns, TriChem and the institute. I thought it had been sold. After I learned about these experiments that were going on, I demanded we defund all that we could and untangle the El Dorado name as much as possible. Ella, I am so sorry. I had a hand in all that happened to you." His voice broke, and he moved toward Ella, who stepped back.

"Stay away from me, Armand. That's what was on the paper you took from my file, wasn't it?" Ella said, and Megan took her hand.

"Yes." Armand's face was murderous and anguished all at the same time. "I will kill you, Ein."

"Yes. Yes. Heard it before. Anyway, Armand, your partner didn't see it that way. So we hid your holdings from you and continued our work. It has yielded some magnificent results." She gestured to the man in the suit.

"He is one of the UnNaturals, then?" Jeremiah stepped toward the man, who waved him back with his gun.

"UnNatural? He's going to be stronger than any of you when I am done with him. His radioactivity is already growing to a point of concentrated devastation."

"What is it you want to accomplish, Ein?" Jeremiah asked her, sounding genuinely interested. "You are one of the most powerful of all the Naturals, tasked with a deed so great as to live through all time, and that has never been enough to satisfy you."

"Oh, Jeremiah, you never could think bigger." She sauntered over to Ryan. "My, my. Don't you look healthy and quite brawny? All the radioactive energy in this place is good for you, just like I thought it might be. Don't worry," she ran a long pointed nail down the front of Ryan's shirt, "mommy dearest is just fine and free to go, now that you've completed your job."

Megan shoved Ella aside and Ein's henchman stepped in front of her.

"Where do you think you're going, girl?" He spit tobacco on the ground.

"Oh, you know, right over there to punch Ryan in the face." Megan's fury filled the room. "What job does Ein mean, RYAN?"

"Get back over there." The distorted Jersey accent came out again, and he pushed Megan backward. Her stature Lilliputian in comparison, she resignedly stepped back.

"Isn't it obvious?" Ein drizzled the words over them. "I needed Jeremiah to bring Ella here. Ryan kept me abreast of every move. Though the plane crash was unexpected."

"Why?" demanded Ella. "I thought you were going to kill me."

"Because," Jeremiah said in hushed voice, "she needs my DNA to open the containers that house the pieces belonging to the other Naturals."

"So you see, Ella, I don't necessarily need you." Ein cocked the gun and pointed it back at her.

"If you shoot her, I will not open the containers." Jeremiah sat down tiredly on one of the crystal formations. It was the first time Ella realized that James wasn't visible. *Where is he? Does Ein know he is here?*

"Ella, your professor friend hid all the materials about you. I knew he was making progress on your condition, and I knew that Jeremiah had found you. Which could only mean he would bring you here, knowing that you would need your piece to understand what and who you are. With the piece and the professor's treatments you would grow more powerful, and well, we can't have that, can we?"

"Ein," Ryan said her name, and the woman walked back up to him.

"Yes, my good little solider?"

"If I can have my mother back, how do I get out of here? We climbed down, but obviously you didn't."

"That's simple, darling. Having found the ship a few years ago, I had a pathway dug here. There's an industrial elevator all the way to the top. No worries. As soon as we're done here, we'll go back up to the surface, and you and mommy dearest can have your reunion. Speaking of which, enough talking. Open the containers, Jeremiah."

"No, thank you," he said it so dismissively Ella almost laughed. Until Ein pointed her gun at Megan again.

"You told me I couldn't shoot Ella, you didn't say anything about the human."

Jeremiah still didn't move.

"I am not joking," Ein started to pull at the trigger. "I am tired of playing games with you. Open the containers."

"I need Ella's help." He stood up and went to what appeared to be a compartment. It had been chiseled out of rock, and broken crystals lay strewn about the bottom of it. "I see you thoughtfully had your men chisel out the panel. How kind of you. Ella, if you would join me please. Back up, Ein, you know that the security measures are probably still in place. Wouldn't want to mess up that pretty, white suit of yours in case they go off."

Ella was shocked to hear Jeremiah being so sarcastic. She went over to him as he put his hand onto the panel.

"Ella, you'll need to take your glove off and also put your hand here."

"I don't remember that requirement, Jeremiah." Ein stepped back over to them. "I hope you're not thinking about trying anything."

"Back up, Ein. Messy, messy. We had to create new protocol for the trip to Earth. Maybe you just don't recall yours," waving a no-no finger at her as if she was child. Ein seemed unsure for the first time and moved back.

"Now, Ella, I am going to open the containers and hand the pieces out one by one. Carefully place them in a bag."

"Okay."

The panel had opened in a way that Ein's view was partially blocked. "Don't try anything," she repeated. Ella realized that something about Jeremiah was putting the woman on edge.

Delicately and conscientiously, he handed her metal after metal. Some of them warm to the touch, some of them cold, some of them seemed to be moving. Out of the corner of her eye, Ella saw him move one to the back of the shelf.

He leaned back. "They are not all here. How is it that they are gone?"

"How could they not all be there?" Ein seemed about to lose her cool. "No one can open your part of the containment but you. Who was here?"

"Ein, if I knew that, I wouldn't be asking you," Jeremiah sounded exasperated. Then Ella realized that, as he was talking to her, his hands were very slowly opening a container. Whatever was in it was yellow in color. He palmed what looked to be a stone in one hand and put the rest of them into the bag. Except for the one he had pushed to the back.

"Ella, I can't reach that one," though she could see he could reach it just fine. "Please pull it out, would you. Take your other glove off, please. They are wet, and I wouldn't want to contaminate it."

"Oh, uh, sure. No problem." Ella hoisted the bag onto her shoulder, and Jeremiah put his head down as if trying to catch his breath. Gingerly, Ella opened the last container, the top of which Jeremiah had already loosened, and took out the silver-blue stones. They instantly came to life in her hands.

"Uh, Jeremiah? What's happening?" Ella stumbled back, wide-eyed, and the pieces broke into bits and absorbed into her skin.

"He gave her her pieces, DAMMMIT," Ein yelled.

As she did, Jeremiah yelled, "HEY, RYAN. CATCH!" Without thinking, Ryan stuck up a hand and easily caught the large, yellowish stone. It, too, broke into pieces and disappeared into his skin.

"NOW!" Jeremiah slammed the panel back and pushed Ryan and Ella together.

There was burst of energy between the both of them that sent a shockwave through the room, momentarily knocking everyone backward. James hit the man in the suit in the head with a crystal fragment, as he had been hiding just out of sight. Megan tried to kick the other man, but he was a wall. She opted instead to hit him with a crystal fragment, too. Ella was pleased to note Megan managed to stab him with the sharp end, as well. It was the last clear thought she had.

She felt a surge of power run through her and Ryan. It connected them. Her eyes became glassed over, and she saw a symbol burn to life on Ryan's chest.

Ein came toward them with the gun. Ryan moved a hand in her direction, and somehow it slapped her back, but not before she got off a shot.

"NO!" Armand jumped at Ella and pulled her to the ground.

"Thank you."

Her words sounded as if they came out of someone else's mouth. She rolled her face away only to see that Megan was the one who had been hit.

"MEGAN!" Ella, for the first time, didn't suppress her rage, she let it overtake every bit of her being, as the memories of millions of years permeated her mind. She bounded up and headed toward Ein.

The woman was laughing. "Don't you know, darling? Naturals can't use their powers against one another."

"Yeah, but I bet I can still punch you." And with that, Ella hit the woman with one hundred years' worth of anger. Ein fell, hitting her head on a jagged rock.

Crystals were starting to fall. Armand and Ryan were fighting Ein's men. The UnNatural kept disappearing and reappearing, making it impossible for Armand to land a hit. James was trying to stop Megan's bleeding. Jeremiah had gathered up everything he could from the ship. Ryan seemed to be having some luck fighting the other man, his bawdy gold chain clanging against him as if he were made of metal. The sound resonated in the room, but power pulsated off of Ryan, and every time he connected with the man, the ship reverberated. More and more crystals were cracking and hitting the ground.

"WE HAVE TO GET OUT OF HERE!" Armand scooped up Megan. "ELLA, JAMES, LET'S GO!" He ran to the elevator. It, too, was starting to shake.

Jeremiah was leaning over Ein. He kissed her forehead.

"I'll get out of this, you know," she said to him.

"I have no doubt." Jeremiah got up and ran to meet them.

The UnNatural started shooting at them, and they all took cover as the elevator rushed to the surface. Ella's head was saturated with thoughts, making it hard for her to pay attention. The elevator slammed to a stop, and they vaulted out just before the cable broke and sent it crashing back into the dark.

"COME ON, ELLA," James yelled with all the strength that seemed left in him. Ella had to force herself to the present. She was the only one still standing in front of the collapsing cave entrance.

"Run for the plane!" Armand commanded.

The ground groaned under their feet as they ran. Armand was carrying Megan, and Ella was trying to hold on to James. Jeremiah was ahead of all of them, looking out for any more of Ein's men.

Ella's blood was falling on the sand, melting into the Earth. Every drop brought her another piece of Earth's memory. Her head swam with images that were becoming harder and harder to contain. She stumbled more than once in the effort to keep going. The pain from the slice out of her leg helped to keep her focused on moving forward. We have to get to the plane. Megan might be dead, but we have to try to get her help.

Someone fired shots at them, and they all dove for the ground. Armand put Megan down and pulled out a gun. He fired off into the distance, unable to see where the perpetrator was hiding. It seemed clear for a moment, so they got up and continued to make a dash for it.

"The plane! I think we can still fly it! There's little damage! HURRY!"

Jeremiah made it to the plane before them and had already opened the door. He had climbed in and readied to take Megan up carefully, trying not to cause any further harm.

Once she was in, Jeremiah pulled Ella up, and they both pulled the rest of them on board. Armand climbed up and ran to the cockpit. Someone started to take shots at the plane. Armand revved the engine and drove the plane as fast as he could to an empty stretch of land.

That's when Ella realized that Ryan wasn't on the plane.

"Where is Ryan?" She ran to a window on the plane and saw the cave falling into the ground as they pulled away. "NO! WE CAN'T LEAVE! RYAN ISN'T WITH US!"

The ground started giving way, seemingly moving closer and closer to the plane.

"ELLA! We have to take off. The ground is going to swallow us whole," Armand yelled.

As he said it, James slipped into the seat next to him, biting his teeth against his pain, and they pulled the plane into take-off. Ella fell, and Jeremiah moved to help her get strapped in. Jeremiah had belted Megan in laying down on a fully flattened seat.

"Please tell me she is alive," Ella cried.

"She is, but just barely. She needs medical attention immediately."

The plane rose and fell several times before it seemed Armand finally had a handle on it.

Jeremiah looked at Ella. He saw her symbol glowing through where her suit had torn. Her eyes filled with the moving parts of their universe, her pieces were filling out the memories that were meant to be hers a long time ago.

"I'm so sorry," he told her. "It wasn't supposed to happen this way. None of it. I'm so, so sorry."

As if in a trance, her voice took on a deeper intonation. "I need Ryan. We must find him and the others."

"Of course. We will go back to find him, and we'll look for the others. Maybe we can live as one, though our destiny is lost."

"Our destiny is not lost," she told him. "Someone altered my piece to contain information about Ein before we left home. I know what we have to do. And I know how to get us home."

27

www.ingramcontent.com/pod-product-compliance
Lightning Source LLC
Chambersburg PA
CBHW022147010726
47493CB00002B/382